P9-BAW-975

# SMOKE AND ASHES

***The Finest in Fantasy and Science Fiction by TANYA HUFF available from DAW Books:***

SMOKE AND SHADOWS (#1)
SMOKE AND MIRRORS (#2)
SMOKE AND ASHES (#3)

BLOOD PRICE (#1)
BLOOD TRAIL (#2)
BLOOD LINES (#3)
BLOOD PACT (#4)
BLOOD DEBT (#5)

The Confederation Novels:
VALOR'S CHOICE (#1)
THE BETTER PART OF VALOR (#2)

The Keeper's Chronicles:
SUMMON THE KEEPER (#1)
THE SECOND SUMMONING (#2)
LONG HOT SUMMONING (#3)

SING THE FOUR QUARTERS (#1)
FIFTH QUARTER (#2)
NO QUARTER (#3)
THE QUARTERED SEA (#4)

WIZARD OF THE GROVE

OF DARKNESS, LIGHT, AND FIRE

# SMOKE AND ASHES



TANYA HUFF

DAW BOOKS, INC.
DONALD A. WOLLHEIM, FOUNDER
375 Hudson Street, New York, NY 10014
ELIZABETH R. WOLLHEIM
SHEILA E. GILBERT
PUBLISHERS
http://www.dawbooks.com

Jacket art by John Jude Palencar.

DAW Books Collectors No. 1365.

DAW Books are distributed by Penguin Group (USA) Inc.

Book designed by Elizabeth M. Glover.



First Printing, June 2006
1 2 3 4 5 6 7 8 9

DAW TRADEMARK REGISTERED
U.S. PAT. OFF. AND FOREIGN COUNTRIES
—MARCA REGISTRADA
HECHO EN U.S.A.

PRINTED IN THE U.S.A.

For Violette and Paul,
who rebuild our house, look after our cats,
and are even attempting to teach me how to
dress. Definitely above and beyond!

# One

ALTHOUGH BOTH MOON AND stars were hidden b-hind cloud, the night was not as dark as it could have been. The light from streetlamps bounced off pale concrete, providing illumination enough to make the two men walking along the empty sidewalk clearly visible.

The dark-haired man shoved his hands deeper into the pockets of his brown suede jacket. "I know we didn't have much of a choice, but I don't like how that ended."

"It ended the way it had to end," the blond replied with a weary smile. And if his teeth were just a little too white and preternaturally long, there was no one there to note it. They might have been the only two men alive in the entire city. Their footsteps should have echoed . . . that's how alone they seemed.

"I don't like circumstances making my choices for me."

"Who does?"

"You don't seem to be having any trouble."

"I've just had a lot more practice at hiding . . ." His voice trailed off and, frowning, he looked up.

"That's it. Good. Lee, follow his gaze. A woman screams and . . ."

A plaid flannel body pillow, clearly weighted, dropped down onto the sidewalk about three feet in front of the actors.

". . . and the unfortunate lady lands. Cut!" Peter Hudson moved out from behind the monitors, pulling off his headset and tossing it back in the general direction of his black canvas chair. Tina, his script supervisor, reached out and snagged the set just before it hit the pavement, her left hand marking the place she'd stopped lining her copy of the script, her eyes never leaving the page. "Mason, I liked the same old/same old thing you had going during the dialogue," he continued as he reached the pillow. "It was a nice counterpoint to Lee's whole mortal indignation thing."

"Nice?" Mason Reed—aka Raymond Dark, syndicated television's most popular vampire detective and star of *Darkest Night*—folded his arms, and curled a lip to expose one fake fang. "That's the best you can do?"

"It's after midnight," Peter sighed. "Be thankful I can still come up with nice. Once Angela adds the echoing footsteps in post, I think the scene'll play . . ." The sound of large machinery revving up reduced the rest of the director's observation to moving lips and increasingly emphatic gestures.

Still standing on the top of the ladder from where he'd thrown the body pillow—Peter liked to be certain about lines of sight—Tony Foster caught one of the gestures aimed at him, clambered down, and ran over to the director's side.

"I want one more take before we bring in Padma!" Mouth by Tony's ear, Peter all but screamed to make himself heard. "Deal with it, Mr. Foster!"

"How?"

"Any way that'll get my footage!"

Any way.

Yeah. Tony headed for the construction site. Like he didn't know what that meant.

Promoted back in August from production assistant to TAD, trainee assistant director, Tony found himself in October still doing much the same thing he'd been doing as a PA—which surprised no one, him least of all, since Chester Bane, the notoriously frugal head of CB Productions, hadn't yet gotten around to hiring someone to do his old job. Still, TAD meant he was now moving up in the Directors Department with a raise in pay and a clear, union-sanctified path to the director's chair. Not necessarily a short path, but he was on it and that was the main thing. Since he'd been in the business less than a full year, he really had nothing to complain about. Besides, CB's penny-pinching ways ensured that he was learning a lot more than he might have on a show with a larger personnel budget.

And on a show with a larger locations budget, he'd have never learned how to take advantage of roadwork in order to get a normally busy Vancouver street cleared of traffic without having to go through all the hassles at city hall or pay off-duty police officers to safely keep it that way. Half the permits. Half the money spent. Digging for a sewer line guaranteed empty streets for blocks away from the actual machinery and city hall had been more than willing to halve the inconvenience to Vancouver drivers.

There was, of course, a downside. They'd been working around the noise—construction seemed to follow the same "hurry up and wait" schedule that television did—but that machine . . .

Backhoe, Tony realized as he drew closer.

. . . seemed to be settling in for a long roar. Sure, they could remove the sound in post, but Peter hated looping dialogue. Mostly because Mason wasn't particularly good at it, and the results always looked as though a big rubbery monster was due to stomp Tokyo.

*Any way* didn't include actually talking to the construction crew. The foreman had made it quite clear earlier in the evening that they needn't bother. He had a job to do and no fancy-assed, la-di-da television show was going to put him off schedule.

With that attitude in mind, Tony stopped about six meters from the backhoe and watched the huge bladed bucket bite through the asphalt. After a moment, he noticed that the operator worked in what was essentially an open cab. Noticed, after a moment more, that her line of sight didn't extend as far down as the keys dangling off to one side of the double bank of bright yellow-and-black levers.

That could work.

Turning on one heel, he started back toward the trailers. There was always the chance the operator might glance down—it was a small chance, but given the size of the biceps on the woman, he wanted to make sure there wasn't the slightest possibility she even began to contemplate the thought of considering him responsible.

Call him a coward, but those arms were the size of his thighs.

Besides, he didn't need to see the key. He knew where it was. Knew the shape it occupied in the universe. Okay, maybe *the universe* was going a little far, but he had local space nailed.

*"Mr. Foster?"*

He had to strain to hear Peter's voice in his ear jack.

*"Any time."*

Now seemed good. He concentrated and closed his fingers around a handful of keys as, behind him, the backhoe sputtered to a stop.

Wizardry, according to Arra Pelindrake, the wizard from another world who'd left him a laptop with instructions both detailed and annoyingly obscure, was all about focus. New spells required words or symbols or embarrassing contortions—Tony suspected that the wizards of Arra's world were either double-jointed or had a vicious sense of humor. After a while—where *a while* generally referred to years of practice—the words, symbols, and contortions could be replaced by the wizard's will.

Back in the summer, Tony had discovered that trying to keep a location crew alive in a haunted house could condense *a while* into one high-stress night. These days, if he wanted something to come to him, it came. Other spells were a different story. He was still trying to forget what happened the first time he tried a clean cantrip on his bathroom. Nothing said, *Hey, I'm a weirdo!* like having a date attacked by scrubbing bubbles.

As far as other spells were concerned . . . Well, there were surprisingly few places in and around the lower mainland to practice Powershots, given population density and the expected explosive results, but just in case he ever had to blast his way out of another haunted house, he had the theory nailed.

He reached the craft services table in time to see Lee—one hand still shoved in the pocket of his leather jacket, the other wrapped around a Styrofoam coffee cup—flirting with Karen, the craft services contractor. As Lee dipped his chin and looked up at her through a fringe of thick, dark lashes, she giggled. Actually giggled. Not a sound Tony'd ever connected to Karen before. Laugh, yes. Also swear like a sailor. But giggle? No. Lee's answering smile and a murmured comment Tony wasn't quite close enough to hear brought a flush to her cheeks, the rosy color under the freckles clearly visible in the double set of halogen spotlights aimed at the table.

"When you're ready, Mr. Nicholas!"

In answer to Peter's summons, Lee winked, drained the cup, and tossed it into the nearer of the two garbage cans, turned, and half smiled as his gaze swept over Tony. Then the gaze kept sweeping, that half smile the only acknowledgment he gave.

Tony watched him walk back to where Mason and Peter were standing by the scene's starting mark. The shadows following hard on the actor's heels were nothing more than the result of solid objects blocking the path of both natural and artificial light. No otherworldly shadow warriors dogged his footsteps. The chill Tony felt on the back of his neck was a fall breeze, a warning that winter, such as winter was in British Columbia, was on its way. If the dead were walking, they weren't walking here. Everything was so aggressively normal it was almost possible to believe he'd imagined Lee screaming, his body tortured from within by an insane dead wizard. Almost possible to believe he'd imagined Lee sitting in the back of an ambulance and admitting that . . . well, essentially admitting that when he'd kissed him, he'd been fully aware of whose lips were involved.

Of course, he'd also said that the show had to go on.

That had been August. It was now early October. The show had been going on for nearly two months and was getting very good at it. Unlike a lot of actors, Lee had always been friendly with his crew and that "friendly" had always extended to Tony. Nothing about that had changed; he treated Tony no differently than he treated Keisha, the set dresser, or Zev Sero, the music director. The kiss and the confession were safely buried under what Tony thought was one of Lee's better performances.

Since the ladder and the pillow had been moved away from the shot, Tony assumed that Peter was doing this last take without his assistance. The backhoe keys slid off his fingertips into the garbage to lie hidden under a half-eaten muffin. Watching the boom operator—a skinny middle-aged man named Walter Davis who'd replaced skinny middle-aged Hartley Skenski who hadn't made it out of that haunted house alive—Tony reached for a handful of marshmallow strawberries.

"Those things'll kill you, you know."

One of them took a shot at it.

Coughing and blowing bits of soggy pink marshmallow out of his nose, Tony glared up into the amused face of RCMP Constable Jack Elson and contemplated several responses that would get him fifteen to life. When he could talk again, self-preservation prodded him to settle for a merely moderately sarcastic, "Aren't you out of your jurisdiction?"

Constable Elson, like CB Productions, was based in Burnaby—a part of the Greater Vancouver area about ten miles east of the city.

The constable shrugged. "I'm off duty. Heard you lot were out on the streets, thought I'd come down and take a look."

"Quiet, please!" Adam Paelous, the first assistant director, began the familiar litany. "Let's settle, people!"

Tony jerked his head back toward the trailers and started walking. Smiling slightly, Jack followed, snatching a couple of cookies off the corner of the table as he passed. He'd been around often enough in the last month or so that Karen, usually pit bull protective of the show's food, no longer tried to stop him and, even more disturbing, sometime in the last few weeks Tony had started thinking of him as Jack.

"Rolling!"

Half a dozen voices, including Tony's, echoed the word.

"Scene 19a, take three. Mark!"

The crack of the slate bounced off the buildings a couple of times and finally disappeared under the distant profanity of the road crew.

As Peter called action, Tony figured they were far enough away and murmured, "Okay, fine, now you're here, what are you looking *for?*"

Jack grinned. "It's been almost two months since you were found next to a dead body. I figured you were about due."

He was probably kidding.

The RCMP constable had been unhappy about the verdict of Accidental Death after the Shadowlord had been and gone, but that was nothing on the way he'd felt when Tony'd finally forced open the doors to Caulfield House on that August night. He'd seen the kind of weird-and-wonderful that even television writers would have had a hard time making people believe, and what he'd seen, combined with a good cop's ability to sift out the bullshit, had left him with no choice but to believe Tony's promised explanation. He'd believed it. He just hadn't liked it much.

Given his adversarial history with the police, Tony still wasn't sure why he'd told Jack and his partner Geetha Danvers the truth about what had happened in the house—slightly edited of personal information and back story. Maybe he'd hoped that it would keep them from hanging around and scowling suspiciously at all and sundry. It had worked on Constable Danvers, not that she'd been the scowling suspiciously sort to begin with, but it had done sweet fuck all to get Jack Elson out of his life.

"Look at them." The constable gestured with a cookie, including actors and crew in the movement. "They're acting like nothing happened."

They were acting like the backhoe was quiet and that meant they could shoot, that was all they cared about. Except that wasn't what Jack meant. Peter, Adam, Sorge—the director of photography—Mason and Lee; they'd all been in the house. Karen and Ujjal, the genny op, had been outside trying to get in. Or get the others out. The rest of the crew had been involved only to the extent that they'd heard the stories.

Tonight they were all working to get the scene in the can as though nothing had happened.

Tony's turn to shrug. "It's been a while."

"That shouldn't matter." Jack had taken to an expanded reality like a fangirl who knew her favorite actor was in town. Now that he believed, he suspected the supernatural of lurking around every corner. Sometimes he even spotted it. Sometimes he called Tony.

*"What's about six centimeters high and can take a bite out of a car bumper?"*

*"What?"*

*"I think I saw one in the impound yard. Maybe more than one."*

Finally recognizing the voice, Tony'd rolled over and squinted at the clock. *"It's three in the morning."*

*"Does that matter? Do these things only come out between midnight and dawn? What are they?"*

*"How the hell should I know?"*

*"You're the . . ."* Elson's voice—he'd still been Elson then, not yet Jack—had dropped below eavesdropping level. *". . . wizard."*

*"Yeah. Wizard. Not a database for things that go bump in the night."*

*"So you won't tell me."*

*"It's three in the morning, for fuck's sake!"*

*"Why do you keep repeating the time?"*

He'd sighed. *"Because it's three in the morning."*

In a just world, Jack would have gotten discouraged by now. Or distracted.

"Bunch of hikers just spotted a Sasquatch up by Hope—probably not a real one," Tony added quickly. "We're old news." A shadow moved just at the edge of the light, and he rolled his eyes. "Well, to everyone but you and him."

Him. Kevin Groves. Their very own tabloid journalist.

Fortunately, after the house incident, Mason had hogged the spotlight, and for Mason it was all about Mason. Unfortunately, Kevin Groves had apparently heard the bits of truth nearly buried under ego.

To his great disappointment, after official statements were taken—and with three dead under mysterious circumstances official statements *were* taken—no one really wanted to talk much about what had happened. They seemed almost embarrassed about having been a part of a paranormal experience, given the kind of people to whom those sorts of things generally happened. In the public perception, haunted houses came just under alien anal probes and slightly above thousand-year-old lizard babies. Group gestalt insisted on a rational explanation for everything that could possibly be given one and refused to admit to the rest, leaving Kevin Groves lurking unfulfilled around the soundstage and being regularly escorted off location shoots.

Although it was clear that an unwillingness to talk didn't mean that anyone had actually forgotten the experience. No one ever seemed to be under a certain place on the soundstage between 11:00 and 11:15 AM or PM and Tony's *abilities* were used whenever they'd save a few moments or dollars. Television people dealt with the surreal on a daily basis and had managed to work a couple more bits in with little difficulty.

It helped that Tony had been a PA back in August, bottom man on the television totem pole, so anything too bizarre coming from his position wasn't exactly hard for them to ignore.

"I wouldn't be so fast to dismiss Mr. Groves, if I were you," Jack observed around a final mouthful of oatmeal raisin. "It mostly got lost in all of Mason Reed's posturing, but don't forget that there were interesting things said about your actions that night."

Tony sighed. "Yes, I have vast and incredible powers."

"You talk to dead people."

"So? I also talk to my car and the bank machine."

"Dead people talk to you."

"What, you never caught an episode of *Crossing Over* back when it was on six or seven times a day? Apparently, dead people talk to everyone."

"You . . ." He waved a hand.

Tony raised an eyebrow, the movement attaching a certain smuttiness to the unspoken part of the constable's observation.

Jack snorted, refusing to be baited. "The word wizard *was* mentioned."

"Yeah, so were the words mass hallucination and gas leak. If I'm such a mighty wizard, don't you think I'd have better things to do than stand around on the edge of a construction zone at one o'clock in the morning?"

"What, and give up show business?" Brushing cookie crumbs off his jacket, Jack grinned, golden stubble glinting in the spill of light from the streetlamp.

The grin made Tony nervous.

It was supposed to. And knowing that didn't help.

"I'll go have a word with Mr. Groves."

"I can't stop you."

"You know, you're not as dumb as you look."

Since *"neither are you"* would be an enormously stupid thing to say, Tony bit his tongue as the RCMP officer walked toward the reporter.

"Cut! Good, that's got it!"

*"Tony."* Adam's voice in his ear. *"Go get Padma."*

The conversation with Jack had moved him nearly back beside the trailer shared by makeup and wardrobe. He leaned in through the open door and saw it was empty but for Padma Sathaye, the victim of the week. Ready for her scene, she was sitting in the makeup chair, absently rocking it back and forth with the pointed toe of one shoe, and reading an Elizabeth Fitzroy romance novel. *Sweet Savage Seas,* Tony noted; one of the older ones.

"Padma? They're ready for you."

She murmured a distracted reply, read for a second longer, and then closed the book around a folded piece of tissue. "I'm afraid I have a bad addiction to trashy romance novels," she told him apologetically as she stood.

"Who says they're trashy?"

"Pretty much everybody."

"I don't."

"But you wouldn't be caught dead reading one."

"I've read a couple."

The caked blood kept her from smiling too broadly. "How very sensitive new age guy of you."

He shrugged and stood to one side to let her pass. He'd read them because Elizabeth Fitzroy was the pseudonym of Henry Fitzroy, once Duke of Richmond and Somerset, bastard son of Henry VIII, vampire, and one of his exes.

Sort of ex.

Sort of . . . not.

Henry Fitzroy—Prince of Man, Prince of Darkness—was just a little on the possessive side. As far as he was concerned, Tony would always be one of his.

Mostly, that was all right by Tony. He liked to keep things friendly with all his exes. Hell, he saw Zev all the time at work and they still occasionally hung out. It used to be like that with Henry. Even a couple of months ago, he'd have given the vampire a heads up on this night shoot so they could hang together for a while, but things had cooled between them since the incident with the house.

Since it had become obvious that Henry'd developed some kind of connection with Chester Bane.

Okay, strictly speaking, things hadn't so much cooled as Tony'd cooled things.

He didn't like Henry becoming a part of his daytime life. He might be Henry's, but this show, this job, was his—and Henry could just piss off and stop bonding with his boss.

He wished he had the guts to ask CB if they were still in touch.

Following Padma across the street, he noted Everett, the makeup artist, standing by the video village, a gallon of fake blood at his feet. Beside him, Alison Larkin from wardrobe sketched costumes in the air; her every gesture threatening to drench the immediate area in coffee. As far as Tony knew, she'd never lost a drop. He placed the genny op, light techs, sound techs . . . the greater part of his job on location was knowing where people were so he could find them if needed.

Jack and Kevin Groves seemed to have left the area. Probably not together. Hopefully not together. Unless Jack had arrested the reporter for loitering with intent.

No. Not even then. Jack knew enough that Tony wanted the reporter nowhere near him for any length of time even if that time involved handcuffs. And not in a fun way.

"Come on, people, let's move!" Adam's voice set the crew in motion. "We've only got the street for one more night and second unit's got it all tied up!"

Padma laughed at something Lee said as she arranged herself on the pavement and Mason smacked his costar lightly on the arm. Peter shuffled the two men into position, Adam called for quiet, and they were rolling again.

Raymond Dark and James Taylor Grant stared down at the body that had just landed at their feet.

They weren't the only ones.

Tony's gaze flicked up to the rooftop.

Something else was watching . . .

Wonderful.

It was like having fucking gaydar for the supernatural.

*"So I have to be careful now because I'm a player?"* It was one of the last conversations he'd had with Henry before he'd stopped returning the vampire's calls. *"What was I before?"*

Henry's eyes had silvered slightly, a sign that the Hunger was near the surface. *"A victim. But there's enough of them that you had a chance of being lost in the crowd. Now, you stand out."*

He'd very nearly responded with something stupidly cliché about how he thought he'd been more than just a meal to the other man. Stomping hard on his inner drama queen, he'd snarled, *"I'm not saying I don't appreciate your help, but I've been taking care of myself since I was fourteen."*

*"You survived . . ."*

*"Yeah, my point. Before you came along to hold my dick, I survived just fine."*

*"Things are different now."*

*"And that gives you the right to bite down on the rest of my life?"*

*"What?"*

The conversation had deteriorated around then, but the point was, if Tony was sensing a supernatural watcher on the roof, he was probably sensing Henry playing Mother Hen of the Night. Sure, he hadn't told Henry about the shoot, but Henry had new contacts in the business now.

He flipped a finger in the general direction of the feeling.

"CB Productions, can I help you? Uh-huh. Uh-huh." Tucking the phone under her chin, Amy waved her left hand in Tony's general direction while she doodled on a message pad with her right. "No, I'm sorry, that's not possible."

He crossed to her desk during the other half of the conversation and noted that up close her fingernails weren't a uniform black. Each nail also wore a tiny, white stick-on skull.

"Look . . ." She methodically scratched out what she'd already written. ". . . why don't I just put you through to our office manager? Okay. Just stay on the line." Pushing the hold button, she hung up the receiver and frowned up at Tony over the blinking red light. "What are you doing here? You're working second unit tonight."

"CB wanted to see me." Tony glanced around to see that Rachel Chou, the office manager, was noticeably absent. "Shouldn't you find Rachel?"

"Why?"

He nodded toward the phone.

Amy snorted. "She's not in the office today. That asshat can stay on hold until she gets back for all I care."

"Nice." Tony picked up one hand and took a closer look at the nails. "Skulls glow in the dark?"

"Uh-huh."

"Hair, too?" White strips of hair bracketed her face. They seemed slightly greenish next to the matte black of the rest.

"Please; too tacky." Lids lowered, she tipped her face up. "But my eye shadow does."

Wondering why glow-in-the-dark hair was tackier than glow-in-the-dark eye shadow—and skulls—he leaned forward for a closer look.

"Don't do it, Amy. He'll make you watch old black-and-white movies."

"Don't do what?" Tony demanded, turning in time to see the door to post close and Zev start across the office.

"She looked like she was about to make an unhealthy commitment."

"As if. And what's wrong with black-and-white movies?" Amy leaned to the right so she could see the music director.

Zev grinned within the shadow of his dark beard. "He keeps pausing so he can comment on the way they used to set up scenes."

She jerked her hand out of Tony's grip. "Is he kidding?"

"No, but . . ."

"Dude, you've got to work a little harder at getting a life."

"I used to have one." Tony nodded toward Zev. "He broke up with me."

"Yeah. Quel surprise."

Shoving his hands into the front pockets of his jeans, Zev frowned thoughtfully in Tony's general direction. "I thought you were doing second unit tonight?"

"I am."

"CB wants to see him." Amy's tone suggested last requests, last meals, last rites.

"Why?"

Tony shrugged. "I don't know."

They turned as one toward the closed door of the boss' office. The scuffed wood gave nothing away.

"He's just running over the stunt with Daniel," Amy murmured.

"Daniel's not doing the stunt."

"Gee . . ." Eyes rolled. ". . . I can't see why not. Daniel'd be so convincing as a not very tall, gorgeous Indian woman."

"Well, the not-very-tall would give him a few problems," Zev reflected, measuring a space some two meters from the floor.

Daniel was the stunt double for both Mason and Lee. He also acted as coordinator for any stunts performed by outside talent. "Why is it when Frank writes an episode," Tony wondered, "we always need to hire a stuntwoman?"

They turned toward the bull pen. From behind that closed door came the rhythmic sound of someone reading aloud.

Zev frowned. "Maybe he thinks the only way he can get a date is with someone used to risking her life."

"Frank dating?" Amy shuddered. "My mind just went to the scary place."

In the awkward silence that followed, Tony heard maniacal laughter. He might've been worried except it clearly came from one of the writers.

"Not a specific scary place," Amy amended quickly.

They both turned to look at Tony. Amy was the exception to the general rule that those who'd been in the house ignored what had gone on and Zev, as an ex, had certain rights and privileges involving shared history and exploded beer bottles.

"So." She picked at the edge of a skull, then looked up hopefully. "Seen any dead people lately?"

He'd nearly seen Henry keeping tabs on him the night before. But Henry, not being exactly dead, just differently alive, didn't really count. "No."

"But you'll tell me if you do?"

At the edge of his vision, Tony could see Zev shaking his head almost hard enough to dislodge his yarmulke. "Sure . . ."

Zev sighed.

". . . I promise."

♠

"Brianna has been asking after you."

"Brianna? Really?" From the expression on CB's face, that clearly sounded as stupid as Tony suspected. Brianna had been asking for him pretty much every time she spoke to her father. "Uh, in what context?"

CB's eyes narrowed as he leaned back, his leather office chair creaking ominously under his weight. "In what context do you imagine, Mr. Foster?"

"Boss, I swear I never told her she was a wizard!'

"So you've said previously. And, once again, I believe you." He steepled fingers the size of well-muscled bratwurst. "However, as Brianna does not, I think it's time we move on."

*"Move on?"* Tony cleared his throat and tried again an octave lower. "Move on?"

"Yes."

No. He was not going to teach CB's youngest daughter how to be a wizard. First, wizardry was a talent more than a skill, and while Brianna had proved sensitive to the metaphysical, he had no idea if that equaled talent. Or what, exactly, did equal talent, for that matter. Second, he was still teaching himself how to be a wizard and, frankly, as a teacher, he sucked. Scrubbing bubbles and one pissed-off cater-waiter had to be incontestable evidence of that. Third, giving this particular eight-year-old access to actual power would be like . . . his mind shied away from comparisons and settled on: the height of irresponsibility. No one, including her father, could control the kid now. And fourth, he'd rather have toothpicks shoved under his nails.

Mouth open to lay everything but the last point out in front of CB—not smart to give the big guy ideas—he closed it again as CB continued speaking.

"I have a friend putting together a PBS miniseries for Black History Month, so I called in some favors, and he gave my ex-wife a sizable part. She's taking both girls to South Carolina with her. Shooting ends December twentieth. You have until then to come up with a permanent solution."

The pause lengthened.

"Was there anything else?"

Like invasions from another world or a waxy buildup of evil.

"Um, no?"

"Good."

♠

"Permanent solution. Permanent solution." Tony paused, one hand on the door leading out to the parking lot, frozen in place by the sudden memory of his mother sitting at the kitchen table twisting her hair onto multicolored rollers shaped like bones. A home perm. And the permanent solution had totally reeked. He remembered because they were called *Tonys* and his mother used to tease him about being a hairdresser.

Later, like around the time he hit puberty, his father stopped finding the hairdresser jokes quite so funny—Warren Beatty's enthusiastically hetero performance in *Shampoo* conveniently ignored.

His father was no longer a problem given that they hadn't spoken to each other for about ten years.

Brianna's father, however . . .

The door jerked out of his hand, and he stumbled forward, slamming up against a solid body on its way in.

His way in.

Tony recognized the impact. And the black leather jacket he was currently clutching with both hands. "Lee." Two fast steps back. He stared down at his arms still stretched out . . . *Right. Release the jacket.*

"Tony."

Just for a second, Tony was unsure of what Lee's next words were going to be. Just for a second, it almost looked as if the show was over for the day and reality was going to get its time in. Just for a second. Trouble was, a second later Lee pulled his hail-fellow-well-met actor-face back on.

"You okay? I didn't realize there was someone standing there."

"Well, why would you? You know, solid door and all and you not having X-ray vision." X-ray vision? Could he sound any more geeklike? "I was just leaving."

"Right. You're doing second unit work tonight."

Everyone seemed to know that. Were they posting his schedule now or what?

Lee shifted his motorcycle helmet from under his left arm to under his right but didn't actually move out of the doorway. "So you were here to . . ."

"Meeting. I had a meeting with CB."

"Good. I mean, it was good?"

"Yeah. I guess. Still dealing with Brianna's reactions in the . . ." Shit. Never bring up the house thing with Lee.

The actor-face slipped. "In the house?"

Unless he brings it up first. "Yeah. In the house."

Lee's eyes closed briefly, thick lashes lying against his cheeks like the fringe on a theater curtain. Only darker. Not gold. And without the tassels. Tony realized he was babbling to himself, but he couldn't seem to stop. They hadn't been alone together, standing this close, since, well, since the house. For a moment, he hoped that when Lee opened his eyes, the actor-face would be gone and they could maybe start dealing with what had happened.

Lee had to make the first move because Lee was the one with the career he could lose. It was Lee's face plastered on T-shirts worn by teenage girls and forty-year-old women who should know better. Tony was a TAD. Professionally, no one gave a crap about him.

The moment passed.

Lee opened his eyes. "Well, I have to say that it's been nice running into you and all, but I need to get to my . . ." Dark brows drew in, and he waved the hand not holding the helmet.

"Dressing room?"

"Yeah." The smile was fake. Well done, but fake. "My memory sucks some days."

Tony reflected the smile back at him. "Old age."

"Yeah." The smile was still fake, but the regret flattening his words seemed real. "That has to be it."

♠

Tony squinted up at the top of the building, trying to count the number of people standing at the edge of the roof. Sorge's request for a steadicam had been overruled by the budget, so there should only be two: Leah Burnett, the stuntwoman doing the fall, and Sam Tappett, one of Daniel's safety crew. Two. Not a hard number to count. Most nights he could even do it with his shoes on. So why did he keep getting three? Not every time—because that would have made sense. Every now and then, he thought—no, cancel that, he was *sure*—he could see a third figure.

Not Henry.

Not tonight.

Not unless Henry had been growing an impressive set of horns in his spare time and had then developed the ability to share his personal space with mere mortals. The same actual space. Sort of superimposed.

Welcome to the wonderful world of weird.

Déjà vu all over again.

The question now: should he do anything about it and, if so, what?

It wasn't like his spidey-sense was tingling or something in his subconscious was flailing metaphorical arms and wailing *Danger, Will Robinson! Danger!* He didn't have a bad feeling about things, and he had no idea if this was a threat or some kind of symbolic wizard experience. Maybe it was something all wizards saw on top of buildings at—he checked his watch—11:17 on Thursday nights in early October and he'd just never been looking in the right place at the right time.

Still, as a general rule, when he saw things others couldn't, the situation went south in a big way pretty fucking fast.

Unfortunately, none of the second unit crew had been in the house. They'd heard the stories, but they didn't know. Not the way those who'd been trapped and forced to listen to hours of badly played thirties dance music knew. If he told Pam, the second unit director, that he intermittently saw a translucent, antlered figure on the roof, she'd assume controlled substances and not metaphysical visitations.

Tony hadn't done hard drugs since just before Henry pulled him off the streets. Point of interest; he'd never seen big, see-through guys with horns while he was shooting up.

He glanced down as a gust of wind plastered a grimy piece of newspaper to his legs. Evening weather reports had mentioned a storm coming in off the Pacific, and the wind was starting to pick up, sweeping up all kinds of debris as it raced through the artificial canyons between the buildings. Before he could grab the newspaper, another gust whirled it away and slapped it up against the big blue inflated bag Leah would land on.

If Daniel thought it was too dangerous, he'd cancel the stunt regardless of the shooting schedule. Tony hurried over to where the stunt coordinator was checking the final inflation of the bag.

"It's getting kind of windy."

"Yes, it is."

"Four stories is a long way to fall."

"Uh-huh." He straightened and bounced against the side of the bag. "That's why they call it a high fall."

"Yeah, it's just that falling four stories the wind'll have longer to throw her off . . ." As Daniel turned to look at him, Tony sputtered to a stop. "But you've taken that into account."

"I have." Stern features under dark stubble suddenly dissolved into a smile. "But I thank you for staying on top of things. It never hurts to have another person thinking about potential problems." He unclipped the microphone from his collar. "Hey, Sam, what's the wind like up there?"

*"Little gusty. Not too bad."*

"What's Leah think?"

During the pause, the antlered figured came and went and came again. It almost seemed to wave when Leah did.

*"She says she's good to go whenever you give the word."*

"We're ready down here. Pam, we can go any time."

*"Glad to hear it."* Pam's voice in the ear jack. *"Let's have a slate on the scene and get started!"*

Tony backed away from the bag as Daniel's people took up their positions. Since a high fall relied 100 percent on the stuntee's ability to hit the bag safely, the stunt crew were essentially there to deal with a miss. Tony wouldn't have wanted to see the backboard so prominently displayed were he about to jump off a roof, but, hey, that was him.

"Quiet, please, cameras are rolling."

A repeat of "Rolling!" in half a dozen voices rippled out from the director's chair.

"Scene 19b, high fall, take one. Mark!"

"Action."

Far enough away now, Daniel's voice sounded in Tony's ear jack. *"On three, Leah. One . . ."*

Up on the roof, Sam would be echoing the count, fingers flicking up to give visual cues.

A gust of wind blew a bit of dirt in Tony's eye. He ducked his head just in time to see that same gust about to fling a ten-centimeter piece of aluminum with a wickedly pointed end into the bag.

*"Two."*

Impact wouldn't make anything as simple as a hole. At that angle, at that speed, it was going to be a gash. And a big one.

*"Three."*

The *wham whoosh* of impact and applause from the crew covered the sound of aluminum slapping into Tony's palm. The jagged piece of debris had probably blown down from the construction site. *Revenge of the backhoe.*

"Cut!"

He looked up as Leah climbed down off the bag, Daniel, grinning broadly, reaching out a hand to steady her. The fall had clearly not been a problem; the high heels, on the other hand, were giving her a little trouble. She was smiling, definitely happy, but less overtly euphoric than a lot of stuntees were after nailing a four-story fall.

She didn't look like Padma. She looked like a stuntwoman wearing the same costume over some strategic padding.

*So much for the magic of television.*

It took a moment for Tony to realize she was staring at him.

No, not at him. At the piece of aluminum still in his hand.

As though she'd suddenly become aware of his attention, she lifted her head. Lifted one dark, inquiring brow.

Even the see-through guy with horns sharing her space seemed interested.

NIGHT SHOOTS ALWAYS THREW Tony's sleeping patterns out of whack. When a guy his age got off work, he was supposed to go out and do things. He wasn't supposed to drive straight home and fall over. It wasn't just wrong, it was old. It was what old guys did.

Except there wasn't a whole lot to do at 2:30 on a Thursday morning in beautiful downtown Burnaby.

Cradling a bag of overpriced groceries from the 7-Eleven, Tony kicked the door to his apartment closed and shuffled into the tiny kitchen. The shuffling was necessary because he'd started sorting laundry back on Monday, hadn't quite finished yet, and didn't want to start again from scratch because he'd mixed the piles. The bread and milk went into the fridge. He tucked the bottle of apple juice under his arm and carried the bag of beef jerky and the spray cheese into the living room—where *living room* was defined as the part of the long rectangle that contained an unmade sofa bed instead of a stove, a fridge, and a sink.

The television remote was not in the pizza box under the couch. It finally turned up on top of the bookcase by the window, half buried in the pot with the dead geranium. Raising it in triumph, he settled back against the pillows, sprayed some cheese on a piece of jerky and started channel surfing with the mute on.

Replay of a hockey game on TSN, end of hurricane season on *Outdoor Life*, remake of *Smokey and the Bandit* . . .

"Which after *The Longest Yard* and *The Dukes of Hazard* pretty much proves there is no God," he muttered, jabbing his thumb at the remote.

. . . some guy eating a bug on either the Learning Channel or FOOD—he didn't stay long enough to see if it came with a lecture on habitat or a raspberry vinaigrette—three movies he'd already seen, two he didn't want to see, a bug eating some guy on either Discovery or Space, someone knocking at the door . . .

His thumb stilled.

Someone knocking at *his* door. Carefully. Specifically. Trying not to wake the neighbors.

It didn't sound like Henry's knock. He checked his watch: 2:57. Besides the vampire, who did he know who'd be up at this hour? Even tabloid journalists eventually crawled back under their rocks for a nap. It wasn't Jack Elson or his partner; the police had a *very* distinctive knock.

Might be Conner, that friend of Everett's he'd met while visiting the makeup artist in the hospital. They'd gone for coffee but hadn't been able to hook up since—Conner worked in the props shop at one of the other Burnaby studios, and his hours were as insane as Tony's. Maybe their schedules had finally matched up.

Of course, Conner'd have no way of knowing that.

Unless Everett had told him.

Hell, if he was going to imagine hot guys, why not drop all the way into fairy-tale land and assume it was Lee, no longer conflicted and unable to deny the blistering passion between them. Okay, for passion substitute a couple of possessed kisses—but they'd been pretty damned hot.

Another knock.

*Of course, I could just get off my ass, walk a few meters, and find out.* Dropping the spray cheese down in a pile of blankets by the jerky, Tony headed for the door.

There was a spell on the laptop called "Spy Hole" that allowed the wizard to see through solid objects. The first time

Tony'd tried it, he'd given it a little too much juice and gotten way too good a look at Mr. Chansky across the hall in apartment eleven. Talk about being scared straight. The experience had convinced him that sometimes the old ways were the best. Leaning forward, he peered through the security peephole.

Leah Burnett.

And the translucent overlay of the big guy with antlers.

She grinned up at the lens and lifted a bag of Chinese food into Tony's field of vision.

All right. She had his attention.

Stepping back, he opened the door.

"Hey." She waved the bag. "I thought we should talk."

"All three of us?"

"Three? If you have company . . ."

"No." He just moved enough to stay solidly in her line of sight, blocking her view of the apartment. "You, me, and the guy sharing your space."

Dark eyes widened. "Guy?"

"Big guy." He held his hand about half a meter over her head.

"Really? What does this *guy* look like?"

"Hard to say, he's a little fuzzy. Got a rack on him like Bambi's dad, though."

"And you can see him right now?"

"Not right now. He kind of comes and goes."

"Uh-huh." A quick glance up and down the hall. "Maybe we should discuss this inside."

"Got something to hide?"

"Just trying to keep you out of trouble with your neighbors."

That seemed fair. Besides, there were precautions in place in case he was actually in any danger from her. Them. Although, given the Chinese food and all, he doubted it. Opening the door all the way, Tony tucked himself up against the wall and beckoned the stuntwoman in.

The glyphs painted across the threshold were supposed to flare red and create an impenetrable barrier if danger approached—it had taken days of fine-tuning to stop them from going off for the pizza girl, Mr. Chansky, and the elderly cat who lived at the end of the hall. As Leah stepped into the apartment, they flared white then orange then green then a couple of colors Tony suspected the human eye shouldn't actually be able to see. The pattern slammed out to fill the doorway, turned gray, and fluttered to the floor.

Leah brushed at the shoulder of her jacket, the pale ash smearing across the damp fabric. "Sorry about that." Her nose wrinkled as the smell of burned cherries momentarily overwhelmed the smell of the Chinese food. "What did you paint those on with, cherry cough syrup?"

"Yeah." When she stared up at him in astonishment, he shrugged. Carefully. His head felt like he'd just been hit repeatedly with a rubber mallet. "Cherry was the only flavor that worked. And," he added, hoping he sounded like he believed it was possible, "I will fireball your ass if you try anything."

"Like what?"

"Sorry?"

She pulled the door out of his hand and closed it. "What are you expecting me to try?"

He had no idea, so he followed her farther into the apartment.

"I suppose I should be impressed that a guy your age actually sorts his laundry," she muttered stepping over a pile of jeans and up to the kitchen counter where she set the bag down, shrugged out of her jacket, and started opening cupboards. "Ah. Plates." And a moment later. "Cutlery?"

"In the drawer by the fridge."

"Right. It's mostly plastic."

"They were free."

"Fair enough." She handed him a full plate and stepped over socks and underwear and stood staring at the rest of the apartment. "Daniel told me you were gay."

"Yeah."

"Way to work against the stereotype."

"What?"

Her gesture took in the walls, the floor, and most of his furniture. "It's beige."

"It was beige when I got here."

"You have a flag tacked up over the window."

"I'm a patriotic kind of guy."

"The only thing on the wall is a poster for *Darkest Night.*"

"It was free."

"I figured. You seem to have spent everything you've made in the last year on that entertainment center."

"Look . . ." Tony pushed the laptop to one side and set his plate down on the small square table. ". . . if you're here on some weird makeover thing, I don't want my apartment redecorated or my life rearranged."

"You sure?"

Her smile changed the whole shape of her face. Made her look years younger. Made her eyes sparkle. Made her look like someone he'd like to get to know. Really well. Made him want to slide the sweater off her shoulders, push back the dark curls and . . .

. . . he suddenly noticed that the translucent antlered guy looked a lot solider. Except for the horns, and the weird way his eyes had no whites, he seemed to be human. His skin tone was a little deeper than Leah's—a regular coffee instead of a double double—he had a lot of long dark hair twisted into dreads, and he was naked. And, although it was difficult to tell for certain, given that he and Leah were still sharing the same space, remarkably well hung.

*What the fuck?*

Tony shook his head and Leah was once again just a not very tall stuntwoman eating chow mein in his living room. Alone. No overlay of antlered guy. Eyes narrowed, he took a step back and raised the plastic fork. "What was that?"

"A test." She caught a bean sprout before it fell off the edge of her plate. "Ninety percent of men fail it."

Tony did the math. "Well, good for me. I'm really most sincerely gay."

"And yet you still can't afford a gallon of periwinkle paint?"

"Yeah, well here's a thought . . ." He moved a pile of old

sides—the half-size sheets with all the background information for each day's shoot as well as the necessary script pages—and sat on the steadier of his two folding chairs. ". . . unless that guy is your inner interior decorator, how about you let the beige thing go and tell me what the hell is going on?"

She thought about it for a moment, then nodded and sat on the edge of his bed. "You're a wizard."

Tony just barely managed to resist coming back with, *I know I am, but what are you?* It was just past three in the morning, for fucksake. He was a little punchy. He swallowed a mouthful of beef fried rice and said: "You're . . . ?"

"Not." A wave of her fork, dangling a piece of overcooked bok choi, cut off his reply. "It's complicated. Maybe you should call your teacher, and I'll only have to go through it once."

"My teacher?"

"Mentor. Whatever you call the senior wizard in charge of your education." Dark eyes sparkled again. "I'm assuming that in this brave new millennium you don't use the word master."

"What makes you think I have a teacher?"

Leah sighed. "You're young. Far too young to be on your own."

"Surprise." He spread his hands.

Brows rose. "What happened to your teacher?"

He pushed chow mein around his plate. "I thought we were going to talk about the naked horny dude."

Fortunately, only a little rice went up her nose. When she finished laughing and snorting and blowing her nose on the crumpled handful of toilet paper Tony'd brought from the bathroom, she said, "His name is Ryne Cyratane. It means: He Who Brings Desire and Destruction. He's a Demonlord."

"Oh, man." The fork bounced as he dropped it on the table. "Not again."

"Excuse me?"

"A few years ago, some friends of mine stopped a Demonlord from coming through in Toronto."

"Coming through?"

"Yeah, there was this lesser demon writing the Demonlord's name on the city in blood and . . ." He frowned, trying unsuccessfully to remember the specifics Henry had told him about how they'd finally defeated it. "It got complicated, but he didn't make it."

"Obviously." Her tone went beyond dry to desiccated. "Well, there's no need for you to worry about this one. I've got him contained." She stood and pulled up her sweater.

"Nice tat."

"Thank you." It circled her navel, row after row of black glyphs spreading almost up to the edge of her ribs like ripples moving out from the point of impact. "It's a Demongate. As long as I live, the gate stays closed and my lord is denied reentry to this world."

"Your lord?"

"Long story."

"Okay. Reentry?"

"He was here about four thousand years ago. For almost five hundred years, worshiped as a god, he ruled a territory in what's now Lebanon. Ish. Same general geography anyway, near as I can figure. He had a temple, he had handmaidens, he had a lot of sex."

That would be the desire part, Tony figured.

"Then something came up—he's never said what—and he created a gate to return to the hell he came from. It took a lot of power. To get it, he killed everyone in the village and, with their blood, anchored the gate in his sole surviving handmaiden."

And that would be the destruction. Tony leaned closer. The tat wasn't black. Not exactly. It was a very, very dark red-brown. "You're the handmaiden."

"Handmaiden, priestess, lover; I was his . . ."

"Girlfriend?" He winced at her expression. "Sorry. I was just channeling *Young Frankenstein,* you know when Frau

Blucher is explaining and . . . Never mind. Sorry. Totally inappropriate interruption. I'll just, uh, be quiet now."

She waited a moment longer.

Tony picked up his fork and ate some more rice and tried to look like there was some *other* idiot in his apartment who couldn't keep his mouth shut.

"I was his most beloved." Leah continued at last. Her fingertips lightly stroked the edges of the pattern, raising goose bumps on her skin. "He cut the gate into my flesh, glyphs written in the blood of my people, because he intended to return but would be unable to open the gate from the other side. Gates from the hells have to be opened from our side or we'd be overrun by demons in a heartbeat."

"And they have to be asked in?" Then he remembered that he'd said he'd be quiet and he shrugged apologetically, but she seemed resigned to the interruption.

"You're confused, that's vampires."

It didn't seem like the right time to correct her. Henry went where he wanted. "Why didn't this Ryne Citation . . ."

"Ryne Cyratane."

"Right. Why didn't he just leave the gate open?"

"Because that would have been just asking for another Demonlord to come along and try to take it over. And, before you ask, the wizard who had opened the original gate was long dead."

"Dead wizard." Yeah, that sounded encouraging. "Nice."

"Probably not. Anyway, Ryne Cyratane figured that I'd be able to stand what he'd done to my people for just long enough for him to finish up his business at home and then grief and guilt would cause me to take my own life. Should I be stronger than my grief, it wouldn't much matter because time was on his side and a human life is pitifully short to the demon kin—and, back then, pitifully short was even shorter. Unfortunately for his plans, he made a small error—although, to be fair, I was squirming a bit while he incised the protection runes." She traced the outer ring. "He intended to protect the gate from me, to keep me from defacing the pattern, thus destroying the gate and preventing him from returning, but he ended up writing in a much more powerful and general protection.

"The gate protects itself and, in protecting itself, protects me. I can't be injured because that would affect the gate. I can't age because that would affect the gate. I am held as I was the day he left this world."

"Four thousand years ago?" And that would make her . . . "You're four thousand years old?"

She shrugged and sat back down on the end of the bed, retrieving her plate and looking mid-twenties at the absolute outside. Jeans. Sweater. High-tops. "More or less. Probably closer to thirty-five hundred. You lose track after a while."

Given the whole vampires, wizards, other worlds, sentient shadows, trapped ghosts deal, he saw no reason to doubt her. Precedent suggested the world was about a hundred and eighty degrees weirder than most people suspected and, these days, nothing much surprised him. Besides, hers wasn't the kind of story a sane person would make up. On the other hand, she did fall off buildings and set herself on fire for a living, so perhaps sanity wasn't a given here.

"So . . ." He groped his way back to the beginning of the story. ". . . this Ryne Cyratane slaughtered everyone you knew?"

"Every single person. Even called the goatherds in from the hills."

"I don't want to bring up old shit, but . . ." Tony pushed a cashew around his plate until it slid off the edge, bounced across the table, and off onto the floor. Only then did he look up and meet her gaze. "He slaughtered everyone, and you don't seem too upset by that."

"What do you expect?" Her shrug was perfect twenty-first century ennui. "It happened a very long time ago. I've dealt. You should have seen me right afterward, I was a mess." She widened her eyes, raised both hands, fingers spread, and shook them from side to side. "I was the crazy lady who lived in the wilderness for about three hundred years. One day I was a warning to misbehaving children, next thing I knew I was being fished out of the Nile by the servants of a priest of

Thoth. He cleaned me up, brought me back to myself. *He* was a wizard." Her eyes unfocused and the corners of her mouth curled into a smile as she examined the memory. "And kind of cute in a shaved head, totally fanatical sort of way."

"What happened to him?"

"He got a little too ambitious and the governor fed him to the crocodiles."

Crocodiles? Tony wished the threats on *his* life were so mundane. "Couldn't have been much of a wizard."

"They were very large crocodiles. And there were a lot of them."

"What happened to you?"

Attention snapped back onto Tony's face. "Do you really want the whole life story? Because until the last couple of centuries, it's been pretty much centered in and around the beds of powerful men."

It'd been more than that—frighteningly more—Tony could see a bloody history lurking behind Leah's glib comment. But he could also see she didn't want to share. Not a problem. He didn't like handing out every detail of his back story either. "So this demon has been trying to get back through the gate for thirty-five hundred years."

Dark brows drew in. "No. What makes you say that?"

"Well, he's . . . you know." He waved at where the translucent image would be and realized it hadn't been around since Leah's little orientation "test."

"Oh, that. We're connected, of course, but after all this time he knows I'm not going to kill myself, so he lives his own life. He's probably hanging around the gate right now because of the Demonic Convergence."

"Say what?"

"The reason I'm here."

"Right."

"And he's usually around during sex."

Tony raised the fork again.

She grinned and rolled her eyes. "Stop panicking, we've already established that's not going to happen. But if it did, the energy created while I adjusted your lifestyle would go through the gate and into my lord—as long as he's close enough to the gate at his end."

"The Demonlord gets off through you?" That sounded just a little ethically kinky.

"Not exactly off. He gains power from sex. Always has. The man/woman variety only, though . . ." Her voice picked up a slightly mocking tone. ". . . which seems kind of limiting for a demon powered by sexual energies, but there you go."

"You're feeding him? With sex?" Scratch the qualifier. Tony liked to think he didn't judge, but there was a definite ethical kink in the stuntwoman's lifestyle.

"Well, he *was* my god," Leah reminded him pointedly. "And," she continued before he could respond, "there've been benefits on my side over the years. Like . . . the years. And a certain . . ." Dark eyes gleamed. ". . . vitality."

"He slaughtered your people!"

"You're going to have to let that go," she sighed.

"Why?"

"Because it's ancient history, it's not important, and we have bigger problems."

"Bigger?"

"The Demonic Convergence." Tony could hear the capital letters in her voice. "Energies are aligning. Powerful energies. Powerful enough to crack the barriers between here and the hells."

He had to agree that didn't sound good. "Hells? More than one?"

"Many more."

"Well, isn't that just fucking great." All at once, Chinese food seemed trivial. He put down his fork. "And these energies are powerful enough to open a Demongate?"

Her hand dropped to cradle her stomach. It was the same gesture Tony'd seen pregnant women make and in this context that creeped him right out. "Not this gate. Like I said, it's protected. New gates will be created. Okay, not really gates, more like access points that can be exploited just long enough for something to come through."

"One to a customer?" That sounded good.

She nodded. "But there could be hundreds of them."

That didn't. "Hundreds?"

"Rough estimate." When her expression grew reassuring, Tony figured he must have looked as stunned as he felt. "But don't worry, most of these holes will only go through a few layers, just to the closest hells. The convergent energy has to hit the same spot over and over before we get to anything much bigger than imps." She got up, walked into the kitchen, and set her empty plate in the sink.

Empty. She'd kept eating while she was telling him about demons, and Demongates, and slaughter. *I guess she really has gotten over it. It's just a story to her now.* Maybe someday the Shadowlord and the house would be just stories to him. Maybe. Probably not. Thirty-five hundred years was a lot longer than he'd get. He watched her rinse the plate, set it on the counter, and turn to face him.

"Well?"

"Well what?"

Her expression slid from reassuring to impatient. "Don't you have questions?"

"Yeah. A couple." Understatement. He had so many questions he could barely drag one free of the mess. "Okay. Imps. They're not a problem?"

"Without a wizard they can be one hell of a problem, pardon the pun, but you should be able to deal with any that manage to get through."

"*Manage* to get through?"

"Didn't I tell you?" Leah's sudden smile had so much wattage behind it, her Demonlord made a brief, translucent appearance, flickering in and out again before Tony fully realized he was there. "We'll be smoothing out reality's potholes before anything can come through. I'll find them," she added when he shook his head, "and you'll close them."

"I don't know how!"

"I do." She all but patted him on the head as she passed on her way back to the sofa bed. "I just needed a wizard to implement the knowledge."

Just. As far as Tony could tell the word *just* didn't belong in any sentence spoken since Leah had walked through his door. Just thirty-five hundred years old. Just got a Demongate on the old tum. Just a Demonic Convergence. Just imps. Just needed a wizard. Wait a minute . . . "How did you know?"

"Know?"

"That I was a wizard?"

"I felt you use your power when you kept that piece of flying metal from puncturing the bag, of course. Over the years I've become attuned."

"To power?"

"Among other things." Her expression as she looked up from rummaging in her purse was subtly smuttier than anything Tony could have ever managed. He felt his ears grow hot. Hotter when he realized she was doing it on purpose.

"Stop it."

"Sorry. Bad habit. Sugarless gum?"

"No, thanks." She seemed more amused than contrite. "Hang on; I thought the . . ." He waved a hand in the general direction of her stomach. ". . . the gate thing was supposed to protect you."

Her hand slipped under her shirt again. "It does."

"Then why did you need me out there saving your ass tonight?"

"What makes you think that you weren't there because I needed you to be?" Three and a half millennia of confidence in the question.

"Well, I . . ."

"They tried to burn me at the stake once—well, actually, they tried a number of times, but in this particular instance, it rained for eight days. The wood was too wet to light, and finally one wall of my cell washed away and I escaped."

"I'm surprised you didn't just . . ."

"Fuck my way free? Devout Dominicans; a little too fond of barbeque but devout. They weren't interested. So . . ." She stood and slowly walked over to stand beside his chair, pushing a pile of laundry out of the way with the side of her foot. She wasn't exactly looming over him—she wasn't exactly tall—but she was so *there* that he had to fight the urge to move away from her, to give her space. ". . . are you going to help me out or not?"

"Help you close up imp holes made by a Demonic Convergence?" He was amazed he got that sentence out with a straight face.

"This isn't funny."

Okay. Maybe not entirely a straight face.

"If a shallow hole isn't filled in and the convergent energies keep hitting it and making it deeper, then something a lot more demonic could get through. If that happens, people will die."

That took care of the smiling. "I figured." Nikki, Alan, Charlie, Rahal, Tom, Brenda, Hartley . . . "They always seem to."

"Yeah, they do." Her palm cupped his cheek for a second and he saw thousands of years of people dying while she lived on. He'd have jerked back, but she was gone before he could move, sitting once again on the end of the sofa bed. It had happened so fast he could almost convince himself he'd imagined it. In fact, he had every intention of convincing himself he'd imagined it.

"So . . ." She leaned back on her elbows, crossed her legs, and kicked one sneakered foot in the air. ". . . what happened to your teacher?"

And here they were back at the beginning. And why not answer? It seemed he owed Leah a confidence or two. "She went back to her own world."

"Her own world. Another world?" Leah asked when he nodded. "Not a hell?"

There were wizards nailed to a blackboard. "Not exactly."

"Damn." Apparently, after living for so long, nothing much surprised her either. Tony appreciated how much that simplified things. "Reality's getting a little crowded."

"Tell me about it."

"No." Her foot kicked out and pointed. "Your turn."

So he told her. About the Shadowlord because that was tied up with the whole wizard thing but mostly about Arra and how he hadn't wanted to leave and she hadn't been able to stay. "But she left a lot of information on her laptop about how to be a wizard and I've been . . ." He stopped when Leah raised a hand. "What?"

"You're learning how to manipulate cosmic energies from a home study course designed by a wizard from another world?"

"Yeah."

"Unbelievable."

"What is?"

"Her cosmic energies aren't your cosmic energies."

"What?"

"She's not from *this* world."

"Duh."

Gripping the edge of the sofa bed, Leah sat up and leaned toward him. "Okay, I'll try and make this simple. It's all about energy, right? This Arra did teach you that?"

"Yeah." He tried not to sound defensive and had a feeling he was failing miserably at it.

"So the energy of her world has to have been different from the energy of this world because the whole . . ." One hand rose to sketch a circle in the air. ". . . world is different. Different planet. Different stars. Her energy pattern is therefore *different.* Following me so far?"

"Yeah."

"So, on this world she had to adapt everything she knew to fit a new pattern. To make a square peg—her—fit in a round hole. What worked for her here won't necessarily work for you. You are not a square peg. You're a round peg. The hole is also round. You need to find a teacher who knows what's going on in this world."

Beginning to get pissed about the distinctly patronizing tone, Tony reached out for the spray cheese and the container slapped into his hand. "I seem to be managing."

"What is *that?*"

She sounded more appalled than impressed. Not the reaction he'd expected but then, he reminded himself, she claimed to have met wizards before. "It's a can of spray cheese." He turned it so she could see the label. "I was eating it on beef jerky."

"On beef jerky?" Leah rummaged around in the blankets,

pulled out the open bag of jerky, stared at it, and shuddered. "I can see I've got my work cut out for me. Never mind, we'll deal with your eating habits another time."

"Hey, I'm not the one with a demon in my belly!"

"Oh, for crying out loud, I didn't eat him! And I certainly didn't cover him in . . ." Leaning forward, she snatched the can out of his hand. ". . . an edible cheese product. Doesn't it worry you that the manufacturers feel they have to define it as edible?"

"No."

"Fine!"

"All right, then!"

Leah glared down at the can in one hand and the bag in the other and her lips twitched. Then her whole body. Just for a moment, Tony was afraid that spray cheese and beef jerky were the secret ingredients Ryne Cyratane had been holding back and now, with them both in close proximity, the gate was opening. Then he realized she was trying not to laugh.

Then she wasn't trying anymore.

She laughed like they hadn't been talking about demons and wizards and the possibility of people dying. She laughed like this moment, the moment when laughter overwhelmed her, was the only moment that mattered. Tony smiled as he watched her; it was impossible not to.

It was just as impossible not to join in.

They almost managed to stop a couple of times, then one of them would wave the can of spray cheese and they'd lose it again. Finally, they ended up lying side by side on the sofa bed, gasping for breath.

"Oh, yeah. I needed that." A long breath in and she sat up, twisting just enough to look back over her shoulder at him, pushing dark curls off her face. "Was it good for you?"

Tony ignored her, frowning as he tugged a familiar plastic bag out from under her butt. "You've crushed my jerky."

The brow he could see lifted in a decidedly smutty manner. "Is that what you crazy kids are calling it now? Damn." And the brow dipped down. "Is that the time?"

He squinted toward the TiVo. 4:46. He had to be up for work in three hours and fifteen minutes. "Fuck."

Her turn to ignore him. He was kind of amazed by that actually, all things considered. "I've got to get some sleep." She slid to the edge of the mattress and stood. "I've got a two o'clock call for a CBC Movie of the Week."

"Stunt?"

"It's what I do." Scooping up her purse, she hung it on her shoulder and headed for the door. "If you're finished with work before sunset—they want the light for the shot, reflections on the water and all that artistic crap—can you come by VanTerm? I'll leave word with security."

"Hang on!" He jumped to his feet and followed her. "That's it? We eat chow mein, you tell me we're having a Demonic Convergence with a high chance of imps, and then we just go off to work?"

"Unfortunately, saving the world doesn't buy the groceries." Rummaging in the depths of her bag, she pulled out a slightly crumpled card and passed it to Tony. "My cell number. Call if you're going to be late or you can't make it."

"And?"

"And we'll reschedule. This isn't going to go away; we've got lots of time to fix it."

"Yeah, but when did it *start?*"

"A week ago Monday afternoon at 2:10."

"Really?"

"No. And yes. Approximately." He could hear her smile even though he couldn't see her face. "You really are gullible for a wizard."

"Maybe." Reaching out, he stopped her from opening the door. "But one thing before you go; are you here, in Vancouver, because this is where the convergence is happening, or is it happening here because it's where you are?"

Her expression was almost proud when she turned; like she was about to praise a puppy. "You're smarter than you look."

"Thank you. You didn't answer the question."

"This . . ." A light, almost reverent touch against her stomach. ". . . is the second oldest and most powerful continuously running bit of magic in the world."

"What's the first?"

"I'm not allowed to say."

"Seriously?"

"No, I'm just bullshitting you again." A firmer pat on the sweater above the tat. "This is the oldest."

He literally felt his heart start beating again. The way his life had been going lately, if there *was* an older bit of magic in the world, he could expect it on his doorstep at any time. "That's a sick sense of humor you've got there; I can see why you were a demon's favorite handmaiden."

"Sticks and stones . . ." Ryne Cyratane flashed as she smiled. ". . . won't actually touch me."

"Lucky you. So if you're walking around with the oldest magic in the world, then the convergence is here because you are? Nothing personal," he added when she nodded, "but I wish you were somewhere else."

"Too late now, things have started. And when I say things, I am, of course, referring to the Demonic Convergence eating holes through our reality into a myriad of hells. Bright side, though, with a wizard in the immediate area, the world stands a better chance." Dark brows lifted as she grinned. "You wouldn't wish a worse chance on the world, would you?"

He made a show of thinking about it but didn't fool her.

"You're a good man, Tony Foster." Taking hold of his shoulders, she kissed him gently on both cheeks and murmured something in a language he didn't know. "Sumerian blessing," she told him stepping away. "Roughly translates as 'the gods help those who help themselves.' I left out the part about the goats. Redo the wards before you go to sleep—they won't stop a Demonlord, but they might stop lesser demons."

"Might?"

"Should."

"Should's not a lot more encouraging."

"Best I've got."

Ryne Cyratane flickered again as Leah went out the door. Head half turned, he seemed to be paying more attention to

Leah's surroundings than to his handmaiden although, since Tony was trying to get a better look at his ass, there may have been subtleties missed.

He had just enough cough syrup left to reset the wards. Finished, he closed the file on the laptop, powered down, and closed the door.

*They won't stop a Demonlord, but they might stop lesser demons.*

He locked the door, put the chain on, and shoved a chair up under the handle. One thing he'd learned over the years—it didn't hurt to take precautions and not taking them often hurt a lot. Where hurt could be defined as, *Oh, look, here I am back in the ER.*

He could still catch two hours and forty minutes of sleep if he fell over right now. When the paper bag the Chinese food had come in rattled as he tossed it onto the counter, he realized that they hadn't eaten the fortune cookies. He grabbed one and cracked it.

"The blow from sunlight is more unexpected than the blow from darkness." That was new. "Cookie guys must have gotten themselves a new Magic 8 Ball." Shoving the slip of paper in his pocket, he stripped off his clothes and dropped onto the bed. As he leaned across to get the light, something crinkled under his elbow.

Somehow a copy of *TV Week* magazine had gotten shoved under the bottom sheet. It had been folded open at "Star Spotting" and the photo of Lee and the blonde du jour. It looked like they were coming out of a club. She had both hands wrapped around Lee's arm, her gaze following the strands of long, pale hair blowing up into his face. He looked like he was saying something clever to the crowd of paparazzi, his hand holding a shape in the air.

"Wizards see what's there," Tony told the picture.

He wasn't touching her. He wasn't looking at her. She was an accessory.

A smoke screen.

A lie.

"Yeah." The magazine hit the far wall and fluttered to the floor. "Bitter much?"

He left the television on a blue screen with the sound off. A high-tech night-light for people who knew there were things to be afraid of in the dark.

"Hey, Tony, I got an e-mail from Brianna."

Tony lowered his coffee and peered blearily across the office at Amy. He must be getting old. Two hours and forty minutes sleep just didn't do it for him anymore. "So?"

"You want to know what it says?"

"No."

"It says, 'Tell that jerk-face Tony to check his e-mail.' You know . . ." She leaned back in her chair and flicked an eraser at him. ". . . you might want to try and establish a relationship with someone your own age."

He should have gotten a larger coffee he realized as the eraser bounced off his forehead. Except that he didn't think they made a larger coffee. "We don't have a relationship."

"No? Then why'd you give her your e-mail?"

"I didn't."

"Sure you didn't. You look like shit, by the way. Late night?"

"Very."

"Hot date?"

"Not even remotely."

"Cold date?"

Henry's body temperature was several degrees below normal. Tony wondered why his brain decided to throw that into the conversation. "No date."

"Ah, so you stayed up drowning your sorrows. Dude, I'm there."

Amy had gone off again with Brian—her on again/off again boyfriend—just after the incident in August. She insisted it had nothing to do with what had happened that night, but Tony still felt vaguely guilty even though nothing had specifically happened to Amy. Of course, given that it was Amy . . . well, that might have been the problem.

Tuning out Amy's litany of dating woe, he negotiated a maze of papier-mâché tombstones and headed for the soundstage.

He wasn't sure how he made it through the morning.

Mason's close-ups.

Lee's close-ups.

Padma's close-ups.

The same lines, over and over.

Sorge's anticipated rant about matching light levels between studio and location.

"Welcome to the thrilling and exciting world of syndicated television."

Peter half turned. "What was that, Mr. Foster?"

Oh, shit. Had he said that out loud?

"I . . . um . . . was just . . ."

"Why don't you go make sure Raymond Dark's office is ready."

"Right."

The next scene would be one of the first scenes in the episode, the scene where Padma's character arrived to hire Raymond Dark, someone or something in an advanced state of decay having been lurking about her windows at night. People who worked in the entertainment industry got very blasé about the dead walking.

"This isn't *just* a stalker, Mr. Taylor. Stalkers don't shed parts of their body . . . Sorry."

"Don't shed body parts behind the hedge," Peter called from behind the monitors. "I like the emphasis on just and we're still rolling."

"This isn't *just* a stalker, Mr. Taylor . . ."

Tony let the words wash over him. And over and over, and the moment Peter called lunch, he dropped onto the office couch and closed his eyes.

"Late night?"

No mistaking that crushed-velvet voice. He opened his

eyes to see Lee gazing down at him from a little over an arm's length away. For one damn-the-torpedoes moment Tony thought about asking, *Afraid I'll drag you down here with me?*—but sanity prevailed and he said only: "Very."

"Hot date?"

Been there, done that, had the conversation once already today. "Not even remotely."

"Hey, too bad."

*Oh, no. You don't get to be all happy my love life sucks.* "Bite me."

"Pardon."

Oh, shit. Had he said *that* out loud, too? So much for sanity prevailing. Miss a few hours' sleep and his sense of self-preservation took off for parts unknown. He shoved his fist in his mouth to block a yawn and, when he could talk again, said, "Sorry. I'm so out of it, I don't know what I'm saying."

"Sure."

What was that supposed to mean?

"Pleasant dreams."

Or that, he wondered as Lee walked away.

Worrying about it probably kept him awake for all of three or four minutes. He tossed. He turned. He realized he was probably dreaming about the time Lee suddenly acquired an impressive and familiar set of antlers. Usually, that kind of awareness woke him up but not today. He heard Leah's voice say something about feeding on sexual energies, and he settled back to enjoy the show.

"Tony!"

No.

"Come on, wake up."

Not going to happen. Not now. Not when . . .

"I haven't got time for this shit."

He didn't have a whole lot of choice about waking up when he hit the floor. Rolling over onto his back, he glared up at Jack Elson. "What?"

"I've got a body I want you to look at."

"What?"

"They found a construction worker just down from where you lot were shooting last couple of nights, torn to pieces."

Tony took the RCMP constable's offered hand and allowed the larger man to drag him up onto his feet. "Sucks to be him, but what's that got to do with me?"

"Something bit his arm off."

# Three

"COUGAR. DIDN'T THEY HAVE one in Stanley Park a couple of years ago? Probably ran out of house pets to eat out in the suburbs and wandered into the city."

"Coroner ruled it out."

"Bear, then."

"No."

"Really big raccoon." When Jack took his eyes off the road long enough to glare across the cab of his truck, Tony shrugged. "Raccoons can be pretty damned big. I saw one once about the size of small dog."

"You sure?"

"About what?"

Jack downshifted and accelerated through a changing light. "About what you saw. Maybe it wasn't a raccoon."

"You think I saw a small dog?"

"Don't tell me what I think."

"Fine." Tony sighed. "If you don't think I saw a raccoon, what do you think I saw?"

Another glance across the cab. "You tell me."

"Oh, for fuck's sake; sometimes a raccoon is just a raccoon!" He sank down as far as the seat belt strap would allow.

Tony hadn't wanted to go look at a dead body, particularly not a dismembered dead body, and he'd half hoped that CB would refuse to allow him the time off. Although CB hadn't been happy about losing his TAD for the afternoon, he was well aware of the benefit of remaining in the RCMP's good graces and he'd waved off Tony's protests that he was needed on the soundstage with one massive hand. *"As difficult to believe as it may be, Mr. Foster, I believe production can continue for a few hours without you."*

*"Boss, there's no PA out there yet. I'm it."*

*"So if an errand needs running, someone on the soundstage will have to run it."*

Tony'd opened his mouth to point out how unlikely it was that grips or electricians or carpenters would do any such thing and then closed it again when CB added: *"They'll do it for me."*

Yes, they would. Because no one who worked for Chester Bane would be suicidal enough to refuse although they'd tell themselves they were doing it because it never hurt to do the boss a favor.

Which was also true.

As Jack pulled into the underground parking at Vancouver General Hospital, Tony's stomach growled. "You made me miss lunch," he muttered.

"You may thank me for that," Jack told him, turning off the truck. "Come on."

The city morgue was in the basement near the end of a long hall made narrow by line of gurneys, wheelchairs, and a locked filing cabinet. Cramped conditions along the outside walls of the outer office made the reason for outsourcing the filing cabinet clear. A middle-aged Asian woman wearing the end-of-her-rope expression common to professionals who fought with bureaucracy on a daily basis sat at one of the cluttered desks forking noodles out of a Styrofoam bowl.

"Dr. Wong."

She waved the fork in Jack's general direction and continued chewing.

"This is the witness I mentioned earlier. Should we just go on in?"

Fork tines pointed toward the set of double doors in the back wall.

"Thanks. We won't be long."

A large hand between Tony's shoulder blades got him moving again in spite of his brain locking things down by suddenly repeating *dismembered dead body* over and over as though it had just realized what that meant.

"Elson."

Jack paused in the doorway, leaving Tony staring into a harshly lit room at a bank of stainless steel drawers familiar to anyone who'd ever turned on a television set.

"If he pukes, you clean it up."

Jack snorted. "If he pukes, he cleans it up."

"Hey!" He turned just far enough to glare back through the open door at the doctor. "I'm not going to puke."

"Yeah." She plunged her fork back into the noodles. "That's what they all say."

And then the door was closed and Jack was walking across the room and opening a drawer.

Pulling it open.

Exposing the dead body.

The dismembered dead body.

For him to look at.

Look at the dismembered dead body.

"Oh, for Christ's sake, Foster. You've seen bodies before."

"I know."

"So get your ass over here."

It wasn't so much the body, it was the morgue and the drawer and the smell—the place smelled like the grade ten biology lab just before the whole fetal pig fiasco; he'd dropped out a week later—the combination made it creepier than he was used to.

*Creepier than a dead baby in a backpack, its life sucked out by an ancient Egyptian wizard? Creepier than a man bouncing off a window, every bone in his body broken? Creepier than watching a wardrobe assistant gurgle out her last breath through the ruin of her throat?*

*Well, if you put it that way . . .*

At least this guy was likely to stay dead.

Fingers crossed about that whole staying dead thing, Tony walked over to the open drawer.

He didn't recognize the construction worker, but then he hadn't seen any of them naked so that might be a factor. The left arm was missing about ten centimeters below the shoulder, the edges of the wound ragged, the end of the bone crushed. "Where's the arm?"

"No one knows."

"Nice."

"Probably not. Losing the arm didn't kill him; whatever took it also broke his neck. What do you see?"

"Dead guy missing an arm."

"Tony."

"Seriously. That's all I . . ."

"What?"

Frowning, Tony walked around the drawer and stared at the construction worker's other side. Head cocked, he spread his fingers and tried to match the tips of the first three and his thumb into a line of gouges ending in deep punctures. "Is there a set just like this on the guy's back?"

"Why?"

Wizards saw what was there. "Because if there is, it's how it held on while it bit the arm off."

There was a set of identical punctures in the guy's back.

"It?" Jack demanded.

Tony shrugged. "Your guess is as good as mine."

"Probably not!"

Yeah, okay. That was valid. He took another look at the body. Something with three fingers and impressive claws had definitely bitten the poor bastard's arm off. And that was all he had.

Not an imp, though. Not unless the Demonic Convergence imps were bigger than the regular kind, and Leah's attitude had implied they weren't. She'd said he wouldn't have any trouble dealing with them and, although his ego was plenty healthy, he suspected he'd have a little trouble dealing with whatever the hell had been snacking on construction workers.

Worker.

So far.

Great. This meant there was something going on in Vancouver besides the Demonic Convergence. And Henry. *Yeah, we're a happening kind of place.*

"If you've got something, Tony, spit it out."

He rubbed the edge of the stainless steel table with his thumb. "It's not about this."

"For Christ's sake, try and stay focused. I've got a dead man here, and . . ." When Jack's voice trailed off, Tony looked up to find the constable's pale eyes locked on his face. "It's more weirdness, isn't it? There're two sets of weird going on. This . . ." He waved a hand over the body. ". . . and whatever you decided didn't do this."

"It's nothing."

"Oh, no. This is something so the other thing, it doesn't get to be nothing until I say it's nothing."

Tony ran over that in his head and wasn't sure where he ended up. "What?"

"Talk. Or we stay in here until you do."

♦

"So this Demonic Convergence thing, it started a week ago but it isn't responsible for this?"

"No. Probably not." Jack's expression suggested he be more definite and since hanging around in the morgue was beginning to freak him out, that seemed like a good idea. "Definitely not," he amended.

"Demonic Convergence says demons to me, and a demon could have done this."

"Yeah, but there's barely even been enough time for it to wear reality away to the point where imps could get through." Tony was improvising now off very little information, but Jack didn't need to know that. "No way the Demonic Convergence had anything to do with this unfortunate man's death."

Jack stared at him for a long moment and then slammed the drawer. Fortunately, the seals absorbed most of the sound. "So what did?"

"I have no idea."

◆

"Layers of hells?"

"Yeah."

"But if hell exists, then . . . just, no."

Tony braced himself as the truck briefly lifted up onto two wheels while taking the exit off Lougheed. "If it helps, it's not hell like a church-sponsored hell. It's hell like a really shitty place to be stuck in, so why not call it hell. If you live there, you probably call it something like Scarborough."

"What?"

"It's a Toronto thing."

"Then no one outside of Toronto cares." Palming the wheel around, Jack hit the gas and set about trying to break the sound barrier heading south on Boundary Road. "So I can expect demons as this Convergence goes on?"

"First, demons would be a long shot even if there was no one around to take care of things. Second, I'm on it."

"Is that a 'no'?"

"That's a no. Although there might be a few imps."

"Imps?"

"Sort of small, mostly harmless demons."

"Can I shoot them?"

"How should I know?"

"You're the wizard. How long is this Convergence going to last?"

"No idea."

Like many very fair men, Jack turned almost purple when upset. Tony took pity on him before he blew an artery. "I'll check some stuff out, okay? When I have answers, you'll have answers."

"What kind of stuff?"

"Wizard stuff."

"This is totally insane."

"Don't blame me, you're the one who decided to go all Nightstalker. You know, a little denial can be a lot healthier."

"Not in my line of work. I'm after the truth." He narrowly missed running down a young woman pulling a two-meter-high Dutch windmill on a dolly and sighed. "That sounded inanely pompous, didn't it?"

"Had a certain Fox Mulder-like quality to it, yeah."

The truck rocked to a stop in front of the studio, momentum fighting brakes hard enough that Tony's face nearly impacted with the dashboard. From his sudden vantage point, he could see other vaguely oily scuff marks. His face hadn't been the first. He supposed it was encouraging that Jack's driving hadn't been aimed specifically at him—he'd been starting to think he inspired a certain lunacy behind the wheel. Some kind of wizard leakage thing.

"I'm fine, thanks for asking," he muttered as he straightened, fumbling for the seat belt.

"You're welcome. You've got my cell number?"

"Yeah." Jack's card was in his wallet right next to Leah's. The cop and the stuntwoman. The RCMP and the Demongate. Small world. He jumped out of the truck and turned to close the door.

"Hey." Jack leaned toward him. "If you find out what killed that guy, you call me."

"I'll call," Tony sighed. He closed the door and looked in through the open window. "But whatever it is, you won't be able to arrest it."

"I can arrest anything I can get a pair of cuffs on," Jack snarled, slammed the truck into gear, and roared off. Traffic stuttered to give him room, and Tony had an instant's unobstructed view of the other side of the street . . .

. . . and Kevin Groves. The tabloid reporter looked like he'd just won a lottery.

♦

"How long until we can shoot at UBC?" Eyes rolling, Amy beckoned Tony over. "You have got to be kidding me! Who? That can't take more than a . . . What, them again? Right. Fine. If anyone cancels, will you call me? Thank you." She dropped the phone onto the receiver and sighed. "Once again, UBC is standing in for every alien city in syndication.

You'd think it was the only place in the lower mainland that looked science fictiony."

He balanced half his butt on the edge of her desk. "So why do we want to shoot there?"

"Giant mutant plants escape from a genetics lab and start blinding people. Raymond Dark goes in at night when they're doing whatever plants do at night."

"Like *Day of the Triffids.*"

"What?"

"RKO movie with Howard Keel and Janette Scott. Although I think it was a meteor shower that actually blinded people. They mention it in the *Rocky Horror Picture Show.*" Frowning, he reached for a plastic six-legged octopus and got his hand slapped.

"So there are no new ideas in television. Quel surprise. Not." She moved the octopus out of his reach. "No one will notice we stole it."

"I'll notice."

"Yeah, and if you spent more time learning wizard shit and less time watching Movie Central, you might be useful."

"For what?"

"That's the question, isn't it?" Leaning back in her chair, she laced her fingers over the line of skulls embroidered onto her raw cotton shirt and smiled. Tony mistrusted the smile. "So, an afternoon off with the new boyfriend?"

And that was why. "You're delusional."

"I just want you to be happy."

"We were at the morgue."

"Cool. Why?"

"He wanted me to look at a body."

"Kinky. Pre- or post-autopsy?"

Tony couldn't remember any stitching, so he guessed. "Pre."

"Kinkier."

Before the conversation could devolve further, they were distracted by a young woman fighting to get a Dutch windmill through the front doors and into the office. She looked familiar.

"This is the last one they have," she gasped over the noise of balsa wood and canvas hitting the floor, "so it better be the right one."

"They?" Tony asked, ducking a flimsy-looking blade. "Windmills R Us?"

"Prop shop over at Bridge," Amy explained. "We borrowed it. And before you ask, I suspect it was part of some bucolic alien landscape."

"I was actually going to ask if they know we plan on burning it down in a blatant *Frankenstein* rip-off."

"With any luck, that would be a big fat no and, according to the writers, it's not a rip-off, it's an homage. Krista, this is Tony, our TAD. Tony, this is Krista, the new office PA."

"Hey!" Krista waved a hand in Tony's general direction. "I don't suppose you could help me get this onto the soundstage."

"Through there?" He glanced toward the scuffed door that led to the hall that led to the soundstage that led to the show that CB built. Lined with racks of extra costumes, the hall was barely wide enough for one and not even remotely wide enough for one and a windmill.

"Well, duh."

"Not possible. You'll have to take it outside and go around to the carpenter's door."

Krista looked at the windmill and then at the bloody knuckles she'd acquired getting it into the office. "You're fucking kidding me."

"He really isn't," Amy told her cheerfully.

The new PA's brows drew in, stretching the blue crescent moon on the left side of her forehead. "This is a test, isn't it?"

As Amy shook her head, Tony leaned close and murmured, "You're lucky. The last two got sent to Starbucks."

"Bad?"

"One of them's still there."

"Right." She took a deep breath and began to force the windmill back outside.

"Need some help?"

"No, thanks. I've got it."

Tony backed toward Amy's desk as something cracked. View blocked by the base of the windmill, it was impossible to tell what.

"Get out of my way, you fucking asshat," Krista's voice snapped out like a whip.

Or who.

"I think I'm starting to like her," Amy said, grabbing for the phone. "She has a way with words. CB Productions."

"I definitely like her," Tony growled as Kevin Groves came into the office cradling his left arm. Anyone who recognized Groves for the fucking asshat he truly was, was a person worth knowing. "Hey," he waved a hand in front of Amy's face. "I'm out of here."

She nodded at him and began explaining the company policy regarding their actors and reality shows. As far as Tony knew, CB didn't actually have a company policy, Amy just enjoyed maligning the intelligence of reality show producers on CB's dime.

"Tony Foster." Groves' voice matched his looks; thin and unmemorable.

"Can't talk." Tony spun on one heel, rubber squealing against tile, and headed for the exit. "Have to work."

"Just a few minutes of your time."

"No."

"Why were you out riding with RCMP Constable Jack Elson?"

"Ask him."

"Is it true you're lovers?"

Tony turned in the open doorway and laughed in Groves' face. "You know, you should ask Constable Elson that—but wait until I'm there so I can watch you get your ass kicked."

"I just intended to get your attention." Groves took a step closer. His jaw worked at a wad of gum. Spearmint from the smell. He was holding up his PDA, the record icon flashing. "Were you with him today because of the construction worker who was killed last night by your location shoot?"

"*My* location shoot?"

"Fine. By the show's location shoot. By the location being used by the television program known as *Darkest Night*.

Whatever. Do the police believe that supernatural forces are responsible for the removal of the man's arm?"

Groves knowing the arm had been removed was better than him knowing it had been bitten off, Tony supposed. Over one of the reporter's polyester-clad shoulders, he saw Amy stick her head in Mason's office. "Are you on cheap drugs?" he asked conversationally.

"Do you use drugs to heighten your senses?" Groves asked in turn.

Tony smiled as Jennifer, Mason's personal assistant, emerged. Part of Jennifer's job was to protect Mason from unwanted press attention. When she was in a good mood, she extended that protection to the rest of the studio. His smile widened as one set of impeccably manicured fingers clamped down on Groves' shoulder and the other reached low to give the wedgie to end all wedgies.

He joined in Amy's applause as Jennifer frog-marched the reporter across the office by the grip she maintained on the waistband of his tighty whiteys—which was now considerably higher than his waist.

"Foster!" Not surprisingly, Groves' voice sounded shriller than usual. "Does this have anything to do with the Demonic Convergence?"

He stopped applauding and ducked quickly through the door, closing it behind him before Groves could see his face.

"Demonic Convergence?"

Too late to hide his expression from Lee who'd apparently been lurking in the hall, one arm draped nonchalantly over a rack of faux Gypsy-wear.

"Tabloid reporter." Tony shrugged, hoping he sounded a lot more dismissive than he felt. "That sort of shit's his stock in trade."

"Like haunted houses."

"Sure." Shit. Not sure. The last thing he wanted was for Lee, who knew damned well haunted houses were real, to start thinking they were about to be involved in an actual Demonic Convergence. Which they were. Tony worked his way past a pair of gorilla suits wondering how the hell Groves had known about the DC. Had Leah spoken to him? And if she had, why? And if she hadn't, how else . . . ?

"Tony!"

He turned just far enough to see that Lee had followed him. Given his ongoing obsession with the actor, not noticing that kind of proximity had to be healthy. Healthier had he not been distracted by the thought of Leah taking Kevin Groves, of all people, into her confidence, but lately he'd take any emotional stability he could get.

"Well?"

From Lee's tone of voice, he'd missed half of an entire conversation. "Sorry. I wasn't listening."

"Yeah. I noticed." And Lee wasn't happy about it. Another time, a time when Tony didn't have an immortal stuntwoman, a gung ho RCMP constable, and a Demonic Convergence to deal with—*and let's not forget there's also something out there that reduced a grown man to snack food*—Lee's unhappiness at his lack of attention would be bringing on a case of the warm fuzzies.

Another time.

Right now, he had rather a lot on his plate. Did Jack expect him to go hunting the snack food reducing monster? Because that so wasn't going to happen.

"Tony!"

"Right. Sorry. Distracted."

Lee sighed and ran a hand up through his hair. "I was just asking if there was anything in what Groves said. That you were out with Constable Elson because a construction worker got killed."

He wanted to be a part of it—whatever it turned out to be. It was obvious in his voice, in his expression, in his body language. Everything said: *Let me help you.*

Oh, yeah, like Tony was going to let *that* happen. In the last six months, Lee had been possessed three times and there was no way in hell—any hell—that he was going to add to that list.

*Let me help you.*

*Why?*

*Because I seem to have a deep-seated metaphysical death wish I'm not even aware of. Maybe it stems from my repressed sexual identity, but since that's tied up with you, too, I guess I'm in the right place.*

No fucking way. He was not going to be responsible for Lee getting whammied yet again. Tony managed a near approximation of a smutty grin and flashed it in the actor's general direction. "Hate to admit it, but Groves was right. I was with Constable Elson because we were having hot Mountie sex in the cab of his truck."

Long pause.

Lee stared.

Tony kept grinning.

Finally, Lee sighed again, the exhalation a type of surrender. "CB let you off work for that?"

"Yeah, the boss is all about keeping the cops happy." He started walking again. Once in the soundstage, Peter'd have them both back at work and this conversation would be over. "Just be thankful Jack's not interested in your ass, or he'd pimp you out, too."

"You call him Jack?"

"When I call him other things, he reminds me he's armed."

"Tony . . ."

Tony sped up just enough to keep Lee's hand from landing on his shoulder. *Goddamn it!* The red light was on, and they were stuck together at the end of the hall, waiting for the camera to stop rolling in a space barely a meter square. They were *not* going to talk about the Demonic Convergence. He was not going to give Lee the chance to talk him into changing his mind, then somehow put himself in danger, and confuse the hell out of both of them when Tony had to ride to the rescue. Again. "So, how's the blonde?"

Lee frowned. "Which blonde?"

"You can't keep track?"

"Sure, but . . ."

"The one you took to the latest premiere." Hands curved out in front of his chest indicated her dominant features. "Nice picture of the two of you in *TV Week*."

"Ah, yeah . . . Judith. She's fine. Great."

"Rented?"

"Jesus, Tony." Lee rolled his eyes. "No, she was not fucking rented."

"Borrowed?"

"Where do you go to borrow a blonde?"

Tony snorted. "Probably not the same place you do. So how was the movie?"

"What movie?"

"The one you went to with the borrowed blonde."

"Obviously, not great; I don't remember it. How was the morgue?"

Nice try. "What morgue?"

"The one you went to with *your* borrowed blond."

"Before or after the hot Mountie sex?"

"Look, Tony, if you don't want me to have any part of this—whatever this is—all you have to do is say so."

A long moment passed, and it was as if all that guy banter hadn't happened. They were back at the Demonic Convergence part of the conversation.

Tony'd never noticed before that the red light made a noise when it went off. Sort of a faint *plock.* "I don't want you to have any part of this," he said, yanked open the door, and stepped out onto the soundstage.

♦

He hadn't expected to be done with work by sunset let alone have time to get from the studio to VanTerm before Leah finished her stunt. But at 5:50, almost an hour before the sun actually went down, he was in his car and heading west on Hastings, squinting behind the shield of his dark glasses.

VanTerm was a container terminal up on Burrard Inlet. Eventually, everyone shooting any kind of shipping in the Vancouver area ended up there because its layout made it easy to crop the shot. For the short time Tony'd been paying attention, it had stood in for San Francisco, New York, New Jersey, Singapore, Gotham City, and at least two alien planets not to mention the half-dozen times it had actually played itself. It was the UBC of shipping locations.

He turned right on Victoria Drive, drove more or less the speed limit to Stewart Street, turned left and then right onto the terminal grounds.

"I'm here for the CBC shoot." He fumbled out his Director's Guild Card, but the middle-aged security guard in the box barely looked up from his laptop before waving him through.

Berth three was past the reefer yard, past the container yard, jutting out into the inlet across the end of the jetty that also held berths one, two, and four. Tony parked by the first truck—freshly purple, the CBC logo bright and shiny on both sides and across the back—locked his car, and started walking. Quickly. It was still a bit of a hike and he wanted to make sure he saw Leah take her dive. It was more of a stunt than CB would ever be willing to pay for—even if the season one *Darkest Night* DVDs sold as well as Olivia in marketing predicted. Since Olivia in marketing was ten thousand or so in debt to a bookie named Icepick Ernie, no one put much faith in her ability to pick a winner.

They had four cameras set for the shoot. One up on the back end of the container ship to catch the fall from above, one in a Ports Canada Police boat about ten meters out, and two on the jetty. The two on the jetty were, Tony was happy to notice, one model older than the cameras used by CB Productions.

"Let's hear it for government spending," he muttered, hands in his front pockets as he watched the second unit director set the shot. "Repaint the trucks before you replace the equipment."

Still, hard to argue with the kind of pull that got clear skies and a totally killer sunset in a city that got roughly three hundred days of rain a year. When the CBC wanted a sunset, they got one.

A familiar voice shouting his name turned his attention away from the water.

"Daniel?"

CB Productions' entire stunt team jogged over, grinning.

"What are you doing here?"

Daniel patted his radio. "I'm on the safety crew. You don't

honestly think I can support a family on the hours I get from CB, do you?"

"I thought your wife supported your family." Daniel's wife was in advertising. Tony wasn't exactly sure what that meant, but it had, at one point, involved Daniel bringing in packages of wieners for everyone on the shoot.

"Ouch. Way to kick a guy in the nuts." But he was still grinning when he said it, so Tony decided not to worry about insulting a man who had black belts in three martial arts and who cheated death for a living. Okay, maybe not death, not most of the time, but he definitely cheated soft tissue damage on a regular basis. "So, you're done early today."

"I am that."

"You here to see Leah's dive?"

"Yeah." Tony nodded up at the container ship. "She going from the back end there?"

"It's called the stern, you ignorant git."

"Looks stern. Also high."

"And this is one of the smaller ones. There's ships out there today that can carry up to and above 8,000 TEU—this one, I'd say no more than 4,000."

"No shit."

"You have no idea of what I just said, do you? TEU stands for twenty-foot equivalent unit and . . . uh, never mind. Essentially, this may look big, but there's lots bigger." He waved a hand; a *Blue's Clues* bandage wrapped around one finger. "Approximately seven meters, railing to surface, into water approximately fifteen meters deep."

"Deep enough?"

Daniel snorted. "More than. And cleaner than usual, too. Ports Canada guys on the boat were saying it was highest tidal backwash they'd ever seen up the inlet. Swept all sorts of crap out to sea."

"And that's good?"

"Very. Hitting a hunk of crap that floated in past the cleanup crew is always a frightening possibility—where always means not today."

*Not today, not for Leah,* Tony thought as Daniel took on the unmistakable characteristics of someone listening to voices in his head. Coincidence or Demongate? He didn't have enough information to answer that. He really didn't want enough information to answer that, but then, it sucked to be him.

"Divers are in the water." Daniel clapped him on one shoulder hard enough to rock him back a step. "We're ready to go. I'll talk to you later."

"You know you've got a burning windmill in your future, right?"

He paused, half turned. "*Frankenstein* rip-off?"

"Homage."

"That's what they all say."

True enough, Tony admitted as Daniel jogged back to join the rest of the safety crew on the jetty. The sunset had painted the tops of the waves red-gold and burned highlights along the edges of the ship. Leah, wearing a short blonde wig and a shorter red dress was standing at the rail talking to a heavyset man with a gleaming shaved head and a down vest. Probably the show's stunt coordinator. As Tony watched, she glanced down and lifted a hand to acknowledge the divers, then positioned herself with her back to the rail. She had to be on a box. She wasn't that tall.

Bald-and-gleaming moved back to stand by the camera.

The entire crew gathered itself up.

"Rolling!"

Tony repeated the word silently as it bounced up and down the jetty. As it faded, he knew the director would be telling Bald-and-gleaming that Leah could go when she was ready.

Leah's arms went out; she jerked back, and went over.

Seven meters later, she hit the water butt first, folded just enough to take the heavy slap off her back. From the pumped fist rising up over the video village, the splash, lit by the setting sun, was everything the DP wanted.

He couldn't see her surface, the edge of the jetty was in the way, but he heard her.

"Damn! That's cold!"

He joined the crew's applause and moved closer as the divers swam up to help her to the aluminum ladder Daniel had just lowered into the water. The strappy, red high heels seemed to be giving her a bit of a problem, but hands reached down to pull her the rest of the way. She accepted their congratulations with a coy and dripping curtsy, waved toward the director's double thumbs up and again to Bald-and-gleaming. By the time she got to Tony, she was wrapped in a thermal blanket.

"You okay?" he asked, falling in to step beside her.

"Please. Went out of the crow's nest once on a pirate ship in the Caribbean—1716, it was. Now *that* was a fall."

"I thought you said you spent your time in the beds of powerful men?"

She winked at him from under a dripping fringe of wet wig. "What do you think I was doing in the crow's nest?"

"Keeping watch?"

"I had my eyes open if that counts."

Tony followed her up into the makeup wagon where she sat, still wrapped in the blanket so that a middle-aged Japanese woman could work the wig off without ripping the lace that attached it to her face.

"Tony, Hama. Hama, Tony."

The makeup artist nodded without looking up.

"Tony works over at CB Productions."

"The vampire show?"

"That's the one."

She looked up then. "Everett Winchester still with you?"

"Yeah. But don't quote me on that."

Hama grinned at Everett's signature line. "Tell him I said hi. All right, that's got it." She tossed the wig onto the counter where it looked like blonde roadkill. Drowned blonde roadkill. "Get into dry clothes, and I'll take out the pins."

Her own hair still up under a net cap, Leah left the towel in the chair and slipped in behind the set of shelves that separated makeup from wardrobe. It was a layout Tony was familiar with and therefore just a bit on the cheap side for any other show. Still, with only Leah on camera, there wasn't a lot of point in bringing out two separate trailers.

"So, you the boyfriend?"

Given the peal of laughter from behind the shelves, Tony didn't see much point in answering.

Hama raised a delicately arched brow. "Apparently not."

"We're just . . ." Then he paused. What were they? Friends? Not yet. Metaphysical accidents? Closer, but hard to explain.

"We're compatriots," Leah declared emerging from behind the screen in jeans, a white T-shirt, and a yellow hoodie, dress dripping from one hand and a pair of yellow high-tops in the other. "Partners in crime. *Paesano!*" She dropped back into the chair and drew her feet up to lace on the sneakers as Hama took the pins out of her hair. Released, it fell in thick black curls reaching just below her shoulders.

"Your mouth is open," she snickered, looking up from tying her second shoe. "What?"

"How the hell do you fit all that hair . . ." He waved at the wig on the counter. ". . . under that?"

"Magic."

Tony believed her.

Bouncing out of the chair, she zipped up the hoodie and turned just far enough to kiss Hama on the cheek. "You are a wizard of the makeup chair. I've stair falls next week, will I see you there?"

"You will."

*"Bueno!"* She scooped the strap of a plaid shoulder bag up and over her shoulder, and grabbed his arm, not quite dragging him out the door. "Come on, Tony, I've got to sign off, then we can go."

"The stair falls for the same movie?"

"Yep. Hell of a way to make a living, eh?"

"Then why do you do it?"

"Are you kidding? It's the most fun I've had with immortality since the thirteenth century." She raised a hand. "Don't ask. And the money's nothing to sneeze at. I mean we're talking $500 a day base rate plus, for this shoot, the CBC increase of 25 percent. I get called for a big budget movie and the increase can be as high as 130 percent—you should maybe learn some basic physical protections and think about it."

"No, thanks, I want to direct."

"Of course you do. Hey, I'm starving. The moment I finish the paperwork, let's head for some food."

"We're eating?"

"And talking. I think you proved last night you can handle both."

Last night. Right. "Where's . . . ?" He gestured at the space over her head.

"Ryne Cyratane? Probably as far from the gate as he can get. He's like a cat, hates water. Shit. Shoelace. Hang on."

Tony who'd taken a couple of extra steps, turned as she dropped to one knee. The sunset was behind her, the last of the light unexpectedly bright. He raised a hand to shade his eyes, and saw something move. At first he thought it was the Demonlord, then he realized it was significantly solider and swinging a human arm directly through the space Leah's head had just occupied.

She dropped flat, warned by the swish or the smell or both, and rolled away from a kick that would have disemboweled her had the claws made contact.

Disemboweled anyone else.

As Leah rose to her knees, he thought he saw a familiar breadth of translucent bare shoulders behind her although with the sun in his eyes it was hard to tell for certain. "Do something!"

"Do what?" There were scales and horns and whoa! Teeth!

"Wizard it!"

Right.

He folded the middle two fingers of his right hand in and swung his right arm back and then around and over his head. He was supposed to shout the eleven words of the spell clearly and distinctly, but clear and distinct got dumped in favor of speed. Things that were mostly serrated edged were fucking motivating! As long as the arm motion and the words finished as the same time it should . . .

Energy surged up from his feet, roared through his body, and blew out of his outstretched arm, arcing between forefinger and little finger then blasting forward.

The sudden flash was impressive.

"Tony?" Leah scrambled across the asphalt toward him. "Are you all right?"

Good question. Bits hurt. Hardly surprising since the spell had knocked him back on his ass. He blinked away brilliant blue afterimages. "I think I broke my tailbone."

"Yeah . . ." She slipped an arm behind his shoulders and levered him up. Fortunately, her Demonlord seemed to have taken a powder because being cuddled by them both would have been too weird. ". . . and your fingernails are smoking."

One last narrow wisp of smoke drifted off into the twilight from the ends of both blackened nails. "Ow."

"Well put. What do you call that?"

"Arra called it a Powershot." His fingers felt scalded, but he could use his hand. "What the hell was that thing?"

"*That* was a demon."

"A demon? Like a Demonic Convergence demon? Like nothing to worry about because we'll only have to deal with imps? That kind of a demon?"

"It shouldn't be here!"

"No shit!"

Still supporting most of his weight, she glared down at him. From this close, Tony could see a tiny scar at the edge of her right eyebrow. "Quit yelling at me! It's not helping!"

He could also see that she was really most sincerely freaked and that threatened to send him into strong hysterics. When thirty-five-hundred-year-old immortal stuntwomen got freaked, it was time for the rest of the world to fucking lose it. Fortunately—for some weird definition of fortunately he didn't want to go into right now—he was too exhausted to start up the whole *oh, my God, we're all going to die* thing. After a couple of deep breaths, he managed a fairly calm, "What happened to it?"

"Ash."

"And the arm?"

Leah nodded toward a long, narrow lump of black on the pavement. "It got just a little overcooked."

"But the demon is ash?"

"The demon was other, the arm was flesh."

That almost made sense. Tony struggled to sit up a little straighter, but someone seemed to have snuck into his body and replaced all his muscles with marshmallows. "I don't feel so good."

"Considering the way you just blew your wad, I'm not surprised."

"Nice imagery."

"Thank you. Can you . . ." Approaching voices cut her off and suddenly it became necessary he sit up on his own as Leah withdrew her arm and stood. "Oh, no, here comes the cavalry. They must've seen the flash. You get that arm packed up and let me deal with them."

Deal? Tony managed to brace himself on one hand and turn enough to see three men approaching from the jetty. Then Leah crossed into his line of sight, hips moving to an ancient rhythm. She laughed in answer to something one of the men said, a low, throaty sound that held heated suggestion.

And if even he could feel the heat, the odds were very high that none of the three men were now paying any attention to anything else.

*You get that arm packed up.*

Yeah. Right. Like that was the sort of thing he did every day. Well, actually, given the content of *Darkest Night,* he'd done it a couple of times helping out the set dresser. He rolled up onto his feet, swayed for a moment, and staggered back to the makeup trailer where he begged a garbage bag from the box on the counter.

"Are you feeling all right?" Hama asked as she handed it over. "You don't look so good." Her eyes narrowed. "You should be a medium beige and you're down to a light ivory."

"I'm fine. Just a little tired."

"You need more protein and less pizza. Especially if you're going to spend time with Leah."

"I'm not spending that kind of time with her." He'd just rest for a moment longer against the open door.

"Uh-huh."

"I'm gay."

"I'm generally fairly cheerful myself," she said dryly. "Trust me about Leah and red meat. Now close the door and go; you're letting cold air in."

It wasn't easy finding the remains of the arm. The banks of overhead lights shining down on the stacks of containers created nearly impenetrable shadow and, half blind, he almost tripped over it before he saw it. It looked like a long lump of charcoal roughly carved into the shape of an arm—a slight bend in the black where the elbow might be and little stubby fingers on one end. Given that the construction worker's other hand had been relatively normal, he had to assume the stubbiness occurred after death. Had the Powershot burned the fingers away? Or had the demon snacked on the end of his weapon?

"Demon snacks. Right. Why can't I ever spend time thinking about cars or getting laid, like a normal guy?" He sighed as he shook out the garbage bag. It was one of the small white ones made for garbage pails under the sink and it smelled vaguely of mint.

The scar on the palm of his left hand twitched as he dropped heavily to one knee beside the arm, and he hesitated, fingers spread out about five centimeters over the burned flesh.

"Problem?" Leah's voice behind his right shoulder.

"The last time I picked up an arm, it wasn't . . . fun." Hello, understatement.

"Well, this one's pretty much pure carbon, so I don't imagine it'll give you any . . . Oh, my God! The fingers moved!" She snickered as he threw himself back so quickly he toppled over and pulled the garbage bag from his hand. "Kidding. Here, I'll get it."

"You seem to be feeling better," he muttered from the asphalt.

"There's nothing like a little slap and tickle to remind a girl of what's important." Slipping the bag over her hand, Leah bent and scooped up the arm like she was scooping an enormous turd. An enormous burned turd. With fingers. Stubby fingers. "I'm going to be feeling better than you will for a while," she added, straightening. "You just ripped that energy right out of your guts, didn't you?"

"I guess." Feet, legs, guts eventually. Tony rolled up onto his knees as Leah closed the bag and reached into his pocket for the twist tie Hama had given him. A narrow piece of paper fluttered to the ground, a small line of white against the dark asphalt.

"What's that?"

"Fortune from last night's cookie." He picked it up and turned it over, leaning back just a little to bring it out of shadow. "*The blow from sunlight is more unexpected than the blow from darkness*. That demon just attacked you in the last of the sunlight," he said slowly as he got to his feet. "And I'd say that was unexpected."

Leah rolled her eyes. "You got a fortune cookie that really tells the future?"

"You've got a tattoo that's a Demongate."

"So you're saying stranger things have happened?"

"You're holding an arm."

She glanced down at the bag. "Good point."

"Can I ask you something?"

"Sure."

It took almost more effort than he had available to pull his car keys out of his jacket pocket. "Can you drive?"

♦

Tony didn't notice the rip in the side of her hoodie until they were going into the steak house and he stumbled. Leah turned to steady him, and he saw the fabric gape. "Looks like that demon almost got you."

She glanced down at the sweater and shrugged. "It's the *almost* that matters; I can't be hurt, remember? Unfortunately, that doesn't extend to my clothes. The important thing is that I ducked at exactly the right moment and you were there in time to blast the little bugger into dust."

"Not so little," Tony grunted. "And not an imp!"

"Would you let that go?" She maneuvered them around a table, toward the back of the restaurant. "So there was a lot of convergent energy hitting the same spot early on, and something a little bigger than an imp got through. It happens."

"Is it likely to happen again?"

She flashed him a sunny smile. "Well, if it does, you'll be there to deal with it, won't you?"

"You said imps," he muttered. "That wasn't an imp."

"And speaking of how much size matters . . ." She waited until she'd helped him into a high booth against the back wall and they were holding laminated menus before she continued. ". . . you might want to dial your Powershot down a bit. I think you're going to lose those nails."

The nail on his pinkie had begun to curl. It wasn't painful when he poked it, but it wasn't a pleasant feeling. Sort of a condensed memory of the energy surge.

When he looked up, Leah was shaking her head. "You don't know how to dial it down, do you?"

Tony thought about lying, but there was an arm in his trunk and transporting detached, carbonated body parts made lying seem a little pointless. "That was the first I ever did. I'll get better with practice."

"Uh-huh. He'll have the sixteen-ounce T-bone," she told the waitress.

"I can't eat a . . ."

Both women turned to stare at him. Leah's gaze flicked down to his fingernails.

He had the sixteen-ounce T-bone.

All of it.

And two baked potatoes with sour cream and chives.

And a side of creamed corn.

And a side of fried mushrooms.

And three huge pumpernickel rolls with butter.

And two beers.

Once he got started, he barely paused to breathe.

Leah had a lot less of the same things.

"So," she said at last when he set the gnawed bone on the plate and sat back with a satisfied sigh, "you got lucky."

"Lucky?" Maybe wizards had a second stomach. He should have felt sick, but he only felt comfortably full. In fact, he felt like dessert. He yawned. And a nap.

"You got lucky with your first Powershot. You didn't blow off your hand."

"And I saved your ass," he reminded her, through another yawn. "Stress the negatives much?"

"Sorry." The dimples flashed. "You did, indeed, save my ass. You got lucky."

"Isn't that what happens around you? My day ends early enough to let the only person who can save you arrive in time to save you?"

"Yes, but . . ."

"I see no buts."

"You've just eaten enough for two people . . ."

"Why is that bad?"

"You needed to replace the energy you used."

"But that's normal for a wizard, right? It's not bad. Demons running around VanTerm are bad. But, like you said, I dealt, so that's good."

"Fine." She rolled her eyes. "If you want bad, I have a hole in my favorite hoodie!"

Tony grinned as Leah shoved her hand through the hole and waved it at him. "You're right, that's . . ."

He stopped grinning.

She frowned. "What?"

"Your T-shirt."

She twisted and looked down, pulling the yellow fabric aside. There was a smaller hole in the T-shirt.

And under that, the very tip of the demon's claw had lightly scratched Leah's skin. Her finger shook as she traced the tiny burgundy beads of dried blood on the centimeter-long scratch. "No. That's impossible. I can't be hurt."

"That's not exactly *hurt,*" Tony began but she cut him off.

"You don't understand. That's blood!"

The scratch was barely visible from across the table. "Not much . . ."

"My blood!" Leah spat the words out through clenched teeth. "I haven't seen my blood in thirty-five hundred years!"

"You must have . . ."

"No!"

Other people in the restaurant were beginning to turn and stare. "Come on. We need to go."

"Where?"

"Back to my place." All of a sudden he didn't feel like dessert. Her eyes were wild and he wondered just how close the "crazy lady in the desert" was to the surface.

"What are we going to do about this there?"

Good question. Too bad he didn't have an answer. Wait . . . "We can start by reading *your* fortune cookie."

# Four

"I HAVE TO SAY THAT I'm not surprised you lost the fortune cookie in this mess."

Tony sat back on his heels in time to see Leah shake her head at the pair of boxer-briefs dangling between thumb and forefinger, then toss them to one side. She'd calmed down a lot in the car, and by the time they got to the apartment, she'd either got a handle on things or slid so deeply into denial she was living in Egypt. Tony wasn't sure which, but that was okay because he didn't care which. Whatever worked. "I told you, I was sorting laundry."

She prodded a pile of jeans with the toe of one sneaker. "Historically, most people sort laundry in order to do laundry."

"I was going to get to it."

"When you get down to a pair of paint-stained sweats and a T-shirt you got free from a promo guy?"

"Pretty much, yeah." He smothered a yawn with the back of his hand and nodded toward the kitchen. "The garbage is under the sink. Try there."

"You said you didn't throw it out."

"I didn't throw it out on purpose." Shoving a pile of old newspapers out of the way, he dropped to his belly to look under the sofa bed. Dead batteries. *Firefly* disk two. Blue silk tie. One dress shoe. *Where the hell was the other one?* Assorted balled-up socks. Empty Timbit box. Three issues of *Cinefex.* As the cheap parquet floor warmed under him, it got harder and harder to stay focused. Empty sample bottle of guava-flavored lube. Empty beer bottle. Unopened can of generic cola. No fortune cookie.

Clutching the can of cola, he shuffled backward until his head cleared the bed frame, dragged himself up onto his knees with a handful of mattress, and allowed his upper body to collapse onto the bed.

Something crinkled.

Setting the can aside, Tony rummaged in the tangle of sheets. "Found it."

Leah stared down at him in disbelief as she turned from the sink. "You slept with it?"

"Calm down, we're just good friends." Although the packaging had maintained physical integrity, the cookie within had been crushed. He got himself up on his feet just long enough to shuffle around and sit down on the edge of the bed. Then he reached out and dropped it into her hand.

Her other hand moved to cover the scratch on her side. "This is foolish."

"Maybe."

"Yours could have meant anything. It didn't have to refer to the demon; that could have been coincidence."

"Could have. But I doubt it. Wizard," he added with a shrug when she glanced at him.

Crumbs whispered against each other as she shook the package, the motion hiding the way her fingers had started to tremble. "Yeah, but this is my cookie, and I'm no wizard."

He understood why she was delaying; a certainty she had held for her whole life had changed and, given the length of her life, that was saying something. Change could be terrifying. He understood; he just didn't have a lot of patience with it since these days his life changed every twenty minutes. "Would you just open the damned thing!"

She hesitated a moment longer, then caught the edge of the plastic between her teeth and ripped. A small strip of paper spilled out of the pile of amber crumbs on her palm.

"*Ambitious change requires help; timing is everything.* Oh, yes, very clear and extraordinarily anticlimactic." Eyes rolling, she dusted the crumbs off into the sink. "That could mean anything."

"It could mean that your Demonlord is getting ambitious and is using the Demonic Convergence to send through minions with the ability to kill you so that the gate opens and he can come through."

"Minions?"

"Demonic minions."

"Yes, I got that." She sat beside him on the bed, dark brows drawn in. "The rest of it, though—you're really reaching."

"I'm really not." Grinding the heels of his hands into his eyes only blurred his vision. The steak seemed to be wearing off. Tony patted the blanket until he found the cola, popped the tab, and took a long swallow. "When you were attacked," he told her, feeling the sugar and caffeine hit his bloodstream, "when that demon drew blood—such as it was—he was there, Ryne Cyratane. I saw him."

"So? I told you last night he'd be close because of the Convergence." Her hand went back to her side. "He had nothing to do with this."

"He likes sex, he hates water. You were with me so that takes care of the sex, or lack of sex, and you were still close to lots of water. He had to be in that parking lot with you for another reason."

"Tony . . ." The paper crinkled slightly as she waved it. ". . . this is a fortune cookie fortune. It's a mass-produced platitude. Ambitious change could mean anything."

"You said he made a mistake on the spell. He's had thirty-five hundred years to figure out how to fix it. He can't get through himself . . ."

"Why not?"

"How the hell should I know? He can't because he didn't, but he can send . . ."

"Minions?"

"Yeah. He's got motive *and* opportunity, and all the pieces fit."

"Based on a fortune cookie."

He snatched the paper from her, crumpled it up, and threw it at a pile of T-shirts. "Wizards see what's there."

"You're learning to be a wizard from a correspondence course. Did it ever occur to you that you're seeing the wrong thing?"

"Okay. Fine. What do you think's going on?" They were sitting side by side. Not looking at each other.

"Ryne Cyratane would have nothing to do with this."

"With hurting you?" When she didn't answer—and given that the Demonlord had carved those runes into her flesh using the blood of her people, Tony figured she didn't really have an answer—he asked, "Would he let another Demonlord use the gate?"

"No."

No question there.

"Then since he's still around, he's got to be the one trying to open it. He probably figured out a way to direct the convergent energy to one spot."

"Okay, fine, you have all the answers . . ." Leah twisted around to face him, eyes narrowed. "Why did that demon bite the construction worker's arm off?"

Tony sighed. "Duh. Demon."

He downed half the can of cola while she thought about it.

"It explains everything."

"Yeah."

"I bet you're feeling pretty smug about figuring this out," she muttered at the toes of her high-tops.

He assumed she was actually talking to him. "Not really. It was kind of obvious." For a long moment the soft squeak of his fingers rubbing the cola can was the only noise in the apartment. "I guess you're feeling kind of betrayed."

"Well, yes!" After contemplating her shoes a while longer, she lifted her head and pushed her hair back off her face. "And no." Her laugh was a bit shaky, but to Tony's surprise, it wasn't faked. "I mean, he is a Demonlord, after all. He did slaughter everyone I knew, so this isn't exactly out of character for him. It just took him a while to make his next move."

"Maybe time runs differently where he is."

"Probably not. He was never very bright." One hand slid under her clothes to stroke the tattoo, and she smiled. "The sex was great, though."

Tony stared at her with as much astonishment as he had the energy for. "And that makes everything okay?"

"Well, no, not okay; but it puts it in perspective, doesn't it? So," she continued before Tony could respond, "assuming that he'll try it again as soon as he's used the convergent energy to open a new hole, how do we keep these minions of his from killing me?"

"And releasing a Demonlord into the world."

"That's part two. You'll excuse me . . ." Her hand moved around from the tattoo to the scratch. ". . . but I'm more concerned about part one."

Since keeping Leah alive would keep the Demonlord out, Tony decided there was no point in calling her on that. They needed a plan. And while they were planning . . . "Can he hear us?"

"No. He says he gets impressions of my life, but our only real conduit is sexual energy."

"Good." Hang on. "He *says?* You have conversations?"

"Sometimes, when he's right up by the gate, I enter a meditative state and we talk."

"Sometimes?"

"Postcoital."

Why did he even ask? "All right, we're not totally helpless; I dusted the demon with the arm."

"And got knocked on your ass," Leah reminded him. "It's been what? Three and a half hours, and you're still too wiped to get it up again."

"I could so . . ." Actually, no, he couldn't. Not even thinking of Lee in his motorcycle jacket and chaps got a response.

"That was a metaphor, Tony."

Her expression suggested she knew what he'd been thinking. He could feel his ears go red. "It doesn't matter. I've got time to recover . . . for another Powershot," he added hurriedly as she grinned. "It'll take him a while to get another minion through, right? So we just have to stick with the original plan. We find out where the weak spot is, and you teach me how to close it down."

"No."

"Why not?"

"If Ryne Cyratane is sending demons through to kill me, my going anywhere near the weak spot would be like waving a steak outside a lion's cage. It might provide enough incentive for a breakout—resulting in a really bad time for the steak."

Tony fought his way through this second metaphor—which was, at least, not about sex. "Fine, you don't have to go near the weak spot. You tell me where it is, teach me what to do, and I'll deal."

"It's not that simple."

He sighed. "It never is. All right, what do we do? How do we stop your Demonlord from opening the gate?"

"We keep me alive."

"Yeah, I got that."

"Seriously, that's all we have to do." She reached out and touched his arm. "I teach you how to send the demons back without destroying yourself, and every time one shows up, you zap it."

"That sounds simple. Or not," he amended when her expression threatened bodily harm.

"One question: what'll the demon be doing while I'm zapping?"

"Trying to kill me." Her expression added a clear and succinct *You idiot.*

"Or trying to kill me, and you can't stop it because, guess what—oh, yeah—it can kill you, too. I'm thinking we need some backup." Leaning forward, he could just barely reach his jacket hung over the back of a kitchen chair. He pulled his cell phone from his pocket, turned to Leah, and grinned. "Who you gonna call?"

She looked confused. "I'm not calling anyone."

He sighed. "No one watches the classics anymore."

♥

"Nelson."

"Nice phone manner, Victory. You always bark at your clients?"

"Good to hear you've regained consciousness, Tony."

"I wasn't . . ."

"You weren't? Then you had another reason for not calling?"

"I was . . ."

"Busy? Hang on a sec." Her voice faded slightly as she moved the phone from her mouth. "Drop the pins and step away from the doll."

"Vicki?"

"Yeah?"

"Are you working?" Victory Nelson had once been a much decorated Toronto cop, now she was a vampire P.I.—just like Raymond Dark only without the sidekick, the contrived plots, and the need to keep the violence under PG-13. Tony heard a couple of muffled thuds and some moaning.

"It's no big. These guys are total wannabes. What can I do for you?"

"I have a friend with a bit of a problem."

"Is this friend another wizard?"

Oh, crap. She knew. He hadn't called because he hadn't known how to tell her and make it sound believable. "How . . . ?"

"Henry told me, idiot."

Right. Because Henry still considered Tony's life to be his. His Henry's, not his Tony's. God, he was too tired for this. "No, she's not a wizard. She's a stuntwoman and an immortal Demongate."

"Cool."

"Not really." He outlined the problem.

Vicki let him talk without interruption. "Okay," she said when he finished. "Here's what you do . . . You listening?"

"Yeah. I'm listening."

"Stop acting like an ass and call Henry."

"I'm not . . ."

"Bullshit. Look, I'm not saying he's not indulging in a bit of testosterone-fueled assness as well, but one, he's out there in Vancouver and I'm not. Two, he owns a grimoire. Maybe more than one. He understands the whole demon thing. And, three, he needs to know what's going on, unless you'd rather he found out that you were dealing with demons in his territory and didn't tell him."

"I don't think . . ."

"I know."

Tony waited and when she didn't say any more, he sighed. Of course she heard it, even three thousand miles away. She could hear the blood moving through the hand holding the phone.

"You know I'm right."

He sighed again. "I guess."

"Tony . . ."

"Fine. You're right. Happy?"

"Ecstatic. Let me know how it turns out. Unless, of course, I find out on the news and then you needn't bother."

"Because then I'll be dead."

"That's not as much of an excuse as it used to be. Now . . . you call Henry, I'm going to grab a bite."

The background moaning grew louder.

Henry paused outside the door to Tony's apartment. He could feel the power painted around the frame. He could smell the cherry cough syrup. It seemed that in the weeks since they'd talked, Tony's studies had progressed. And adapted.

Tony had always been adaptable. It had helped him survive on the street. It had helped him accept that the world held wonder and darkness beyond the barriers most people thought marked the edge of reality. It had certainly helped him working in an industry that created yet another reality and very nearly believed in it.

Yes, adaptable was good.

Young, arrogant, prickly, possessive; not so much.

And if Tony didn't exactly go out looking for trouble, he certainly seemed to call it to him.

A noise pulled Henry's attention to the far end of the hall, and he turned in time to see an overweight tabby slip out of the last apartment. The cat's owner kept the door open on the safety chain so that the cat could wander in and out at will. Henry had never met the owner, but he and the cat had come to an understanding months ago.

The tabby's yellow eyes narrowed; he raised his tail and sprayed the wall just outside the apartment door.

*Mine.*

Henry sighed and raised a hand to knock. That was exactly the sort of welcome he was anticipating.

He could feel a life on the other side of the door. Hear a heart beating. Feel power . . . When the door opened, he smiled. It was more of a warning than a threat. "Leah Burnett?"

She was no more than five foot five, Mediterranean looking—south side of the inland sea. Almost, but not quite, Arabic. Under black-and-yellow clothing she had the kind of curves most women in this age dieted away. Thick dark hair fell in soft curls just past her shoulders framing a face with full lips, high cheekbones, and dark eyes narrowed in a frown.

"You're Henry Fitzroy?"

"I am." He could feel old power clinging to her like smoke. No, not merely old. He was old. This was ancient.

"I thought you'd be taller."

At six feet, his father had been huge—even before his girth had expanded to fit his ego. At five six, Henry was more typical of his century. "Sorry."

"No, it's all right. I like a man I can look in the eye without getting a crick in my neck."

And she *was* looking him in the eye. Wondering what she was trying to prove, he let a little of the mask fall and a little of the Hunger rise.

She smiled in a way that told him she knew exactly what she saw. Then she drew her tongue over her lower lip, leaving it glistening, and tossed her hair back off her face to expose the curve of her throat. Looking up at him through thick lashes, she drew in a deep breath and exhaled a challenge.

Henry felt himself respond and only barely managed to keep himself from moving toward her. He dragged the Hunger—both hungers—back under control and asked, "Should we be doing this in the hall?"

She laughed and stepped aside, her power masked as his was. "Tony's asleep."

The wards on the doorframe stroked against him as he stepped over the threshold but made no attempt to keep him out. Leah seemed satisfied with that as she closed the door, and Henry wondered just how sensitive to Tony's wizardry she was.

"Did he tell you he dusted a demon this evening?"

"Dusted?"

"Well, specifically ashed. He called it a Powershot. Took a lot out of him," she added quietly as they stood together looking down at the young man on the bed. "How much did he tell you on the phone?"

"He told me your history. Your pertinent history with the Demonlord," he added when she snorted. "He told me of the Demonic Convergence, and he told me how this Demonlord is planning to use it to kill you."

Pushing her hair back off her face, she nodded. "Demonic minions. As long as the spell controlling the Demongate holds, they shouldn't be able to hurt me, but they have."

Minions. He could hear Tony in the word. "May I see the spell?"

Moving away from the bed, she unzipped her hoodie and raised her T-shirt. "Be my guest."

It was an amazing tattoo. Even . . . no, *especially* knowing what it was. He dropped to one knee to get a closer look. And frowned. "I have seen the language of the damned," he said softly, head cocked to one side as he followed the curve of the characters, "and this writing I do not recognize."

"There is more than one hell, Nightwalker." She matched his formal cadence. "And more than one heaven, I suspect."

"Blasphemy."

The two fingers she placed under his chin were warm, and he allowed her to lift his head. "A religious word. And a strange word coming from a man whose church believes him soulless and damned. I say there is more than one hell and I am in a better position to know. By the time your lord was born, I had been carrying mine for over a thousand years."

"Your *lord* is . . ."

"I *know* what he is. You take yours on faith."

"Mine is not trying to kill me."

"His . . ." And she grinned, breaking the mood, suddenly looking no more than the young woman she appeared to be. ". . . minions would."

Again with the minions. Henry strongly suspected Tony had provided it. "The church does not think of itself in that way."

"Yeah, like that matters."

She had a point. "They would kill you as well."

"Oh, they've tried."

Which brought them neatly around to the matter at hand. Holding her hips, he moved her around so that he could see the wound. It was small, a minor flaw on the smooth curve of café-au-lait skin and only barely deep enough to bleed. Not worth noting had it not been the first blood drawn from this body in over three thousand years. Bending closer, he drew in a long, slow breath. The scent of her blood was familiar, neither the demon that had attacked her nor the demonic power that enveloped her had marked it. The scent around the blood, her scent, was almost smoky and he found himself wanting to taste. To lick a moist line along the curve from hip to ribs. Could he feed? Would the protective power perceive the threat or the seduction?

The flesh of her hips was warm and yielding under his grip. The air between them began to heat. Henry caught the scent of her arousal and growled low in his throat. She wound her fingers into his hair and subtly shifted her weight to bring bared skin closer to his mouth.

♥

The growl snapped Tony fully awake. One moment he'd been dreaming of driving his car from the backseat and the next he was up on his elbows staring at Leah and Henry at the foot of his bed.

Actually, Henry on his knees, his hair wrapped around Leah's fingers, his mouth about to descend to skin was pretty damned hot. Tony could feel his body responding like it always did when Henry got the vampire mojo going. His responses had gotten a bit kinky after all those years of teeth and, under normal circumstances, he'd be more than happy to lie here and watch while they went at it.

Unfortunately, the word normal had sweet fuck all to do with his life.

"Not a good idea, Henry."

Oh, yeah, interrupt a vampire when he's about to chow down. Not the best way to live a long and happy life. Henry's eyes were dark, and he had the whole Prince of Darkness thing on full blast.

Too bad.

Their history helped him hold Henry's attention but only just. "Ryne Cyratane is in the building and he doesn't look happy." In fact, for a guy who supposedly fed off sexual energy—and there was enough floating around that Tony strategically draped a fold of blanket over his boxer-briefs as he sat up—the Demonlord looked decidedly unhappy. Possessive even. Possessive and pissed. Tony recognized the expression even when he could see the wall of his apartment through it. "Henry! I'm guessing he doesn't like to share with other powers! He's already sending demons after Leah; it won't help her if he starts sending them after you, too."

Henry's lips drew back off his teeth.

Great. Vampire, prince; they both saw the whole thing as a challenge.

"Leah! Turn it off!"

Yeah. Like that was going to happen. Her head was back, her skin practically glowed, and even he was starting to find her tempting.

Henry was after blood. Leah was after sex. Together, they'd

make a bad situation worse. As far as Tony could see, there was only one thing to do. He picked up a pillow and threw it as hard as he could at the vampire's head.

The next instant, he was flat on his back, Henry's hands around his wrists, Henry's body driving his down into the thin mattress. Tony's hips bucked up as Henry's teeth closed through the skin of his throat and concerns about demonic interference abandoned ship . . . along with pretty much anything else resembling cognitive thought.

♥

"Oh, please, there's no need to be embarrassed, it's not like I've never seen ejaculate before."

"Make her shut up," Tony muttered as Henry handed him a glass of juice.

"How?"

"I don't know, vamp her or something."

"I don't think we want to go there again."

Tony wasn't sure he *could* go there again. At least not for a couple of days. Provided those days included thirty-six hours of sleep and a lot of liquid. He handed the empty glass back to Henry, wrapped the sheet and the shredded remains of his dignity around him, and stomped off to the bathroom to clean up.

The shower helped. Although he had to brace himself against the tile to keep the water from pounding him down onto his knees.

After, wrapped in his one thinning bath towel, he wiped the mirror clean and studied the mark on his neck. It was . . . noticeable. In spite of the coagulant in Henry's saliva, the actual bite within the impressive bruising still seeped blood. Fortunately, in the almost empty medicine cabinet, he had one sterile pad remaining from the exploding beer bottle incident. No gauze, but there was a rolled-up tensor bandage with very little *tense* left that should do, provided he kept it fairly loose.

Tomorrow . . .

Crap.

He didn't think he even owned a turtleneck.

"Tony?"

Henry outside the bathroom door. Worrying.

"I'm okay."

It seemed a little pointless to balk about being seen in a towel, all things considered, so Tony squared his shoulders, stepped out into the hall and across it to his closet. He'd have gone back into the bathroom to dress except Henry needed a few moments in there. Leah was out of sight, so she had to be in the kitchen end of the room where the angle was too tight to see or be seen from the hall. He pulled on jeans—Henry had destroyed his last clean pair of underwear—a T-shirt and a sweatshirt over that, then socks and shoes. Dressed, he walked into the living room and quickly stripped the bed, throwing the bedding onto a pile of dirty laundry in the corner and folding the mattress up into the sofa. It was a little stiff; he didn't close it often. The two cushions went back on as he shoved debris that had been under it out of the way with the side of his foot.

There.

That ought to help bring things back to what passed for normal.

He turned to find Leah standing behind him. "Could you not fucking do that!"

"Sorry." She offered him a large glass of what looked like chocolate milk. "It's an instant breakfast. I dropped a couple of packages from the craft services table into my purse."

"That's not . . ."

"Please, it's a CBC show. Think of it as your tax dollars at work."

It didn't seem worth it to argue. Tony sat at one end of the sofa and took a cautious swallow. "It's a little slimy."

"How old was your milk?"

"Oh, ha." Another swallow. He frowned as she pulled a chair out from the table and dropped onto it. "Are you . . . um . . . Tall, dark, and naked is gone, did you . . . um . . ."

"Get off?" She crossed her legs and smiled at him. "Don't worry. I took care of it. Although, if truth be told, you guys almost took care of it for me. Woof!"

His blood pressure was too low to raise a decent blush. "Could you not talk about it?"

"At all?"

"Ever."

"You know, you're weirdly prudish for someone with a Nightwalker as a lover."

"It's not . . . it's having an audience." A memory of a night in an alley off Charles Street back in Toronto surfaced. "No, it's having *you* as an audience."

"Hey. You will never find a more appreciative audience than me. Although the audiences for this live sex show I was in back in London in . . ." Dark brows drew in, and the yellow toe of the sneaker in the air drew circles. ". . . 1882 were great."

"At the Midnight Lily?"

Tony was childishly pleased to see her jump as Henry appeared behind her.

"The what?"

"The Midnight Lily—was that the name of the club?"

"Yes . . ."

Henry nodded thoughtfully and walked past her to sit on the other end of the couch. "I thought you looked familiar."

Rolling his eyes, Tony reached for the remote. "I'll just watch a little TV while you two trade flashbacks."

Then the remote was gone. "I don't think so." The fingers of Henry's other hand gently touched the rough bandage on his neck. "You took a chance."

Shaking his head hurt. "Not much of one. You never really damage what you consider to be yours." He was impressed by how nonchalant he sounded about the whole thing.

"A good thing you stopped us, then." Fingertips lingered a moment longer then withdrew. "A good thing you saw the danger."

"Yeah, well, wizard. We see what's there."

"True." Henry sat back against the sofa cushions. "And occasionally what isn't there."

It might have been wiser to just let that go but, given what he'd already survived tonight, Tony was feeling a little reckless.

He turned and faced Henry, eyes narrowed. "Are you telling me you're not doing CB?"

"And are you deciding who I can and cannot feed from?"

"You have the whole damned lower mainland. CB, the studio, that's mine!"

"Your employer might argue that."

"Are you two always such drama queens," Leah demanded, "or is this special for me? And," she continued before either of them could respond, "while it's painfully obvious you two are dealing with the kind of personal shit that would give Dr. Phil reason to retire, this isn't the time. Let's concentrate on the important thing here. Me. You," she pointed at Henry, "are here for backup. Tony seems to think you'll be useful—the brawn to our brains and beauty combination although there was some mention that you might have access to information we can use. I doubt you're going to know anything about demons I don't, but, hey, better safe than sorry. Also, given what you are, and given how stupidly territorial vampires can be, I'd rather have you with us than against us. You . . ." Her finger moved to Tony. ". . . need to conserve your strength. Between that spell you threw earlier and your ex's feeding habits, you haven't got energy to spare for arguing." She paused just long enough to ensure she had their full attention. "Now then, who has a plan?"

"I think," Tony said slowly, "we should bring Jack Elson in on this."

One red-gold brow lifted as Henry drawled, "Now, do I say anything about you and Constable Elson?"

"There *is* no me and Constable Elson; the man is straight!"

"You're doing it again," Leah snapped.

"Fine." The look Henry shot her would have caused strong men to run. Leah rolled her eyes. "Why Elson?"

Tony finished swallowing the last mouthful of liquid breakfast. "I have an arm in my trunk."

♥

"This is a human arm."

"And he's what? Only four hundred and sixty-ish?" Leah

shot an anime-sized look of wonderment in Tony's direction. "What amazing deductive powers!" And to Henry. "I have to know; how did you work it out?"

"It smells like burned pork," Henry told her dryly, not rising to the bait. "Not to mention, it's wearing the remains of a watch. From what you said about Tony dusting a demon, I had assumed it was a demonic arm."

"We wouldn't need Jack for that." Tony yawned and nodded toward the arm. "This got bitten off a construction worker. Jack took me to see the body this afternoon."

"Why?"

"Because he doesn't believe in giant raccoons and he wanted some answers."

"I'm moderately disturbed by how much sense that makes," Henry muttered. "And you think we should give this arm to him?"

"Sure. He can put it with the rest of the body."

"And you don't think that would cause more questions?"

"Well, we'd . . . I'd . . . answer his questions. Mostly. He knows what's going on. I mean, he knows there's stuff going on. I told him about the Demonic Convergence." Tony yawned again. "He's still at least one version of the script behind, but it won't take long to bring him up to speed."

"I wasn't actually thinking of questions from Constable Elson," Henry pointed out. "I was thinking of the coroner and the victim's relatives. It might be best if they continue to believe that the arm was bitten off by a wild animal and eaten. Another urban myth of man-eating cougars in the city would be preferable to an investigation. Modern forensics can be remarkably thorough."

"Let me guess, you've been watching *CSI.*" This time, Tony yawned so widely his jaw cracked. "Besides, we'll need Jack to work backup in the daylight."

"Demons don't . . ." Henry began and stopped.

"The last one did. Which leaves us kind of screwed if you're all we have."

"Thank you."

Crap. "Sorry. That was . . ."

"Tactless," Leah offered. "But true."

Henry nodded, graciously acknowledging the point. "And you think Jack Elson can stop a demon?"

"He has a gun."

"Will a gun have any effect on these creatures?"

Forgetting the wound in his throat, Tony shrugged and ground out, "I have no idea," through gritted teeth.

"Then perhaps we'd best not involve Constable Elson until we know more. Why don't you start by telling me *exactly* what happened this afternoon."

"I've got it." Leah lifted a hand to cut off Tony's protest, but he hadn't actually planned on one. Exhausted, he sagged back against the sofa cushions half listening to the immortal stuntwoman tell Henry about the demon attack but mostly thinking how *immortal stuntwoman* sounded like a cool idea for a show and wondering if he should pitch it to CB.

Hell, at some point someone had to have thought that *vampire detective* was a good idea.

"Tony?"

"I'm awake."

"Of course you are."

Leah's eyes were so dark a brown he could barely make out where the irises ended and the pupils began. "What?"

"Henry's going to get rid of the arm."

Tony shot Henry, still standing by the arm, a thumb's up. "How?"

"Leave that to me," Henry said quietly, "Leah knows a better way of returning the demons to hells, one that won't nearly kill you. She'll teach it to you. But not tonight," he added. "Tonight you need to regain the energy you spent." *And the blood you lost.* Tony felt his heart beat just a little faster. Henry's eyes darkened slightly, aware of Tony's response.

"You're doing it again," Leah sighed.

"You are not totally without fault here," Henry told her, masking the Hunger. "Your presence is provocative."

"Why, thank you."

"What about more construction workers?" Tony asked.

Dimples flashed as Leah turned her attention to him. "I'm very much in favor of construction workers."

"Yeah, funny. Remember the arm. That demon that attacked you killed someone else first."

The Vampire and the Demongate exchanged nearly identical glances.

Tony sighed. Figured that he'd be the only one who thought of the little guy. "If either of you says the words collateral damage, I'm going to be really pissed."

"Tony . . ."

Henry cut her off. "If we concentrate on keeping Leah alive, on keeping the gate from opening for this Demonlord, we prevent mass slaughter. With the demons focused on her, there will, hopefully, be few other lives lost." Henry's tone suggested this was the last he was prepared to say on the matter.

*Can't make an omelet without breaking eggs. God, I must be tired if I'm thinking in bad clichés.* "So tomorrow I learn a better way to return demons to hell and then I become Leah's bodyguard for the duration of the convergence. As each demon pops out and attacks, I send it home. If it attacks at night, are you willing to make sure I stay alive long enough to do the spell?"

"I am."

"And if it attacks in the daytime . . ."

"It is ultimately your choice if you involve Constable Elson."

"Sure it is." Both Leah and Henry looked as if they wanted to respond. Tony ignored them. "Okay, I'm seeing one big problem here. I already have a job."

Henry folded his arms. "I will talk with CB."

"And get me some time off."

"It seems like the best idea."

"With pay."

"You have a high opinion of my powers of persuasion."

"Am I wrong?"

"No. And now, you need to sleep. Where do you keep your clean sheets?"

Tony glanced around the room at the piles of laundry. There were less of them than there had been, but that was only because they'd been unsorted over the course of the evening. "I only have one set."

"Then we won't worry about it." Henry crossed the apartment at close to mortal speed and knelt by the sofa. "I don't suppose one night without sheets will hurt you."

Tony nodded. "Once I was pissed off about having no sheets, then I met a man with no blankets." When the only response was confusion, he sighed. "It's a variation on the shoe/feet thing." The confusion deepened. He waved a hand; hardly his fault if he was being profound and they were being dense. "Forget it."

"I don't think that'll be hard," Henry murmured slipping one arm under Tony's legs and the other behind his back.

"Hey, don't . . ."

Henry ignored him and straightened. Big surprise. Tony squirmed a bit but nothing he could do was going to change the fact that he was being held in Henry's arms like an overgrown infant. "I hate it when you do this."

"I know. Leah, would you fold the bed out, please."

"Sure thing. I'm good with beds."

Too tired for innuendo, Tony let that go. Besides, it seemed to be the simple truth. In a remarkably short time, he was shoeless but still dressed and stretched out under a blanket.

"Okay, it's a long shot, but what if another demon attacks tonight?" he asked as Henry turned off the overhead lights.

"These are lesser demons, not the Demonlord himself. They may not even be able to get through your wards and, if they can, I'm sure I can at least slow them until you wake."

"At least slow them?"

"Good night, Tony."

♥

"So . . ." Leah pushed a curl back off her face. ". . . what do we do while we're waiting for dawn?"

"I suggest you sleep." Henry nodded toward the bed. "Tony won't even know you're there."

"And you?"

"I'm going to get my laptop from the car and do some work."

She slid out of her sweater. "You can do that; work with me lying right over there?"

"I am perfectly capable of maintaining control regardless of your provocation—however involuntary that provocation is most of the time."

"Maybe together we could provoke Ryne Cyratane into making a fatal mistake."

His lip curled, showing teeth. "Since the only person in this room likely to be a fatality is Tony, I'd have to say no, thank you."

# Five

TONY WAS CHASING A PENGUIN around the *Darkest Night* set when the phone rang. Which was when he realized he was dreaming. Given his experience in television, penguin chasing was a distinct possibility; a phone ringing on the soundstage was not. The last time it had happened, Peter had promised to castrate the next recipient of an incoming call, and he'd promised it with such sincerity that even the women on the set had been nervous.

It was almost fortunate that Arra's gate reopening had destroyed cell phone reception, downgrading the threat to a moot point.

As the penguin shuffled off past Raymond Dark's coffin, Tony dragged himself up out of sleep and groped amid the debris on the bedside table. Lukewarm liquid splashed onto his shoulder as he attempted to answer the half empty can of cola. When he finally found the handheld, he sank back against the pillows.

"What?"

"Mr. Fitzroy just explained your situation, Mr. Foster."

None of his three functioning brain cells allowed him to mistake CB's less-than-dulcet tones. "Uh . . ."

"He seems to think that it will be too dangerous for you to be Ms. Burnett's bodyguard at the same time as you're being my TAD."

"Demons . . ."

"Yes. Mr. Fitzroy mentioned that there may be demons and, as I'd just as soon not have demons on my soundstage disrupting my production schedule, you may have the time you need to deal with them."

"Thanks, Boss, I . . ."

"Don't make a habit of this, Mr. Foster."

"No, I . . ."

"And while you're sitting around waiting for something to attack Ms. Burnett, I suggest you answer your e-mail."

"Boss, I won't exactly . . ."

But he was talking to the dial tone. Wondering what Henry had said, or more importantly, what CB had heard, Tony tossed the phone down onto the tangle of blankets on the bed beside him.

The tangle snorted and swore in a language he didn't recognize.

*Three guesses who and the first two don't count.*

He grabbed one of the tangle's rising curves and shook it. When it gave under his fingers and kept shaking on its own, he snatched his hand away. "Hey! Where's Henry?"

"He left about an hour ago . . ."

Tony squinted toward the entertainment unit. 6:55. Sunrise was at 6:49. He must have called CB from his car.

". . . he said I should wake you, but I figured the wards would give enough warning."

"Why didn't he wake me?"

Leah's head and shoulders emerged from beneath the covers. "Hey, you guys have issues I'm not going near." When she stretched, Tony had an epiphany.

"You're naked!"

"I hate sleeping in my clothes."

He was still in his jeans and T-shirt although someone had removed his socks and sweatshirt.

"Relax." She yawned. "Although I've contaminated your space with girlie bits, your honor remains safe."

"It's not my . . ." Taking a deep breath, he sat up and swung his legs out of bed. "I just think you got naked a little fast."

Warm fingers patted his arm. "Sweetie, I've gotten naked a lot faster."

*Okay. Should've seen that one coming.*

Another deep breath as he shifted his weight forward. He seemed fine. Internal fluid levels had to still be low, but he wasn't feeling faint or light-headed. In fact, he was feeling pretty good. If he had to, he could probably toast another demon.

Three. Two. One.

When something with horns and scales missed its cue to break down the apartment door, Tony stood and made his way past the piles of laundry to the bathroom.

The bite on his neck still looked like hell. A hickey of the damned. In all the years he and Henry had been together, Henry'd never lost control like that.

Issues.

Yeah. Right.

Leah was up and dressed by the time he got out of the shower. The bed had been reconverted into a sofa and she was stuffing clothing into a pillowcase. "I've got a washer and dryer. You can do some laundry at my place."

"Your place?" Had he missed something?

"You didn't think we were staying here, did you?"

Tony shrugged.

It seemed to be the answer she'd expected because she grinned and tossed the stuffed pillowcase down beside its equally stuffed mate. "Get together everything you can't leave behind. We'll grab some breakfast on the way."

"So those files your wizard mentor left you, they're cued to you, right?"

Tony resisted the urge to glance toward the laptop case in the back seat, keeping his eyes on the road instead. "You booted up after I fell asleep?"

"I was curious. All I got was spider solitaire."

"She used it to tell the future."

"It?"

"Games of spider solitaire."

"Well, who hasn't used *that* excuse to justify not working? Hash brown?"

"Sure."

Leah lived out in Sullivan Heights and the fastest way there from Tony's apartment was to get onto Lougheed and head west. When they crossed Boundary, Tony had to remind himself not to turn. It was weird driving almost right past the studio on a Thursday morning.

*I should be there. They need me.*

*Or worse, they don't really need me and I should be there so they don't find out.*

"Did you see that?"

"See what?" Caught up in his concerns about remaining employed, Tony had no idea what Leah'd seen.

"There was a spot back there, by the gas station, where the rain wasn't."

He glanced over at her, but the back of her head didn't tell him a lot. She'd twisted around in her seat and was staring out the window, back the way they'd come. "Say what?"

"I saw an interruption in the rain. Some demons don't like to get wet."

Tony snorted. "Man, are they converging in the wrong place." And then the program loaded. "Hang on! There's another demon through?"

"Looks that way. Drive faster," she commanded, throwing herself back into the seat.

"What? No! I can get off Loughheed on Douglas and back on at Springer."

Leah turned to stare at him. He could feel incredulity hit the side of his face as he changed lanes. "And do what?"

"If there's a demon back there, it might eat someone. Or part of someone. I can't let that happen."

"So if we go back and wave me around like bait, and you Powershot it, what happens then?"

"No one gets eaten."

"Yeah, but you're out on your ass for another twelve hours. You're too wiped to learn the new spell and you're not able to protect me. Then, during those twelve hours, another demon shows up and eats me, opening the Demongate and ending the world as we know it."

"If it eats you, will the gate open inside it? Ow!" He rubbed his thigh where she'd smacked him.

"If you drive faster, we'll put more distance between us and it, and it'll take that much longer to find me. During that time, you can learn how to send it back to hell so that, when it finally catches up, you'll be able to save me without taking yourself out of the fight."

They were almost at the off ramp.

"I can't just let a demon run around loose."

"You can't just let a Demonlord into the world either."

Valid point.

Past the ramp. Too late to go back.

"If someone else dies . . ."

"Better them than me."

He fought the urge to hit the brakes and skid to a dramatic halt. It was the kind of reaction that would look great on screen and accomplish absolutely nothing in real life. He wanted to snarl, *It isn't all about you!* but, until the Demonic Convergence was over, it was. He wanted it to be about imps again. He'd kind of been looking forward to that.

"All right." Deep breath. No option but to deal. A little more gas and they were matching speeds with the fastest car on the road. "Why won't this new thing you're going to teach me knock me on my ass?"

Her seat creaked as she shifted her weight, tucking her knees up to brace her feet against the dashboard. "You'll be manipulating energy instead of just hurling it."

"Say what?"

She sighed impatiently. "Well, I'm no wizard, but that Powershot of yours looked like the magical equivalent of picking up the biggest rock you can find and crushing your enemies with it. Of course you're exhausted afterward; you're also looking at pulled muscles, back trouble, and probably hernias."

"Hernias?"

"Magical equivalent of. What I'm going to teach you is more like rolling the rock to the edge of a cliff and pushing it off as your enemies pass under it. There's a lot less effort involved and result is the about the same."

"Really?"

"No, not really." Slouching as far as the seat belt would allow, Leah propped her yellow high-tops up on the dash. "It's actually a pretty lousy analogy and only applies to the amount of power involved. Powershot lots. My way, less."

"Yeah, but you said you're not a wizard . . ."

"No, I'm not. I'm just the one who stands to be eviscerated if you don't get it right." She gave his leg a patronizing pat, her fingers lingering just a little too long. "And then the world as we know it ends."

Yeah. Yeah. No pressure.

Leah's condo was in a clump of high-rise concrete towers overlooking the TransCanada and a railway ravine, and it wasn't hard to understand why she objected to his beige. Her walls were shades of yellows, oranges, and reds. Her furniture was large and heavy and predominately wood and leather with cushions the same shades as the walls softening the angles. Every piece looked sturdy enough to take the weight of two moving adults.

From the sparsely furnished second bedroom on the north side of the corner unit, Tony could almost convince himself he could see Simon Fraser University high on the heights of Mount Burnaby—where *height* was a relative term given the actual peaks of the Rockies less than an hour's drive to the east.

He couldn't see any interruptions in the rain.

♠

"All right." Leah opened the bottom of the white silk shirt she'd changed into after an impressively quick shower and, pushing her black track pants dangerously lower on her hips, stepped closer to the gooseneck lamp they were using as a spotlight. "The innermost circle of runes defines the actual gate. All you have to do, because we're not talking about creating an actual gate as much as reminding reality that demons don't belong here, is burn these four into the air . . ." One finger, a careful distance from skin, indicated the runes in question. ". . . each rune more or less an equal distance from the other, with the demon in the middle of the pattern. When you finish the fourth rune, reality will reset itself and no more demon."

With his nose so close to her skin, she smelled like soap and cinnamon. Or cinnamon soap. Which was a weird choice, but it suited her. "*All* I have to do?" Tony muttered, peering at the intricate tattoo.

Leah chose to ignore the sarcasm. "Because the demon doesn't belong here, you don't have to be specific about its name or its ultimate destination. Once you weaken the barrier, it'll snap back to where it belongs. It's a variation on what we were going to be doing before Ryne Cyratane upped the stakes—only then you'd have been pushing the runes through the weak spot to reinforce it."

"Yeah. Okay." The individual runes were a lot more complex up close than they were when they were just a part of the larger pattern. "What happens if I screw one of these up? Squiggle when I should spiral?"

"Probably nothing . . ."

The *probably* was a little worrying.

". . . although if, by chance, you re-create an entirely different power definition . . ." She shrugged, the curve of her belly rising and falling with the motion. "Maybe death. Destruction. Perpetual reruns of *The Family Guy*."

"Hey, that show's a classic!"

"Every now and then," Leah muttered, flicking Tony on the top of the head with one finger, "I think, why not let him in? How much worse could things get? You'd better draw the runes on paper first."

"Sure." He straightened. "But what did . . ." Tucked into the front pocket of the laptop case, his cell phone played the *Darkest Night* theme; Zev had made a digital file available to anyone in the studio who wanted to use it. Tony suspected he was hoping it would get picked up as a download by one of the big online ring-tone sites, but so far there were no takers. Flicking the phone open, he checked the display. "It's Amy."

"Who?"

"Assistant office manager at the studio. I should take it."

"Why?"

"It might be about work."

"You're a TAD." Leah allowed her shirt to fall closed. "Nothing you do is more important than learning how to keep me alive."

Since she put it that way, he answered the phone.

"Tony?" Amy had conspiracy in her voice. "You okay?"

"I'm fine, why?"

"Because CB said you weren't coming in today. Or tomorrow. CB. The boss. He didn't show up at your place last night and beat you into a coma, did he?"

"No. Why would he?" Did Amy know something about CB's feelings toward him that he didn't?

"Why would he carry your messages unless he was feeling like mondo guilty?"

"I asked him for some personal time."

"Personal time?" Amy snorted so vehemently, he had to move the phone away from his ear. "Loss of consciousness is CB's definition of personal time. It's not . . ." She lowered her voice dramatically. ". . . the other stuff is it?"

"The other stuff?"

"This isn't a secure line, nimrod."

"It isn't a line at all."

"Exactly my point. Well?"

And who was to say that Kevin Groves wasn't crouched in a bush outside the studio attempting to intercept his phone calls? It was the kind of sneaky underhanded, not exactly legal thing that tabloid reporters did, wasn't it? "It's sort of the other stuff."

"Bastard. Just so you know, if you have any . . ." Her voice moved away from the phone. "CB Productions, please hold." And back. ". . . extracurricular fun without me, I will kick your ass up onto your shoulders."

"It's not . . . fun." He said the last word to no one in particular.

Leah sat down and pushed the lamp out of her line of sight. "So Amy, the assistant office manager at the studio, knows you're a wizard?"

"Yeah."

"And your boss knows?"

"Well . . ."

"Well," she mocked, fingers tapping out annoyance on the polished tabletop. "Most people who have, let's say, *unusual* powers don't go talking about it to all and sundry since all, and particularly sundry, don't usually deal well with unusual."

"Thing is, we were trapped in a haunted house together."

"All three of you?"

"No, CB was outside."

"But he knows?"

"He knew before, during the Shadowlord thing."

"So Amy and your boss . . ."

The *Darkest Night* theme interrupted.

Tony glanced down at the screen. "It's Zev. He's the music director at the studio."

"Does Zev know?"

"He was in the house."

"Along with how many other people?"

"Not many."

"Good."

"About thirteen."

Dark brows rose almost to her hairline. "About?"

"Three of them died."

"Yay." Her fingers stilled.

*It's when the drums stop that you have to worry.* The *Darkest Night* theme looped back to the beginning and kept playing.

"Tony, answer the damned phone."

The conversation with Zev paralleled the conversation with Amy minus the speculation about a coma and the final threats.

"You'll call me if you need me?"

"Sure."

"And you'll be careful?"

"Count on it."

"Because you're an annoying pain in the ass, but I'm used to you being around."

"I'm used to being around. Don't worry." As he hung up, Leah slid a sheet of blank paper in front of him.

"Practice," she snapped, handing him a pencil. "Before someone else . . ."

The *Darkest Night* theme.

Once.

Lee's cell number.

Tony had, of course, memorized it even though he'd never used it. He stared at the phone, but Lee had obviously reconsidered calling.

"Earth to Tony." One bare foot kicked him, not particularly gently, in the shin. "Let's try and remember we're on the clock here!" Leaning back, she reexposed the Demongate. "Now that your fan club has checked in, can we get on with this?"

"Sorry." He peered at her belly, put pencil to paper, and stopped. "Look, when you said, burn these four runes into the air, what did you mean?"

"You know." The tip of one finger sketched invisible circles. "Draw them in the air with lines of energy."

"Okay." He remembered Arra creating golden lines of power as she called on light to banish shadow. "I don't actually know how to do that."

♠

"Everything in here is about energy. There's just nothing specifically about energy."

"Well, that's useless." Leah pushed a curl away from her face and tried to shove Tony away from the laptop. "Look up drawing."

Tony flicked the same curl away from *his* face and refused to be shoved as he scrolled up the file list.

Drawing, of the Dark.

Vaguely familiar but not helpful.

Drawing, Down the Moon.

Also familiar. He opened the file.

**This is woman's magic. You don't need to know it.**

*Then why the hell did you list it, you crazy old . . .*

Drawing, Blood.

"What did she think she was training," Leah snorted, "a wizard or a paramedic?"

"So she was a bit rushed when she put this together."

"A bit rushed? Da Vinci was a bit rushed when he was finishing the *Mona Lisa*. This wizard of yours seems more like a complete incompetent." Her breath hit the side of his head, warm and impatient. "You scroll; I'll stop you if I see anything useful."

Storms, Calming.

Poison, Checking for.

Water, Purifying.

Demons, Banishing.

"Hold on. Right there." One fingertip tapped the screen. "You have a spell to banish demons." The fingertip moved to tap him on the forehead. Hard. "You think maybe you should have mentioned that? Just in passing, perhaps?"

"I forgot it was there." He jerked away before she could tap him again and opened the file.

*Calling demons is among the stupider things you can do with your power. I am inclined to allow stupidity to be its own reward; however, it is possible that someday you may need to clean up another's mess. Begin by drawing six drops of blood from the idiot who called the demon. Do it quickly before the corpse cools.*

"This is useless." Leah straightened, turned, and dropped onto the edge of the table. "These demons weren't called, they're being sent. There's nothing we can use in there . . ."

"It says we should use an unnatural rope to hold the fiend."

"And then do what with it? Why don't I just kill myself and save them the bother?" Dragging both hands back through her hair, she began to pace. "I can't believe this wizard of yours would leave out something so basic."

Tony scrolled up and down the list one more time and frowned. "Hell, if it's all that basic, maybe there's something about it in the instructions."

The sudden silence was so complete, he could hear the traffic passing on the TransCanada six stories down and almost a half a kilometer away. He twisted around on his chair to find Leah staring at him from across the room. "What?"

"There's instructions?"

"Yeah. I didn't read them, but . . ."

"You didn't read the instructions? Of course you didn't," she continued before he could answer. "You just opened the spell list and started trying things out, didn't you?" While he was thinking about denying it, she closed the distance between them and smacked him on the back of the head. "Men!"

"Hey!"

Leaning back she flashed him a narrow-eyed glare. "Hey, what?"

"Nothing." It just seemed like a bad time to go into the whole gender stereotyping thing.

"Good. Now then . . ."

He could feel every one of those thirty-five hundred years leaning over his shoulder with her.

". . . let's have a look at the instructions, shall we?"

Power, Responsibilities of.

Power, the Focusing of.

Her finger touched the screen. "That's got subdirectories."

"On it." The next layer down had been divided into basic, intermediate, and advanced. As Tony moved the cursor onto advanced, Leah's hand closed around his wrist and moved it back to basic. "I thought we were in a hurry."

"We are. But as much as I don't want to be killed by a demon, I'd also rather not be killed by you. Start at the beginning. Read fast."

Fortunately, the lesson was, well, basic and it seemed he'd been instinctively doing most of it already. The rest of it seemed simple enough. When he mentioned that to Leah, she snorted.

"Lots of things seem simple when you read the instructions, but it's an entirely different story when you actually try to hook up the DVD player."

Fair point. "It doesn't seem that complicated, though. Mostly, I just have to shift my internal focus to external."

"Do you even know what that means?"

Tony pushed his chair out from the table and stood, forcing her to take a couple of steps back. "It's sort of like choking up on the Powershot."

"Choking up on the Powershot?" Muttering under her breath, she moved around until she stood behind him. "Your keen grasp of description fills me with confidence."

"I need to practice."

"You think? Make it fast and don't destroy my apartment."

"Your faith is underwhelming," he muttered, bouncing lightly on the balls of his feet and shaking the tension out of his arms. He could do this. He called things to his hand by knowing where they were, by being aware of the space they defined. According to Arra's notes, focus meant being aware of the space *he* defined and pulling in energy to fill it. That was the part he'd been doing instinctively.

Once he had the energy, all he had to do was pick a spot outside his body, shift the focus to that spot, and re-form the energy in his chosen pattern. Like writing with sparklers only the images would stick around longer. Arra's notes suggested he practice with a neutral symbol, something that could only be what it was.

Okay.

Right index finger extended—best not toss the scar on his left hand into the mix until he had a better grip on what he was doing—he picked a point about halfway to the window, refocused until his right eye started to water, and began burning his chosen symbol onto the air.

Leah's curtains caught fire.

Crap! That wasn't supposed to happen. Glancing down at the laptop, he checked the screen. No, definitely not supposed to happen.

He opened his left hand. The fire arced toward it.

The curtains separated at the char line, the lower third dropping to the floor.

Tony coughed, smoke pluming out on his breath. Back in his teens, although he couldn't afford the habit, he'd bummed the occasional cigarette from other guys on the street. The coolest guys could always make the biggest plumes of smoke. Apparently, for wizards, the cigarette had become optional—although he wasn't sure that the present circumstances were any healthier.

He was sure blowing out a nice big plume, though.

Leah crossed the room and picked up the burned fabric. Ash crumbed off between her fingers, drifting to lie like dirty snow on the hardwood floor. She stared at the ash, at the curtain, and finally at Tony. "Damn. What did you do?"

"It was an accident."

"*After* the accident. When you put the fire out."

"Oh." He coughed again. There was a little less smoke this time. "I called it to me."

"The fire?" Still holding the piece of curtain, she started back toward him. "You called the fire toward you?"

"It's just another kind of energy, right?"

"Yeah. Right." Her fingers left dark gray smudges behind when she patted his arm. "You just keep believing that, okay?" A wave of the ruined curtain for emphasis. "Try dialing it back this time."

"It?" One last puff of smoke as punctuation. "You want me to do it again?"

"Curtains can be replaced," she reminded him as she returned to her place out of the line of fire, "I can't. Once more, with less feeling."

"I don't think . . ."

"Good. You think too much and we're running out of time. Do what you just did, only less."

"Less. Right." Tony wiped damp palms on his thighs, extended his finger again, and very carefully refocused. To his surprise, a bright blue light burned in approximately the right position and then went out. Okay, almost there. He needed less less. *That's more, right?* Licking dry lips, he tried again. The blue light burned longer. *A little more.* And again. This time the light maintained; became a line; the line bent into a circle; the edges of the circle sputtered, but the shape held. Within the circle, two dots of power for eyes. The curve of a smile.

It was slightly lopsided but recognizable.

"What is it?"

Or not.

"It's a happy face." Even when he turned away, the power he'd used to create the symbol hung in the air. It was bone useless but way cool. "I told you it would be . . ." His voice trailed off as the sound of laughter filled the condo.

Tony whirled around, both hands up, expecting some kind of demonic clown charging in from the balcony. There was only his happy face, all blue and glowing and hanging in the air. Given the way it was laughing, it seemed to be very, very happy indeed.

"Simple," Leah said, raising her voice enough to be heard. "You said it would be simple. I think you meant to tell me that you were simple. And when I say simple, I don't mean that you're easy, I mean that you're . . ."

The *Darkest Night* theme joined the laughter to drown out her last word.

Since he couldn't think anything else to do, Tony answered his phone.

"Tony! There's something in the soundstage! It's ripping the place apart. There's crashing and screaming and . . ."

"Lee!"

"No, it's Amy, you ass!"

He knew that. "I meant . . ."

"I don't give a good goddamn what you meant! Get in here!"

"What . . ."

But there was only the dial tone. Over by the window, the happy face kept laughing.

Shoving the phone back in his backpack, Tony hung it over one shoulder as he ran for the door. "The demon's at the studio!"

"Tony! Wait!"

"Forget it, Leah. You want your body guarded, you come with me."

"I intend to." She grabbed his backpack and dragged him around. "But you can't leave that thing hanging in my condo!"

The happy face kept laughing.

Tony stretched out his left arm and sucked the energy back through the scar. He had the giggles all the way to the underground garage.

♠

Leah's driving made it difficult to practice the four runes he needed to know. He'd taken half a dozen pictures of the tattoo with the camera on his phone and, with his knees pressed against the dash and the phone open on his knees, he tried to memorize the swoops and curls as he sketched.

Tried to sketch.

"Leah!"

"You want to get there in time or what?" Considerably over the 100K limit, she cut in and out of westbound traffic in order to maintain her speed.

The TransCanada was a slightly less direct route back to the studio, but it had no lights and they were making amazing time—even considering the amount of lateral movement. Flung right then left, Tony wondered again why every time something metaphysical came down, he ended up in a car with people who drove like complete maniacs. Henry, Arra, Mouse, Jack, Leah . . .

"Hey!" The car started to hydroplane on the wet pavement, the back end fishtailing for about thirty meters before Leah got it under control. Tony caught the phone before it hit the floor but lost his pencil. "We're not all immortal here!"

"Trust me. I'm a professional stunt driver."

"They aren't!" The drivers of a late '90s Buick and a little imported hybrid flipped them off in quick succession. Hoping Leah's protective coating would work against road rage, he bent to find the pencil. He'd just about decided to take off his shoulder belt when he heard the siren and straightened so quickly he cracked his head on the dash. "Shit. Is that for us?"

"Seems to be. Are you crying?"

"No. My eyes are watering, I hit my head. You're not stopping!"

"Neither is the demon at the soundstage."

Good point. He wasn't looking forward to explaining it to the police but, still, a good point.

"If it is a demon." She slid between two transports, passed on the right shoulder, and somehow ended up back in the left lane.

"What do you mean if?" Tony demanded.

"If it's a demon, why is it at your soundstage? Why isn't it hunting for me?" As they passed the Kensington on ramp, an unmarked car squealed onto the highway in front of them, siren also wailing, the light on the dash just barely visible through distance and rain. "They're trying to cut us off!"

He grabbed the wheel before Leah could change lanes. "No. Follow them."

"Are you insane!"

"They're not slowing down, and the car behind us has fallen back."

"I lost him."

"No." There was no mistaking Jack Elson's pale blond hair in the unmarked car. "I know these guys."

Leah shot him a quick glance. "Your Mountie buddy?"

"Eyes on the road! My Mountie buddy and his partner," he expanded when his heart started beating again. An East Indian woman was driving and he was willing to bet she had to be Constable Danvers regardless of how much ethnic recruiting the RCMP did.

"I forgot to add them to the list of the people who know what you are, didn't I? Why didn't you just tell the papers?" she continued before he could answer. "It'd save time."

As the two cars sped toward the studio, he tried to remember if he'd told her about Kevin Groves. And what it was *about* Kevin Groves that he'd intended to tell her. "Well, technically . . ."

"I don't want to know."

They fishtailed off the ramp onto Boundary, squealed tires through the gate of the industrial complex, and sprayed gravel in tandem as they pulled up in the parking lot at CB Productions.

Jack was out of the car, gun in his hand, before the gravel hit the ground again. "When they called in your plates, I figured something was up. What is it?" he demanded falling into step as Tony sprinted for the building.

Tony hesitated, wondering if Jack had kept his partner in the loop. Television cops never kept secrets from their partners. "There's a demon ripping up the soundstage!"

"A what?" Danvers yelled as the four of them pounded in through the office doors.

"A demon!" Tony skidded to a stop as the dozen or so people in the office turned to stare.

He stared.

They stared.

"Jesus, Tony . . ." Amy's brows dipped to nearly touch over her nose. ". . . what the hell happened to your neck?"

"Not important." Trust Amy. He couldn't stop himself from touching the bite as he hurriedly counted heads. "Not everyone's out."

"Such a grasp of the obvious," she said to the room at large. "This is why I called him."

"Amy." Tina's tone suggested that was enough. "A few people got out the back," the script supervisor continued, rocking the new and teary assistant set decorator in the circle of her arms. "There's a few still in there."

"CB?"

All heads turned toward CB's office as though they were on a single string.

"He went in as we came out."

Of course he had. Tony took a quick mental inventory of CB's office but could think of nothing that the big man could use as a weapon.

"Okay." Deep breath. A quick, purposeful crossing to the door—made slightly less purposeful by the people milling about in his way.

"You brought the cops?" Zev asked, pushing through to his side.

"They brought themselves." He reached for the door and paused. This wasn't a case of reacting to an attack, blasting before he could consider the consequences; this was deliberately going after a demon. Deliberately going after something with teeth and claws and attitude. *Try not to look like you're nearly pissing yourself.*

*You went after the thing in the basement,* a little voice reminded him.

*Did you miss the part about teeth and claws?* he asked it.

A quick glance back over his shoulder. "You guys don't have to . . ."

Jack reached past him and shoved the door open. "Move!" he snapped.

So he moved.

They ran in single file between the double racks of costumes—a wizard-in-training, two RCMP officers, and an immortal stuntwoman/Demongate bringing up the rear. It sounded like the punch line of a bad joke. All they needed was a duck. Tony'd been a little afraid that either Zev or Amy would follow, but they both seemed to have more sense.

The door to the soundstage was closed.

When Tony reached to open it, Jack stopped him, hand without the gun wrapping around his wrist. "You don't just go charging in! Listen first."

Leah raised an eyebrow in Tony's direction, sharing her amusement. "The door's soundproof. We might as well go charging in."

"Fine. We . . ." Jack used his weapon to indicate that "we" in this case meant him and Danvers. ". . . go in first."

"Good idea."

The constable fixed Leah with a pale stare. "Who the hell are you?"

"Leah Burnett."

"And?"

"I'm a stuntwoman."

"Let me rephrase. Why are you here?"

"I don't even know why *we're* here," Danvers muttered.

"Believe it or not . . ." She pointed at Tony. ". . . the safest place I can be is next to him."

"Not," Jack snorted.

Tony could feel momentum slipping away. Once it was gone, he was afraid he'd never be able to force himself onto the soundstage. Ignoring the others, he yanked open the door and charged through, heading for the area under the gate.

The Demonic Convergence was happening on the lower mainland because Leah and the oldest spell in the world currently lived here. But she didn't have the only spell around. It might not even be the strongest. It sure as hell wasn't the freshest.

*Looking for that nice, fresh demonic feeling?*

*Oh, man, I seriously need some downtime with my brain.*

In the last few weeks, the set under the gate that had brought Arra Pelindrake into this world and then taken her out again had been the living room of grieving parents, a medieval dining hall, and a veterinary office—anything they could fit into the space without moving the walls or windows. CB disapproved of unnecessary rebuilding.

The end wall had been reduced to a jagged bit of framing and a dangling piece of plywood. Standing surrounded by debris, one sleeve ripped from his suit jacket and the exposed arm hanging limp by his side, CB shook a length of pipe up at the lighting grid. "Get your scaly red ass down here so I can kick it back to whatever overblown special effect it crawled out of!"

A shriek of tortured metal from above.

One of the big lamps plummeted toward the floor.

Time was supposed to slow as certain death approached. That was the theory. Total bullshit as far as Tony was concerned. The lamp exploded against the painted concrete floor, CB dove out of the way, swinging the pipe to deflect a shard of glass away from his leg, and Tony barely had time enough to realize he should do something. No time at all to think of just what he should do.

The sound of another lamp ripped from the grid made one thing clear; he had to get the demon down.

Tony held out his hand and called.

The demon was about the size of a ten-year-old but remarkably heavy for all that. The impact knocked the breath from them both and for a moment they sprawled together on the concrete, arms and legs tangled in interspecies intimacy. Then it blinked orange eyes, and a mouth, far too wide for the face that held it, opened.

Black teeth.

Shiny and black like that lava rock Tony could never remember the name of.

Lots and lots of black teeth!

Pain flared in his left shoulder, something squeezed around his right leg, and the demon's head snapped forward.

*Fuck! Teeth!*

Four shots jerked it back far enough for Tony to get his left leg free. He kicked out, hard. It reared back, hissing and snarling, still attached by the tail wrapped around Tony's leg. He kicked it again, a little lower, and black claws on the hind legs shredded his jeans below the knee.

Jack took another shot. The tail whipped away. Danvers grabbed his shoulders, dragging him up onto his feet.

"Why are you wrestling with it?" Leah screamed, crouched behind a yellow chaise lounge. "Get those runes in the air!"

Tony ducked as the demon launched itself over him, heading for Leah. Ducked a little lower as it returned the other way, arms and legs flailing as CB yanked it back by the tail.

It folded back on itself, squirmed free, and leaped straight up.

If it regained the high ground . . .

No way in hell he remembered the runes.

*So we stick with what we know.*

Miraculously still standing, Tony made a mental note that a Powershot released inside was blinding. Hopefully, *temporarily* blinding.

"Mr. Foster!"

Patterns of blue light danced across the inside of Tony's lids. At least, he thought he had his eyes closed. "Yeah, Boss?"

"Was that you?"

"Yeah."

"Did you hit it?"

"I don't know."

"Is anyone being disemboweled?" Sarcasm dripped from Leah's voice.

It seemed that no one was.

"Well, isn't that lucky." Not so much dripping now as flowing freely.

"What was that?" Jack's voice, demanding an answer.

"The demon? Or Tony's pyrotechnical answer to the demon?"

"Hey!" He turned toward where Leah's voice put her. "We were all screwed if it got back into the light grid."

"Damned right." Danvers this time. Nice that someone understood.

A hand closed around his arm and by blinking rapidly he could almost make out the silhouette of the person attached to the hand. At least he hoped it was the person attached to the hand.

"You're bleeding." Danvers again.

"He should count his blessings he's alive to bleed." Leah, closer now, sounded distinctly unsympathetic. "What happened to the plan, Tony?"

"You guys had a plan?" Jack didn't sound like he believed her.

"There's a way to send the demons back where they came from without wiping out our best defense."

"If this ash is all that remains of the demon, he's out of the picture." CB. From near the floor. "Except for a few minor punctures, I believe Mr. Foster—who, I assume, you were referring to as our best line of defense—is fine."

"Tony, can you see yet?" Leah. Right in his face.

He could sort of make out shapes, but he got a little dizzy when he turned his head. "Uh . . ."

"No. He can't. We can. He can't." Probably Leah's hand on his cheek. The fingers were trembling a little. "Someone had better grab him before he cracks his skull open on the floor."

On cue, Tony felt his knees buckle.

"I've got you, kid." A dark Jack-shape with blond highlights.

"These holes look clean, and they're not as deep as they could be." Danvers, as she pulled his shirt off and started working on the punctures in his shoulder. Tony was starting to really like her. "Damp denim seems to make decent body armor. I don't think he did much damage to your leg either. Is there a first aid— Thanks."

No mistaking CB's presence up close and personal. There was a sudden lack of open space in the immediate area.

Jack shifted his grip to give Danvers a better angle on the shoulder. "So what's wrong with him?"

"You mean besides the holes? It was the Powershot. Not the smartest thing to do."

Jack answered Leah's question with one of his own. "Who *are* you?"

He'd keep asking until he got an answer, like the world's biggest, red serge-wearing terrier. Given Leah's earlier opinion of all and sundry, and given that Jack was definitely one of the sundry, the odds were good she wasn't going to tell him. The trick was figuring out how much of the truth would shut him up.

"She's a demonic consultant," Tony told him, trying not to think about what Jack's partner was doing to his shoulder.

"A what?"

"Demonic consul . . . OW!"

"Sorry."

"It's okay." And it was. The flash of white light accompanying the pain seemed to have cleared his vision. Where cleared meant he could see people standing around him and pretty much figure out who they were. Beyond about three meters, things were still a little fuzzy—like his focus had been pulled so he had no depth of field—which likely meant there'd be something with teeth and scales charging in from the fuzzy any minute now.

"Tony?"

Or not.

Lee gradually came into focus as he came closer. Then

came into focus a lot faster as he broke into a run and dropped to one knee.

"What happened?" he demanded, his hand closing around Tony's wrist.

Tony opened his mouth, but Jack filled the words in. "It's the aftereffects of frying a demon."

"You're hurt!"

"It's uh . . ." He glanced over at the blood-soaked pad in the RCMP officer's hand and decided not to bother with the whole manly denial thing. "Yeah."

"It's not as bad as it looks." Danvers' matter-of-fact tone made it convincing. Given that it was his blood, Tony wasn't entirely convinced, but Lee seemed to be.

Seemed to be glaring at Jack.

Who still held Tony cradled against his body while Danvers finished with his shoulder.

Lee was glaring?

Tony had no idea how Jack was responding, but something in the way his grip shifted and the way muscles moved in his chest, made Tony think he felt amused.

"How are the others, Mr. Nicholas?" CB's bulk reappeared like a mahogany wall at the end of Tony's feet, the force of his personality enough to break through Lee's . . . well, to break through whatever the hell was up with Lee.

"Fine. They're good." The actor sat back and turned, visibly distancing himself from the scene on the floor—although his fingers maintained their grip. "Mouse thinks the gaffer's nose might be broken."

"And Mason?"

"Would be on the phone to his agent if there was a phone around to be on."

"I'll speak with him in a moment."

"I can't say that I blame him, CB."

"Demons." Jack ignored Lee's reinstated glare, but there was nothing that suggested amusement this time. He shifted Tony's weight onto his partner, who caught it, steadied it, and raised a skeptical eyebrow when Tony muttered, "I can sit on my own."

"What about them?" CB demanded as Jack got slowly to his feet.

"She said *demons*. As in more than one. They had a plan to send the *demons* back where they came from. That . . ."

All eyes turned with his gesture to the smear of ash on the floor. Tony could just barely make it out. ". . . isn't the end of this. Is it?"

And all eyes turned to Leah.

Who looked at him.

His stomach growled.

# 

"HOW LONG IS THIS Demonic Convergence going to last?"

"I don't know."

"You don't know?" CB repeated Leah's answer as a question, an eyebrow raised for punctuation. There were rumors that eyebrow had once caused a loan manager to wet himself—a rumor that Tony, having more than once been on the receiving end of said eyebrow, was inclined to believe.

Leah proved to be made of sterner stuff, but then she'd already survived plagues, the Inquisition, disco. . . . "Information on the last Demonic Convergence was passed on as an oral history for centuries before finally being written down by an insane monk in 332. He was a little vague on duration."

"Rather an important point, don't you think?"

"As a matter of fact, I do." She matched his dry, sarcastic tone precisely and then sat back and crossed her legs. "Fortunately, we know that the Convergence is of limited duration, just not exactly how limited. My best guess would tie it to the moon through one full cycle. A month, no more. Maybe a little less."

"And your worst guess?" CB growled.

She shrugged. "The planets change position slowly and the stars slower still."

"You're saying this could last years?"

"It could."

"Demons could be dropping into my studio for years?"

"Or the one Tony destroyed could be the only one you'll see. There's no way of knowing for sure."

*Liar,* Tony thought. He was impressed by how much like a consultant she sounded and less impressed by how heavily edited the story had become. She hadn't mentioned that the demons were only coming through because a Demonlord was directing the convergent energy. Nor had she said anything about being an immortal Demongate, confident that Tony would keep her secret. Since he'd already lied for her once today, he supposed she had reason for the confidence. After all those years with Henry, he was good at secrets. And given that the residue of Arra's spell seemed to be exerting a stronger pull than Leah, the whole Demongate thing seemed a little less relevant than it had.

"I have a question!" Perched on the edge of CB's desk, Amy waved her hand above her head, the charms hanging off the polished bicycle chain she wore wrapped around one wrist glinting under the fluorescent lights. "How does one become a demonic consultant? Exactly?"

Amy hadn't been included in the "we" when CB'd growled, *"We need to talk."* When those who'd been involved in the battle—plus Lee who'd arrived on the scene before anyone thought to adjust the story—followed CB into his office—where followed, in Tony's case, meant hanging off Jack's arm and more or less putting one foot in front of the other—she'd invited herself along, dragging Zev behind her. Tony was glad they were there. Although the odds were good Zev would have understood, keeping Amy out of the loop had limited survivability, and even CB seemed to realize it would be easier in the long run to let her stay.

"I have a better question," Constable Danvers sighed, rubbing the bridge of her nose. "Who the hell is going to believe all that damage in the soundstage was caused by a deranged fan?"

"Drugged fan," Lee corrected. He'd suggested the cover story.

"Whatever. Drugged, deranged; no one will buy it."

"Mason did," Lee reminded her. Mason had been thrilled to think that one of his fans had gone berserk and trashed the soundstage. Mason was thrilled to believe pretty much anything that made it all about him.

"Once Mason starts talking about it," CB explained, "everyone else will believe it, too."

"Like he'll give them a choice," Amy snorted.

CB nodded. "My point exactly. You should use the tools you have to hand."

Everyone turned to look at Tony.

"You calling me a tool?" he roused himself enough to mutter.

"Yes."

So much for humor.

"I shall sum up, then." CB leaned back in his chair which creaked alarmingly under his bulk. "We are in the midst of a Demonic Convergence of indeterminate length. The demons are attracted to this building because of . . ."

Tony hoped no one had noticed the slight pause—where *no one* referred to the RCMP officers who hadn't been told about the gate or Arra or the Shadowlord when they were told about what had happened in the house. Given that they'd been standing on the front lawn when the heavens opened, the story of the house had been unavoidable, but—so far—Tony'd managed to avoid filling in the whole metaphysical backstory.

". . . the residual energy; energy most likely connected to Mr. Foster's abilities."

*That's right. Make it believable. Blame me.*

"Ms. Burnett," CB continued, "who has made a study of demonology . . ."

No one seemed to have any trouble believing in a stuntwoman as a student of demonology.

". . . just happened to have recently contacted Mr. Foster to inform him about this Demonic Convergence and to instruct him on how to return said demons to the hell they came from—although, as circumstances have forced Mr. Foster to fry both demons he has already faced, whether or not he *can* return them remains theoretical."

Tony rubbed the bandage on his shoulder. Nothing much about this seemed theoretical to him. His whole body ached.

"Because both demons have been reduced to ash, we have no proof should we decide to make the story public, so rather than be mocked by those who have not shared our experiences, we are maintaining that today's incident was caused by a drugged fan of Mason Reed's. Constables Danvers and Elson will support that story in their reports."

"I can't believe we're going to falsify a report!" Constable Danvers punctuated each word by banging the back of her head against the wall.

CB laid both hands flat on his desk. The fingers of the left hand started to tremble. Muscles tensed in the arm the demon had dislocated and Jack had snapped back, and the trembling stopped. "Given that you arrived here in an official capacity, the report is unavoidable. You may, of course, choose to tell the truth."

Danvers looked at CB, she looked around the room, and, finally, she looked at her partner. Who shrugged. Jack had been remarkably quiet since he'd brought up the point about multiple demons. Tony wondered what he was thinking. His partner seemed to be wondering the same, but after a long moment, she sighed and muttered, "Fine. But what happens if these things go public? You know, suddenly show up on the six o'clock news climbing the Lions Gate Bridge?"

"They don't show up on camera," Leah told her.

"Why not?"

"They don't have souls."

"What?"

"A camera steals a piece of your soul," Leah explained. "Demons have no souls, so they don't show up on camera."

"That's total bullshit."

A raised hand cut off the murmur of agreement. Leah leaned toward the constable, smiling slightly. "Why *don't* demons show up on camera, then?"

"Because they . . . I mean, they . . ." When no one seemed willing to help, Danvers' shoulders sagged. "I can't believe I'm even having this conversation." *Bang. Bang. Bang* against the wall.

Jack reached out and grabbed her shoulder, stopping the motion. Once she'd stilled, he stepped past her, swept a narrow-eyed gaze around the room—which would have been more effective had most of the people in the room not recognized it as having been inserted for effect—and finally locked his eyes on CB. "As long as demons are attracted to your soundstage, for *whatever* reason . . ."

Translating the emphasis, Tony could see another "talk" with the constable in his future. Probably accompanied by shouting.

". . . you'll have to close the studio."

Zev hummed a few portentous bars of music under his breath.

Amy moved off CB's desk and out of the line of fire as the producer smiled. "I have an episode and a half of a show still to shoot, Constable. I *have* to do no such thing."

"People are going to get hurt. Someone's already been hurt. Someone besides Tony."

"It was the gaffer," Tony murmured. "He's the guy who sets the lights to get the effect the DP wants," he expanded when Jack turned to glare. "When things get weird, it's good to hold onto the stuff you know. Not you, personally," he added quickly. "Us you."

"Did you get hit on the head?"

"I don't think so."

"Check." Jack's attention relocked on CB. "Your gaffer's nose is broken. He's on his way to the hospital. You were lucky no one was seriously hurt. Or killed. You're closing the studio."

"I am contractually obligated to provide twenty-two episodes of *Darkest Night* within a specific time frame," CB told him. "If I close the studio, this won't happen, and we will be in violation of our contract. There will be no season two. My people will be let go. Most will not be able to find new work as many of the network shows that were filming in Vancouver have moved back across the border."

"So you think your 'people' . . ."

That was the most sarcastic set of air quotes Tony had ever seen.

". . . would rather be exposed to demonic attacks than unemployment?"

"Speaking as one of his people . . ." Perched now on an arm of the couch, Amy waved again. ". . . definitely."

"You are not the average employee," Jack pointed out.

"I am," Zev broke in before Amy could respond. He shuffled forward to the edge of the couch cushion. "I vote we finish the season."

Jack stared at the music director for a long moment. "Why are you even here?" he asked.

A nod toward Amy. "I came in with her."

"That's not helping your case, you know that, right?"

"Yes, but . . ." He winced and fell silent as Amy smacked him on the arm.

"And," Jack continued, "as I understand things, neither of you spend much time out on the soundstage where the demons are going to be."

"I do." Lee rose slowly off his end of the couch and moved until he stood face-to-face with Jack. "And I say we don't close the studio."

Tony had a feeling that, right at that moment, Lee would say black if Jack said white. He cleared his throat and was more or less gratified when it drew everyone's attention back to him. "Look, I'm going to be here anyway . . ." He tried to sit forward like Zev had, found he didn't have the energy, figured *screw it* as he fell back, sagging slightly into the warmth Lee had left. ". . . and it would be a lot easier on me if I didn't have to waste time and energy . . ." A short rest for emphasis before he finished. ". . . keeping friends and coworkers from being eaten while I deal."

"Eaten?" Amy and Zev together. Lee came in a little late.

"We've got a dead guy without an arm in the morgue. Killed by a demon who ate the arm." Jack folded his arms triumphantly.

He didn't know the arm hadn't been eaten, and since he was helping Tony make his point, Tony wasn't planning on mentioning it.

"So . . ." CB steepled his fingers and peered over the mahogany triangle at his TAD. "You think I should close the studio."

"No." Leah jumped in before Tony could get his mouth open. "I don't think you should close the studio." She stood and spread her hands, looking earnest. "We don't know how long the Demonic Convergence will last." Tossing her hair back over her shoulders, she adjusted her posture subtly. "There's no reason to risk putting so many people out of work. Tony will be here. I've taught him everything he needs to know."

The simple statement sounded pornographic.

Lee, who was closest to her, made a sound low in his throat. CB and Jack leaned in.

Ryne Cyratane flexed translucent muscles and ran his hands down Leah's arms.

"Then it's settled." CB's voice slipped past Barry White and headed toward registering on the Richter scale. "We'll keep the studio open."

Jack nodded, absently drying his palms on his thighs. "That sounds reasonable."

"Nothing about this sounds reasonable," Danvers muttered. "What the hell are you talking about, Jack?"

"She's the demonic consultant." A nod and an appreciative smile toward Leah. "We're out of our depth—we should listen to her."

"You're out of your mind."

Charms chimed as Amy waved. "I'd like to second that, except I want the studio open, so I won't."

All right. Enough was enough. If Leah didn't want her secrets told to all and sundry, she needed to lay off taking advantage of all and sundry. Tony frowned at Lee. Especially this particular sundry. "She's using demonic sex appeal to convince you."

Leah's dark eyes widened, and her lower lip went out. "Tony!"

"Do you have proof of this accusation, Mr. Foster?"

"No, but . . ."

"Then don't make it."

"Hello! Wizard!" He tried to stand and fell back onto the couch. His second attempt was more successful but only because Zev helped. "Okay. Wizard. Let's assume I know more about what's going on here than . . ." The room shifted out of focus and back in again. ". . . than not-wizards, okay? And let's assume that I can . . ." Whoa. His head felt like a raw egg balanced on a strand of cooked spaghetti. ". . . I can . . ."

"You can barely stand, Tony." Lee didn't sound particularly sympathetic, but then Lee was as enthralled by Leah as Jack and CB.

*Okay, forget the room. Focus on Lee's face. You're good at that.* He was. But it had never been so hard before. His brain attempted to toss in a smutty innuendo but didn't quite manage it. "Behind her . . . there's a big . . . a big naked . . ."

On *naked,* Lee turned his attention back to Leah.

Crap.

Tony's knees gave out, and Zev was a second late keeping his head from bouncing off the floor of CB's office.

"That sounded like it hurt." Amy frowned down at him.

Way to state the obvious.

"He needs to see a doctor."

Constable Danvers was rapidly becoming one of Tony's favorite people.

"No, he just needs rest. A Powershot uses a lot of personal energy, and that's not something a doctor can fix. No wonder he's babbling." Leah sounded convincing. Tony would have been more convinced if when his head fell to one side, he hadn't been looking through a bare foot. An enormous bare foot.

"What happens if another demon attacks before he recovers?" Jack demanded.

"We're screwed."

Tony wondered if he was the only one who heard, *You're screwed.*

"I can shoot it."

"That's sweet, but bullets will only slow it down. All you can do is hope Tony recovers and that from now on, he does things *my* way."

Tony was starting to think Leah had some serious control issues. He closed his fingers around Zev's wrist. "All . . . about . . . sex."

As darkness claimed him, he heard CB snort. "Welcome to the wonderful world of television, Mr. Foster."

He came to, stretched out on the couch in CB's office, all his attention on the vegetable soup in a Styrofoam bowl steaming on the coffee table beside him. Ignoring the spoon, he grabbed it with shaking hands and downed it in four swallows. Or, more accurately, three since a good portion of the fourth he coughed out his nose.

A familiar hand passed over a wad of paper napkins.

"Where's everyone gone?" he asked when he could talk.

"Back to work." Ryne Cyratane had vanished and Leah looked no more than normally attractive. "Your friends on the force have reports to file and a nonexistent drugged fan to pretend to track down. Your coworkers are finishing the day's pages—well, except for Mason Reed who leaked news of the incident to the press and is now giving interviews."

Tony snorted out an alphabet noodle; an F or maybe an E deformed by its passage through his sinuses. "The studio's staying open."

"Yes."

"The demons will come here."

"Yes."

"Because the gate is putting out the kind of residual power that attracts them more powerfully than you do."

"Yes."

"If there're people in the studio, the demon won't just

check out the gate, realize it's not you, and go hunting as instructed by its boss. It'll try for a snack and make itself obvious. If it's distracted by a meal, it'll be easier for me to send it home." His subconscious had put the pieces together while he'd been out. "You're setting up the people here as bait."

She stared at him for a moment, then she smiled. "Only during business hours. Your vampire can still deal with it after dark. More soup?"

"Sure." Tony drank, slower this time, and considered his options. His brain felt like it was wrapped in barbed wire. It hurt to think and, as far as he could tell, he didn't actually seem to have any options. Sucked to be him. "I could tell them."

"About what?"

"About them being bait. About you being a Demongate. About the Demonlord's plan to kill you and take over the world. I could tell them everything."

"And that would accomplish what?" she asked reasonably, crossing the office and perching on the edge of the coffee table so she could stare earnestly into his face. "CB has very good reasons for not shutting the studio down. I agreed with him, so I helped him convince your friend Jack. Yes, your crew will be in a bit of danger, but if you get your head out of your butt and learn how to deal with the demons, it's all incidental anyway. You'll send them back before they do any damage."

"Yeah, tell that to Ritz."

"Who?"

"The gaffer." He waved at his nose.

"Your gaffer's name is Ritz?"

"Probably not, but that's what he goes by."

"Right." She tucked a strand of hair behind her ear. "If you'd been here, instead of at my place . . ."

"I was protecting you!"

Leah ignored him. ". . . Ritz wouldn't have gotten hurt."

"So what happened was my fault?"

"It was no one's fault." Leaning forward, she patted his

knee. "Tony, this is working out perfectly. The gate obviously has a more powerful signature than I do or that demon wouldn't have come here first."

First. He frowned. First? "That wasn't the first demon."

Leah wrapped a curl around a finger. "Well, no, but . . ."

"And the first demon didn't come here first."

"Ah!" She held up a cautioning finger. "We don't know that."

"It killed a guy, ripped off his arm, and *then* came after you."

"It probably came to the studio at night when there was no one here, then it found my scent at the stunt site where it killed the construction worker. It was the next day before it found me. If there'd been a wizard in the studio prepared to send it back . . ." Her voice trailed off dramatically.

"I'm seeing a problem with that."

"I'm not saying it was your fault that man died."

"Yeah. Bite me. Let's consider the word 'probably.' "

She frowned as she went back over what she'd said. Then she rolled her eyes. "Fine. But the second demon definitely came here first—even though we drove right by it—so the odds are certainly in favor of the first demon having done the same thing. Demons at this level aren't known for independent thought. They're just big scary, scaly killing machines. Fortunately, this lot has been given a mission, so there's less random killing."

"That's comforting." Tony's head hurt, his shoulder was throbbing, the soup had barely taken the edge off his hunger, and at some point while he was in la-la land, his torn and bloody clothes had been replaced by geek wear off the costume rack. He couldn't decide if he was pissed off, resigned, or just hungry, and he was doing it all while wearing polyester. "So I'll be sitting under the gate, 24/7 until the convergence is over."

"You'll have breaks between demons. It takes time to divert enough convergent energy to get a demon through even a thinned barrier, and I can't imagine that my lord will be able to pop them out any closer together."

"He's not still your *lord!* He's trying to kill you!"

"Sure, now, but he's been my lord for thirty-five hundred years. It's not going to be an easy habit to break."

"And you like using his power."

"Well, duh."

Kind of a hard response to argue with. Tony wasn't sure if he admired her honesty or was appalled by it. Bit of both, probably. He dropped his head into his hands and scrubbed at his face. "I took out demon-with-the-arm last night and red-and-toothy this morning, that's barely twelve hours apart."

"No, it's closer to twenty-four. Demon-with-the-arm acquired the arm the night before he attacked us," she reminded him. "And look at the bright side, when you're not sending demons back to hell, you can do your job and, more importantly, collect a paycheck. You couldn't work or get paid if you were still following me around."

He didn't really have an argument for that either. "My laundry is at your place."

Sensing the win, she smiled. "I'll deal with your laundry."

"Yeah." The edge of the Styrofoam cup flaked apart under his fingernails. "Look, the only way I can see ruling out that probably—as in probably the demons will come here first—is if you're here with me. Then the demons will *definitely* come here first."

Her hand dropped to her side, and the smile disappeared. "Tony, I bled."

"So?" When he moved, the adhesive tape holding the gauze pad over the hole in his shoulder pulled at sensitive skin.

"The demons can hurt me."

"Yeah, well, big scary killing machines, remember? You got off easy." There were three deep scratches under his polyester pant leg. "We both did."

Leah's eyes narrowed. "Are you being deliberately stupid, or did you hit your head harder than I thought? They're the *only* thing in the world that can hurt me!"

Ah. "So, given the chance, you'd rather they weren't given the chance?"

"And a second brain cell comes online!"

He supposed he could understand her reaction. Except . . .

"You came to me so that I could help you deal with the Demonic Convergence, and now you're putting other people in danger."

"Oh, no!" Both hands went up, palms toward him. "Don't put that on me. I came to you so we could spackle the weak spots and maybe deal with a few long-legged beasties that'd scuttled in from the closest hells. I never intended to face down demons. And people? People are in danger every time they step into the shower. Do you know how many household accidents happen in the bathroom? Should they stop showering? Or what about the chance of choking and dying? Should everyone stop eating? These demons are the *only* things that can hurt me, and I don't think it's unreasonable that I should avoid them!"

"But they can't *only* hurt you! You've lived for thirty-five hundred years; don't you think shorter lives should be protected because they are shorter?"

She sat back and frowned. "No."

Actually, he should've seen that coming.

"Look, let's forget about me for the moment and talk about you. You're a wizard, and wizards pretty much have three options." She flipped up a finger. "An ascetic life of learning." A second finger. "World domination." A third finger. "Or supporting the greater good. What's it going to be?"

"World domination."

All three fingers snapped down. "Wrong answer."

Was it fair that she could go for so long without blinking? Finally, he looked away and sighed. "Do I get a big red W on my chest?"

"Why would I know about your skin problems?"

"Just asking."

Her expression bordered on triumphant as she patted his arm and stood. "You really shouldn't waste any time learning those runes. CB says you can stay here and use his office."

"Me? Where are you going?"

"To get your laundry." Tone and expression together suggested that if he was all that stood between the world and demonic domination, the world was doomed.

"Right. Laundry." He watched her walk to the door. "Leah?"

She paused, holding the door handle.

"What if you're wrong? What if the next guy doesn't come here first? What if it goes after you?"

She chewed the corner of her lower lip, looking a lot younger than someone who'd seen her entire village slaughtered thirty-five hundred years ago. Then she tossed her hair back over her shoulder and smiled. It wasn't a particularly believable smile, not when one hand dropped to rest against the curve of her belly. "Then I race back here and you get to be my hero again."

"But if . . ."

"Tony, relax, we drove right past that demon this morning and it still came here first. Since I seem to have another option, I'm not going to spend the rest of the Demonic Convergence, however long it lasts, cowering behind you. Nor will I let this latest plan of Ryne Cyratane's control my life any more than I let his first plan control me. You'll deal with the demons; I'll get on with living."

"And my life?"

"Do you have a life that doesn't involve your job?" Her wave gathered in the studio beyond CB's office. "And, hey, here you are."

The door closed behind her. Tony stared at it a moment longer. He felt like he should have argued harder. If Leah stayed at the studio, then the demons would head here guaranteed, and he had a feeling there weren't many guarantees in demonology. But even on short acquaintance it was obvious that Leah was all about having things happen for her, her way. It'd likely become habit after the first couple of millennia—right about the time she'd got out of the habit of relying on other people who inconveniently died just when they were needed.

Still, at least she wasn't cowering behind him. That was a good thing, right?

The four sketches he'd made in the car were spread out on CB's blotter. His weight on the edge of the desk, Tony picked up the least complicated and stared at it for a long moment, his thumb leaving a vegetable-soup-colored print on the paper. He raised his other hand. He focused. He picked his spot. He drew the pattern.

Or not.

The blue lines sputtered and broke apart, tumbling out of the air like fireworks.

Tony braced himself and somehow managed to neither slide to the floor nor end up sprawling and drooling across CB's desk.

Afterimages floated across his vision. Blue sparks tumbling and falling. Tumbling and falling. Tumbling and . . .

He swallowed hard, belched vegetable soup, and didn't throw up.

"Go me," he muttered, staggering forward to stomp out a bit of smoldering carpet. Going actually sounded like a good idea. He needed food. Lots and lots of food.

Who the hell had moved CB's door so far from his desk?

Since Amy'd never let him live down a little heavy breathing, he clutched at the door handle and tried to stop panting before he went out into the office. It was quiet. Too quiet. The hair lifted off the back of Tony's neck . . .

. . . and settled down again as he realized that Amy wasn't at her desk. That always lowered the noise level. She'd probably sent Krista out to the soundstage to find someone and then, with the office PA still gone, had to deliver the next urgent message herself. Given the belt of red lights blinking across the bottom of her phone, she'd been gone for a while.

Even though there seemed to be a perfectly mundane reason for the unnatural calm, Tony walked carefully out into the middle of the room, his heels barely touching the floor. Caution, yes, but also he had a suspicion that the wrong step would cause his head to fall off his shoulders. After the year he'd had, rhetorical statements became frighteningly possible and he much preferred his head where it was.

He could hear voices raised in the bull pen as the writers bashed the last rough edges off the season's final script. It didn't take much concentration to make out the actual words.

"Because we need a little physical action here! It's a classic bit and it always gets laughs. We can't lose!"

It sounded like Mason was going to get nailed in the nuts again. The writers never got tired of slipping physical humor into the script. So far, Peter and the other directors had managed to keep this particular piece of physical humor from actually happening to their temperamental star, mollifying the writers with guest stars and bit players curled around their crotches and moaning. The writers had some issues.

He could hear Rachel Chou, the office manager, talking quietly to someone in the small kitchen.

"And just what, exactly, do you mean by that?"

Mason's voice boomed out of his small office on the other side of the main doors. Was he still with the press? And, if so, shouldn't he be back on set by now? Tony tried to remember Raymond Dark's call sheet for the day and drew a blank.

He shuffled a couple of steps forward but still missed the reporter's reply.

Mason, however, had done Bard on the Beach and knew how to project above the sound of flapping canvas and not so distant traffic crossing the Burrard Bridge. One hollow-core door was nothing to him. "How dare you insinuate that about my fans!"

Mason's fans were predominantly middle-aged women with Web sites and frighteningly explicit imaginations. Less common were those who believed that vampires truly lurked in the darkness—beyond that, they couldn't seem to agree on the particulars. Tony was fairly certain he'd never seen Henry actually lurk. Rarest of all were the fans who admired Mason's acting.

"My fans are the salt of the earth!"

Who really talked like that? Tony wondered, moving closer still. Although, in all fairness, some of those Web sites had some pretty salty language, not to mention an interesting concept of male anatomy. Or at least of Mason's anatomy. And, while he was hardly one to complain about hot man-on-man action, he was a little confused by all the Raymond Dark/James Taylor Grant stuff out there. Leaving the actors' preferences out of it entirely, Raymond Dark was a tomcat with a new conquest every week and half a hundred tragic love affairs in his past. Even James Taylor Grant had buried one true love and staked another.

Lee'd dated the second actress for a while until a chance to star in a remake of *Time Tunnel* had drawn her to Toronto.

The door of Mason's office flew open, snapping Tony's attention back to the matter at hand. He barely had enough time to look like he hadn't been eavesdropping when the star of *Darkest Night* made a dramatic exit—or entrance, depending on point of view—announcing, "This interview is over!"

"Mr. Reed, you have to be aware that this show has been attracting an unhealthy amount of paranormal attention."

Tony knew that voice.

"I don't have to be aware of anything," Mason snapped as Kevin Groves followed him out of the office. "And I very much dislike what you're implying!"

"Which is?"

Lip curled, Mason turned on his heel and headed for the exit. "My assistant will deal with any further questions."

Groves blanched—which wasn't surprising given his last encounter with Jennifer—and allowed Mason to leave unimpeded. Physically unimpeded. "I will discover the truth, Mr. Reed!"

Even from across the room, Tony could tell Mason was considering whether or not he should respond.

*Please, not the Nicholson!*

After a long moment, Mason snorted and walked out of the production office.

Tony released a breath he didn't remember holding, then looked up to see Kevin Groves heading his way.

"We need to talk."

About to suggest a biological impossibility, Tony suddenly remembered just what exactly it was about the reporter he'd wanted to pass on to Leah. Kevin Groves knew about the Demonic Convergence. Tony had to find out how much. "Okay."

Groves opened his mouth and then closed it again, looking confused. "Okay?"

"But not here." He had to work here and the last thing he needed was for someone to see them together. Where someone meant Amy. He'd never live it down, especially since his breathing was decidedly still on the heavy side. "I need to eat. We'll go across the road."

Still clearly taken aback, Groves shrugged. "Sure."

"So let's move!" Before Amy got back. Tony led the way out to the street and almost didn't make it. Had that outside door always been so heavy? Groves reached past him, laid a surprisingly large hand against the glass, and shoved. "Thanks."

"Are you all right?"

"I'm fine." If anyone saw them, he could just say he was doing a bit of follow-up damage control. It never hurt to know what Mason had told the press before the headlines made it onto CB's desk.

The green light barely lasted long enough for him to shuffle across Boundary.

"We're not heading to the Duke's?" Grove asked as Tony turned and walked past the damp and deserted patio.

"Man, you really *are* an investigative reporter, aren't you? You don't miss a thing."

"I thought all you guys always went to the Duke's."

"Thought wrong."

The Duke's was a gathering place for the various actors who made the Burnaby area their home, or at least their place of employment—actors, directors, producers, but seldom crew. Crew had their own place cut from the front of an old warehouse, three quarters of the building still used by one of the bigger studios for storage.

"Okay, here's the deal." If he concentrated, he could talk without panting. "You only talk to me, and you keep your voice down."

"Or?"

"Or you'll never know what's going on."

"You don't look so good."

"Who asked you?"

"I'm just saying," Groves muttered as Tony led the way into the Window Shot, adding as they paused to allow their eyes to adjust to the gloom, "You'd think there'd be more windows."

"That's not what it means." He could feel Groves waiting for an explanation. Why not give him a freebie? "Crews used to get paid daily. They'd get what they were owed in cash from a payroll window after shooting ended, so the last shot of the day was called the window shot."

"And now you come here after the last shot of the day for the first shot of the day."

"You're smarter than you look." Bigger, too, Tony realized as they made their way across the scuffed tile floor to the empty booths under the single window. Tony was five ten; Groves was a couple of inches taller and broader through the shoulders. Not much meat on him, though, and the cheap gray suit did a lot to hide what size he had as did the way he curled in on himself as though he expected to be hit. All things considered, not an unreasonable expectation.

The booth smelled like beer and fries and damp clothes, but Tony felt a lot more secure with the dark wood supporting him. If he craned his head just right, and the traffic on Boundary cooperated, he could see the main entrance to the studio parking lot through the streaked glass. Leah seemed pretty sure that nothing would happen for a while, but he felt better being able to keep an eye on things. Even a minimal eye.

"Tony!" The owner of the bar approached, drying her hands on a green apron. "What can I get for you?"

"Large poutine and a glass of milk, please, Brenda." Milk was like food. He'd seen a PBS program about it.

"Oh, yeah, that's healthy. And your friend."

"He's not my friend," Tony put in quickly before Groves could speak. "He's a reporter for the *Western Star*."

"Ah." One steel-gray brow rose as she turned and gave the reporter the once over. "That cover picture last week, the creature of the night? It looked like a raccoon in a Dumpster. You guys aren't even trying."

Groves' lip curled. "I have nothing to do with the cover photos."

"Yeah, I bet I'd have a little trouble finding someone who admits they do. What do you want?"

"Coffee's fine."

"My coffee's better than fine," she snorted and headed toward the kitchen.

"Why did you tell her who I was like that?" Lacing long fingers together, Groves braced his forearms on the table and leaned forward.

"So she'll watch what she says around you."

"You think she knows things?"

Tony shrugged and sucked air in through his teeth as the claw holes in his shoulder pulled with the motion.

"What is it?"

Pointless to lie about the obvious. Lies should be held against need when they could be camouflaged by bits of the truth. "I hurt my shoulder."

Behind the glasses, dark eyes narrowed at the straight answer. "How?"

Tony's turn to snort. "You were talking to Mason, how do you think?"

"I can say you were hurt in the attack?"

"Go ahead. I'm a TAD . . ." He remembered pain in time to cut off the shrug. ". . . no one will give a shit."

"You *saw* this deranged fan?"

"Duh. You know it's funny. You believe in all sorts of paranormal crap, yet you don't believe that one of Mason's fans could go bugfuck."

"It's not that I don't believe . . ." He paused and leaned closer still. Tony got a whiff of mint and wondered, since there seemed to be no gum chewing going on, if it was a default odor. "I've met some of Mason Reed's fans," he said, "and it's a short trip to bugfuck. But there's more going on."

"More?"

"Why are we here?"

"I wanted some poutine," Tony told him as the food arrived.

Groves waited until they were alone again, until he'd emptied three creamers into his coffee, and said, "Why are we here together?"

"You said we needed to talk."

"You agreed with me."

"You've been stalking us since August."

"Because I know when I'm being lied to."

"About what?"

"Anything."

"Like creatures of the night?" Tony asked. His tone implied he couldn't believe they were talking about stuff no one in their right mind believed in.

"Yes."

Tony nearly choked on his mouthful of fries and gravy and cheese curd. "You're serious?"

"It's a . . ." Groves stared into his coffee as though he could find the missing word. Finally, he raised his head and met Tony's eyes. ". . . curse."

"You know when you're being lied to?"

"I do."

He did. And more, he expected Tony to believe him.

"What are you doing?" he asked as Tony frowned at the scuffed wood beside his bowl.

"I'm trying to decide if beating my head against the table will be worth it."

"Why?"

Because like drew to like. The Demonic Convergence was in Vancouver because Leah was there and the gate was there and he was there and—oh, yeah—Henry was there. Since he'd first met Henry, there'd been ghosts and werewolves and walking mummies. . . .

It was like murders always happening around Jessica Fletcher. Who the hell would want to live in the same town as a little old lady who solved crimes?

*Or never noticing a white van until you owned one and then they were all over the goddamned place.*

There was a gate to another world in the studio where he worked.

The house they used for a location shoot just happened to be haunted.

When *Darkest Night* needed a stuntwoman, they hired an immortal Demongate.

It was like eight o'clock on the WB.

And Kevin Groves, who knew when he was being lied to, was still waiting for an answer. Tony sighed. "I'm having one of those days." Absolutely not a lie. "So let me guess . . ." He took a swallow of the milk. ". . . you went to work for the tabs because they're the only ones who dare to print the truth?"

"That's right." After a long moment, Groves rolled his eyes. "Now what?"

"Sorry." Tony blinked and started eating again. "Just having an MiB moment. You'd like the regular papers to print the truth?"

"Who wouldn't?"

Good point. "Under your byline."

"I don't do what I do for the good of my health, Mr. Foster. I'm a journalist."

Or he wanted to be seen as one, which, for all intents and purposes, amounted to the same thing. "So, are you saying Mason lied to you?"

"Mason Reed believes everything he says."

"That's not an answer."

Groves only shrugged and took a long drink of his coffee. Waiting.

*He knows I have something to say or we wouldn't be here together.*

*He believes that I have metaphysical powers, that weird metaphysical shit is happening around the studio, and he's looking for proof.*

*Let's not be too impressed by him sharing his lie detecting ability since I'm guessing he tells everyone. Of course he probably doesn't expect everyone to believe him.*

*Probably.*

"Yesterday, you said the words Demonic Convergence like you expected me to know what they meant. Why?"

Groves smiled. "Because I expected you to know what they meant."

"Why?"

"Nope. You asked a question, now I ask a question. That's how these things work."

Maybe it was. Almost able to feel the calories in the poutine winging off to various body parts, Tony pushed his empty bowl aside, laid his forearms on the table, and leaned forward, deliberately mirroring the reporter's earlier position. "Not this time," he said quietly. "I ask the questions, you answer them, and if I'm happy with the answers, maybe I'll tell you some of what you want to know."

Groves started at him for a long moment, then he sneered and stood. "I don't have to . . ."

"Yeah, you do. This is your only chance, Kevin. Screw it up and you spend the rest of your life on the outside looking in. Knowing things are happening but never being a part of it."

His lips drew back off coffee-stained teeth. "Idiot. I want to expose it, not be a part of it."

Tony locked their gazes and refused to let the other man look away. "Bullshit."

"Everything okay here, gentlemen?"

"Fine, Brenda. I could use a coffee now if you wouldn't mind. And Mr. Groves could use a refill."

"He's not leaving?"

"No." He sat down, hands shoved under the edge of the table a little too late to hide the trembling. "I'm not leaving. Refill would be good. Please."

Tony sat back feeling powerful. Feeling like a wizard in control. Feeling like he'd just kicked a puppy. A mangy, annoying, nippy puppy that no one liked but a puppy nevertheless. He shot what he hoped was a reassuring smile at Brenda who frowned at them both as she set a clean mug on the table and then filled it before refilling Kevin's. She frowned once more, just at him, before she walked away.

"You thought I'd know about the Demonic Convergence

because of what you believe I did last summer at that location shoot, right?"

"Witnesses said you spoke with the dead. Witnesses agree you . . ."

"Yeah." Tony raised his hand. His right hand. No point in flashing the rune burned into his left at this point in the game. "I don't need to know what you believe I did. Just answer the question."

"That's what I thought." Sullen but cooperating. Wanting desperately to be on the inside. With the cool kids.

"How do you know about it?"

"I was researching you, what you might be involved in . . ." Black masses and deals with the devil were strongly implied by his tone. ". . . and I found an old book in a used bookstore. It was written in German. I could read just enough to recognize that it was about talking to the dead, so I bought it figuring I could get it translated." The sullen started falling away. Tony had a feeling that being taken seriously was a new and exciting sensation for Kevin Groves. "There was a piece of folded paper in it . . . except it wasn't paper. It was vellum. You know what that is?"

"I have no idea."

"It's a piece of calf hide tanned really fine for writing on. Point is, it's old. Really old. On the vellum was a chart drawn up by some astrologer. He wrote that the powers would align to create a Demonic Convergence and the walls between the world and hell would thin. I took his calculations to the astrologer at the paper and she worked out the dates."

"Is she the real thing?"

Groves snorted. "Not hardly. She's got a Ph.D. in math, but she hates teaching."

Damn. Tony scrapped his idea of a metaphysical Justice League.

"It's happening now, isn't it? The Demonic Convergence?"

Why not? He'd already done the math. Or had the math done for him. Mouth open to admit that yes, the Demonic Convergence was in fact happening now, Tony got distracted by the sight of his own car driving by and turning into the studio lot. Then he realized that if Leah had gone back to her place for his laundry, of course she had to take his car.

Then he noticed that there was a spot by the entrance to the parking lot where the rain wasn't quite falling.

# Seven

"WHAT THE HELL IS UP with you?"

Tony ignored Kevin Groves yelling behind him, concentrating on getting through the traffic on Boundary without being killed. Wizardry wouldn't keep him from dying under the oversized wheels of some guy's SUV—or under the wheels of one of the new hybrids for that matter. He might be more environmentally dead, but he'd be just as dead. Horns blared, tires skidded sideways on the wet pavement, creative profanity blasted out of half a dozen open windows, but he made it to the other side alive. From the continuing sound of horns, tires, and profanity, Kevin was right behind him.

Great.

In about thirty seconds, deciding how much to tell him would no longer be a problem.

Tony could see the headlines now: IMMORTAL STUNTWOMAN SLAUGHTERED IN BURNABY; DEMONGATE OPENS AND THE WORLD ENDS! Bright side—he'd be dead and someone else would be cleaning up the mess.

He could see his car at the far end of the lot and thought he could see Leah twisted around, rummaging in the back seat. Then the driver's side door opened and an enormous white-and-red umbrella emerged, tipped down to keep the rain from blowing up under the outer edge. Unfortunately, tipped down, it was also keeping Leah from spotting the anomaly moving across the parking lot toward her.

Lifting his left hand, Tony called the umbrella. The demon appeared as nylon and wire and wood passed through the same space it was occupying, and Leah, mouth open to demand answers, had just enough time to fling herself back inside the car as claws struck sparks off the closing door. For a heartbeat the car filled with a translucent, naked, and very pissed-off Demonlord, then it was only Leah.

*Yeah, well, I'd be pissed, too, if my way back into the world kept ducking at the last minute.*

"That's a . . ."

"No shit." Tony thrust Leah's umbrella into Kevin's arms. "You might want to get behind something solid."

"I don't . . ."

"Or not. Just stay out of my way."

Fortunately, the demon was intent on peeling his quarry out of her strange new shell. Where *fortunately* didn't refer to the damage being done to his car. As he started focusing energy, Tony realized he'd pretty much run out of options. Another Powershot would use all the energy he'd regained and then some—the "and then some" was the worrying bit. He'd done a little gaming in his day and he knew what happened when stats fell into negative numbers. Leah's runes were his best chance. He was pretty sure he could remember the first one and then, with any luck, the others would fall into line behind it.

Except he couldn't quite remember the first rune.

*Curves here. Crosses back. And there's sort of a circle thing . . .*

*Crap!*

The demon shot him a disdainful sneer over one shoulder—given the excessive teeth and the glowing yellow eyes, it was a pretty damned effective sneer—and then slammed its palm down on the window. The window cracked.

He could hear Leah screaming.

*Fuck!*

No time to get this wrong!

He wiped out half the glowing symbol, realized it now looked sort of like the word *go* . . .

Palm against glass. A louder crack. More screaming.

. . . and went with plan B. The rune on his left hand grabbed ghosts. Ghosts were energy left over when flesh rotted. Therefore, the rune should allow him to grab this energy.

Grab it and throw it.

The glowing blue *go* hit the demon between the shoulder blades and sucked into the scaled skin with a disconcerting sizzle.

The demon spun around . . .

*H*

. . . shifted its weight onto two different legs . . .

*O*

. . . and charged.

*M*

Tony didn't have to keep throwing the letters. The demon charged through them, no longer sneering, clearly intent on ripping apart this puny mortal who dared to interfere.

*Puny mortal?* Where the hell had that come from?

*Sizzle.*

*Sizzle.*

*Sizzle.*

Too close!

The world had not gone into slow motion. Too bad because he could have used a bit more time. Eyes locked on the charging demon, his breath coming fast and shallow; he was only going to get one chance. Panic lending speed, more focused than he'd ever been in his life, he scrawled the last letter in the air.

*E*

Not so much a *sizzle* as a *ZAP*. Like the world's biggest bug hitting the world's biggest bug zapper.

The impact threw Tony backward as the demon flared a brilliant lime green and disappeared, leaving nothing behind him but a piece of smoking pavement and the smell of charred fish. It was over before his ass hit the parking lot; a large, deep puddle absorbing most of the impact.

"What was that all about?"

He could feel power racing over his skin as he peered up through the afterimages at Leah. "You're welcome."

"It was kind of hard to see what you were doing . . ." Her voice grew shriller with every word. ". . . but those weren't the right runes!"

"They worked."

"They shouldn't have!"

Tony would have shrugged, but his shoulder hurt way too much and, from the line of warmth dribbling down his chest, he had a feeling the bandage had come loose. He should have felt like crap, but he didn't. He felt invincible. It was like the way he knew where things were when he reached for them except . . . more. He knew where the whole world was. He knew where he was in the world. No. More still. He *was* the world. Just him, no backup singers.

It was the most incredible feeling. There was nothing he couldn't do, and no one could stop him. Without really thinking about what he was doing, he healed the puncture wounds in his shoulder.

And was amazed by the new and exciting levels of pain.

"SonofafuckingBITCH!"

Then world was a big ball of rock again, and his place in it involved a puddle and a parking lot.

"Tony!" Leah was right in his face. "What did you *do* to the demon?"

"I told it to go home."

Her mouth opened and closed a couple of times. She took a step away. "Go home?"

"Yeah." Even on the lower mainland, October rain was *cold.* As the water soaked through the cheap polyester, his balls tried to climb up and sit on his lap. "You said it yourself, the demons don't belong here. I sent it back where it belonged."

"It's not that easy!"

"It is if I want it to be." Teeth clenched, he checked to make sure his arm still worked, then he got to his feet. "This is my world, not *his.*" No need to define the pronoun. "*He* may need to slaughter whole villages and draw complicated esoteric symbols, I don't." Rain ran under his collar and down his back. "Intent is nine tenths of the law."

"No, it isn't!"

"It is," he repeated slowly and deliberately, "if I want it to be." He could feel the world waiting for him. What was it Leah had said earlier? He was the round peg in the round hole and, here and now, it was a perfect fit.

She shook her head, rain flinging from the ends of dripping curls. "It isn't . . ."

"Is."

"No."

"He's telling the truth."

"Who the hell are you?" Leah snarled as Kevin Groves and her umbrella emerged from behind a parked van and joined them.

Tony smiled. This might be fun. "Leah Burnett, Kevin Groves. Kevin is a reporter for the *Western Star*."

"The press? You brought in the press?" She grabbed a double handful of white and red and yanked the umbrella out of the reporter's hands. "This is mine! Why does he have it?"

"So my hands were free and I could save your ass. Again."

"Save my ass?" Her eyes widened and her posture changed subtly, her focus shifting from him to Kevin. "From a special effect? Don't be silly."

"It wasn't a . . . a special effect." Kevin scrubbed his palms against his suit. Kind of pointless given that the suit was soaking wet, but Tony had to admire the fact that he was still thinking for himself. No other straight boy had managed as much when Leah turned it on.

"Of course it was." She moved a little closer. Tony amused himself by watching Kevin's Adam's apple bob up and down as he reacted to Leah's proximity. "What else could it have been?"

"D . . . demon."

Speaking of demons, Leah's Demonlord seemed more present than usual. He noticed Kevin, frowned, and dismissed him—although Tony wasn't sure how he knew that since Ryne Cyratane hadn't actually focused on anything in this world. There was just something in the way he stared through the space Kevin was occupying that said, *I know you and you mean nothing.* Then the antlered head went up and his nostrils flared as he searched for . . .

*Me.*

*He's searching for the power that sent his demon home.*

But the Demonlord's—attention?—slid right past him.

*Like I'm not even here . . .*

And he wasn't, Tony realized suddenly, not according to the Leah-filter Ryne Cyratane experienced the world through. He wasn't reacting to Leah's *I'm an enormous metaphysical slut* performance, so to the Demonlord he didn't exist. Except that he obviously did since there was a demon back home blubbering about the big mean wizard who'd kicked demon butt. The Demonlord had come looking for the wizard but wasn't finding him.

Two possibilities.

Straight woman. Gay man. In the far end of both options where there was no attraction at all to what Leah was offering.

A kind of strangled moan jerked his attention back to the here and now. Offer accepted; lip lock commencing.

"For crying out loud, get a room, you two!" Rolling his eyes at such blatant and public heterosexuality, Tony took four steps back and yanked open the side door of the van Kevin had been hiding behind. Peter never locked it. He was hoping some lowlife would jack it so that he could replace it with wheels a little less suburban.

It wouldn't be comfortable, but it would be private. Privater. More private?

Leah, in spite of being quite clearly in the midst of giving a fairly thorough tonsillectomy with her tongue, acknowledged the open door, gave Kevin a shove, steered him through half a dozen stumbling steps, pushed him into the van, climbed in after him, and pulled the door closed.

*Let's hear it for centuries of practice.*

Kevin yelped once, the muffled sound verging on desperate.

All that adrenaline had to go somewhere, Tony figured, walking away. Leah probably just wanted to forget she'd been attacked by yet another demon and, more importantly, she wanted Kevin to forget the demon entirely. It was a more physical solution than Arra's memory erase spell, but both parties involved had to be enjoying it more.

He hadn't even reached the back door of the soundstage when a shout stopped him in his tracks and he turned to see Leah emerging, adjusting her clothes.

"That was fast," he observed when she joined him. Not that he'd been moving particularly quickly or anything since every step sent reminders of extraordinary pain up from his feet to his skull, but still . . .

"Tell me about it." But she looked happier. Grounded. The familiarity of sex erasing the terror evoked by the possibility of death and dismemberment.

*Jesus, that's profound.*

"He still knows what happened," he said, nodding past her to Kevin who was hoisting his backpack up over one shoulder and looking a little happier himself.

Leah glanced over her shoulder and looked smug. "He knows what I told him."

"And you told him it was special effects." Tony waited until Kevin had crossed the parking lot, anticipating what was about to happen with a certain amount of petty glee. "So, Kevin, what did you think about those special effects? Not Leah's special effects," he clarified hurriedly, "before that, in the parking lot."

The reporter shrugged and, at Tony's gesture, blushed and zipped up. "It was a demon."

Tony leaned against the building where he was out of the rain and less likely to fall over. "He has a power," he explained before the astounded immortal Demongate found her voice. "He knows the truth."

Leah frowned at him. "Seriously?"

"Yeah."

Turned and frowned at Kevin. "Seriously?"

"Yes."

Back to Tony; still frowning. "So, what? You got yourself a sidekick?"

Wizardman and Reporterboy!

That was wrong on so many levels.

The glee evaporated as he looked up and realized the shooting light was on and they were stuck outside. Only a few meters to the back door and warmth and coffee and it might as well be in Alberta. "No," he told her flatly, "I got myself someone who may know how long the Demonic Convergence is going to last."

"Wait a minute, the *Western Star*." Leah's fingers closed around Kevin's wrist and she hauled him around to face her. "You know someone's lying and you still print crap like 'I was impregnated by a Sasquatch'?"

He chewed on a corner of his lower lip. "Who says that was a lie?"

"And you're going to report on all this?"

"I don't . . ." More chewing. Tony thought he seemed torn. He was inside the story now, he'd had a look at what Tony could do, and had to believe Tony's threat about stuffing him back outside with his nose pressed against the glass. But demons, actual demons and wizards, that was a byline on the front page. "I mean, if someone noticed . . ."

"No one noticed," Tony assured him. "And if anyone did, they'll think it was a special effect. Even without Leah's . . . reinforcement."

Kevin stared at him like he had oatmeal coming out his ears. "They'd think a charging demon disappearing in a flash of lime-green light was a special effect?"

"You should see what the guys at Bridge get up to in their parking lot," Tony snorted as he pushed off the wall. The demon had obviously rattled him more than he'd thought. The craft services truck was parked no more than three meters from the back door—he didn't have to go inside for sustenance, he could go to the source. He paused on the metal stairs that led into the back of the truck and glanced down at the other two who were watching him like he might do something interesting. Like blow something up. Or fall over. Or fall over while blowing something up.

"You guys want a coffee?"

"Are you sure you should be touching stimulants?" Leah asked.

"Yes."

"Okay, then. Double cream, no sugar."

"Kevin?"

"I'm good."

Tony didn't quite hear what Leah muttered as he went inside and he was just as happy not to given that, when he came out holding the two coffees with a muffin in his pocket, Kevin was still blushing.

"All right," he said, pushing back in under the scant overhang. "When we go in, you guys go straight through to CB's office. Leah, tell him what happened. Kevin." He held up a hand for emphasis. "Don't talk to anyone in the soundsta . . . What?"

Kevin pointed to the rune on his palm with a shaking finger. "The demon had one of those. I saw it when it was charging at you!"

"Like this one?" Tony demanded, turning his hand so he could see the rune.

"How should I know?"

"Right. Sorry." He pointed the rune at Kevin again, who ducked. "Relax, it's for making energies solid enough to hold."

"Yeah, well, she has them, too. All over her . . . um . . . her . . ."

"Stomach? Jesus, Kevin, you just had sex with her in the back of a van. You ought to be able to name body parts."

"I don't do that." The reporter looked seriously freaked, like reality had finally caught up and smacked him on the back of the head. "I don't have sex with women I don't know. My God! We didn't use protection! Do you know what the STD statistics are in this city? I could have caught somethi . . . OW!"

"You were hysterical," Leah explained, picking her coffee up again.

He rubbed his cheek. "I was not! I was reacting in a perfectly . . . A cult!"

Tony blinked at him over the edge of his cup. "A what?"

"You belong to a cult! You and her, and that's why you've got those things and that's why the demon did, too. You're both mixed up in something that's out of your control!"

"It's not a cult." Tony waited for Kevin to realize the truth of that and carefully said nothing about things being out of his control. Although, technically, they'd never been *in* his control. "The Demonic Convergence brought us together, and now, with or without your help, we have to save the world."

Kevin straightened, grabbing his backpack just before it hit the ground. "You don't scare me."

"He should," Leah snorted. "He doesn't know what he's doing. Making it up as he goes along. Wild cannon. Could go off at any moment. And speaking of going off at any moment . . ."

"Don't," Tony told her. This was not the time to hit back at the reporter for that STD comment. To his surprise, she didn't. "Was this the rune on the demon's hand?" he asked Kevin again.

He shook his head. "No. It was more . . . squiggy. And fresher."

"Fresher?"

"Not a scar, a wound. And not burned, cut."

Tony finished his coffee and started on his muffin while staring down at his palm. If the demons were coming from Ryne Cyratane, why would he be marking them? "He's marking them so they can hurt you," he said at last. "Slipping them between the runes in the existing spell."

"Yeah." Leah brushed crumbs off her sleeve. "I got that." She grabbed a double handful of the track top and the shirt under it and pulled them up. Her track pants were riding low on her hips and most of the tattoo was exposed. "Did it look like one of these?"

Kevin stared. And blinked a couple of times, overcome by memory. "I . . . uh . . . I . . . that's not . . . I don't . . ."

"Would you concentrate!"

"No?"

"No you won't concentrate, or no it wasn't one of these runes?"

"Forget that for now," Tony sighed as the red light over the door finally went out. *What had they been shooting in there? Raymond Dark meets* The Fellowship of the Ring? "Show him again in CB's office when you've got a chaperone. Right now, let's move before we're stuck out here for *The Two Towers.*"

"What?"

"Just move."

He got them most of the way across the soundstage before anyone noticed, and by then they were close enough to the other exit that he gave them a shove and turned to face the approaching first assistant director.

"Was that who I think it was?" Adam demanded as Tony moved to block his line of sight.

"The stuntwoman we used the other night? Yeah. That was her."

"Not her. The guy. That was that reporter that's been hanging around. Graves."

"Groves."

"Right."

"Mason called him in to brag about the deranged fan." As the star of the show, Mason was pretty much untouchable. Made him handy to blame things on. "I saw him hanging around out back and had Leah take him in to see CB."

Adam had no special lie detecting powers, but he was responsible for seeing that actors and crew managed to get their collective shit together long enough to produce a weekly show. He didn't need to know the truth as much as he needed to know what would get the job done. "Mason needs his goddamned ego examined. Why is the stuntie hanging around?"

"She's with me."

Dark brows rose. Adam had been on the haunted location shoot and on the soundstage when the demon attacked—even if he hadn't been part of the battle or its aftermath. He knew . . . things. Maybe not specifics but definitely *things.*

Arms folded across a barrel chest, he frowned at Tony for a long moment, but all he said was, "Good enough." Then his eyes unfocused.

Recognizing the expression, Tony reached for the volume on his radio, remembered he wasn't wearing one, and waited, growing increasingly twitchy. It was one thing to be momentarily aware of his place in the universe and another entirely to be on the soundstage unplugged. He hated not knowing what was happening.

"It's the same goddamned coffin lining we've used since the beginning, Sorge," Adam barked into his microphone. "Why is it making Mason look ruddy now? No, I don't know. Hey! Don't be calling me names in French; you want to call me names, you do it in English. Or Greek. Fine. I'll be right there." He pivoted on one heel, paused, and turned back. "Get your ass back to work as soon as humanly possible."

"I'll do what I can."

The set under the gate had been cleaned. The broken wall had been cleared away and, from the rhythmic spit of nail guns in the distance, was being repaired. The painted plywood floor had been swept. Tony dropped to one knee and dragged a damp fingertip over the floor where the demon's ashes had been. Nothing.

Crap.

"You look disappointed."

He looked up. Lee wore a pale khaki golf shirt tucked into darker khaki Dockers under a black leather jacket, over black ankle boots. James Taylor Grant was supposed to look preppie-tough; today, they'd gotten it right. Other days . . . well, no one looked tough in tennis whites. Except maybe Serena Williams. "I wanted to look at the ash." No need to lie to Lee; he knew as much as any of them. Besides, there were enough lies between them already. *And cue the world's smallest violin . . .*

"The demon ash? Why?"

"I don't know. I guess I thought maybe it could tell me something."

"Because you're working for *CSI: Second Circle of Hell?*"

Tony snickered and stood. "You want to bet they pitched that?"

"No bet. Tony, you . . ." Lee frowned, his gaze tracking up from the damp spot Tony's knee had left on the floor. "You're wet."

"Yeah." Reaching back, he yanked the cheap polyester pants away from his body. "I'm just glad I'm not wearing underwear."

Green eyes gleamed.

Had he said that out loud? Crap again. "Sorry. TMI."

"A little. Maybe." The actor shifted his weight as Tony wondered what he meant by maybe. "So, uh, your friend is . . . attractive."

"My friend?" He ran over the friends he had that Lee knew. "Jack? For the last fucking time, man, he's straight."

"I meant Leah." The *asshole* was silent but understood.

"Oh. Right." Duh. Attractive to Lee.

"She's got a certain . . . I mean, you can't help but react to her."

That almost sounded like an apology. Tony rubbed his temples and tried to figure out what Lee was apologizing for. Demons were fairly straightforward compared to most conversations he and Lee had these days.

"And I saw you with Kevin Groves."

Half a smile. "He's straight. too."

Half a smile back. "You sure?"

"Well, he's never had his tongue down my throat."

*Unlike you.*

The actor's expression suggested the subtext came through a bit louder than Tony intended.

"I didn't mean . . . Look, I wasn't . . ."

"It's okay. It's not like I thought you were hitting on me or something." Lee tried to make it a joke, but neither tone nor grin matched the way he shoved his hands in his pockets looking suddenly young and unsure.

Which was weird because Lee wasn't young, he was—Tony frowned as he did the math, Lee's birth date being all over the Internet. Only a year older? It was just he was always so self-assured and Tony always seemed to be scrambling to survive that the gap seemed a lot larger most of the time.

Not this time.

In fact, there wasn't much of a gap at all.

Between them.

No gap.

Which one of them had moved? Tony didn't remember moving.

"Jesus, Tony. You're bleeding again."

"I was." He could feel the heat of Lee's fingers through the shirt. "It stopped."

"Hey!"

Lee jumped back, his ears crimson. It was the most awkward movement Tony had ever seen him make.

Adam scowled at them both from the edge of the set. "You," he said, pointing at Raymond Dark's mortal sidekick, "are needed, and you . . ." His finger moved to Tony. "Peter wants to know if you'll ever be doing any actual work again any day soon."

"I have to talk to CB."

"Whatever. By the coffin, Lee."

"Yeah, I'll be right there." When Adam was gone, he said, "Someday, you're going to tell me what's going on, right?"

"You know . . ."

"I meant all of it. Details."

"What, you didn't like Leah's explanation? Kind of looked like you did."

Long pause. Probably not as long as it seemed. *Time slows when you have both feet in your mouth.*

"Just let me know if I can help, okay?"

Been there. Done that. Got the T-shirt. And since Tony knew from sad experience how the conversation would go if he said no, he decided to take the path of not having yet another argument with Lee. "Sure," he lied.

Lee looked surprised. "With the . . ." He gestured at the floor. "You know."

"Yeah."

Wizardman and Actorboy.

Nope. Not going there either.

♦

"Tony! Why is Kevin Groves in CB's office?"

Tony glanced down at the hand holding his arm. Specifically at the large black spider that covered the back of it. "New tat?"

"Don't be ridiculous," Amy sneered. "A new tat would still be all red and puffy and gross. Now, answer the question; has CB agreed to give that creep an interview?"

"No."

Her grip tightened. "Stop being coy."

"He . . . Kevin . . . saw something, in the parking lot."

Brown eyes rolled between the double fringe of thickly mascaraed lashes. "Saw what?"

Tony jerked his head toward the door to the bull pen, currently open a suspicious six inches. "The walls have ears."

"Yeah? Well, they also have the coffeemaker from the office kitchen." Amy's voice rose to *don't fuck with me* levels. "So unless they want me to take it back . . ."

The door slammed closed with near panicked speed.

"Start talking," she continued, "before my phone . . ." Her phone rang. "Bugger. Talk fast."

"Amy . . ." She'd filed points onto her fingernails and those points were now dimpling the sleeve of his borrowed shirt. Considering how much his amazing new healing ability hurt, it didn't seem smart to just jerk his arm free.

"Faster than that."

Talking seemed to be his only route to freedom. "Groves saw me vanquish a demon in our parking lot. I thought CB'd be the best guy to deal with it."

"Vanquish?"

"Amy!" Rachel Chou stuck her head out of the finance office. "Are you going to get that?"

Not really a question.

She let go of Tony and snatched up the phone. "CB Productions! Our mailing address? Okay, but I'm warning you right now that we use unsolicited scripts in the porta john on location shoots. Yeah, exactly for what you think. Hello? Ha!" The receiver went back into the cradle with a triumphant clatter. "Tony!"

He'd have been safely inside CB's office if he hadn't stopped to knock. Knocking seemed like a good idea given that Leah was behind closed doors with two men. Although the thought of CB and Kevin Groves as two parts of a threesome made him want to scrub his brain out with bleach. Since no one had commanded/invited him in, he turned to see Amy standing by her desk, hands on her hips. Even the PowerPuff Girls on her T-shirt looked annoyed.

"Vanquish?" she repeated, pointedly.

"I sent it home."

"Leah's way or *BOOM! SIZZLE!* ASH!" Her hands flicked open on each of the last three words.

"Sort of Leah's way." He shrugged. "Sort of not."

"Can it come back?"

"It's not dead, so I guess it can." Just in time he remembered Amy knew the *Reader's Digest* version and stopped himself from saying, *It'll come back if Ryne Cyratane sends it back.*

"I want to help."

Thanks to Lee, he knew how to cut this off. "Sure."

"Don't bullshit me," she snorted. "I mean it."

"I know." Tony tried to sound like he'd meant it, too, even though they both knew he hadn't.

Her eyes narrowed. "Well?"

Odds were good she wasn't going to take *I'll get back to you on that* for an answer. What did it mean that he could lie to Lee but not to Amy? Was it some sort of weird psychological thing or was it just because Amy was scarier? A memory poked at him. Jack had shot the red demon, at least twice. "Bullets can hurt them. Can you find us a gun?"

"Are you insane?"

A good question and one he'd been considering himself lately. "Just for backup. In case I fall over again."

"Are you likely to?" she demanded as the door opened behind him.

Odds were good. Whatever he'd done in the parking lot

had healed his physical injuries but had left him feeling weirdly fragile. Not tired, exactly. He reached out with his round peg, looking for the round hole in the universe. . . .

"Tony?"

*Okay. Definitely way past time to ditch* that *analogy.*

"Tony!"

Leah this time, not Amy. She grabbed his arm, dragged him into the office, and closed the door while he tried to decide if she looked any more disheveled than she had. He decided she didn't but only because the alternative was too disturbing.

Kevin was sitting on CB's couch poking unhappily at his handheld. "I can't get an uplink."

"I told you," CB growled from behind his desk as the reporter set the PDA on top of his open backpack. "We're in a dead zone."

"Your phone won't work either." Tony crossed the room and dropped onto the other end of the couch. His trousers squished, and he realized a little too late he should have stayed standing. But since there was *already* a damp imprint of his ass on the cushion, he remained where he was.

"You seem confident, Mr. Foster."

"Phones haven't worked since . . . Wait. Not confident about the phone thing?"

"No."

Confident. As in filled with confidence. Hey, why not? He'd just sent a demon home by force of will alone. His will. His will alone. He had been the world. He had the power! *Although it might be best to play that down a bit in front of the boss.* He shrugged.

"Ow!" The lines of blood on the shirt had dried, sticking the fabric to his skin. Specifically to his right nipple. Shrugging had ripped it free.

"I'm pleased to see that this new confidence hasn't changed you," CB growled as Tony clutched at his chest.

Weirdly, in spite of the sarcasm, CB actually did seem pleased. What had he expected? What had Leah told him?

Tony repeated the latter question out loud as Leah perched on the far edge of CB's desk.

"Ms. Burnett told me what happened in the parking lot. That you returned a demon to its hell without using the proper runes. That wizards who feel they can ignore the rules are dangerous."

"I saved her ass." It seemed so obvious and yet he kept having to bring it up.

"She doesn't dispute that, Mr. Foster, but she considers it a matter of luck that you've injured no one but yourself to this point."

Tony frowned at Leah who was looking . . . smug. Not overtly, but it was there. "She doesn't like that she can't control me."

To Tony's surprise, CB smiled. "No, I don't imagine that she does."

"That's not—" Leah began, but CB raised a hand.

"Mr. Foster," he said, "has always been able to see what is in front of him. It's a rare skill. Mr. Groves . . ."

Kevin jumped.

". . . has identified the rune cut into the demon's hand as this." The sheet of paper he lifted held a new swoop and squiggle. "It is on the third circle of Ms. Burnett's interesting tattoo . . ."

Interesting? That was a bit of an understatement. Tony glanced at Kevin who was blushing again. He'd have heard a lie even with his ears that interesting color of puce, so if Leah hadn't told them what the tattoo actually was, what had she told them?

". . . and it seems to indicate," CB continued, "that she was its primary target."

"Why?" Tony prodded.

"Because it's on my tattoo," Leah told him, smiling. Ryne Cyratane flickered behind her.

Rune-to-rune attraction was apparently true enough for Kevin's gift and banal enough to give nothing away. Looked like Leah still hadn't given up her backstory, using her demonically-fueled sex appeal to keep CB and Kevin Groves from asking inconvenient questions. It seemed only vampires and Demongates got to have secret identities while wizards were left flapping in the breeze. Tony frowned at the rune. "Did the demon in the soundstage have one?"

"There was something," CB acknowledged. "But it moved too fast for me to get a good look at it."

"I knew it wasn't a fan," Kevin muttered.

"Actually, Mr. Groves, there is nothing that says the demon isn't also a fan."

The reporter snorted. "You think they watch syndicated TV in hell? Never mind," he continued before anyone could answer. "I withdraw the question."

"Mr. Groves was attempting to access the electronic copy of the page he found." CB set the rune to one side and laced his fingers together. "His astrologer friend was only able to work out the time of the Demonic Convergence in a general way, so I suggest he retrieve the original and bring it here for our demonic consultant to study it. Perhaps, with her experience, she'll have more luck." The look he shot Leah said he figured she could do anything she put her pretty little head to.

Eww. Tony felt slightly sick.

The look Leah shot CB in turn sat just to one side of *Are you nuts?* "You're going to let him walk out of here?"

"Why not?"

"With this story?"

"Your story is safe with me," Kevin told her.

Tony snorted. The ringing tones and the hand over the heart detracted somewhat from the believability. Seemed that twenty minutes or so removed from the demon, being inside the story was no longer enough to suppress old habits. "Safe doesn't mean out of the paper, does it?"

Kevin's betrayed expression was slightly less believable than his sincere expression. After a few moments of reorganizing his face, he ended up in the general vicinity of resigned. "Okay, fine. But we're a weekly. I've got until next Tuesday at 3:00 to file, so you've got until then to change my mind, right?"

"Yeah, that sounds fair except that you've been digitally recording on that handheld, so you've got blackmail material if nothing else."

"Kevin!"

As Leah's shocked exclamation—heavy on the second syllable—caught his attention, Tony grabbed the PDA from the backpack. When Kevin lunged for it, Tony held up his left hand. "We can't trust you."

Back in the corner of the couch, as far as he could get from Tony's hand and still be on the couch, Kevin glared over the barrier of his backpack. "I'm a journalist!"

"Essentially." Still working the rune, Tony stared down at the screen and double-tapped the record icon with his right thumb. "If he'd got the uplink, he'd probably have shot the sound file back to his office."

"No, I . . ." The weight of disbelief cut him off. "Yes. Fine. I would have. But you don't understand." He lowered the backpack onto his lap and fiddled with a strap. "This is a complete validation of my entire life. Demons and wizards and sex!"

"Sex?" CB asked. One eyebrow rose.

Tony suppressed a shudder. "Don't ask." Sounded like CB's virtue was intact at least. Back to Kevin. "So you've been validated, big whoop; you've still got questions. You want to know why the demons are attacking Leah. You want to know where they come from." Tony took a moment to study the rune on his palm, then he grinned at the reporter. "You want to know how I sent something capable of smashing its way into a car out of this world using only the finger of my right hand. Hell, that's not even my good hand." He waved his left, feeling power ripple with the movement. "Not even my wizard hand. You've got to be wondering *exactly* what I'm capable of."

Not *exactly* a threat.

"Are you threatening me?"

Okay, maybe it was.

"I don't even know you guys," he continued. "Why should I do what you want?"

"Because we're trying to save the world here, Kevin."

"By suppressing the truth?"

"If that's what it takes."

"And what kind of a world will that give us?"

"One not strewn with dismembered bodies, you short-sighted jackass."

"You want that page I found." His chin lifted. "I think I've got bargaining power."

"Yeah? I think you've got . . ."

"Mr. Foster."

Tony sighed. At this rate the Demonic Convergence would be over before the conversation. "Here's a thought: you let us look at that page, you don't talk about this to anyone, and I don't erase your memory."

"No one is erasing anyone's memory!" CB's protest added a certain verisimilitude to the bluff.

Tossing her hair back over her shoulders, Leah crossed to kneel gracefully by Kevin's feet. Reaching out, she took both his hands—and his backpack straps—in hers. No sign of Ryne Cyratane and no sign CB was reacting.

*She's playing the long shot. Appealing to Kevin's better nature.* Given what he did for a living, wondering if he even had one seemed redundant.

"Kevin, please. Work with us. Don't just report the truth, become a part of it. Make a stand against the darkness you *know* exists. Be one of the heroes."

He rolled his eyes. "Heroes die young."

Yeah. Redundant.

"Mr. Groves, if you don't want to help, we cannot . . . will not force you." CB sat back in his chair and laced his fingers together. "Mr. Foster, return his equipment and show him out."

"Just like that?" Ragged unison from everyone in the room who wasn't Chester Bane.

"Yes."

Kevin pulled free of Leah's hands and stood. "You're just going to let me go and tell the world what I've seen?"

"Mr. Groves, I have spent my entire career ignoring what

the tabloids print about me. I think I can manage to ignore this as well."

"You don't think anyone will believe me."

"Have they ever?" As the reporter sputtered, Tony caught Leah's eye and shook his head. Kevin could spot a lie and, so far, he hadn't accused the boss of lying. She closed her mouth as CB sighed. "People have no interest in the truth, Mr. Groves. They'll enjoy the story while it's being told and forget it the instant the next story comes along. It's why television is so successful."

"Reality TV . . ."

"Isn't. Now, if you don't mind, in spite of delays . . ." Somehow he made the delays seem like they were Tony's fault. ". . . I have a show to produce."

"No. You need the page I found!"

"I expect we'll continue to manage without it."

"It could have important information!"

"Mr. Foster, tell Ms. Chou to arrange to have my couch cleaned. Ms. Burnett . . ." He frowned at her. "If you intend to continue hanging about my studio, find something to do."

Kevin didn't quite stamp his foot. "You need the information I have!"

"And you haven't convinced me of that. Good afternoon, Mr. Groves."

"Then I will convince you!"

"Fine."

"I'll prove it to you!"

"Very well."

"I'll be back with that page. It has important information!"

"I look forward to you proving it to me. You will, however, have some difficulty returning if you don't actually leave." The final word carried enough volume to lift Tony and Leah to their feet as well and move all three of them across the office and out the door.

Kevin pointed a finger at the two of them. "Don't go anywhere." Then he turned and ran for the street.

"Don't let the door hit you on the way out, asshat!" One hand covering the phone, Amy flipped him off with the other.

"Thank you for holding, Father Thomas; we really need to use that graveyard . . ."

Leah smoothed down her clothes; not because they needed it, more because she needed something to do with her hands. "Your boss is an impressive man."

"Yeah." Tony carefully detached the rest of the shirt from his chest. "All his ex-wives think so."

"I meant he's a manipulative s.o.b."

"They'll probably agree with that, too."

Amy hung up and grinned at them as they drew even with her desk. "I got you the g . . . u . . . n."

"I can spell," Leah sighed.

"I'm not spelling it out for you." She jerked her head toward the bull pen. "I don't want that lot to get excited. It's never pretty. Anyway, the guy's bringing it over later."

"Tonight?" Tony asked incredulously.

"This very."

"That was fast."

"I'm the best."

"You're kind of scary."

"Just part of my charm." Head cocked, she examined him through narrowed eyes. "So what are you going to do now?"

"I don't know what she's going to do," he nodded at Leah as he pulled polyester away from his body. He might have the whole world in his hand, but he also had wet fabric in the crack of his ass. "But *I'm* going to talk to Rachel and then I'm going to get my laundry out of my car and change my pants."

# Eight

"ALL RIGHT, THAT ONE works for me." Peter tossed his headphones onto his chair and walked out into Raymond Dark's office, one fist pressed against the small of his back to knuckle out the stiffness of a fourteen-hour day. "Mason, you happy with it?"

"I'm happy with anything that lets me get rid of these damned teeth," Mason muttered around the fingers shoved into his mouth. "I bit my lip again."

"Bad?"

"Nothing that'll show on camera, thanks for the sympathy."

"You're welcome. Lee?"

Lee, sprawled on the red velvet sofa, waved a weary hand. "It was art. Emmys all around. Are we done?"

"We're done. That's it, people . . ." Peter raised his voice as he turned to face the crew. ". . . good work, thanks for staying late, and make sure you have tomorrow's sides before you leave."

That wasn't it, of course, but with the last shot in the can the mood lifted as everyone found enough energy to get them through wrap-up and out the door. With no demons currently ripping either place or people apart, Tony did what he always did. He made sure the radios were back where they belonged, put the batteries in the charger, ran an errand for

Peter, helped Tina close the trunk she locked her computer gear into, had a short meeting with Adam about an error in the advance schedule—where meeting would be defined as Adam pointing it out and telling him to see that it got fixed—and then he was done and the rest of the crew were heading for cars and home and the soundstage was empty.

Nearly empty.

Leah was somewhere around.

And Lee was standing just inside the door, watching him, his face expressionless enough that it was kind of creepy.

"What?" Tony demanded. He'd stopped just a little too close, almost inside the other man's personal space, but if he backed up now, he'd look like a dork.

"You're staying in case another demon shows up."

"That was the plan."

"It's not a great plan."

"Yeah? So far it's wizard three, demons big fat zero—nada, zilch, and three asses kicked. I think it's a workable plan."

"Workable," Lee snorted, rolling his eyes. Expressions were catching up to him—concern, disdain, and exasperation chased themselves across his face. "You're just going to live in the soundstage until this Demonic Convergence is over?"

"It won't last forever."

"You don't know that."

Shrugging, Tony tried to look like a wizard on top of things. "When it happened before, it ended. Precedent suggests it'll end this time."

"Precedent suggests? Precedent?" A twisted smile appeared to punctuate the silent but obvious *give me a fucking break.* "What? You've been watching Court TV?"

Tony chose to answer the actual question. "Nah, CITY's had *Ironside* running Mondays at midnight. Raymond Burr," he added at Lee's blank stare. "Wheelchair lawyer? Black-and-white lawyer show ran from '61 to '68? Dude, it's classic television."

"I'm not big on the classics." Lee sketched air quotes around the word classics, body language relaxing as they moved away from demons and wizards. "I don't watch anything older than I am."

"Your loss. You're missing your own history."

"My history?"

"As an actor."

"Ah. Well, maybe someday you can expose me." Challenging eyes. Flirty smile. Tony took an involuntary step back, not caring how it made him look. *Never a demon around when you need one . . .*

Hang on. Flirty smile?

Was Lee possessed again?

Tony cleared his throat. "Expose you?"

"To my history."

"Ah."

The pause stretched toward uncomfortably long, and Tony frowned as the expression left Lee's face. *And how am I supposed to respond? We don't do that joking around with sexuality thing anymore, remember? Not since you took that one step too far—and may I point out that it was you and not me. But, hey, you responded to Leah this afternoon, so now you're comfortable in your sexuality again and I'm fair game.* His brain just wouldn't shut up about it. "Look, some guys like black and white, some guys don't. Some guys try it but end up holding on to the whole Technicolor thing." Great. Now his mouth was in on it.

Any chance the anvil missed?

"Tony . . ."

No chance in hell. In any of the hells.

*The coyote wouldn't have missed with that anvil.*

*And now it's his turn to pause—except his pauses seem to be meaningful instead of empty. I wonder if I hurt his feelings by reminding him of how he gets indiscriminating under stress? Now that's an idea; he should hang around, and if the next demon's big enough, I could do him up against the wall after the fight.*

*Shut* up, *brain!*

". . . I just want you to be careful. Okay? Since there's seems to be nothing I can do to help—even if I thought you meant it . . ."

*Martyr much?*

". . . I just, well, be careful."

Without waiting for an answer, he was gone.

Tony stared at the door for a moment, wondered what he'd been reaching out for, and let his hand drop to his side.

"He wants you."

"Bite me."

"And you have some unresolved aggression toward him." Leah fell into step beside him as he turned and headed for the area under the gate. "You want to talk about it?"

"No."

"There's not a lot I don't know about the psychology of sex."

"There is no sex."

"Why not?"

"Because he's straight."

"Please."

"Why are you even still here?" he demanded moving into her path and stopping suddenly, forcing her to stop as well. "I thought you were off to live your life, to take a chance, refusing to be held hostage by your Demonlord's expectations."

"That sounds like bad country music."

"You said you weren't going to cower behind me."

"I'm not cowering," she snapped. "But given what happened this afternoon, I think staying behind you might be my best option. You're here, so I'm here."

"The demons . . ."

"The demons won't be sneaking up on me if I'm sitting here waiting for them, will they?" Something in Leah's face told Tony not to press it. Told him she'd been a lot more freaked by the demon in the parking lot than she'd let on, and what she didn't want to be was alone. "Besides," she added, pushing past him, "I've got nothing that pressing to do until Tuesday anyway. What on earth makes you think that Lee is straight?"

Tony scrambled to catch up. "He sleeps with women."

"Oh, yes, that's conclusive. Moron."

"He got stupid over you."

"Ninety percent of the male population does. Means nothing. Didn't you see *Kinsey?*"

"Sure. Liam Neeson totally got screwed by the Oscars that year."

"Granted, but my point is that if most of the world's population is neither completely gay nor completely straight, then even the odds are in your favor. I'm not sure why he'd choose you to break cover with; I mean, you're just passably attractive, reasonably intelligent, excitingly powerful, remarkably pleasant, appealingly broad-minded, definitely loyal, and appallingly self-sacrificing."

Reeling under the torrent of adjectives, Tony opened his mouth to respond, but nothing came out.

"Next to a man like, say, Liam Neeson," she continued before he could find his voice, "you're practically invisible. He's someone I'd do in a minute."

"Right," Tony snorted, finding his voice. "You'd do ninety percent of the male population in a minute."

She shrugged. "Eighty max."

"Kevin Groves."

"Fine. Eighty-one." She dropped down onto the end of the chaise lounge. "It's always amazed me," she sighed, "that two men can ever manage to get together at all given the whole lack of being articulate. Maybe he's scared."

"Lee? Scared? Of me?"

"Don't be dumber than you have to, okay?

Tony dragged his jeans back up over his hips—they were a little big and shoving his hands in his pockets dragged them low—and sat down beside her. "You sounded like Amy."

"You discuss your sex life with Amy?"

"Okay, first, Lee has nothing to do with my sex life, and two, are you insane? Give Amy an inch and she'll take a kilometer."

A dark brow rose and one hand patted his thigh. "Mixed metaphors, that's what's wrong with the world." Leah glanced around the empty soundstage as though she'd lost something. "Where *is* Amy? Based on our very short acquaintance, I would have thought she'd be here."

"She left with the rest of the office staff. She had a date."

"On a Thursday? Good for her. I'm all for a sister getting some."

"Big surprise. Not. But it's just for coffee at Ginger Joe's—it's a Goth coffee place she likes. She's meeting a guy she knows from the net."

"You told her to be careful because she didn't know this guy, right?"

"Yeah."

"And she told you that you were the one waiting for a demon, so you should be the one being careful, right?"

"Not in so many words, but yeah."

Leah nodded, smug. "After a few thousand years, people get predictable."

♥

"So where's your partner?"

Jack jumped and only just resisted spinning around and answering the question physically. He put most of the energy into slamming the door of his truck and managed to turn with something approaching calm. "She's home with her kids. Tony call you?"

Henry Fitzroy nodded and Jack wanted to wipe the smug, superior look right off his face. Which wasn't fair because all the guy had done was nod, but there was something about him, something that made Jack want to fall in behind him and charge the shield wall. He wasn't even sure what a shield wall was, but he fucking hated the feeling.

"Tony tell you what's going on?"

"Yes."

*Yes? That's it? Fine, you want to be mister one word answer, we don't need to talk.* But the dark eyes were strangely compelling, and Jack's mouth kept moving without any apparent prodding from his brain. "He thinks the demons are attracted to the soundstage, to his accumulated power at the soundstage."

"But you don't believe that."

"He's not telling me everything."

"Why would he?"

"Because . . ." Jack had a feeling that *because I told him to* wouldn't fly. "Because it's my job to protect the public!"

"I think we've moved some distance away from your actual job description, Constable."

"No, we haven't. Look . . ." He folded his arms, unable to look away but unwilling to appear compliant. ". . . I catch the bad guys; that's what I do. These are bad guys. In order to catch them—all right, deal with them," he added as a red-gold brow rose, "I need to have all the facts. Which I don't."

"Perhaps he doesn't think you can cope with all the facts."

"Well, he should try me."

"Yes. Perhaps he should."

Distracted by Fitzroy's too-charming smile, it took Jack a moment to realize that the other man's eyes weren't dark at all but hazel. Frowning, he matched his shorter stride as they headed toward the studio's back door.

"I assume you're here as backup muscle? He sent me out to buy cherry-flavored cough medicine," Fitzroy continued before Jack could answer. "A specific brand that's, unfortunately, not particularly popular." He hefted a bulging canvas bag. "I had to visit nearly every drugstore on the lower mainland before I found the volume he asked for."

"What's Tony going to do with that much cherry-flavored cough medicine?"

"He's going to do magic, Constable Elson."

♥

"What the hell was that!"

"I think someone's at the back door," Leah sighed.

"Right." On his feet, heart pounding, Tony could barely hear short, sharp bursts of the buzzer over the thrum of blood in his ears. "Do you think it's a demon?"

"I think demons seldom ask to be let in. And I think that your boss gave the security guard the night off, so you'd better get it."

"Right." Tony headed for the back of the soundstage, his breathing almost returned to normal.

There was no security hole in the door and since Leah hadn't actually said it *wasn't* a demon, he took a moment to find his focus and wrote "go home" as small as he could manage it an inch or so from the pitted steel. If there was a demon, and the demon charged when he opened the door, it would charge right through the command and that would hopefully be that.

Except that the door opened inward.

"Having a fish fry?" Jack asked, grimacing as he stepped over the threshold. "Because if you are, your fish are burning."

"I'm not." Given that the door was in the only home it had ever known, nothing had happened but sizzle and smell. At least he hoped it was because the door had no other home to go to because a bad smell wasn't much of a weapon against claws and teeth. "Hey, Henry." Calmly. Business as usual. *Do not touch the bite on your . . . Crap.* He forced his arm down. "Did you get the stuff?"

"Every bottle left in this part of British Columbia."

"Thanks." He took the bag and turned his attention back to Jack. "What are you doing here?"

"The nutbar who works in your front office called me."

As a general rule, that wasn't a specific enough description, but . . . "Amy?"

"She said you needed a gun."

"You brought me a gun?"

"I'm carrying a gun. My gun. You're not going anywhere near it."

"A gun?" Henry asked, in a tone that managed to squeeze *are you insane* into the two small words.

"You can shoot demons," Jack told him before Tony could answer. "It may not stop them, but it sure as shit slows them down. I shot one this morning half a dozen times. Exactly six shots. I know that because there's one fuckload of forms I have to fill out when I fire this thing, so . . ." Half a pivot and he was facing Tony. ". . . you can thank me for coming back and risking yet another three hours of paperwork—involving, let's not forget, lying. And, while we're on the subject, let's not forget the interviews with my superiors during which I will also have to lie."

"You didn't have to come."

"Yeah, and risk you actually getting your hands on a weapon? Like that's going to happen."

"I think you're taking the greater risk being here, Constable. Your career . . ."

"Bugger my career. I got a one-armed dead guy in the morgue."

Tony watched Henry study Jack for a moment and then turn and flash him a smile. "Perhaps you should just thank him, Tony. After all, you wanted to bring him in."

"You did?" Jack's brows rose but he looked pleased.

"I did. Past tense. But Henry . . ." He glanced over at Henry who was wearing his blandest expression. Like blood wouldn't clot in his mouth. "Fine. Whatever. Thanks. Come on." He led the way back to Leah and the chaise lounge wondering if he'd actually been in control for that short time in the parking lot or if he'd been delusional.

Circumstances were pushing him strongly toward the latter belief.

♥

"And this is supposed to do what, exactly?" Jack demanded at last. He'd been amazingly quiet until they were two thirds of the way around the soundstage, so points for patience. Or he was just too stubborn to ask until the frustration levels rose sufficiently.

Tony was betting on the latter. He finished the last ward along the side wall—or as close to the side wall as he could get, which meant, in a couple of places, two to three meters into the soundstage. "It's an early warning system," he said as he dipped the number two brush back into the bowl of cough syrup Henry was holding and bent to paint the more complex rune in the corner. "Something crosses the line with ill intent . . ." He paused, squinted up at his laptop open across Jack's hands, then added a final flourish. ". . . and we'll know it in time to brace ourselves."

"How?"

"Will we know? I have no fucking idea. I've never done this before."

"The wards on your apartment—" Leah began.

"Were meant to keep things out," Tony interrupted. "But we don't want to keep them out of here; we want them in here, so I can deal with them. This is new."

"Then aren't you moving a little fast?"

He twisted around just far enough to scowl at her. "This is the fourth wall. They're long walls. I'm getting the hang of it."

"Okay, but the end of that squiggle has always turned left before."

"Fine." A little more cough syrup turned the squiggle to the left. "Happy?"

"Who wouldn't be?"

"I'm not," Jack grunted. "What happens if demons drop in from above?"

"It's covered. Just give me a minute to finish."

"And if something with claws and teeth attacks before you're finished?"

"Then we won't know until someone gets eviscerated."

"No one gets eviscerated!"

"Not if you'll shut up and let me work."

Arra's instructions said he should visualize the complex corner runes and then mentally draw a line from corner to corner, the lines crossing overhead in the middle of the square. Okay, so the space enclosed wasn't exactly square, but it did offer the biggest bang for the buck, so Tony was still going with it. He closed his eyes. Saw the runes. Drew the lines.

"Cool." Leah sounded as though she was smiling.

When Tony opened his eyes, there was a cherry-cough-syrup-colored translucent dome over the soundstage.

And then there wasn't.

Although the scent of expectorant lingered.

"Is it gone?" Jack asked, breathing through the neck of his T-shirt pulled up over his mouth.

Tony checked. "No. It's still there. That was like a test pattern to show that it worked."

A red-gold brow rose as Henry studied his face. "Really?"

Made sense, so why not. "Yeah. Really."

♥

The second time the buzzer went off, Tony sighed and headed for the back door as though he'd never been startled, never jumped to his feet at the sound. Not that it mattered much since he could hear Leah telling Jack and Henry about how he'd reacted the last time. Jack seemed to think it was pretty funny.

First demon that showed up, Jack was going to be out in front.

When the door opened, the pizza delivery girl handed him a plastic shopping bag containing two bomb bottles of cola and began pulling the extra large pizza out of the insulated pouch. "You Tony Foster?" she asked without looking up.

"Yeah, but I didn't order a pizza."

"Come from your boss, Chester Bane. He order. He pay." She shoved the box into his hands and grinned as his stomach growled. "He say I give you message, too. He say you should answer your damned e-mail."

"Pepperoni, sausage, olives, tomatoes, mushrooms, green pepper, and double cheese; your boss knows how to order a pizza." Jack pulled a slice from the box and bit off the tip with obvious enjoyment. "None of this good-for-you broccoli crap."

"Personally, I could have done without the olives," Leah muttered, flicking a piece off her slice.

There was always someone who bitched about the toppings, Tony reflected as he chewed. It was practically a requirement of pizza eating. Three people in the group, one person bitched. Five to seven people, two bitching. Unless there were anchovies, and then everyone but one person bitched, regardless of numbers. Of course, in this particular group, the stats were kind of skewed. . . .

"You not having any, Fitzroy?"

"No, thanks. I ate before I came."

Jack shrugged and took another piece. "Great. More for me. Where are you going?"

Barely two steps away from the chaise, Henry turned and smiled at Jack. "Why?"

"Because, I think, given all the weird shit going down . . ." Jack paused to wipe a bit of grease off his chin. ". . . that if we're going to work together, we shouldn't leave each other in the dark about what's going on."

"Fair enough. I'm going out to the office."

"Why? There's no one there."

Henry's smile grew a little edged. Tony shuffled back just far enough to be out of the line of fire—just in case. Better Jack caught that look than him. "Television people," Henry explained pointedly, "don't keep the same hours as mere mortals. There's probably a few people still working on post-production . . ."

Post? Tony stiffened.

". . . and Chester Bane never leaves his office before midnight."

"You and Mr. Bane friends?"

"We've dined together a few times."

"Son of a BITCH!" Tony tossed aside his crust and clawed at the hot cheese and pizza sauce that had slid off it and onto his crotch. By the time he finished scraping and swearing, Henry was gone.

*Just as well. Not like I was going to call him on making stupid vampire double entendres in front of Jack.* He took another handful of napkins from Leah—who had almost stopped laughing—and scrubbed at the denim.

"You guys have some issues," Jack snorted.

Tony snatched the last piece of pizza out from under his hand. "Do not." Great. Even straight Mounties were noticing.

"Uh-huh. So why here?"

"Why not here?" Leah wondered. "They have issues everywhere else."

"No, why are we waiting here?" Jack's gesture took in the

immediate area, empty but for two folding chairs, food debris, and the chaise he shared with Leah. "There's a lot more comfortable places to wait in this soundstage, so why *specifically* here?"

"I did a spell here," Tony told him, gesturing with the pizza crust. "A big one. It left a mark."

"What kind of spell?"

"I'm not sure." Teeth slightly clenched, half a shrug—Tony was a very good liar. "I screwed it up."

"It had something to do with the ceiling?"

Had he looked up? He didn't remember looking up. "Yeah. It had something to do with the ceiling. But the rest is classified. If I told you, I'd have to turn you into a frog."

"You can do that?"

He swallowed and smiled. "I could try."

Jack shook his head, but what exactly he was denying wasn't clear. "Like I said to your friend Fitzroy, I don't think we should be keeping secrets."

"Is this a police thing; asking so many questions?" Leah leaned in. Tony figured she'd suddenly remembered she had a few secrets of her own. "Or are you naturally so curious?"

No sign of Ryne Cyratane, so at least Jack had a fighting chance, but Leah on her own, being intense and interested and brushing breasts against bicep, was enough to attract male attention.

She attracted Jack's. He probably wasn't even aware he'd straightened his shoulders. "It's what cops do, ask questions."

*And spout bad cop show dialogue.*

Tony cleaned up while they flirted and tried not to think about what was happening in the boss' office. *Figures. The one time I could use a little e-mail distraction from a psychotic eight-year-old, I'd never get an uplink.* Even if he had a cable, there wasn't a phone jack on this side of the soundstage.

"I was thinking."

Since he'd gotten used to Henry suddenly appearing by his side years ago, Tony enjoyed Jack and Leah's reaction.

"Wasn't your original plan to find the weak points between this world and the hells . . ." Four-hundred-and-sixty-odd years of Catholicism gave him a little trouble with the plural. ". . . and have Tony close them before they open and expel a demon?"

"Where the hell did you come from?"

"The original plan?" Henry repeated pointedly to Leah, ignoring Jack's question.

"Yes, that was the original plan. So?"

"So I'm not sure we shouldn't return to it."

"Hello!" The eye roll was dramatic. "What happened to hunker down, protect Leah, and save the world? I'm not going on walkabout across the lower mainland if demons are coming after me personally."

"Hang on," Jack interrupted. "Why are the demons coming after you?"

Tony reviewed various meetings in CB's office and realized that only he and Henry knew Leah was anything more than a stuntwoman who did demonology as a sideline. CB and Kevin Groves knew demons were coming after her, but Jack, his partner, Amy, Zev, and Lee knew only the basics of the Demonic Convergence. *Fuck this; I need a scorecard!*

"Maybe they want my recipe for goat cheese pizza," Leah snapped. "Duh! They're trying to kill me!"

"Why are they trying to kill you?" Jack was using his "don't even try to bullshit me" voice now. Interestingly enough, it worked.

"Because I know things and that makes me a threat."

"How do they know you know things?"

"What difference does it make?"

Jack sighed, ran a hand up through his hair, and took a moment to get comfortable on his end of the chaise. "Until you jokers listen, I'm going to keep repeating that, under the circumstances, I don't think we should keep secrets from each other."

"Oh, I see." Leah's second eye roll was more sarcastic than dramatic. "You show up with a gun and suddenly we should trust you?"

"Under the circumstances, I don't think we should keep secrets from each other."

"It's the Mountie thing, isn't it?" she sneered. "How can we not trust the stalwart in red serge?"

"Under the circumstances, I don't think we should keep secrets from each other."

She spun around to glare at him, their faces inches apart. "You have only the faintest idea of what's going on here!"

"Under the circumstances, I don't think we should keep secrets from each other."

"Stop saying that!"

"Dinner and a floor show," Tony snickered quietly, well aware that Henry could hear him even over the sound of shouting. "I'm having a lot more fun than I thought I would."

"Good." Henry flashed him an affectionate grin, then turned his attention back to the battle. "But we're not getting much accomplished." He stepped closer to the chaise.

Tony didn't need to see his eyes go dark. He could read the change in the set of Henry's shoulders. In the stillness that accompanied him. The Hunter was in the building.

"Jack Elson."

Names held power. Unable to resist the pull, Jack looked up and was caught. Safely behind Henry's left side, Tony saw his eyes widen, his cheeks pale, and his hands clutch compulsively into fists. Jack would never willingly show his throat, but Henry wasn't giving him the choice.

"Some secrets are too dangerous to be lightly shared. You know what you need to know. Accept that and move on. And," he added in a lighter voice, "I've changed my mind about the validity of the original plan. Stopping the demons before they emerge now seems to me to be the safest way to deal with them."

"He has a point," Jack acknowledged slowly, frowning as though he was searching through the conversation to discover how they'd gotten this far. Tony knew the feeling.

"No, he doesn't," Leah argued. "It's not safe putting me right up next to a hole. It could goad the demon to burst through prematurely."

"So? Tony'll be right there."

"*I'll* be right there."

"Tony?" Henry's use of his name drew all of Tony's attention. To be fair, he didn't think Henry could help it. "What do you think?"

So they were going to play that game. Pretend that Tony was making the decisions until he made one Henry didn't like. Pretend that the wizard was in charge and the vampire was *just* backup muscle. Fine. Leah and Henry had ditched the original plan when he was asleep. Unconscious. He forced himself not to touch the mark on his throat and realized he'd get absolutely nowhere if he brought any of that up now.

"Leah, how do you find the weak spots?"

She shrugged. "Gut feeling."

Considering what was on her gut, he'd let that stand. "Can you mark them on a map?"

"It's not that exact. It's more like playing hot, warm, cold; the closer I get to them, the stronger the feeling gets."

"But it should be easier now that there's not a lot of them, right? Because the convergent energy has to be slamming down on only a couple of spots in order for the holes to be going deep enough for demons to come through," he tossed to Jack before the awkward questions started.

"Not exactly easier," Leah began. Paused. Frowned. Sighed. "Okay, easier to find. But harder to close."

"Harder than facing down the actual demon? These weak spots have teeth? Claws? Other unidentifiable sharp bits?"

"They will if you screw up."

"No, *if* when I'm facing an actual demon." He started pacing. He was onto something. "How many weak spots out there now?"

"I don't think . . ."

"Come on, Leah. Try, please."

"Fine." She slid a hand under her clothes and closed her eyes.

"I thought she was a demonic consultant?" Jack stage-whispered dramatically.

"She's consulting," Tony told him.

"Yeah? Who? Or should I say, what?"

"There." Leah cut off Tony's answer. "There's a strong feeling that way. Deep hole." She pointed. "And a weaker one, that way. Still nice and shallow. That's all."

"So two?"

"Deep. Shallow." She looked down at the fingers she'd raised as she spoke each word. "Yes, that's two. Your grasp of higher mathematics makes me feel so much safer."

"We'll go to the shallow one first."

"No."

Tony turned just enough to frown at Henry. "What?"

"We need to go to the deeper one first because it is closer to expelling its demon. You'll have more time to close the shallow hole."

"Except that I'm making the decisions and I say we go to the shallow hole first to see if Leah has an effect. If she does, there's no chance of a demon getting through immediately. No harm, no foul. If she doesn't, then we take her near the other one."

Henry shook his head. "Reckless."

"I think you've forgotten what reckless means," Leah told him as she stood. "Tony's playing it safe."

"Tony risks allowing a demon to break through while no one is here to protect the soundstage."

"Then you stay." He tried not to feel pleased about how startled Henry had looked if only for an instant. "Jack, you'd better stay with him." If this worked, they wouldn't need muscle out on the street. "Leah says these things are just killing machines, there's nothing magical about them, so if one does show up, you two ought to be able to knock it on its ass and hold it until I get back."

"Us two? He's a romance writer." Jack shot Henry an incredulous look.

Tony didn't see the look Henry shot back, but it wiped the incredulous right off Jack's face. "Unnatural rope's best for holding them, and there's a whole lot of the yellow nylon shit over with the carpenter's gear. Don't worry about hurting them. Apparently, there's not much actual damage you can do. Don't get eaten. You know, by demons," he added as Henry frowned.

"Eaten." Not a question, but then Jack had seen the one-armed man.

"Welcome to the wonderful world of the weird and metaphysical," Tony told him, shrugging into his jacket. "Remember, you're the one who insisted on playing; I'd have happily kept lying to you."

"You're still lying to me."

"Yeah, but not happily. And not about anything that counts." It was important Jack believe that. Tony refused to look away until he nodded an acknowledgment. "Leah, where are you going?"

She sighed as she turned. "In the interests of not having any secrets between us—before we hit the streets, I'm off to the little stuntwoman's room where I'll pee and then wash my hands. Maybe I'll put some lip gloss on while there's a mirror handy. Or do you need a definitive answer on that?"

"Great," Tony muttered to Jack as Leah spun on one heel and strode off. "You see what you started?" He jiggled his car keys, stopped when he saw Henry wince. He'd made his point, no need to annoy sensitive ears.

He wanted to say: *If something does show up, don't let Jack be a hero. He breaks easier than you do.*

He wanted to say: *Don't you be a hero either. Let Jack shoot it a few times before you move in.*

And he wanted to say: *Maybe we do have issues, but we also have history, and so we've got to work through them. Because you're not going to let go, and I don't think I am either.*

He settled for saying, "Be careful."

And was pretty sure Henry heard all the rest.

♥

"So, what do I do?"

"Go west; toward the city. Drive slowly. I'll tell you when to turn."

Tony pulled out around an ancient chartreuse minibus covered in lime-green religious slogans. More than one kind of weird ended up on the west coast. "Can I ask you a question, or do you have to concentrate?"

"After thirty-five hundred years, I've learned how to multi-task, so ask."

"Ryne Cyratane's been doing this from the beginning of the Convergence, right? Directing the energy to where he needs it? So, if you only ever felt a couple of weak spots at a time, why didn't you expect the first demon that attacked you?"

"Why didn't I expect a demon to charge out of the sunset swinging an arm on a CBC Movie of the Week location shoot?"

"Yeah."

"Who the hell would *ever* expect something like that?"

Tony glanced over to the passenger seat. Leah had her shirt up and her hand resting on the exposed tattoo. "Fair enough."

♥

They found the shallow hole in an alley off Hastings Street between Gore and Main. The Chinese restaurant along one side was just closing, so they waited while a bored young man in kitchen whites tossed yellow plastic bags of garbage into the Dumpster. Then they waited a moment longer while a pair of Dumpster divers retrieved the edible bits.

"We're wasting time," Leah hissed as Tony grabbed her arm and yanked her back into the shadows.

"So we'll waste a little," he said quietly, watching the two women who looked middle-aged but were probably younger sort through the restaurant waste. "This might be the only meal they get all day. What?" he asked when she turned to glare at him. "In thirty-five hundred years, you were never hungry?"

The glare softened to impatience. "Maybe once or twice, but . . ."

"We wait until they're done. They'll want to go someplace safe and eat, so it won't take long."

It didn't.

"Why do these kinds of metaphysical things always happen in alleys," Tony wondered as they walked past the Dumpster.

"Why not in the middle of the TransCanada? Or a meter over the sock counter at Sears? Or in someone's apartment?"

"Who says they don't?" Leah asked, looking ready to bolt. "All that's necessary is that something be missing to anchor the convergent energy." She indicted a rough-edged pothole in a remarkably filthy bit of pavement. "We're just lucky this one's where we can get to it."

"So?"

"So what?"

"So are you affecting it?" The pothole didn't look like it had changed since they arrived. It didn't look like the weak spot between realities either. It smelled like rotting melon and Kung Pao Shrimp.

Frowning, she prodded the air over the pothole with one foot. "I don't feel any . . . Oh, no!" Arms windmilled as her foot slammed down. "It's got me!"

"Leah!" Tony grabbed her, dragged her back, and nearly dropped her in a particularly pungent bit of rotting garbage when he realized she was laughing.

"Kidding. It's fine. I don't feel anything different." She pulled out of his grip and tucked her hair back behind her ears, still snickering. "You should close it up now."

"I don't know how," he reminded her, folding his arms.

"Oh, cranky." A raised hand stopped his step toward her. "Okay, okay. Forgive me for being relieved. Before you can close the hole—or, this early in the game, just strengthen the weak spot—you have to see it."

"I see the pothole."

"Look harder."

There wasn't a lot of light in the alley; a couple of yellowing, bug-speckled bulbs over back doors and the spill from the streetlights. "I can't see . . ."

"Yes, you can. Wizards see what's there." She sighed and folded her arms, shifting her weight onto one hip. "Look harder."

"I can see where the smell of Kung Pao Shrimp is coming from," he said after a minute. "And you're scraping off your shoe before you get back in the car."

"But you don't see the weak spot?"

"No."

"Okay, don't look *as* hard. I guarantee it's there, in the pothole, a place where the absence of what should be there has left an opening."

"An absence of what should be there? Dial it back a bit, would . . ." Tony froze, half turned away from the scum encrusted bit of pavement in question. From the corner of his eye, he saw a heat shimmer—except, of course, it wasn't actually a heat shimmer—stretched horizontally across the top of the pothole. "I see it. What now?"

"Burn the runes one at a time and push them through the weak spot."

"Through?" Even cracked, the pavement seemed pretty damned solid. "Right. Why don't I just burn *close up* or *keep out?*"

"Tony, use the runes."

He shifted his foot a little farther away from a particularly nasty bit of melon. "Why? *Go home* worked fine on that charging demon."

"I know. It shouldn't have."

"But it did." He was definitely taking his turn to be smug.

"But it shouldn't have."

"But it did."

"Yes, it did. It shouldn't have, but it did. And is this the time to be experimenting with new techniques that may or may not work? That may or may not make things worse? No. The fate of the world is at stake. You risk my life and everyone else's on a whim!"

"But it worked!" Wasn't that the important bit?

"That time. Under those circumstances!" A deep breath, both hands against the clothing over the tattoo. When she spoke again, she wasn't shouting and she sounded sincere. "I promise you that the runes will work every time. Under any circumstances."

Tony wasn't sure how to take sincere. "Swear this isn't just part of your whole control issue thing."

"You want swearing?" Garbage squelched under her sneakers

as Leah stepped toward him. "I'll give you thirty-five hundred years of swearing in a minute! Write the runes and push them through!"

"One at a time?"

"Now you're being deliberately provoking."

Yeah. He was. "If it means that much to you, I'll do it your way."

"Sometime soon!"

"What's the hurry?" The shimmer was kind of pretty in an "entrance to hell" sort of way. "You said this one was shallow."

"It was when we got here," she snorted. "Why are you standing like that?"

He'd shifted to stand angled at the pothole, facing Leah, eyeballs rolled into the lower left corner of each socket. "I can see it better if I don't look at it straight on."

"You know where it is; do you have to see it?"

"I guess not." He turned to face the pothole, rubbing his eyes. "Problem. I don't think I remember . . ."

"I know you don't," Leah interrupted, pulling four sheets of folded paper out of the back pocket of her track pants. "So I brought your cheat notes."

Considering how tight she wore the upper part of those pants, fitting four sheets of folded paper in the back pocket was one of the most impressive things Tony'd seen all day.

He ended up shoving the runes through physically with the scar on his left hand, ignoring his companion's sotto voice commentary about cheating. "Is it cheating for a basketball player to use their height?"

Okay. Maybe not so much ignoring.

"You're not a basketball player, you're a wizard."

"And I'm using what I have. It's not my fault other wizards haven't had it."

"You should be moving them with power."

"Why?"

"Because that's how it's done."

Since he was the wizard and she wasn't, he decided to ignore her. As the last line of energy vanished, there was a soft, almost soggy *pop* that lifted all the hair on the back of his neck. The skin around his eyebrow ring suddenly began to burn.

"I wouldn't touch your face with that hand," Leah cautioned.

His left hand had been pressed flat against the pavement. Or more specifically, flat against elderly grease and rat droppings and more recently deposited bits of chow mein. "Gross . . ." He wiped it on his jeans as he stood. One knee was damp and he smelled like rotting bean sprouts. By no means as wiped as he would have been after a Powershot, he still felt a little hungry. "So, on to the next one or back to the studio?" he yawned.

"Why is that my decision?"

He shrugged. "You're taking the biggest risk."

Her fingers stroked the edges of the tattoo and she smiled. The smile said *we can beat this,* and for the moment at least she completely believed it.

Tony smiled the same smile back at her.

"Let's close the second one," she said.

"Great. You're driving. And I need something to eat." As they passed the Dumpster, he swerved to miss a small pile of suspiciously moving rice. "But not Chinese."

At a quarter after midnight, they were in Richmond, driving slowly south on No. 3 Road past the old Canadian Pacific Railway lands.

"Feeling's getting stronger," Leah murmured, drumming her fingers against the steering wheel. "It feels like I have slugs writhing in my navel."

Tony hurriedly chewed and swallowed his eleventh glazed chocolate Timbit. "Thank you for that image."

"Any time." She turned left on Alexandra, slowing further. "We're close."

They found the weak spot halfway up the side of a building, anchored on a crack in the masonry. There were a few taxis down the street by a hotel, but other than that, the street was empty. Quiet. Once they parked, nothing moved.

"Is this because of the weak spot?" Tony wondered as

they crossed the street. All the empty was beginning to creep him out.

"No, it's because it's Thursday night and the bars don't let out for a couple of hours."

"Right." Head cocked to one side, eyes rolled up and over, Tony frowned and lost sight of the blazing line of energy spilling out of the crack as his face realigned.

"See, this is why you learn to do it properly." Hands on her hips, Leah glared up at the building. "Unless we break and enter and dangle you out the third-floor window—which I'm not philosophically against—you're going to have a little trouble just shoving the runes through this one."

Feeling he should protest, more on principal than because he actually had something valid to say, Tony squinted the crack back into alignment. "This one's a lot brighter than the last one."

"It's a lot deeper. Better hurry."

"I could probably throw them into it."

"Whatever. Just do it."

Her tone, bordering on panic, pulled his attention off the weak spot and that, he realized as he took Leah with him to the ground was probably all that kept him from being blinded as light flared brilliantly purple and something big burst out of the crack.

She slapped the asphalt on impact, grunting as Tony's weight drove the air out of her lungs. "Get! Off!"

"You're welcome!" As the light show from the building dimmed, he rolled off, scrambled to one knee, and aimed his left hand down the road, blinking away afterimages and breathing heavily. He wouldn't be able to see the cheat sheets through the sparkly purple blotches, so he'd have to do this his way.

Not that sparkly purple blotches suggested imminent danger.

On the other hand, the large asymmetrical shape in the middle of the road did.

Bright side, large was easier to hit.

Eyes watering, he scrawled a very quick *go home* and threw it.

Blue sparks on impact.

*Blue sparks, purple blotches. It's like demonic Lucky Charms.*

A sound like wet sneaker tread dragged against tile. A giant wet sneaker tread.

"What have you done?"

"I told it to go home!" He grabbed Leah's hand and dragged her with him as he rose to his feet.

"It didn't work!"

"I know!" Rapid blinking brought the street into partial focus. The demon still looked a little blurry around the edges, but Tony had a bad feeling that wasn't his eyes.

"I told you it wouldn't work!"

"You're not helping! Just stay behind me and . . ." He squinted. "I must've done some damage, it's . . ." Running seemed as close a description as he was going to get. ". . . running away."

Leah grabbed for his sleeve as he started moving. "Where are you going?"

"After it. To stop it from killing people who aren't you," he added when she didn't seem to understand. "Come on. It's not going that fast." Mostly because bits of it seemed to be moving in opposite directions.

Her fingers tightened to the edge of pain. "What part of 'if I die the world ends' are you still missing?"

"The part where it's not after you." When attempting to jerk free only proved that Leah was stronger than she looked, he waved his free hand toward the demon. "Hello! You're here, it's there!"

She frowned. "Right." And let go. And smiled. Well, showed teeth. "Come on!"

They were no more than three meters behind it as they rounded the corner onto the section of Alexandra that curved to meet up with Alderbridge Way. The demon turned an eyestalk toward then, put on a surprising burst of speed, and crashed through a poster-covered door into the only lit building on that end of the street.

Ginger Joe's.

"Raise your hand everyone who's surprised by this," Tony grunted as they ran after it.

"According to Chekhov," Leah panted, "you should never hang a coffee shop on the wall unless you plan on using it."

"Chekhov? The navigator with the bad wig on classic *Trek?*"

Leah took a moment to sneer. "Read a book." She paused as they reached Ginger Joe's. "Didn't this used to be the Café Cats Escape?"

"How would I know?" Tony asked her. "For that matter, how do you know?"

Inside the coffee shop, cymbals crashed and someone screamed.

"Never mind."

They jumped the debris of the door together and skidded to a stop. The demon had gotten tangled in a drum kit left on the small stage when the night's live music had ended and lay half sprawled across two tables—although since it still had two legs on the floor, it wasn't exactly lying. Just past the wreckage a young man crouched, leather-kilted butt in the air, head to the floor, hands over his head, the chrome studs on his heavy leather wristbands gleaming in the dim light. Tony could just barely make out two more pale faces up against the back wall, their terror lending the whole Goth look a certain authenticity.

It took him another agonizingly long moment to find Amy because the demon's bulk blocked his view. A meaty squelch gave her position away just before she danced into sight, black-rimmed eyes locked on the enemy, the hand holding the skull shaped candle holder raised to land another blow.

"Enough staring already!" Leah snapped, racing by him. Seemed that the relief of not being the target was making her a little reckless. "Make with the runes!"

Tony pulled the papers out of his jacket pocket as Leah went up and over the demon, planting her hands between the spikes and flipping in the air to land on her feet on the coffin shaped bar. Possibly not just coffin *shaped* . . .

The first rune formed as Amy smacked the demon again while Leah kicked it in the head.

It roared, lunged at Leah, got tangled in the snare drum

stand, and stumbled, allowing her to leap over the clawed tentacle whipped around toward her.

The world rearranged itself in Leah's favor.

Amy wasn't so protected.

As Tony threw the last loop on the second rune, it wrapped a hand—or whatever the hell it was on the end of its arm—around Amy's neck and squeezed.

*Screw the runes!*

One more Powershot probably wouldn't kill him.

As he pulled his right arm back, Amy reached behind her, scrambled amid the debris, grabbed a full cup of coffee, and threw it in the demon's eyes.

It shrieked.

Dropped her.

And charged for the door.

One meaty appendage smacked Tony in the chest, lifting him off his feet and slamming him into the side wall. He spent a moment really, *really* hoping the crack was one of the fixtures and not a rib, then spent the moment after that trying not to scream.

He could sort of hear Amy yelling that the demon had broken into the wrong damned coffee shop as he raised his left hand and sucked the two runes he'd finished back into his body. It wasn't exactly hard to find his place in the universe now given how well pain seemed to be defining it.

*This is me.*

*This is everything else.*

*Everything else doesn't hurt.*

*I do.*

Turned out the crack hadn't come from one of the fixtures.

Breathing shallowly, he focused his attention on the broken ribs, smoothing the jagged halves. Pain exploded into a thousand razor-edged shards.

When he regained consciousness, Leah was kneeling beside him and frowning down into his face. "When you heal yourself," she said softly—not kindly, but softly, "you still experience the same amount of pain you would have had the injury healed normally."

"I do?"

"Every last bit of it. All at once."

He supposed he was glad of the explanation. "That totally sucks."

"It's why most wizards don't do it."

"Most wizards," he muttered, pushing himself up into something close to a sitting position. "Right. Why don't we get some of those fuckers to help?"

"Can you stand?"

Since there was only one way to find out, Tony let her help him to his feet. It was a little lopsided, but it was standing. Except that Amy's date was now having hysterics on a chair instead of the floor, nothing looked like it had changed. "How long was I out?"

"Couple of minutes."

"You really . . ." It wasn't as easy to mime jumping a demon as he'd expected. "You know, went after it."

"You destroyed the rune that would have let it damage me back there on the street when you burned *go home* right across it. After that, I was safe enough. Although," she added pointedly, "it didn't go home. We need to get back to the studio."

"Hang on." He shuffled toward Amy who left her date to meet him halfway. The hug nearly knocked him on his ass, but he appreciated the sentiment. "You okay?" he asked as they pulled apart.

"Not really, but I'm faking it well."

"This is going to need a creative explanation."

Her eyes regained a bit of sparkle. "I'm all about creative explanations."

"Good, 'cause we've gotta . . ."

"Go. I know." She waved a shaking hand in the general direction of the door. "So go! Kick ass."

The demon was nowhere in sight as they emerged onto the sidewalk. There was a taxi pulling into the hotel on the corner but no other people in sight. After what had just happened, the whole area seemed strangely quiet. Strangely normal.

Totally devoid of demon.

"We'll never catch it."

"We don't have to," Leah reminded him. "We just have to get to the soundstage." She took him by the shoulders and leaned him up against the side of the nearest building. "I'll go get the car. You wait here."

As she ran off, Tony concentrated on staying upright. He knew why the *go home* hadn't worked—it had come to him just before he healed himself. Standing out on the street, blinking away the aftereffects of the demon's entry, he hadn't been connected to the universe. Well, no more than usual anyway; not in a round peg/round hole kind of way. Back in the parking lot, panic had pushed him into place. Here, just now, it had been pain. Actually, there'd been pain in the parking lot, too. Pain seemed to be compulsory.

*I bleed therefore I am.*

*To bleed or not to bleed, that is the question.*

*Ultimate cosmic power! Itty bitty bandages!*

*This could be the beginning of a beautiful laceration.*

*Man, I really need a coffee. . . .*

# Nine

"CLOSED COURSE. Professional driver. Do not try this at home."

"What are you muttering about?" Leah demanded as, with a screech of rubber against pavement, she deftly maneuvered the car around a corner at significantly more than the posted speed.

"Nothing." The best part about the level of exhaustion Tony'd reached; he just didn't care. He didn't care when Leah ran two stop signs and a red light. He didn't care when she passed on the right using four empty parking spaces. He didn't care when she ignored a detour and took a shortcut through some roadwork, fighting the car through six blocks of chewed-up pavement and scraping the undercarriage on an exposed sewer grate. Actually, he cared about the last bit since he'd be the one paying for repairs but not enough to do anything about it.

Licking the last of the chocolate donut crumbs off his fingers, he watched the streetlights go by so quickly they were very nearly a continuous blur. If he turned to look through the driver's side window, the cracks in the glass refracted them into a thousand flares of moving light. "When you said before you were a stunt driver . . . you went to stunt driving school, right?"

"Top of my class."

"Because you knew you couldn't be hurt?"

"That, and because I really like to drive fast."

For a Thursday night not long after midnight, the streets were unusually empty. Tony wondered if that was Ryne Cyratane's spell helping to keep his Demongate from dying in a fiery car crash. "So that was a wicked move you made, back in the coffee shop when you used the demon like a vault and flipped up over its head. Where'd you learn to do that?"

"I played second bull dancer in a Greek production of *The Minotaur* once. Except that I wasn't in a loincloth and the demon wasn't tranked out of its little bovine mind, it was essentially the same stunt. With less ouzo, of course."

"I thought you said the bull was tranked."

"Him, too."

That probably made sense in a world where he wasn't so tired his eyes kept crossing. "Do you think we can beat the demon to the studio?"

She snorted. "In *this* car?"

"Since it's the car we're in, yeah."

"There's a chance. After all, it's not a speed demon." Snickering, she flashed him a smile. "Speed demon. Get it."

"Yes." The chance to fight back had put her in an interesting mood. Using the *may you live in interesting times* definition of the word. "Please watch the road."

With a cop's nose for contraband, Jack had found the deck of cards shoved in the back of a drawer over in the carpentry shop. Wiping the sawdust off them, he whistled softly.

"Now these," he said, returning to the chaise, cards in hand, "are hard core. You wouldn't be interested," he added as Henry stood, "it's all man/woman action."

"Why wouldn't I be interested?"

"I thought you and Tony were . . . You know."

"We were. That doesn't prevent me from being interested in women."

"I thought not being interested in women was the point?"

"For some men. Not for me."

"Yeah. Thanks for shar . . ." About halfway through the deck, he froze. "Holy crap. I don't think that's possible!"

Henry leaned around Jack's shoulder for a look. "It's possible, but the second woman has to be very flexible. And his back's going to ache afterward."

Jack stepped away, turned, and stared at the other man. "How the hell old are you, anyway?"

"Older than I look."

"Let's hope so." If he'd been asked an hour ago, he'd have said the guy was Tony's age, early twenties, maybe a couple of years older. Now, he wasn't so sure. There was something strange about him, something more than just being ass-deep into the weird shit that went with having a wizard for an ex. Maybe it was the whole romance writer thing—that was definitely a little creepy. Maybe he'd researched exotic positions for one of his books. More comforting a thought than the possibility he'd spent his teens as a pornographic gymnast. Jack sighed. "You play rummy?"

"Penny a point?"

Because he'd noticed that the queen of hearts was unnaturally worn—noticed and then refused to think why—Jack was up forty-two dollars when Henry stiffened and dropped his cards.

"What is it?" Damn if it didn't look like the guy was sniffing the air.

"Something's coming."

"Something?" Jack tossed his cards aside and stood, pulling his weapon from his shoulder holster. "The something we're here for?"

"Probably."

To Jack's surprise, Henry flipped the chaise up on its side and shoved it toward the wall. "Get behind that."

"Up yours."

"You'll have a place to brace your weapon as well as some small amount of protection."

"And you'll be where?"

A loop of rope dangled from one hand. "I'll be attempting to . . ."

A rain of cherries cut him off.

"What the hell?"

Henry looked up and moved just enough to avoid being hit. "It's our warning. The demon is through the wards."

Jack winced as a cherry bounced off his cheek. "You think?"

And then there was no time for thinking as all at once, tentacles and claws and spikes dangled from the light grid, filling the space between the grid and the floor. It took a moment for the parts to become a whole and when it did, Jack wished it hadn't. Monsters didn't scare him—over the years he'd seen too much of what people could do—but this one gave it the old college try.

With a shriek of rending aluminum, one of the struts tore free and Jack decided that maybe being behind the fancy sofa wasn't such a bad idea. It had seemed solid. Well made. Likely to survive. He dove over the piece of furniture, rolled, and came up on his knees, ready to fire. Suddenly a line of yellow nylon rope was around the bulk of the demon's body. And then around most of the legs, snugging them in tight.

The demon screamed.

Something snarled an answer.

Jack's hindbrain sent up flares. *Fight or flee! And flee seems like the better idea!*

Right at the moment, denial seemed like a much better idea, but it was way, way too late for that.

Jack popped off three quick rounds at the demon's . . . head and held back the fourth when Henry Fitzroy caught a heavily muscled arm in another loop of rope and began fighting it to the demon's side.

It seemed the not very tall man was stronger than the demon.

Stronger.

Faster.

More fucking scary.

"That's not possible." Under the circumstances, a stupid

thing to say, but Jack was having just a little trouble coping. *Romance writer, my ass.*

The demon hit the floor with a noise somewhere between a crash and a squelch.

A writhing tentacle-like arm split the air where Henry had been seconds before, twisted around for another blow as a second clawed tentacle came straight up out of the demon's body. No way Henry could avoid both. No way Jack could get off a clear shot. Trying not to think about what he was doing, Jack went over the chaise and tackled the arm.

Pinned under the length of his body, it was warmer than he'd expected.

Warmer, and a little damp.

It took him a moment to realize why it smelled so strongly of crushed cherries.

Heavy muscles bunched up to try and throw him off and, with the right leverage, Jack was pretty sure it'd be able to toss him across the soundstage.

It shifted within the confining rope.

Suddenly the floor was farther away.

*Oh, fuck . . .*

♠

Henry had faced a Demonlord and bled to keep an ancient grimoire from falling into the taloned hands of the lesser demon it commanded. In comparison, this creature seemed no more or less than it appeared. Strong. Fast. Other. But not necessarily evil.

*If there are, as the Demongate supposes, a multitude of hells*—he slid under a clawed tentacle that would have disemboweled him—*then perhaps, in some of these*—another loop of rope secured the limb—*we name the inhabitants demon based on appearance not motivations.*

As the creature hissed and writhed, he spun about in time to see Jack Elson lifted into the air on the largest of what seemed essentially its arms.

And then the arm flipped over and Constable Elson was heading back toward the concrete floor at high speed.

There were no visible joints to act as weak spots—or rather too many joints to attack in the little time he had. Racing in toward the creature, Henry grabbed the arm just under the front set of claws and kept moving, dragging it—and the constable—around until he could brace himself against the creature's own body.

Teeth bared, he managed to stop the momentum of the limb and snarled, "Let go!"

♠

Letting go seemed like a fine idea to Jack. He dropped and rolled and crushed a little fruit, finally turning in time to see Henry drag the tentacle down to the body of the creature and secure it with another loop of the yellow rope.

No one was that fast. Or that strong.

"What the hell *are* you?" he panted, pulling himself up onto his knees.

He knew when Henry looked up and smiled. He couldn't put it into words—hell, he didn't think he could form words right at that moment—but he knew. He knew it in the way the hair rose off the back of his neck, in the way a sudden drop of sweat ran down his side under his shirt, in the way he couldn't seem to catch his breath or hear himself think over the pounding of his heart. He knew it in his bones.

No, in his blood.

And then he fell into dark eyes and he forgot that he knew.

"Hey! You guys! There's a demon heading this . . ." Tony skidded to a stop, dragging Leah, who was half supporting him, to a stop as well. He stared at the demon—which may or may not have been staring back. The eyestalks were flipping around in a way that made it hard to tell. "Never mind."

"What's with the cherries?" Leah demanded, scraping pulp off the bottom of her high-top.

"Tony's early warning system," Jack grunted, getting to his feet.

"It made cherries?"

"Apparently."

She turned to Tony, who shrugged. They had bigger problems than fruit. He shook free of Leah's hand and shuffled carefully toward Henry. Trouble was, when a romance writer slash vampire fought a demon, it wasn't the romance writer that then had to be dealt with. He could see the Hunter in the set of Henry's shoulders. In the way he was standing, his back to them, perfectly, impossibly still.

At Henry's side, he leaned forward, careful not to touch, and murmured, "If you need . . ."

"Not from you." A quiet voice. Barely audible. A voice that stroked danger against Tony's skin. "Not after last night."

Last night. This time, he didn't stop himself from touching the mark on his neck. No wonder he was exhausted; it wasn't just the wizardry. "Then who?" The emotional kickback was as important as the blood and Jack, as he'd been insisting to all and sundry, was straight. Leah was far too dangerous.

"Give me a moment."

"Sure." Terror was as valid an emotion as any other and the shadows in Jack's eyes suggested he'd seen something more frightening than the big rubbery monster tied up on the floor. Tony tried not to wonder what would have happened had they got there a little later and had pretty much buried the question by the time Henry turned, the mask of civilization firmly back in place.

Pretty much.

A red-gold brow rose.

Tony shrugged.

"So . . ." Leah sighed loudly. ". . . if you two are finished with all the silent communing, you think we could get going on sending Maurice here home?"

"Maurice?" Jack snickered, the sound just this side of hysteria.

She pushed a handful of curls back off her face and smiled, deep dimples appearing in each cheek. "What? You don't think he looks like a Maurice?"

About to tell her to knock it off, Tony realized what she was doing as Jack's shoulders squared and he rubbed a hand back though his hair, standing it up in damp, golden spikes.

"If you're asking, I think he looks like a Barney."

"Isn't Barney a dinosaur?" Her tongue licked a glistening path along her lower lip.

Jack's eyes half closed. "Barney, Fred's neighbor."

The only thing keeping them from consummating the repartee was the demon, tied and pissed off, filling the space between them.

When Ryne Cyratane made his expected appearance, Tony frowned. The Demonlord looked . . . frustrated?

Because Leah wasn't actually getting any in the here and now?

Because his demonic minions kept failing?

Because he couldn't find the wizard who kept defeating him?

Except this demon hadn't been sent back to hell, so how would he know it had been defeated? And why did he look frustrated rather than angry? A glance down and Tony realized the Demonlord wasn't even particularly interested in the whole Jack/Leah dynamic. Interested, yes, but not, well, fully.

"Tony!"

"Sorry." He shook his head as Leah turned her attention to him and Ryne Cyratane faded. He was missing something, something important, but he was just too damned tired to make the effort and figure out what it was. "I'll start drawing the runes."

"Are you strong enough?"

"Sure." Why not lie on the side of truth, justice, and the wizardly way given there was a distinct lack of choice regardless of how he felt. The demon was fighting against the ropes, rocking back and forth and in a few other less easily defined directions. "Although . . ." His stomach growled on cue. ". . . I wouldn't say no to food."

"There's half a bomb bottle of cola left," Jack offered, clearing his throat and looking everywhere but at Leah. "And some cherries."

"Close enough." Or not. The cherries had no pits and tasted like cough syrup. Fortunately, the cola, essentially sugar and caffeine, faked nourishment.

"It's weird how it can't break the rope." Jack circled the

demon slowly as Tony began to burn the first rune on the air. "We know it's strong and the rope isn't that thick."

"It's an unnatural rope," Tony reminded him, squinting through the blue lines. "What's weird is that Arra would know that it would work. She never faced demons here in this world."

Leah snorted. "Where do you think her demons came from? Wal-Mart?

"These are not the demons I know from the past," Henry said quietly as Tony started the second rune. "This poor creature is nothing more than an animal out of its place."

"Let's not forget these things are killers," Jack pointed out.

"They kill to eat," Henry told him. "So do you."

"Yeah, well, so far I've managed to avoid ripping any arms off while I'm having lunch."

"Good for you."

"You're not entirely wrong," Leah broke in before Jack could respond. "Neither of you. These guys are on the low end of the demonic pecking order." She waved a hand at the demon on the floor. It writhed at her. "They're all about the rending and the killing and, yes, the ripping off of arms, but they're not really very motivated by anything other than the rending and the killing. Relatively speaking, they come from fairly close by. The hell that the ancient mystics saw . . ." She turned her attention to Henry. ". . . the hell adopted by your religion, that was considerably farther away."

"Your Demonlord is no beast. If he uses these creatures, then he has moved closer without using the gate."

"There's some movement within the hells," Leah admitted. "But he can't get here without help. If you want the big guys, the demons with dialogue and motivations, then you have to call for them specifically. It takes a lot of power to punch a gate through to their level, a couple of artifacts that aren't easy to get, and, if you want to survive it, a will of iron."

"Actually, it's not that hard." Henry folded his arms. "I know a not very bright young man who brought through a creature capable of speech and independent evil with a small barbecue and a few cheap candles."

"Did he survive?"

"Not ultimately, no."

She spread her hands. "I rest my case." Before anyone could demand to know what that meant, she added, "And with that kind of power he was probably an untrained wizard."

"Not likely," Henry snorted.

"Outsider?"

"Yes, but . . ."

"It's been my experience . . ." A twitch of her sweater hem directed attention to her abdomen and the physical evidence of that experience. ". . . that potential isn't particularly rare. Actually accomplishing something with it, now that's unusual. If Tony here hadn't met Arra, he wouldn't be fighting demons today. Heroes rise when we need them."

Tony let the observation pass without responding as he finished off the third rune, going over the last curve three times before it stopped sputtering. The buzz from the cola had burned off and it was getting harder and harder to focus.

"Tony?"

A cool, familiar touch against his wrist. He blinked a couple of times in Henry's general direction. "I'm okay."

"Can you finish?"

"Do I have a choice?" The demon was writhing again, bulging around the rope. "Why doesn't it make any noise?"

"Perhaps it communicates by motion."

"No, it made a noise before. Although . . ." weak sneaker-against-tile noise could have easily been made by rubbing demon against asphalt. "So we've tied and gagged it." He snickered, but he didn't really think it was funny. It was just easier to laugh than run screaming from the room. Besides, he was starting to feel sorry for the big squishy thing. That burned in *go home* looked painful.

"Tony."

"I'm okay."

"Look at me."

"Henry, I'm . . ." Henry's eyes were dark and the masks were gone. Hunger. Danger. Tony felt his heart race and a sudden wave of energy flood his body. He jerked back, blinked, and Henry's eyes were hazel again.

"Can you finish now?"

"Oh, yeah. Word up for adrenaline."

The red-gold brows dipped. "I have no idea what that . . ." A silent pivot toward the soundstage door. "Someone's coming."

"Tony? You around?"

"Zev?" Damn. It was Thursday. Zev left midafternoon Fridays, so he always worked late Thursday.

"Good, you're still here. I was finishing up the score on that last episode, and I just wondered if you were on the soundstage." Rising volume suggested he was walking toward them. "You know, given the possibility of demons and all. I've got this great complicated harp piece and . . ." His eyes widened as he came around the corner of the set and he stopped so quickly he rocked back and forth. ". . . never mind. So." The pause extended almost a beat too long. "That's a demon?"

No reason to deny it. "Yeah."

"Really? Okay. It's, uh, you know, big." He frowned, opened and closed his mouth a couple of times, shoved his hands into his front pockets, and took a bravado-inspired step forward. Then glanced down at the floor. "What's with all the cherries?"

"They're part of the early warning system," Jack said dryly, picking one up and flicking it into the wall.

"They must have cost a fortune. They're out of season," he added when it became obvious no one got the point. "Apples would have been significantly more cosahhhhh!" Yanked off his feet by the tentacle around his ankle, he screamed as he slid along a path of crushed fruit toward the demon.

"Don't shoot!" Tony grabbed for Jack's arm as Henry grabbed for the tentacle.

Still screaming, Zev slapped into the demon's side.

Henry twisted a loop into the excess flesh, tightened it, and shoved the music director away with the side of his foot as the demon went after more immediate prey, driving the end of the tentacle spikelike toward Henry's head.

The possibility of the demon getting free, not to mention

eating his ex, added a whole new burst of adrenaline. Tony sketched the fourth rune. "Crap!" Erased the last line. Drew it again.

There was a sudden, intense smell of sulfur and Henry hit the floor beside Zev and a tangle of yellow nylon rope as the demon disappeared. Fortunately, the runes only worked on creatures not native to this reality.

Fortunately.

Really, really fortunately. Tony wiped sweaty palms on his thighs and tried to remember if he knew that.

"I assume there's a reason for all the noise?"

Swaying, he fought to focus on CB's face. "Demon."

"Screaming?"

"That was me!" Zev scrambled to his feet and thrust his arm toward his boss. "It had a mouth in its side! In its side! Not its face! It bit a hole in my sleeve!"

"How fortunate it didn't remove your arm." As Zev absorbed the truth of that, CB stepped forward and caught Tony as his knees unlocked and he began to topple. "And the smell of sulfur?"

"Tradition?"

"Are you asking me?"

Tony sneezed. "No."

"And the cherries?"

"Long story."

"I see. Mr. Fitzroy, if you could place the chaise upright again, please. Constable Elson, there should be food of some kind in the office kitchen."

Tony managed to remain on his feet as they crossed the set, but he suspected that had more to do with the grip CB maintained on his arm rather than any macho shit on his part. Although the chaise looked hard and lumpy, it was the most comfortable piece of furniture he'd ever collapsed on. No need for anyone to worry; he was just going to take a few minutes to recover the feeling in his extremities.

A little easier to do, actually, after CB let him go and moved away.

"Ms. Burnett, I thought your technique of dealing with the demons would use less energy and leave Mr. Foster on his feet."

"It did use less energy," Leah protested indignantly. "After the day he's had, any other way—his whole mano a mano way, for instance—would have killed him."

Yeah, yeah. Déjà vu all over again.

"We'll have to take your word for that. Mr. Groves is in my office with the page of demonology he found. If you could bring him here, I'd appreciate it."

"Kevin Groves?" Tony lifted his head to check if the disapproval he could hear in Henry's voice matched his expression. It did. "The tabloid reporter who's been hanging about the show?"

"That's the one." Leah answered, walking backward toward the exit. "It turns out he knows about the Demonic Convergence and may have primary source information."

"How does someone like that get hold of primary source information?"

"The easy way," she snorted, one hand against her belly as she turned and left.

"She's an odd one," Zev muttered. He had a plastic broom in his hand, the kind with a scraper along one edge. "Even for a stuntie."

"He's right," CB murmured, stepping closer to Henry as Zev began sweeping up the cherries. Tony strained to hear him; this was not a conversation he was going to miss. "There's something about that young lady that's . . . different. Unusual."

No shit.

Fortunately for Leah, Henry had secrets of his own. "She studies demons; that's got to skew things a little."

And again, no shit.

"It seems to be time," CB said, still talking quietly to Henry, "for Mr. Foster to put some serious work into that memory erase spell of Arra's."

Henry glanced down at Tony and then up at CB. "It's like you're reading my mind."

"It wouldn't be the strangest thing that happened today."

"Word." Tony snickered at their expressions, or at as much of their expressions as he could see through eyes that kept sliding closed. "You two need to get out more."

♠

"Mr. Foster?"

"Let him sleep."

"Are you certain he's sleeping?"

Henry laid a hand gently against Tony's chest, listened to his heart beating slow and sure. "I'm certain."

"I've never seen anyone eat that fast. I mean, that was almost a whole carton of potato salad and almost a liter of milk, gone between one blink and the next." Jack brought his hands together, crushing the empty milk carton. "I don't know why he didn't choke. Or puke. Or both. You know, choke and puke. Especially considering it was potato salad and milk, for Christ's sake."

Henry exchanged a glance with CB.

"Are you all right, Constable Elson?"

"Me?" Jack's chin lifted and his chest went out. Henry hid a smile. Although the RCMP officer wasn't a small man, there was no way he could avoid being dominated by CB's bulk. "I'm fine. Why wouldn't I be fine?"

"You have been exposed today to not one, but two demons."

"So have you."

"Yes, but I'm in television."

Jack jerked his head toward Zev who was sweeping up the last of the cherries in the immediate area and muttering quietly. "He's in television and he's freaked."

"He was nearly eaten."

"Yeah, well, I'm fine." Arms folded, he swept a scowl around the soundstage. "I'd be better if I knew how that thing got in."

"That's easy enough to answer; we left the door to the carpentry shop unlocked. I didn't want any more of my property destroyed," CB added as the constable's scowl lit on him.

"We wanted it in here," Henry reminded him, coiling the

yellow nylon rope, "so it could be taken down without risking innocent lives."

"Right. We wanted it in here." A glance toward the place where the demon had lain. "Okay. Then tell me this? If we knew it was coming in a specific door, why did Tony put his warning thing around the whole place?"

"For the same reason we're ankle-deep in fake fruit," Leah snorted coming around the edge of the set, Kevin Groves following behind like a puppy. "Tony doesn't know what he's doing. He's making things up as he goes along."

Jack shifted slightly so that he was between Leah and Tony. Familiar with the protective instincts of the police, Henry decided to let it pass. It was interesting that on some instinctive level the constable thought Tony needed protecting from Leah. "He's doing *fine*."

Stopped about two meters away, Leah folded her arms, metaphysical seductress buried under indignation. "Well, according to you, everything's fine. You're fine, Tony's fine. Everything is *not* fine. We have demons . . ."

"Who don't always use doors," Henry interjected. "Leaving a door open does not guarantee they'll go through it. Tony laid out his wards wide enough to take that into account."

"And the cherries?" she asked, kicking at a piece of fruit Zev had missed.

Henry waited until it rolled to a stop. "I'm not saying he doesn't need to refine his technique."

"Perhaps it would be a good idea . . ." CB's tone had nothing of *perhaps* about it. ". . . if we move to another part of the soundstage and leave Mr. Foster to his rest."

Jack shook his head. "We shouldn't leave him alone."

"No, we shouldn't."

"I'll stay with him," Zev offered, stepping carefully over the pile of fruit he'd collected and walking to the chaise. "You guys can go make plans for dealing with demons and just leave me out of them."

"If you're sure, Mr. Sero."

"Oh, yeah." He held the broom across his body like a weapon. "I'm sure."

"If you hear or see anything, anything at all . . ."

"Trust me. I'll yell."

♠

Henry had always liked Raymond Dark's office. It was, he thought, the kind of office a vampire should have—all dark wood and heavy velvet curtains and shelves of ancient knick-knacks. It had weight. Authority. It wasn't anything like his office, which tended toward beech veneer, piles of research books, and stacks of author's copies he hadn't been able to give away, but that was the difference between artifice and reality.

The black leather desk chair creaked as CB lowered himself carefully into it. "Now then, Mr. Groves; your documentation."

But Kevin Groves was staring at Henry. He swallowed once, punctuated by his Adam's apple rising and falling in the column of his throat. "You're not . . . I mean, you're . . ."

"He's what?" Jack asked from where he leaned against the corner of the set, positioned so that he could see both the desk and a bit of Tony's head on the upper end of the distant chaise.

"Good question." Frowning, Henry caught Kevin's gaze and held it. The Hunger had been buried deep, the masks were in place disguising the Hunter, and yet this reporter knew exactly what he was—which was both disturbing and useful. He smiled and then a little more broadly as, behind his glasses, Kevin's left eye began to twitch. "I'm what?"

"Nothing." Kevin started to shake as his muscles tensed for a flight not permitted to him. He stank of fear. Fear and . . .

Henry's attention flicked for an instant to Leah, tucked up in one corner of the red velvet sofa. That explained why it had taken her those extra moments to retrieve the reporter from the office.

She blew him a one finger kiss.

"Nothing," Kevin repeated as he staggered, released but still unable to run. "You're nothing."

"You didn't see him earlier," Jack muttered.

Before Kevin could turn, Henry shook his head and the reporter froze.

"The page, Mr. Groves."

His head jerked around toward CB. Then back to Henry.

Still smiling, Henry stepped away. "We'll talk later, you and I. Right now, I think you should get Mr. Bane that page."

"Oh, for pity's sake," Leah sighed as Kevin dropped his backpack off his shoulder and began to rummage frantically in its depths, "leave the poor guy alone."

"*I* have done nothing to him. Which is more than you can say."

"Hey, I did nothing to him. *With* him, yes. Not to."

"Are you so sure of that?" *Demongate.*

She straightened. "Don't push me." *Nightwalker.*

CB cleared his throat.

Silence fell.

"What the hell is going on?" Jack demanded.

"Mr. Groves has brought us a piece of a manuscript that seems to define the Demonic Convergence."

"From the crazy monk guy Leah mentioned this afternoon?"

"That has yet to be determined." With the page on the desk in front of him, CB leaned back and steepled his fingers. "Mr. Fitzroy and Ms. Burnett are going to have a look at it."

"What; is he a demonic consultant, too?"

"In a manner of speaking." CB shot a look at the reporter that cut off an already somewhat strangled laugh.

"Tony's the wizard," Jack said pointedly. "He should examine it."

"Later," Henry said as he moved around the desk. "Right now, he needs to regain his strength." The vellum was badly yellowed, the edges touched with water damage.

"That's not from the monk's book," Leah sighed as she joined him. "It's all numbers."

"It's astrological charts." Kevin looked up from fussing with Raymond Dark's inkwell and added defiantly. "I told you that."

"How did you know it had to do with the Demonic Convergence?"

"It says so on the other side."

Frowning, Leah carefully turned the page over. In the margin, about halfway down, someone had written *charts Demonic Convergence* in pencil.

"Not me!" Kevin protested quickly. "That was there when I found the page."

"An earlier researcher?" CB suggested.

"Probably. Hang on." One hand holding back her hair, Leah leaned forward and squinted at the bottom of the page. "There's more writing, but it's faint." She carefully flipped the page. "It's on both sides. I think it was done at the same time as the charts."

"It looks around the same age," Henry agreed, when she moved out of the way so he could examine the barely visible brown marks. "But those aren't words; that's a pattern."

"Just because you don't recognize them, junior . . ." With one finger, she spun the vellum around and bent to breathe gently on the lettering. "Damp will sometimes bring the ink up a bit."

"Or damage an irreplaceable artifact."

"I think the margin notes have already lowered the value a bit."

"Still."

She flashed Henry a smile he'd very nearly seen in his mirror. The dimples were noticeably absent. "I know what I'm doing. Breath gives life to death."

"That's a total . . ." He let his protest trail off when it became obvious the ink was growing darker.

"It's a prayer," Leah announced after a moment. "Or part of one. *Keep us safe, Guardian of the West.*" She turned the page again. *"In light and life I beg thee."*

"Let me see the other side again."

She sighed but complied. "You're still not going to be able to read it."

"No." Frowning, he traced the largest of the letters, its loops and swirls now visible. "But I recognize it."

"How?" CB demanded.

Henry straightened. "I'm not entirely positive, but I think I own the rest of the book."

"You own an ancient book on the Demonic Convergence?" Arms folded, Leah raked him with a disbelieving stare. "You don't think you might have mentioned this earlier?"

"I didn't know it earlier. But this lettering . . ." He tapped the air above the prayer. ". . . is the same. The same shape and in the same place on the page." The document as an object was familiar. It was only the content he didn't recognize. "Unfortunately, because I couldn't read it, I didn't know what the book was about. If this is a page from it, I do now. And *you* can read it."

Slightly mollified by his acknowledgment of her ability, Leah shook her head. "Why would you own a book you can't read?"

"He owns it so others can't," CB said quietly.

"Oh, my." Her eyes widened in mock outrage. "Censorship. I need to see that book," she continued when Henry didn't bother denying it.

He looked at his watch. "It's almost three. I've time to get it and bring it back here."

"Bring back coffees, too," Jack told him, reaching for his wallet. "Hit a Timmy's. Extra-large double double and whatever anyone else wants. Oh, and grab some of those special Halloween donuts with the black and orange sprinkles."

"Way to work the stereotype," Leah snickered as Henry suggested the constable call it a night.

"No." And if Jack didn't meet his gaze, he came closer than many who'd seen what he'd seen. "I'm here until this ends."

"You don't have to work tomorrow?"

"I'll take a sick day. I'm not leaving until I know what's going on."

"You know . . ."

"And," he interrupted stubbornly, "until you can guarantee no more horror movie rejects will be out and about on my streets."

"Your streets?" Leah asked.

"It's a cop thing," Henry told her before Jack could answer. "They're all remarkably possessive."

"Well, you'd know possessive. I should go with you," she added crossing the office as he took Jack's money and folded it into the front pocket of his jeans. "Just in case."

"In case there's an attack on you while Tony sleeps?"

She moved a little closer and tossed her hair back over her shoulder. "With Tony out, you're my best bet."

Henry stared for a long moment at the creamy flesh below the curve of her ear. "No," he said at last. "Too great a risk."

"You think *that's* a greater risk than running into a new demonic minion?"

He gave her back the smile she'd given him earlier. "I do."

♠

"What the hell is going on between those two?" Jack muttered as Leah returned to the astrological charts on the desk and Henry headed for the back door.

"You don't know?"

He turned to see Groves standing tucked in behind his left shoulder. "No," he snapped, putting some decent distance between them. "I don't know."

The reporter shuddered. "Lucky."

"You know?" Stupid question. He obviously thought he did. "So, what's going on?"

*And why is a romance writer a better choice to protect her than an armed police officer?*

Groves answered the actual question instead of the subtext. "She tried for power over him. He threatened to kill her."

Jack blinked. "You're completely bugfuck; you know that, right?"

♠

It wasn't so much a book Henry dropped on the desk as a collection of loose pages stuffed between wooden covers. The pages were paler and the writing darker, but that, Jack realized, had more to do with the way Groves' page had been stored than any actual differences.

He wasn't a big believer in inanimate objects having an aura—in the last few months new and unusual animate objects had pretty much used up all available ability to believe—but under oath on the stand he'd say this book felt unpleasant. He was just as glad he wasn't the one with his nose barely an inch above the writing.

"Do you think you could avoid dropping sprinkles on a priceless literary artifact?" Henry carefully swept a bit of orange icing off the top sheet.

Jack backed up a step. Not like he minded being farther away from that book. "So what's it say?"

"I'll let you know when I've got it in order." Leah sat back, rubbing her eyes, then bent forward again. "This page seems to be more dates. This is a description of a body, the injuries, and how it was found. Oh, this is about the woman who found it and what relationship she was to the . . . well to either the dead guy, a dead guy who might not be *that* dead guy, or to the person writing. Boring stuff so far."

"It sounds like a police report."

She looked up and nodded. Jack barely resisted the effort to reach out and push her hair off her face. "It could be. Somewhere in here, there's probably information on who's writing and why. It's going to take a while before I can find anything that's going to do us any good. If there's anything in here." She yawned. "I'm beat, and my eyes hurt. I need some sleep."

"We need the information."

"Then you stay up and get it."

"He can't read it," Jack reminded her as Henry checked his watch. "And we're all tired."

Dimples flashed. "Then we should all find a bed."

"Cute." A strangled noise flicked his attention momentarily to the reporter. From the expression on Groves' face, he couldn't take a joke. "But you're right . . ." Back to Leah. ". . . we've got to sleep sometime." And finally to Chester

Bane. "If you closed the studio, we could make this our command center."

The big man shook his head. "I can't afford to lose a day's work. Make it your command center with the studio open."

"And if a demon shows up when the director yells quiet, we all just pause until the camera's off?"

"Yes. That should be sufficient."

Jack studied his face and realized: "You're not kidding."

"I don't kid. The studio stays open."

"We should be safe enough tomorrow," Leah told him, covering another yawn. "One way or another, we dealt with the two weak spots I could sense."

"Fine." Since no one was listening to reason and since the RCMP wasn't backing his play, giving him no official weight to throw around, he'd just have to make the best of things. "Tony's security system has been breached. Is it still functional?"

"No." Leah pulled the sleeves of her sweater down over her hands and folded her arms. "I crossed it with no reaction when I got Kevin from the office."

"Why would it respond to you?"

"Everything responds to me."

She sounded so matter-of-fact about it, Jack decided not to argue. "All right." He drained the last sweet dredges of his coffee. "If we can get some more cough syrup, Tony can resecure the perimeter when he wakes up."

"Cough syrup?"

Jack explained quickly, and Chester Bane nodded.

"Get me an empty bottle, and I'll see that he has what he needs."

"Good. And tell your people that a rain of cherries is the sign to hit the deck." He glanced around the office set. "You got a shower in this place?"

"Two." The producer held up the requisite number of fingers. "There are en suites in both of the large dressing rooms although I'd advise you not to use Mason's. Mr. Nicholas is likely to be much more reasonable, particularly as he is aware of what's going on."

"Maybe you'd better talk to him, then." Jack tilted his head back and stared over the tops of the walls, up into the grid hanging from the ceiling. "It's a big place. When your crew shows up, we'll just stay out of each other's way. We'll send . . ." He paused, leaned back until he could see the end of the chaise and frowned. "What the hell is the name of the guy with Tony?"

"Zev Sero. The musical director. Although he and Mr. Foster are no longer . . ." A pause. "Ah. With. Currently. Never mind."

"Send him home. Whether he comes back is up to you two." If it was up to Jack, he'd send Chester Bane home as well. The last thing they needed was more civilians around. "You . . ." Groves jumped. "I'm not inclined to let you out of my sight in case this all shows up on page one next to the cow that does Elvis impersonations."

"It won't." He was facing Jack but looking at Henry, picking at the cuticle around his right thumb, two spots of color high on each cheek. "I promise."

The look was either terror or love, and in this crowd, Jack figured the odds were pretty much even. "You break that promise and . . ."

"Trust me, Constable Elson," Groves interrupted, his Adam's apple bobbing as he swallowed, "there's no need to make threats. I know what's at stake. Oh, God!" Both hands rose to cover his mouth. "I didn't mean to say stake!"

Clearly, Tony wasn't the only one a little brain fried. "Go home. Sleep. Come back."

This time Groves turned to face Henry as he asked, "Now?"

This time Jack wasn't going to put up with it. "Hey. *I'm* telling you to go." And then he decided not to notice that Henry nodded, an almost friggin' regal incline of the head before Groves finally got off his ass and started moving.

Pausing. "My page . . ."

"Stays."

Leah leaned forward and caught the reporter's eye. "I'll take good care of it."

How the hell did she make that sound pornographic? Jack

shifted his weight to make an adjustment. And it wasn't just him. There was shifting going on all over the room.

"I'll be leaving as well." Henry came out from behind the desk. "I have commitments I cannot break."

"Hey." Jack stepped into his path. "If I can break mine, then . . . uh . . ." It was too damned dark and he couldn't find his way out. He had no backup. No weapon. He was . . . was . . . Eyes, they were just eyes. "Fuck. Okay, go."

"I'll be back as soon as I can. Mr. Groves, I'll walk you to your car."

Jack watched them leave, wondering how high Groves would jump if Henry Fitzroy reached over and tapped him on the arm. He turned to find himself under examination by Chester Bane.

"You seem to be taking this in stride, Constable."

He reached for another donut and realized there were bruises on his back that were going to hurt like hell come morning. "Well, the perps are uglier, but it's hardly the first stakeout I've been on."

"You are serving and protecting?"

"Yeah. That's what I'm telling myself."

# Ten

TONY HOPED HE WAS dreaming although, given the way his life had been lately, he figured there was a fifty-fifty chance he was actually physically standing somewhere . . . white. White up above, white all around, white and solid underfoot. At least he was dressed. One of those naked and somewhere white dreams would be more than he could handle right about now.

If he *was* dreaming.

"Hello?"

No echo. No bounce at all. Not inside, then.

Unless he was under a giant white insulated dome that was sucking up the sound of his voice.

Yeah. That was likely. It'd be like *The Truman Show* only without Jim Carrey. Or a set.

The air was warm and smelled like . . .

Well, that was embarrassing. The whole place smelled like him. Still, he supposed a guy who'd had a three-demon day was entitled to stink a bit if anyone was.

He lifted his left hand to run it back through sweaty hair. Stopped it at eye level.

The rune burned into the palm of his left hand—usually a thin white line—had turned a dark blood red. The rune allowed him to hold energy. Energ*ies*. Did the color change mean that the rune was holding all the white in place or was that too much of a leap?

*Okay, let's go over what we know.*

*White place.*

*Red rune.*

That was about it.

As far as Tony could figure, there was only one way to find out if there was a connection. He dropped to one knee and poked at the ground. It felt like a really good kitchen countertop, that stuff where the pieces got melted together and couldn't be scratched. Henry had it in his condo.

And that was as far as he got for a while.

Hard to tell how much time had passed because nothing changed, but Tony was fairly sure he'd been kneeling there for hours. Or he'd gone somewhere else and was just getting back because that sort of thing could happen in a dream. This kind of a dream anyway. The truly weird kind.

Before it could happen again, before he could convince himself that this was a remarkably bad idea, he raised his left hand and slapped his palm down on the ground.

It gave slightly. A noticeable ripple moved out from the point of impact. He rose and fell as it passed beneath him, like riding a solid wave. He watched the shadow that followed the crest until it was too far away to see. His time in television had taught him that a shadow meant a definitive light source, but apparently that rule didn't apply in dreamland.

"That was productive. Not." Rubbing the rune against his jeans, he stood.

And squinted.

A black dot marred the perfect white of the horizon. Or of the distance anyway since *horizon* might be giving the distance more credit than it deserved.

Tony waited and when the dot didn't get any bigger, he started walking toward it.

And walking.

And walking.

And not really getting anywhere.

Of course, it wasn't like he had anything else to do.

"Hey! You want to meet me halfway? And I'm an idiot," he said in a less carrying tone. "What," he asked his immediate surroundings, "is the one thing I'm good at? Yes, I am amazingly good at my job, but I'm speaking metaphysically here, here being somewhat metaphysical. I can call things into my hand. I say 'come here' and things come. Now, admittedly I don't know what this . . ." In spite of squinting until his eyes ached, the dot remained a dot. ". . . is, but it appeared after I smacked the white with the rune and so, therefore, if I call it to the hand with the rune that should make up for a lack of defining characteristics. Right?"

Nothing disagreed with him.

He waited a moment longer.

"Okay, then."

Holding up his hand, reaching, Tony could feel . . . something. Something that was either bigger than anything he'd ever moved before or something that didn't want to come to him. Since the first theory allowed for a little more peace of mind, he went with that and pulled harder.

He hadn't had to use the words that focused this particular ability since the haunted house extravaganza back in August. He used them now.

Shouted them out, one at a time. By the sixth word, he could feel movement. By the seventh the black dot was longer than it was wide, kind of person-shaped. Panting, he lowered his arm and squinted again.

Person-shaped with antlers.

Seemed like he'd been trying to call a Demonlord to his hand.

So, now he knew that, the question was: Did he keep doing it?

Was *Darkest Night* the highest rated vampire detective show on syndicated television?

Duh.

His whole arm shook as he raised it, lowered it, raised it again. Apparently his arm wasn't convinced this was a good idea, but if he wasn't dreaming, Ryne Cyratane might be his only way out. Hell, if he *was* dreaming, Ryne Cyratane still might be his only way out.

This time when he called, the Demonlord didn't move. He did. His feet skittered along the countertop surface until he could see the Demonlord's face and then stopped so suddenly he nearly pitched forward. Too far away to touch—and that was probably a good thing—close enough to see expression. The Demonlord didn't look happy, that was for sure. He looked frustrated. Like he knew the thing he was looking for was right there, right in front of him, but he couldn't find it.

*Me again.* Tony couldn't have explained how he knew. It was like when he was on the street and some nights when the cops cruised by they were just out and about and some nights they were actively looking to score some law-and-order points, and it got so he could tell the difference. This feeling felt like that feeling.

Although, if Ryne Cyratane was looking for the wizard who kept sending his demons back to hell with their dicks in their hands, shouldn't he be angry?

"Hey!"

No response.

"Dude! If you want to talk to me, I'm right here!"

Here and not moving any closer. He could step back but not forward. There didn't seem to be any kind of an invisible barrier, he just couldn't do it.

Tony slid his gaze down Ryne Cyratane's body, got distracted for a moment or two—*Damn!*—and realized that the Demonlord's feet were likewise held in place. Back up the long expanse of skin, another moment of distraction—*Damn, damn, damn!*—and this time he saw that the Demonlord's mouth was moving.

"Okay." He ran a hand back through his hair. The frustrated expression was beginning to seem like a good idea. "You can't hear me. I can't hear you. So what the fuck is the point?"

When no answer was forthcoming, Tony reached into his pocket and pulled his only twoonie out of a handful of change. Two bucks seemed a small price to pay if this worked.

It didn't.

The tossed coin went through the Demonlord as if he wasn't there, hit the ground behind him, and rolled for a couple of meters before toppling over to wobble into stillness.

"Heads or tails?"

No answer to that either.

"Yeah, well, from what Leah says, you'd prefer tails, wouldn't you?"

He was a big guy; powerful looking with great muscle definition and enormous hands. Tony wasn't much for gym queens, but these muscles had a purpose and that made all the difference. It looked like he could rip the heads off small animals and what was more, looked like he'd do it, too, if the mood struck him. Although thick dreads covered the base of the antlers, the curved horn didn't look glued on. They looked like weapons.

He was proportional.

*Oh, come on, it's hanging out there. I'm supposed to not look at it?*

Fortunately the whole rip-the-heads-off-small-animals observation was putting a damper on his completely understandable reaction.

Or not.

The inside of his right arm was suddenly very warm. Lines of warmth trailing over the skin applied with the perfect amount of pressure. It felt really good. Had he not been stuck in a dream with a frustrated Demonlord, it would have felt like foreplay.

He closed his eyes for a moment, and when he opened them again, he had an instant's flash of Ryne Cyratane's face, onyx eyes actually focused on him, then the onyx turned to jade and the Demonlord became Lee kneeling beside the chaise, one hand wrapped around his upper arm, fingers rubbing the soft skin on the inside just under the edge of his T-shirt.

Dream, then.

Hell, maybe dream *now*. He'd had this dream before, he realized as his brain took the opportunity to repeat, *felt like foreplay* half a dozen times.

"Hey."

Tony thought about pretending to still be asleep because it felt so good to have Lee touching him. Sure, it was kind of taking advantage, but he'd had a rough day and he knew that the moment he showed any awareness Lee was back in the happy hetero land of denial. Why shouldn't he take a moment's advantage? Because, unfortunately, he was one of the good guys.

So he blinked and focused and said, "Hey" back.

Weird. Lee kept up the caress. Not that it was a big deal or anything, but it was definitely a caress.

Maybe Lee didn't realize he was awake. So he added, "What time is it?"

"Almost three." Although the fingers quit moving, the hand stayed where it was, and since Lee was smiling right into his face, it seemed like he knew who he was holding.

Hang on. If it was almost three, then he'd only been asleep for about an hour and what the hell was Lee doing at the soundstage when he'd been told to stay out of danger?

"Friday afternoon," Lee added, smile broadening.

Had he said any of that out loud? Or was he really so easy to re— "It's when!"

Lee's grip on his arm kept him pinned to the chaise. "Leah says you can't do the 'with one bound he was up and away.' She says you'll fall over."

His brain kept repeating, *Friday afternoon!* but he managed to catch the last two words. "Fall over?"

"Seems like your busy day turned into a busy night," Lee explained, fingers tracing tiny circles. "Leah said you needed to recover, so we've been keeping an eye on you."

Tiny circles. Warm fingers. *Focus damn it!* "We?"

"Me, mostly." He shrugged. "I finished up just before we broke for lunch and I was going to head home, but Jack said that as long as Leah was tied up in translations, I might as well make myself useful."

"Jack?"

"Sound asleep in CB's office with his jacket over his face."

Tony ran down the list in his head. "CB?"

"Has a meeting with his insurance people." Lee glanced at the pile of broken lumber that had been part of the set on Thursday morning. "Can't think why."

"Zev?"

"I assume he's at his board." The tiny circles stopped as dark brows drew in. "You know, it's interesting, I seem to be the only person who knows about this who wasn't here last night."

"You'd be surprised at what people who think they know don't know."

"Pardon?"

Yeah, Tony wasn't sure he understood that either. "Amy wasn't here."

"Apparently, Amy was a part of the road show." He sighed and the frown morphed from annoyance to frustration. "I just don't seem to be getting through to you. I am over what happened last summer . . ."

*Then why all the touchy-feely now? Oh. Right. Over being possessed.*

". . . and I don't want you to protect me. I don't need you to protect me. In case it's escaped your notice, I'm a fair bit bigger than you."

"Whip it out and prove it," Tony muttered. "Size isn't the point," he added quickly. "When you're . . ." No. "I don't . . ." Uh-uh. "This is . . ." Nope. Probably shouldn't go there either. He closed his eyes and sighed. *When you're involved, I think about you. Not about saving the world or whatever part of it's in danger this month. You. I don't think I can handle seeing you in danger again. This is hard enough without all that extra emotional baggage.* How hard could it be to say that out loud? When he opened his eyes, Lee was watching him. Still holding his arm. Waiting.

Stupid question.

It was fucking impossible to say all that out loud.

Lee's turn to sigh. "Asshole. Come on, sit up slowly. I've got you."

The world made a few interesting adjustments as, with Lee's help, he dropped his feet to the floor and managed to get at least partially vertical. The soundstage slipped sideways for a moment and, true to his word, Lee was right there, his arm around Tony's shoulders. Waking up was turning out to be even more surreal than his dream. Although one thing hadn't changed.

"I stink."

"You do. Think you can make it to a shower?" He pulled away a little, half turned to face the far side of the soundstage. "Props might still have that wheelchair. I don't think we completely destroyed it."

"We set it on fire, pushed it down the ramp at a parking garage, and it slammed into a concrete block wall."

"Still . . ."

"No." Deep breath and a surge upright. "I'm fine. I'm just a little stiff."

"Whip it out and prove it." Almost under his breath. Almost not loud enough to hear except that his mouth was close enough to the side of Tony's head for the words to brush against his ear.

If he wasn't before, he was now.

He didn't close his eyes, although he wanted to. He wished he knew what Lee was thinking. What Lee'd *been* thinking when he'd been sitting and stroking and waiting for Tony to wake up. Conscious of every point of contact, he said, "Stop screwing around, Lee. Unless you're ready to cross the line, it's not fair."

The other man flushed and suddenly there were half as many points of contact. "Can't a guy help a friend who's been fried?" he asked, his mouth twisting into an approximation of a smile.

Were they friends? They'd been friendly although they'd never been the "go out for a beer together" kind of friends. Made sense. Beer and subtext was a bad combination. For the sake of getting where he was going, he supposed he could fake friend if that was how Lee wanted to play it.

"Sure. Speaking as the friend who got fried, I'm glad of the help."

As they shuffled across the soundstage, Tony nodded toward

the back wall of Raymond Dark's office. A couple of grips were opening the trap and wrestling the camera through the space where the imitation Turner had been. "What's up?"

Fortunately, Lee'd had enough of innuendo. "Mason's doing the existential moment that leads us to the final episode and all those frigging flashbacks." He wasn't in the flashbacks, which cut his time in the final episode to the teaser and the tag. There'd already been discussions about an extra feature on the DVD to make up for it. "Mason and existential," he snorted. "Those are two words I never thought I'd put together."

"Does Mason even know what existential means?"

"It means it's about Mason. He's happy with that. He's an uncomplicated guy, our Mason."

*Uncomplicated would be nice.* Tony leaned against a Gothic revival pillar as Lee reached for the door. *It'd be a nice fucking change.*

Before Lee's fingers closed around the doorknob, it moved. They shuffled back as the door opened, shuffled back a bit farther as Adam came into the soundstage carrying a huge sheet of white foam board.

"So, how's the fallen warrior?" he asked, peering around it at them.

Wizard. But it seemed pointless to protest. "I'm fine," Tony told him and when Adam snorted, expanded it to, "a little unsteady."

The 1AD craned his head until he could get a line of sight on Lee. "Don't drop him," he told the actor as if he was saying, *Don't miss your mark.* "We've got one more episode to shoot and I'd like to have a roof to do it under." Without waiting for a response, he adjusted his grip and walked away muttering, "Demons want to invade, they can bloody well time it for hiatus like everyone else."

"He knows . . ."

"CB did a little explaining when the crew arrived this morning."

"I don't think . . ."

"CB thought," Lee interrupted again, "that the known isn't

half as likely to be gossiped about as the unknown. Also, given what some of us have already been through, we deserved better than bullshit."

"That explains it," Tony muttered, as they proved that it wasn't entirely impossible for two people to get through the costumes that lined the hall outside the soundstage. Best to just ignore the implication that CB had given Lee permission to be involved in the fight.

"What does?"

"Your sudden attention. We're fighting a kind of a war here, so it's a two guys in the trenches thing."

"That sounds vaguely pornographic."

"I meant like in episode fifteen."

"That *was* vaguely pornographic. Mason's fan mail jumped seventeen percent after the World War I episode." Maneuvering around the gorilla suits pressed Lee's body tight against his.

Safest to blame the gorillas. It'd keep him from punching Lee in the face. "You know what I mean. Helping a fallen comrade is very butch. Very safe."

One rack of costumes ended at the door to the women's washroom, opening up enough room for them to stand side by side—face-to-face with a little distance between them. Albeit a very little distance. Tony wanted to mutter, *Take a picture, it'll last longer.* except that would be childish and there was nothing even remotely childlike about the look on Lee's face. For a long moment, he was convinced that Lee was going to kiss him. Right there. Right in front of the women's washroom and the tattered sign about no fucking when the red light was on.

Then the moment passed.

Lee nodded toward the dressing rooms, still half a dozen meters down the hall. "Come on, you need to get cleaned up."

Maybe it came from facing demons. Maybe he was lightheaded from hunger. "Chicken."

"Fuck off."

Lee really sounded pissed, but to Tony's surprise, he didn't let go—although his grip on Tony's upper arm tightened until his fingers were digging into flesh. They walked in silence to the door of his dressing room where Tony balked.

"I'm using your shower?"

"You'd rather have Mason walk in on you?"

He was a heartbeat away from saying what he'd rather have. He said nothing as Lee opened the door. Nothing as he walked inside. Nothing as Lee released his arm, stepped back, and asked, "You going to be okay?"

"I'll be fine."

Well, that was something but not exactly relevant.

He said nothing as Lee tossed him a towel. Said nothing as Lee left.

As he dropped to the end of the couch and bent to fight with his shoes, he muttered, "Who's chicken now?"

At least if they were *both* chickens that was sort of a species step in the right direction. Or possibly he'd moved beyond light-headed to completely fucking insane.

Amy was setting a tray of food on the battered coffee table as he stepped out of the tiny en suite, the towel wrapped around his waist. There was no sign of Lee.

*And the repressed gay interlude seems to be over; back to business as usual.*

"Just so you know, I'm not accepting a supporting role." Amy stuck a fork upright in the lasagna. "I lied my ass off to the cops last night," she continued, straightening, "and I demand a spot in the front . . . Whoa, Tony, those are some interesting scars."

It took him a moment to realize she meant the crosshatching on his left pec. Most people who saw him with his shirt off didn't mention them.

*"Who did this to you?" Henry traced cool circles over the damaged skin.*

*"If I tell you, what'll you do?"*

*His smile had been like a knife in the dark. "Make them pay."*

So Tony'd told him. Hell, he was eighteen. Revenge had seemed like a good idea. He still didn't regret it.

Zev had said nothing, merely acknowledged the evidence of old pain with a gentleness that had broken Tony apart. And then acknowledged that by putting him back together again more gently still. *I so didn't deserve him.*

"Are they tribal markings?" Amy asked as he rummaged a shirt out of the garbage bag of his clean laundry.

"Sort of." They were what happened to those who got caught on the wrong turf.

"Cool."

Not really, no. But Amy was looking at darkness from the outside where it was a lot safer and practically branded. "What the hell are you wearing?"

She pulled the front of her T-shirt out far enough to be able to look down at the picture of a nearly skeletal man climbing out of the bisected body of a rotting bear. "New movie shooting in the park. I scammed it off one of the publicity guys. Werebear!"

"Where castle?" He shimmied jeans up under the towel and let it drop.

"What?"

"Are you kidding me?" When she continued to look blank, he shook his head and dropped down onto the couch. "No one cares about the classics these days."

"Yeah, yeah, tell it to your next boyfriend. And speaking of, that cutie cop wants to see you on the soundstage when you've eaten; he's taken your spot on the chaise. Lee says you can leave your clothes in here as long as you need to. Zev says try not to get killed before tomorrow sunset because he'd like to say good-bye. Adam wants to know why you can't work since you're in the building anyway. And I'd be kind of pissed about taking messages for you except I'm sucking up in the hope you'll take me demon hunting."

He muttered a negative around a mouthful of lasagna.

"I can get my hands on some holy water."

"Wrong kind of demons."

"There's a right kind of demon?"

"Damned if I know." He smiled up at her.

"Ew. Mouth closed while eating, pig person." Wiggling her

fingers at him in what may have been a sign against the evil eye although it looked more like she was trying to flick a booger free, Amy backed out the door. "Don't forget the cop on the chaise," she warned as she closed it behind her.

Sometimes, Tony acknowledged, stuffing another forkload of pasta and cheese into his mouth and this time chewing with his mouth closed, the tricks a guy learned grossing out girls at twelve ended up helping him out for the rest of his life.

♣

"Your friend Fitzroy doesn't answer his phone."

Tony shrugged in Jack's general direction. It had been Henry last night. Now it was Fitzroy again. At least he hadn't shortened it to Fitz—Henry reacted badly to diminutives. "He's probably on deadline."

"Oh, yeah. Romance writer." Reclining on the chaise, fingers laced over his stomach, wearing the pale blue dress shirt with the handprint scorched on to it that Mason had worn in episode five, Jack crossed his legs at the ankles. "I don't know many romance writers who can do what he did last night."

"How many romance writers do you know? And how many of *them* have you seen deal with a demon?"

"Good point. Points."

He crossed to the chaise, fighting the urge to look up at the gate as he passed under it. Technically, he fought the urge to look up into the lighting grid at the place the gate would be if it was still opening, but that was more complicated than he was up to right now. "Amy said you wanted to see me?" His attempt at not sounding defensive failed miserably.

Jack grinned. "Thought you'd like to know what you missed after you went all Sleeping Beauty on us last night and before Prince Charming showed up this afternoon."

"Who?" So much for defensive—now, he was just trying not to sound confused.

"Leah sent that actor guy you're so hot for in to watch over you." The grin broadened in a decidedly shit-disturbing manner. "I suggested he wake you with a kiss. How'd that go? I'm curious," he added as Tony opened and closed his mouth a couple of times, "because he looked like he was considering it. Good-looking guy if I was interested in guys, which I'm not."

"Neither is he."

"Bullshit. I pointed out that the place is being overrun by demons and we could all be dead tomorrow, so he should take the chance."

"He's st . . ." Tony couldn't get the word out. Apparently his subconscious would only allow hypocrisy to take him so far. "He's not interested."

"The hell he isn't. I'm a trained observer . . ." Jack unlaced his fingers and thumped himself on the chest. ". . . your tax dollars at work. The girls are either camouflage or he's willing to switch hit."

"Spare me the lame sports analogy, Dr. Ruth."

"Shut up, I'm not done. He's decided he wants you, but he's too fucking freaked to take that final step. Can't say as I blame him, him being in the public eye and all." A thoughtful frown. "Or he would be if anyone actually watched this dumbass show."

"Hey! We've got the highest numbers of any vampire detective show in syndication."

"That and a buck seventeen will buy you a bad cup of coffee." Swinging his feet to the floor, Jack sat up. "So, the story thus far: Your reporter buddy Groves showed up with that page of his. Your romance writer buddy Fitzroy went home and got the rest of the book. Your very hot stuntwoman buddy Leah knows how to read the book, and she's working on the translation. Basically, we're all waiting to find out what the hell is going on. Oh, and your freak buddy, Amy, kind of grows on you. Is she seeing anyone?"

"Not right now." He dropped onto the end of the chaise. "And forget it."

Jack made a noise Tony couldn't identify—although he was pretty sure it wasn't agreement—and said, "So, who's Arra?

"Arra?" He needed to find out how much Jack knew, then he could craft the lie. "How do you know about Arra?"

"You mentioned her last night."

Crap.

"We were talking about the rope, the unnatural rope, and you said it was weird that Arra'd know it would work since she'd never faced demons here in this world. Then Leah said that if you'd never met her, you wouldn't be fighting demons today."

"You remember all that?"

"It's part of my job to remember the details."

That wasn't the part of his job Tony had trouble with. It was more the parts that involved the government and arresting people and sure he'd been willing to falsify reports and get involved on his own time, but how long before the weird built up past the point he could justify not mentioning it. Justify not bringing out the big guns to try and stop it. And would that even be a problem? People had died. Tony stared at the toes of his Doc Martens. They were in the midst of a Demonic Convergence; odds were good that more people would die.

"You want me to take a guess?" Jack leaned forward, forearms balanced on his thighs. "I'm guessing she was the wizard who fingered you as a wizard and that she was from another world, like the demons are. I figure this happened back last spring when I got fed a bullshit line about what happened to Charlie Harris and Rahal Singh."

He didn't need to be reminded of their names.

"I figure she either died then, too, or went home since she wasn't around this summer while you were talking to the dead and she isn't around now."

Tony opened his mouth and closed it again when Jack kept talking.

"At first I thought you may have made some kind of mistake when this Arra was starting you out as a wizard and that's how those two men died—and that's what you've been hiding from me."

He could feel Jack's gaze on the side of his face. He didn't turn. "It's not."

"I know. Leah said something else last night."

"Um . . . take me? Take me, I'm yours?" A weak attempt to lighten the mood but pretty much a gimme.

"She said that heroes rise when we need them."

That forced the turn. "You think I'm a hero?"

Jack shrugged. "I did a background check on you," he said matter-of-factly. "I know what battles you've already won."

"Holy after-school special, Batman," Tony muttered, cheeks flushed. He hadn't won any battles; he'd done what he'd had to in order to survive.

"So what happened last spring?" Still matter-of-fact.

Why not. "Arra and I fought off a guy called the Shadowlord invading from her world. After we won, she went home." Cole's Notes version.

"The Shadowlord was responsible for the deaths?"

"Yeah."

"What happened to him?"

"He got eaten by the light."

"Is that some kind of wizard metaphor?"

"Not really."

"Here?" His gesture took in the immediate area.

"Yeah."

"Good." Jack nodded. "Good," he said again, sounding more satisfied the second time, as though he'd taken that moment to consider things and now was able to let it go.

They sat silently for a moment, Jack staring down into his loosely clasped hands. Voices across the soundstage sounded like they were coming from another world. Tony glanced up into the lighting grid and then back down at his shoes. "An old friend of mine says there's too often a difference between law and justice."

"Would that old friend be Detective-Sergeant Mike Celluci?"

"Christ, no!"

Fortunately, any discussion that might bring up Vicki Nelson was cut off by the bell and calls of "Rolling!" from the permanent sets. It sounded like they were shooting by Mason's coffin—far enough away for quiet conversation but just as well Jack didn't know that. Tony did not want to talk about Vicki Nelson with Jack.

Talking about Vicki would only lead to more lying and basking in the warm glow of even a truncated confession, Tony didn't feel like lying. With any luck, the feeling wouldn't last, but for the moment he decided to go with it.

"Cut! Reset! We'll go again from the top."

They heard the door open almost immediately after the light went out.

"Must be nice," Constable Danvers muttered, stopping at the foot of the chaise, arms folded over her damp, brown corduroy jacket. "Sitting around, head up your butt, not actually accomplishing anything."

"We had a demon last night," Jack protested.

"Yeah? I had a six-year-old who disassembled the DVD player, an eight-year-old who wants a tattoo, and dog vomit all over the living room rug. Trade you."

When she motioned for Tony to move over, he stood. "I'll get a chair." No way he was sitting between two cops. That brought back bad memories.

". . . good news is, no bodies," she was saying as he returned. "No body parts either. We had Sammy Kline making his biweekly call about lights in the sky and, this time, he might actually be onto something since there was a slightly more credible report about a flash of light across the Arm from the airport." She turned the page of her occurrence book and squinted at her notes. "Pilot saw it when he was circling for his final approach and thought it might be an explosion. Richmond detachment sent a car over, and it turned out to be some kind of gas leak and blow in a Goth coffee shop. Goth coffee shop," she repeated with a snort. "That almost qualifies as weird shit on its own."

"A demon knocked the door down." Tony told her. He hid a grin as her head jerked up. "That flash by the airport was the weak spot opening."

Her eyes narrowed and suddenly he didn't feel much like grinning. "Weak spot?" she demanded.

"Between here and the hells."

"You were there?"

He shrugged. "I was trying to cut it off at the pass."

"Great," she smiled insincerely, the expression barely reaching her mouth let alone her eyes. "You're a cowboy now. So there was a demon at a Goth coffee shop? They must've been thrilled."

"Not really. Not all of them," he amended, remembering Amy.

"You'd think that the sort of people who'd drink at a Goth coffee shop . . . What?" she demanded as Jack growled something under his breath. "I just like saying it. We, where we refers to the police in general as opposed to our detachment in particular, also received a number of calls about vandalized satellite dishes, a couple of downed power lines, a destroyed pigeon coop, and, not far from here, a balcony railing ripped right off the twelfth floor. No one saw anything, though."

"It took the high ground between the coffee shop and here," Tony realized. "That's why there were no casualties."

"Not a lot of healthy pigeons left in that coop," Constable Danvers pointed out dryly. "And when you say *it,* you're talking demon, right?"

"Right. They move really fast."

"No shit."

"Can you check for more flashes?"

She shook her head. "There was only the one reported last night."

"Not just from last night," Jack broke in. "Go back at least a week," he told his partner, then turned to Tony. "You want to compare the flashes to the demons you dusted, get a count, and find out if there's any still hanging around."

"It'll get us the timing, too. Unless the intervals are completely random, we'll know when to expect the next one."

"You're smarter than you look."

"I hate to put a damper on the mutual congratulations," Danvers sighed. "But last night's report was a fluke. Pilot just happened to be passing over at the right time. No one else called it in."

"There's not much around there." It was on the edge of an industrial park, as far as Tony could remember and, that close to the airport, what locals there were would be used to blocking out lights and sound. The guests at the hotel down the street wouldn't know what passed for normal in that part of Vancouver and the staff would be too busy to care. "If a weak spot opened where there were more people, someone probably called the cops."

Looking thoughtful, she snapped the occurrence book closed, slid it into an inside pocket, and pulled out her PDA. "Worth a try, I suppose. I can access the electronic files from here."

"Not from here, you can't. You can't get an uplink any closer than the other side of the road," he explained in answer to the questioning curl of her lip, impressed by the amount of information she could convey in a sneer.

"Fine." She stood. "I'll check and then I'm gone. Some of us can't waste precious sick days saving the world. Oh, hell, I'm going to have to come back, aren't I? I can't just call you with the info."

"Let's settle down, people!" Adam's voice, rising from around Raymond Dark's coffin, dampened the ambient noise. "Quiet on the set!"

Tony glanced over toward the door. The light was still off. "You won't get to come back if you don't go away."

"You can talk after he says quiet?"

"Yeah, but you can't leave after the red light goes on."

She took two steps toward the door and half turned, one hand rising to touch the loose knot of hair at the back of her neck. "Lee Nicholas?"

"Is in Chester Bane's office with the demonic consultant," Jack told her. "I thought you didn't have time to hang around and save the world."

"I may need to ask him a couple of questions about that deranged fan." She flashed him a "two can play at this game" look and ran for the door.

"Lee's with Leah?" Tony asked when no one yelled rolling. He was aiming for nonchalant. He suspected he missed.

"That's where I left him. I took over out here, remember?" Leaning on the curve of the chaise, Jack raised an eyebrow. "You think he's in there shoring up his increasingly dubious heterosexuality?" He snickered as Tony shrugged, once again missing nonchalant. "Yeah, it's all right there on your face. Except the increasingly dubious bit. I added that myself."

"So what's with the lights in the sky?"

Jack straightened, allowing the subject to be changed. "Sammy Kline's a janitor out at SFU. Every payday he goes on a bender and reports lights in the sky." Pale brows drew in. "Any chance he could be right?"

Another shrug. "Beats me. I don't do aliens."

"I can't work like this!" Mason's protest cut off whatever smart-ass response Jack was about to make. When he wanted to get his point, across the star of *Darkest Night* fell back on skills he'd learned doing summer theater unmiked in leaky tents situated by a major highway that was uphill—both ways—from his drafty and unheated garret room. No one had suffered for their art like Mason. "Look! Right there! There is a cherry in my coffin!"

"Mason . . ." Peter's voice faded just below where they could hear it.

Mason and a cherry; that was just too easy. Even across the soundstage, Tony could hear the snickers.

"I called quiet, people!" Adam had been around the business too long to allow any amusement to show in his voice. "Settle down! And rolling!"

"Rolling," Tony repeated softly.

"Mark!"

They couldn't hear the scene called, but they heard the clapper.

"Action!"

"Action . . ." He wanted to be by the camera watching Mason overact, the only demons on the set the metaphorical demons in Raymond Dark's past. He wanted bad coffee and long hours and he very much didn't want to be tucked off to one side while he dealt with the weirdness du jour. He wanted his life back. There had to be a way he could deal with this shit instead of just reacting to it. Leah's original idea of preventing the demons from crossing over was a good one, but finding them by driving around the lower mainland was stupid and inefficient.

He had to stop thinking like a TAD and start thinking like a wizard if he ever wanted a chance to be a TAD again.

*Yeah. That's it. Aim high.*

"So this is the infamous game of spider solitaire."

"Infamous?" Tony smacked Jack's hand away from the keyboard and winced as it returned to impact against the back of his head.

"The game that masks the wonders of wizardry."

Tony shot him a sideways look as he scrolled down the index. "You've been talking to Amy."

"No law against it." He winked over the cardboard lip of his coffee cup. "And like I said, she's cute."

"She's not your type."

"You don't know that."

"You're not her type. You're way too normal."

A pale brow arced up. "I took a sick day to hunt demons."

"Maybe normal isn't the right word." Tony paused and frowned at the screen. "Here it is. Finding."

"What? Nemo?"

Tony double-clicked the icon. "There're a few files in here. Finding Living Creatures . . ."

"The demons are living."

"Yeah, but we're not trying to find demons, we're trying to find where demons will be."

"Time travel?"

"Not allowed."

Jack finished his coffee and crushed the cup. "Too bad."

"Finding Inanimate Objects."

"I've lost my TV remote."

"It's in the sofa cushions."

"I am in awe of your power. Nothing on finding your way to hell?"

"Wrong reference material." Tony grinned as Jack snorted. "Here it is. Finding a Power Source."

"You need to be plugged in?"

"I don't think so." He scanned the instructions. "I need a map."

"I've got one in my truck."

♣

The wardrobe department needed more space. Which was pretty much true of every department but finance; they had plenty of space but needed more money. Wardrobe made it obvious with a leaning tower of shoe boxes, shelves six deep in hats, and bolts of fabric piled by color and weight. Since most of the fabric had been bought as remainders, some of the colors were a little frightening. A huge chart delineating what costumes were needed and when covered one wall. Sketches had been pinned up to every nonmoving surface as well as a couple of surfaces that weren't moving now but would be later. The actual clothing hung out in the hall.

When Tony came in with Jack's map, he found Alison Larkin on her knees in front of the thinnest of the staff writers adjusting the length of an apron over a full peasant skirt. Dana, her most recent assistant, sat bent over one of the three sewing machines.

"I need to iron a map."

"We're busy," Alison snapped without looking up.

"I don't need *you* to iron it," Tony amended, wondering if she'd ever swallowed a pin. "I need to iron it."

"Why? Never mind. Don't touch that dirndl on the ironing board! Toss the sheet of white felt down on the cutting table and do it there. And Roger . . ." She slapped a hairy calf. ". . . stop fucking moving, or I'll stick you on purpose. We've got another eight of these to get through."

*Be sure the map is free of creases.*

Ironing the map, not a problem. Not much of a problem anyway. Getting it back to the soundstage without folding it was a little trickier. Tony shuffled sideways through the costumes, arms outstretched, swearing softly under his breath and wondering why they had half a rack of silver lamé jumpsuits.

The door out into the production office opened as he passed and only a last second, desperate lunge to the right kept Leah—and Lee right behind her—from slamming new creases into his map.

"Tony! Good news!""

He continued shuffling toward the soundstage. "I could use some."

"It's possible that because of the way the energy is being used this Demonic Convergence won't go on as long as it has in the past."

"According to?"

"According to the book that your friend Henry provided last night." Following close behind, she waved it in his general direction.

Tony peered at it over the upper edge of the map. It didn't look much like a book. It looked more like a lot of loose, yellowing pages crammed inside a worn, brown leather cover.

"While you were sleeping," she continued, "I was working on a translation."

With first Jack and then Lee in the office with her, Tony doubted that was all she'd been doing. A glance past her at Lee showed the actor was looking a little ruffled. And wizards saw what was there, didn't they? Hey, more power to him. Tony was all in favor of everybody getting some. A happy Demonlord was a . . . well, he was a happy Demonlord, that's what he was, and a happy Demonlord was probably less likely to send over demons to slaughter his favorite handmaiden. *More's the pity.*

"Are you grinding your teeth?"

"No." He stepped over a pair of old steel-toed work boots painted in patterns that might look like urban camouflage on a thirteen-inch TV. In HDTV, not so much.

"Ryne Cyratane is using the energy up."

That was enough to stop him. The ironed paper rustled. "What?"

"The Demonic Convergence produces a limited amount of energy. Usually, it's spread out more and the world is dealing with small shit for months. One or two demons show up near the end."

"Because the energy burns through the hells like acid rain," Lee expanded. "As time passes, stronger drops burn right through the upper layers and end in deeper, nastier places." From his tone, he'd been the one to come up with that bit of description.

*Before or after the two of them tested the strength of CB's coffee table?* They wouldn't have used the couch, or the floor, or the desk . . . it had to have been the coffee table. *Why am I thinking about this?* he asked himself as he started moving toward the soundstage again—which meant moving away from Leah and Lee. Giving them room. They, of course, followed. *So much for symbolism.*

And hang on . . .

Another look at Lee. "She told you?"

The actor nodded. "End of the world as we know it."

Was he blushing? The light in the hall was so bad Tony couldn't tell. Not that it was any of his damned business. "So all this means the Demonic Convergence is going to end . . . when?"

"Sooner. We're not talking months; a month maybe. Maybe not even that if he keeps up this pace. Which raises the question, why is he going to all this effort? If demons always show up at the end of the Convergence—which, according to this . . ." The book was waved for emphasis. ". . . they always do."

"Always?" Tony interrupted.

"According to this book."

"Didn't you tell me they *sometimes* show up at the end of the Convergence?"

"That was before I had a first-person account to read. And they happen more often than I thought, too." She smiled. It was a remarably sarcastic expression. "So now I've proved I'm not infallible, can we move on?"

He shrugged, careful not to crinkle the map.

"Ryne Cyratane is not big on . . ." Dark brows drew in. "Why are you carrying a map of the lower mainland and why you are carrying it like such a spaz?"

"It's for a spell."

"Oh. All right, then."

He managed to hold back a bitchy *Glad you approve.* long enough for Leah to continue talking.

"Ryne Cyratane," she repeated, "is not big on personal effort. It would be more like him to wait and use whatever was going to get through at the end regardless. This is bigger than we thought. He's really motivated."

"Why?"

"How the hell should I know?"

"Okay." Good to know the time frame had been shortened—a half season of Convergence instead of the full twenty-two episodes—but from where Tony stood, that didn't make a lot of difference. He flattened against the soundstage's outer wall to give them room to get past. "Can one of you get the soundstage d . . ."

The soundstage door opened.

". . . never mind."

"Hello, pretty lady!" Framed in the doorway, Mason smiled unctuously down at Leah. "If you're here to watch me tape, we're done for the day, but I'd be happy to make the trip worth your while and sign a few photos. I have some in my dressing room . . ."

"She's not a fan, Mason," Tony interrupted before Leah took him up on it. Not the signed photos but the other nonverbalized offer. "She's a stuntwoman here to talk to Peter about the last episode."

"Ah." Red-gold brows drew in as he visibly retreated back out of sexual harassment territory. Fans wanted his attention. Coworkers weren't fans. "Am I throwing you off the windmill?"

"Very likely."

Gray eyes gleamed. "I'm sure I'll enjoy having you in my arms."

Ryne Cyratane flickered as she smiled up at Mason. "You have no idea."

"Leah! The *stunt!*"

"What st . . . oh. Right." She reluctantly dialed it back and the Demonlord disappeared. "It was nice meeting you, Mr. Reed." Dimples flashed. "My mother loved you in *StreetCred!*"

Tony winced as Mason deflated. This was the first he'd ever seen Leah turn off a guy's interest as fast as she turned it on. *Nothing like a reminder you used to be a network cop and now you're a syndicated vampire,* he mused as Mason stepped into the hall and squeezed past his costar. With the soundstage open before him, he could move a little faster.

Too fast to catch just what Mason muttered to Lee that Lee denied so vehemently. Given the salacious tone to the muttering, and the source, it wasn't hard to fill in the blanks.

*"I hear stuntwomen are very athletic and flexible."* Wink. Wink. Nudge. Nudge.

*"I would never take advantage of a coworker, you cad!"*

Great. His brain seemed to be lifting dialogue from Henry's books.

"What's the spell?" Leah demanded, catching up.

Tony listened to be sure Lee's footsteps were following behind them. "I'm going to search for the power signatures of the weak spots. The spell should tell us not only where they are but how close they are to opening, so we'll know which ones to close first. It's possible . . ." Not very likely, he admitted silently to himself, but possible. ". . . that it'll also map out where the next few weak spots are going to be."

"Predictive magic? Wow. You worked that out yourself?"

"Thanks for sounding so surprised."

"No." Hand against her heart. "I'm impressed. You're taking charge."

Hey, he was a hero. "Yeah, I am."

As they crossed to the chaise, Sorge left Jack's side with a wave and instructions to have a good weekend.

"What were you two talking about?" Leah demanded as Tony carefully laid the map on the floor.

Jack snorted. "I have no idea."

Somehow, staring down at the map lying flat made Tony intensely aware of how thin most people's versions of reality were. Most people believed that this was all there was. He kind of missed believing that. Dropping to his knees, he bent carefully and began to breathe on the paper.

Leah broke off explaining demonic acid rain to Jack to ask him what he was doing.

"The instructions say that the map must know the wizard. This was the least gross option." He finished up by panting at Richmond and stood. "Jack, could you . . ." His open laptop appeared at the edge of his peripheral vision. "Thanks. Now everyone step back. I need to circle the map three times."

"Shouldn't you be naked? What?" Leah protested as he turned. "So nothing would happen; I still like to look."

Jack waved a hand. "Pass on the naked: public indecency. I'd be forced to use the cuffs."

"Don't worry about the naked," Tony snorted. "I'll just be reading some words out loud while I walk. Long, complicated words so, once I start, no interruptions."

"You don't go through this when you call things to you," Lee reminded him. "You just reach for things and they're there."

He'd reached for Lee once.

"That's a good point." Jack nodded an acknowledgment at the actor. "What makes this different?"

"Do you play an instrument?" Tony asked him, grateful for the redirect.

"Yeah."

"What?"

The RCMP Constable glanced over at Leah and Lee and dragged a hand back through his hair, fingering it up into pale spikes. "Accordion."

Much mutual blinkage.

"Okay," Tony said quickly before Leah found her voice. "You know how, when you were learning, you had to think about everything you were doing—right hand, left hand, bellows, melody, words, rhythm, and mostly, you had to wonder why you didn't learn a cool instrument? And then, after a shitload of practice, a song clicks and you could just play without thinking about the bits? Come to Me is like that. It clicked. Other spells, I'm still figuring out as I go."

Since that was as good a cue as any, he started his first circle. The words were not only long and complicated, but there were a shitload of them and he barely managed to get them all in. Third circle complete and the last few words crammed in tongue twister fast, he knelt by the edge of the map, breathed on his fingertips, and pressed them down on the edge of the ironed paper.

"What are you . . . ?"

"Shhh." Leah. Who'd worked with wizards before.

He concentrated. Nothing happened. He could feel the map waiting. Could feel the information he needed just beyond his fingertips. He concentrated harder, focusing power. He could do this. He *had* to do this. *This is what I'm* supposed *to do.* Wait. Not do. He didn't do wizardry. He *was* a wizard. Something shifted and blue light spread out from his fingers pouring like water across the map. Then, suddenly a flare. And another.

And a burst of light.

Coughing and waving away streamers of smoke, Tony looked down at the light dusting of ash on the concrete floor. "I think I'm going to need another map."

♣

The four of them stared down at the pattern of little burns on the second map. Bad news, there were a lot of them. Maybe he was pissed about losing so many demons, but Ryne Cyratane was definitely motivated. Good news, most of the burns were very faint. Only three were significantly darker than the rest.

"What's it mean?" Lee asked, arms folded.

"If it worked . . ." Tony rocked back off his knees, picked up the map and stood. ". . . it means there's a lot of weak spots building at the same rate, and when they break through . . ."

"Wall-to-wall demons," Jack finished grimly.

Leah shook her head. "That can't be right. Henry's book said the Convergence had a limited amount of energy."

"Atomic bombs have a limited amount of energy," Jack snorted. "You need to define *limited*."

"We know for sure that Ryne Cyratane wants you dead and his gate open," Tony reminded her over the upper edge of the map. "I'm guessing he's working the convergent energy to create a lot of weak spots, so he can send through a whole bunch of demons at once, figuring at least one will get through me to you."

"And these darker ones?" Lee tapped the back of the map where the darker burns showed through.

"Best guess; they're distractions. I figure these guys won't be after you, they'll be free agents. If even one gets through, it'll start rampaging through the lower mainland and keep me too busy to close the multiple weak points before they open."

Arms folded, Leah sighed heavily. "That's one complicated assumption there, Tony."

"He's smarter than he looks." Jack gently pushed the top edge of the map down and stared at Tony. "Now, let's fill in the blanks. Who is Ryne Cyratane?"

"He's a Demonlord."

"Tony!"

Whoa. If looks could kill. "Jack's involved in this, Leah. He has a right to know." Still holding the map, he jerked his chin toward the actor. "You told Lee, and he's less involved."

"Whose fault is that?" Lee muttered.

"You're a civilian," Jack snapped. "Tony had every right to try and keep you safe."

Lee took a step forward, chin up. "He's a civilian!"

"He's a wizard!"

"He has no secrets," Tony sighed. "Leah?" He didn't need her permission, but he didn't want a fight either.

She dropped to the end of the chaise and crossed her legs. "Fine. Whatever."

"Ryne Cyratane's a Demonlord who used Leah as a part of

a gate spell more than three thousand years ago and, if he kills her, he gets to come back."

Jack turned toward the chaise. "You're three thousand years old?"

Her turn to sigh. "More or less."

"You look great!"

The dimples made a brief appearance. "Thank you."

"If he kills you, he gets to come back?"

She spread her hands. "The gate opens."

"I'm guessing it's going to take more than a yellow rope to hold this guy?"

Tony shrugged. "From what I've seen, it depends on what part you're holding."

# Eleven

"ALL RIGHT, THIS is what we're going to do." They'd moved across the soundstage to Adam's office—three wooden stacking tables arranged in an L shape, a home for unavoidable union forms, the battery chargers, and a decapitated head from episode three that the 1AD had grown inexplicably fond of. Tony carefully moved a stack of ACTRA forms and spread out the map. "These three spots . . ." He tapped the darker burns. ". . . have to be closed fast, so I can get as many of the rest shut before the shit hits the fan. The Demonlord knows there's a wizard on this side, but he doesn't know about you lot and he doesn't know that the residue in the studio is drawing his demons. Those two things might give us an edge."

He glanced around at the world's best chance to remain demon free. CB and Amy, Lee, Jack, and Leah. And Leah was pulling double duty as probable cause. They were watching him like he knew what he was doing, and he could only hope they weren't delusional.

"We'll break up into three teams. Amy and CB, Jack and Lee. Leah stays with me because she's safest there even if it turns out this lot's not after her, just here for general, all-purpose mahem. We'll go to this spot here . . ." He tapped the map. ". . . closest to the studio and shut it down. The rest of you, you're my eyes and ears. CB, you and Amy will go here, due south down Boundary to North Fraser Way."

"South to north," Amy snickered. When everyone turned to stare, she shrugged. "Well, I thought it was funny."

Amy had come from the office with CB and refused to leave. *"Either I'm in or not, and after last night, the train to not has left the station."* Reluctantly, after he'd figured out what the hell she was talking about, Tony'd agreed.

"Jack, you and Lee are heading out almost to Simon Fraser." It was insane, completely and absolutely insane for Lee to be a part of this given that metaphysical energy looking for a home seemed to consider his body prime real estate. It really pissed Tony off that his *I don't want you involved* had been canceled by one *you should stick around* from Leah. He was trying to keep Lee safe. She just liked having attractive men around. And, okay, he liked looking up and seeing Lee on the other side of the table, too, but he'd also seen Lee on his knees screaming, tortured by the dead to force him to cooperate, and he never wanted to see that again. He'd stuff Lee into a closet and lock the door—fuck the symbolism—if it was up to him. But it wasn't.

"The burn's showing in this industrial park here off Eastlake Drive. It's late enough that there shouldn't be anyone around."

"So no one out there except us to get eaten," Jack put in.

"No one gets eaten," Tony snapped. "It's entirely possible that nothing will happen tonight, but . . ." He raised a hand and cut Amy off before she could speak. ". . . if it does, get clear and then call me, and I'll haul ass back to the studio instead of heading out to the next weak spot."

"We'll all haul ass back to the studio."

Heads nodded at Jack's statement.

"Fine." A grudging admission that he couldn't stop them. "But don't go charging in until I'm here. Jack, you know how hard it is to take one of these things down." Jack nodded reluctantly as Tony continued. "We go after them with everything we have, or we leave them alone. You go in without metaphysical backup, and these things could take you out like that!" He snapped his fingers and something large hit the floor on the far side of the soundstage with a sustained crash.

After a long moment of silence, CB folded his arms. "Mr. Foster."

"I didn't do it!" He frowned. "At least I don't think I did it."

"Well, this is filling me with confidence," Leah muttered as Jack pulled his gun and moved to check it out.

"Maybe I should . . ."

CB laid a heavy hand on Amy's shoulder. "You should let the police handle it."

"Chairs!" Jack called, heading back. "A pile of those metal folding chairs fell over."

"They were stacked pretty high," Lee recalled. "Last couple of days, Adam's been talking about restacking them before they fell."

"Coincidence," Amy snorted. "No boogeymen in the shadows?" she asked as Jack rejoined them at the map.

"Not that I saw."

"But you wouldn't see them, would you? Was I the only one who heard skittering?" She glanced around the group. "Okay, I guess I was."

"Can we just deal with the trouble we know we have instead of looking for more?" Tony sighed. "Or are three demons not enough for you?"

Lee raised his hand. "Enough for me."

"Thank you. When Leah and I finish closing the first weak spot, we'll join CB and Amy and then, when we're done there, head east. Remember, if anything happens, don't try and be a hero, just call me."

"The whole 'you shall not pass' thing always ends badly," Amy added, shrugging a plaid plastic raincoat on over a black hoodie.

"Isn't that what you're telling these things, Tony? That they shall not pass?"

He turned to Lee, intending to deny it, and heard himself say, "Yeah."

"And if it ends badly for you?"

"I'm hoping for weeping, wailing, and gnashing of teeth. Joke," he added when no one seemed to appreciate the humor. "If it ends badly for me, throw everything you have at keeping Leah alive. The hell with secrets, the hell with not causing mass panic. Mass panic sucks less than mass slaughter."

"Do we know there'll be mass slaughter?" CB asked.

He sounded as though he was requesting confirmation so that he could hire enough extras to make *mass* a valid description, but it was still a good question. Tony let Leah answer it.

"Demons gain power from each life they take, and there are a lot of lives crammed onto the lower mainland." Her right hand lay against the tattoo, her left pushed her hair back off her face, tucking it behind her ear. "Enough lives for a satisfactory number of worshipers with plenty left over to spend on other things. Also," she added, the words gaining emphasis, "since any mass slaughter will start with *my* slaughter, I'm all in favor of stopping it."

"Start with?" Amy was on the words like a terrier.

Right. Amy didn't know that Leah was the Demongate.

"CB."

The producer nodded. "I'll give her the new information in the car."

Jack folded his arms, leather jacket creaking as he ignored the exchange, his attention locked on Leah. "People are a lot more powerful than they used to be," he pointed out flatly.

"True," she acknowledged. "And you may have powerful enough weapons to stop him, but don't think for a moment that with this many lives to feed on, he'll be the only one coming through an open gate. The last time, he was called and the gate was destroyed behind him. This time, he'll control it."

"And we already know that Demonlords have demon minions," Amy put in, shifting her weight back and forth, heel to toe. "He could, like, throw them at the military while he feeds and gets too strong to stop. Then the only option would be a surgical nuke. Pow! Hundreds of thousands more die, radiation spreads, one of his minions escapes the blast and absorbs the radiation and mutates so that nothing . . .

CB returned his hand to her shoulder, cutting off the flow of words. "I don't like the thought of leaving the studio unprotected," he growled.

Tony didn't much like the thought either. Even if he knew where to send the bill, it seemed ethically questionable to charge for saving the world, so he'd really like a job to come back to on Monday morning. However, if he had to choose between a building and warm bodies . . . "I don't want anyone out there alone."

"Perhaps I can help with that."

Lee, Amy, and Jack jumped; Jack's hand dropped to his gun. Leah looked like nothing much surprised her anymore. CB looked unimpressed. Tony tried not to give in to nerves and snicker.

"Where the hell did he come from?" Jack demanded as Henry walked up to the table and studied the map. "No one moves that quietly."

"Clearly, someone does," CB told him as Tony started in on the highlights of what Henry had missed.

When he finished, Henry nodded. "I'll stay here. If unnatural rope works on all demons, I can work on securing anything that might show up until Tony arrives to deal with it."

"More metaphysical backup," Jack announced almost too quietly to hear. And then he point-blank refused to explain what he meant, cheeks flushing as Henry caught his eye.

Tony could see that CB wanted to say he'd stay behind. It was his studio, and he was, in his own way, as possessive as Henry. But he was smart enough to know he couldn't do what Henry could, and so he said nothing. That pretty much proved he knew what Henry was, but Tony found he didn't much care. Sometime in the last couple of days, he'd gotten over it. Hell, if CB wasn't big enough for them to share, no one was.

"Let's go." He folded the map and stuffed it into his jacket pocket. "Those three holes were almost burned through. We don't have much time."

"I thought you said that nothing should happen tonight?" Amy reminded him.

"Yeah, well." Tony shrugged. "I was trying to raise morale. And nothing should. Maybe. But we probably still don't have much time."

"Have you *any* idea of what's going on?"

"Bite me."

Amy flipped him off and headed for the door. "Be vewy vewy quiet," she muttered as Jack fell into step beside her. "We'eh hunting demons."

Jack did a passable Elmer Fudd laugh.

"Mr. Groves will be by later," CB told Henry as he followed.

Lee opened his mouth. Closed it. Sighed and finally said, "I'd be better at this if I had a script."

Since that was pretty much a given, Tony said nothing.

"Look, I just want . . . I mean. Fuck it. Be careful, okay?"

"Yeah. You, too."

He nodded and hurried after the others.

"You know," Leah said thoughtfully as she zipped up her jacket, "I was thinking it was just you, but I was wrong. You're both pathetic."

"Leah . . ."

"Don't bother saying it. I'll meet you in the car."

Tony listened to the soft sound of her footsteps die away. He shrugged a backpack strap up onto one shoulder and looked Henry in the eye. "Vicki told me to call you. You know, back when this started."

Henry smiled. "I know."

"You're a hard man to be separate from." Tony wasn't sure he understood that, but Henry seemed to.

"I know."

"With any luck, I'll close those three spots before they open, and you'll have a quiet night." Didn't cost any more to look on the bright side.

"Good luck, then."

Cool fingers rested for a moment against his cheek and, just for a moment, Tony longed for the days when he was the sidekick. "Yeah. You, too."

♦

"I can't believe you don't know how to pick locks," Leah muttered, one hand flat against the steel door, the other working the pair of straightened bobby pins back and forth.

"Why would I know how to pick locks?" Tony demanded quietly.

"Well, you're clearly a man with a past."

"And my entire B&E career consisted of heaving a brick through a grocery store window and then sprinting two blocks carrying a watermelon."

"Two blocks?"

"Ran into a cop. Big guy. Splat. Knocked me flat on my ass."

"Hmmm."

The noise may have been in response to his story or to the lock on the apartment door, Tony wasn't sure. He glanced down at the open laptop, silently ran over the words to the Notice Me Not one more time, and hoped he wouldn't have to use it. Not only because new magic was always an exciting crapshoot, but also because he needed to hoard as much personal energy as possible given what the immediate future was likely to hold. Although he'd topped the tank with a double bacon cheeseburger and large fries on the way to the first site, he had no idea how long that would last. He probably should have bought a second milkshake, just to be on the safe side.

Leah's dimples had gained them access to the highrise as an elderly gentleman was leaving. Ignoring Tony entirely, he'd held the door open and waved her through, making a rather explicit suggestion that Tony very much doubted he—or any man over sixty—would have the stamina to carry out, little blue pills or no little blue pills.

*Dude, if yours are lasting more than four hours, someone should check for rigor mortis.*

Finding the right floor had been simple. They'd taken the elevator up one floor at a time until Leah's gut had pinged. Finding the actual weak spot had been a little trickier, but they were about 90 percent certain it was inside apartment 708. Unfortunately, it seemed the tenants weren't.

Or fortunately, given how little he'd been looking forward to explaining what was going on.

"You'd think it'd be in apartment 666, wouldn't you?"

"Like I keep telling the vampire," Leah snorted. "Wrong kind of demons."

"Hey!"

"I'm picking a lock here, Tony. If someone hears us, the words vampire and demon will be the least of our problems."

She had a point.

He could hear at least one television—maybe two—and a couple of different kinds of music, but at just after nine on a Friday night, most of the people who lived on the seventh floor seemed to still be out. Or they were sitting silently in the dark behind their locked doors. Tony had no intention of ruling the latter out.

The hall smelled like sausages and a spice that bounced around the back of his nose like a pinecone, doing multiple points of damage with every landing.

"That's it." Leah rocked back off her knees and stood, reaching for the door handle. "But if there's a chain . . ."

There was. It was dangling down inside the door, unlocked.

"Nice to see they're taking home security so seriously."

"You come home drunk and the chain's a pain in the ass to get open," Tony explained as they moved inside and closed the door behind them. "And why do *you* know how to pick locks?"

"I hang around with a bad crowd in the fifties."

"You mean hung around."

"No. I mean that every century, I hang around with a bad crowd in the fifties. I like having a schedule." She didn't sound like she was kidding. Reaching back, she flipped on the lights. "Good lord."

Tony snapped his laptop closed and raised his left hand, palm out, rune in defensive position. "What!"

"It looks like your place: beige walls, cheap furniture, and an overpriced entertainment system."

"That was it? I thought you saw something dangerous." He started breathing again and his heart rate began to slow.

"No, just bland." Walking out into the living room, she shook her head. "And if it wasn't so bland, the similarities would be frightening."

"First of all," Tony muttered, sliding his laptop into the backpack, "that's a sheet on the window not a flag, and second, this has a separate bedroom."

"Which is probably beige."

"Hey, he has a set of RexTeck speakers—3-D sound effects and an awesome bass boost." Leah's silence pulled him around. "What? I've heard great things about them."

"Heard great things about demons taking over the city?"

Oh, sure. But she could take the time to discuss interior decorating. Half turned from examining the speakers, he paused. "The weak spot's right there." He could see the shimmer hanging just in front of the floor-to-ceiling shelves of DVDs. "But I thought there had to be something missing?"

Leah moved closer and examined the shelves. "He's missing the third *Aliens* movie."

"He's not missing much."

"And *Star Trek, the Motion Picture* although he has all the rest."

"Motionless picture," Tony grunted.

"Oh, my God, he's got a copy of *The Princess Diaries*. One and Two!"

"Maybe I should just close this up before he comes home and finds you dissing Julie Andrews." Setting the backpack on the floor, he wiped damp palms on his thighs and pointed a finger to start the first rune. A horrible groan came from the far wall. "What the hell was that?"

"The elevator."

"Is it . . . ?"

"Him?" Her gesture made it clear she meant the usual occupant of the apartment. "How should I know? Just wiz."

"Wiz?"

"Wiz!"

The first rune went through the wall of DVDs with no problem. So did the second. The third got stuck.

"Stuck?" Leah moved away from her listening post by

the door and glared at him. "It can't get stuck if you've done it right."

"It's right."

"Are you sure? Check the cheat sheet."

"I didn't bring it."

"Oh, for . . ." She came farther into the apartment, and hauled up her track jacket and the shirt under it. "Check the original, then."

Tony gave the rune another ineffective shove and dropped to his knees, thumbs hooked behind the waistband of Leah's track pants to pull them low enough to see the rune. Head cocked to one side, squinting a little, he moved so close he could feel the air between them warm.

The apartment door opened.

Tony glanced up to see a young man blinking at them blearily, keys dangling from one hand. When he finally managed to take in the tableau, he grinned and flashed a double thumbs-up. "Dude!"

"Ignore him," Leah snapped, tapping the tat with one scarlet-tipped finger. "Check the rune."

"Wait a minute." He was sounding less bleary by the word. "Why are you in my . . ."

"Got it."

". . . apartment?"

Tony stood as Leah turned, dimples flashing an offer no straight boy could refuse. He tugged the center of the glowing blue line farther out from the center of the pattern then pushed. With a sizzle and a faint smell of burning plastic, the rune slipped the rest of the way through.

One more.

Half finished with the fourth rune, refusing to be distracted by what was happening on the sofa, Tony felt the hair lift off his body—his entire body, not just the back of his neck. *Man, never going to get used to that.* Turning, he got an eyeful of Ryne Cyratane and had barely made the very short trip from appreciation to apprehension when a spray of red-and-purple sparks arced out into the room.

They were coming from the shelves of DVDs.

Crap!

Tony finished off the fourth rune so fast he nearly sprained his wrist. Left hand flat against it, he shoved it after the others.

And stumbled forward unable to lift his hand.

A heartbeat later, he was wrist-deep in the DVDs.

"Leah!"

"Busy."

"I don't care!" Yanking back only threatened to dislocate his elbow. "Le—!"

Hands closed on his shoulders, fingers digging in painfully tight. Next thing he knew he was flying. A short flight and a bad landing. Lying in a crumpled heap on the ruin of a cheap coffee table, Tony checked to make sure his arm had actually come with him.

"Time to go."

"Ow. Ow! OW!" Protests didn't seem to matter. Leah hauled him to his feet and hustled him toward the door. Seemed like everything worked. Not quite to the original specs, but he was up and moving. He snagged his laptop case as they passed. "What about . . . ?"

"He got a great memory and a broken coffee table," Leah snapped, dragging him out into the hall and shutting the door. "I think he came out even. Come on. If we get into the elevator before he gets his pants back on, he'll never know what we looked like."

"What if we have to wait for the elevator?"

They didn't.

She shoved him in, charged in after him, hit the button to close the door, hit the button for the first floor, and sagged against the stainless steel wall. "What did you do?"

"Me?"

"That spot wasn't close enough to blow like that."

"It was plenty close."

"Not close enough. I'd have felt it!"

They glared at each other for a moment.

"Okay." Tony flexed the fingers of his left hand. The scar felt hot. "Let me think about this for a minute."

"Don't strain anything," she muttered, adjusting her clothes.

"Nice. I think we hit a metaphysical overload."

"A what?"

"Between that weak spot being so close, you and your tat, me and my . . ." He waved the scar. ". . . power, then the whole distracting with sex invoking your Demonlord, I think we reached a point where things started to happen."

"That actually makes a certain logical sense."

"Yeah. Thanks." Sighing, he mirrored her position on the opposite wall. "And thanks for hauling me out."

She stopped buttoning her shirt long enough to shrug. "Even I can't get a guy to ignore you if you keep hanging around."

"Not then. When you pulled me out of the DVDs."

Dark brows rose.

"You didn't pull me out of the DVDs?"

"I didn't pull you out of the DVDs."

"Then who . . ." His gaze dropped to the tat, disappearing under white silk.

"No." Leah shook her head as the door opened and they moved quickly across the apartment building lobby. "First of all, he has no corporeal form on this plane and second, why would he help you? You're trying to stop him."

"Maybe I'm not."

"What? Stopping him?" She linked her arm through his and dropped to a sedate walk as they moved away from the apartment building and toward his car. He wanted to run, but he made himself match her pace. "Since I remain unslaughtered, I think you're stopping him fine so far."

"Not what I meant. Maybe . . ." The theme from *Darkest Night* cut him off. Sliding his cell phone out of the pocket on his backpack, Tony flipped it open and glanced at the screen. "It's Amy." Thumbing it on, he held it to his left ear.

"Tony! It's out! There were all kinds of wild lights, and then it was like a bomb went off! This tanker by Ballard Power Systems totally blew! I had to call 911 before I called you!"

Shit. Shit. Shit. "CB?"

"He's making sure everyone's out of the building. I'm heading to the Future Shop warehouse to do the same!

Tony, this thing was nasty looking. It took a swipe at me as it went by."

The metaphysical taint! He'd totally fucking forgotten it when he'd sent Amy out to face a demon.

To observe a harmless little weak spot.

Yeah. Big difference.

"Are you okay?"

"It knocked me on my ass, but it was like I wasn't worth its time. I'm . . ."

Call waiting beeped out the last few words.

He checked the screen. Lee. Who'd been shadow-held twice. And possessed. If Amy had a faint taint just from acting as an anchor while he spoke with a dead housemaid, Lee must have a big red metaphysical target painted on his chest. "Amy, tell me you're fine!"

"I'm fine!"

"Stay that way!" Left hand thumbed the link. Right hand unlocked the car. Stomach twisted as he fought the urge to puke. "Lee?"

"Tony! The tear ripped just after we got to it!"

"Are you hurt?"

"What? No! Jack emptied half a clip into the demon, and it lost interest in us."

*Lost interest in you.* "My fault."

"What the hell are you talking about?"

"I sent you out there."

"Hey, grown man here. I knew the risks."

He didn't know all the risks because Tony hadn't thought to tell him. *How could I have forgotten about . . . Hang on.* There were alarms going off in the background. "What's happening?"

"Our demonic buddy didn't so much explode out of the building as explode the building!"

"Fire?"

"No. Rubble. I thought there was smoke, but it was steam. Jack says there must've been a boiler plant in the basement. A few of the surrounding buildings took some collateral damage. The whole place looked empty; the lights were off and all, but Jack's checking for casualties. I called it in before I called you. Tony, we're going to have to stick around here. We won't make it back to the studio before . . ."

*Good, because there's going to be demons at the studio!* Where it looked like it would be just him and Leah and Henry, and that was how it should be. No normal people—however tainted—getting hurt. Circumstances had stepped up to the plate.

"Don't sweat it." Phone clamped between ear and shoulder, he slammed the car into gear and roared out of his parking space and down the empty street. "You're sure you're okay?"

"Yeah, we're good!"

We? Right. Jack. "Stay good."

"Can you handle . . . ?"

"Yes." Tony took his hand off the gearshift long enough to turn off the phone and toss it toward Leah. "Both of the other weak spots blew."

"Another metaphysical overload?" She didn't seem to be making fun of him.

"Probably the same one. They were timed to go off together, remember. When ours tried to open, theirs did, too, but only ours got closed. We're heading for the studio."

"I guessed." At the edge of his vision he could see her clutching the dashboard, knuckles white. "Is everyone okay?"

"Yeah. Things blew, but no one got hurt."

"No one we know."

"Hey, if you know how I can fucking save everyone, tell me now!"

"I was just . . ." Her protest trailed off as he ran a stop sign. "Sorry."

"We know where they're going, and if they do any more damage, it'll just be en route."

"And once they arrive."

"Yeah." A light rain speckled his windshield. He flicked on the wipers. Trashing the studio meant trashing a lot of expensive equipment.

"They won't be expecting a vampire." Her tone suggested she was trying to cheer him up. It almost worked.

"Who does?"

The damp roads were greasy. Speeding around a corner, the car started to fishtail. Tony stomped on the gas and fought to straighten out, cursing under his breath. Something crunched as he passed an old blue Buick Regal, but he convinced himself it was garbage on the road and not a door panel.

"You just . . ."

"No, I didn't."

"Why are you driving? Specifically, why are you driving instead of me?"

"Good question."

"Okay." After a moment, she said, "Ballard Power Systems is a hydrogen fuel development company."

"How do you know that?"

"I did some wire work around one of their tanks."

"Big boom?"

"Then, no. Tonight, very."

"Good thing CB and Amy were right there to call it in." It made him feel a little less guilty about sending them.

"Seems strange that there were two sites that led to explosions plus a . . . Jesus, Tony!" Her fingers locked back down on the dash. "What was that for?"

"Squirrel."

"You swerved into oncoming traffic to miss a squirrel?"

"He's not protected by a Demongate."

"You don't know that."

"Very funny." Not much farther. Napier Street would take them right to Boundary. "Two explosions plus a what?"

"An apartment building." He heard her settle back in the seat and wondered about her expression, but it didn't seem smart to take his eyes off the road.

"So? You said the weak spots happen anywhere something's missing."

"Well, yes, but if these three are deliberate, aimed for maximum shit disturbing, as it were, why an apartment building?"

"Population density. Lots of people screaming." Boundary traffic was annoyingly heavy. Tony slid between a truck and a hatchback and sped south toward the studio. "Furniture thrown off balconies. A distraught mother screaming that the monster has her baby."

"You had me at population density."

"I like to be thorough."

"Tony . . ."

And sometimes, just one word was enough. South of the studio, the streetlights were blowing out all along the east side of the road. *Bam. Bam. Bam.* Heading north. Shards of glass showered down, glittering in the passing headlights. Tires screamed. Horns blared. No accidents yet.

*No accidents in sight,* Tony amended, barely slowing to head into the studio parking lot. There was a whole lot of road in between the Fraser and CB Productions. The lot lights blew as he parked the car, and a shadow passed between him and the building.

A big shadow.

So much for beating it back to the studio and setting a trap.

♦

Feeding off Kevin Groves had been reflex. The reporter had walked into the soundstage, realized they were alone, and bared his throat, a desperate desire rolling off him like smoke.

Henry could have stopped himself, but the emotional need drew him as much as the blood. He expected the sharp intake of breath as his teeth met through soft skin. The look of peace as he swallowed a single mouthful of blood then drew back was less usual.

"Complete truth," Groves sighed. "No codicils, no compromises." Then his eyes snapped open, and he stared at Henry in rising panic. "It's just, you know, lies. I get so tired of them. Everyone lies. You don't. Even when you are. Lying. Please don't hurt me." He stared at the drop of blood rising from the puncture on his wrist and his eyes widened. "You really did it. Oh, God." Shaking fingers fumbled his PDA from his jacket's inside pocket. "I need to ask you some stuff."

"No."

The PDA fell from nerveless fingers, the plastic case cracking against the concrete floor. "Okay."

"Go to Raymond Dark's office and sit down. Stay there. Don't move unless you're avoiding a threat." He could hear glass shattering outside.

"What about . . ."

"Now."

Raymond Dark's office was safer, given that it was not directly under the power residue drawing the demons. Safer. Not safe.

Concrete block walls, no windows into the soundstage. The weakest point was the large door the carpenters used. It had, once again, been left unlocked.

Metal screamed.

Henry raised a speculative brow. Apparently tonight's demon would rather go through the door than open it.

Expected, the shower of cherries was no less annoying.

♦

"Son of a fucking bitch!"

The big sliding door had been pulled half off its track, the steel scored in three parallel lines. CB was going to be pissed.

Something howled. A cherry bounced out into the parking lot.

Tony dropped his laptop case by the wall and took a deep, steadying breath. "Get in there and see if it's marked for you. If not, help Henry."

"And if it is?"

"It won't be. Maximum mayhem, remember? There's a lot less mayhem if it heads right for the person standing beside the guy kicking demon ass back home."

"That was actually very convincing."

He glanced up to see her staring speculatively down at him. "Thank you. Now haul ass." Without waiting for a response, he turned his attention back to the laptop, clutched the pull thing on his fly—the spell needed a metal ground—and recited the words of the Notice Me Not.

♦

This demon was no tentacled monstrosity. It walked on two legs like a man and had a caricature of a man's face—two eyes, one nose, and a mouth. Except the eyes were orange lid to lid, the nose nearly invisible under a plate of its chitinous body armor, and the mouth lipless, with more of the body armor growing up into gleaming tusks. The armor changed color to match its surroundings, and it was now fading down from night-sky black to concrete gray. Henry got a close look at one of the arm plates as it knocked him across the soundstage to slam into the outside wall. When it withdrew the arm, it dangled a length of yellow nylon rope from one thick wrist.

It was fast but no faster than Henry.

Strong, but no stronger.

*Four arms, however, that's a bit of a problem.* This time, at least, he managed to keep hold of the rope. He rolled back under a slash that gouged the floor and managed to get a loop of rope around one leg as it lifted to stomp him. Ducked. Whirled.

"Nightwalker!"

Threw the coil of rope over the left arms to the Demongate.

She caught it. Whipped it back along the floor.

Henry kicked at the side of the demon's knee. Heard chitin crack. Scooped up the rope as he took a blow hard enough to crack even his ribs. He crashed to the floor and thought just for a moment he heard his father's voice bellowing at him to get up. His father had never approved of him being unhorsed. Snarling, Henry caught the next descending arm and threw himself back still holding it, trapping it under another loop of the rope.

Too close!

One of the lower tusks raked his shoulder, ripping through shirt and skin and filling the room with the rich scent of his own blood. At first he thought the flash of light was based in pain, but then he saw the rune take shape.

The demon veered away from the lines of blue fire, giving the Demongate a chance to slam it in the side of the head with what looked like a microphone stand.

Closing three hands around one end of the metal pole, the demon yanked it from her hands, raising it over its head to bring it down in a killing blow. At the apex of its backswing, the microphone stand went flying from its grip to land with a clatter behind one of the false walls.

"You must hate it that your master's spell protects her even from you," Henry growled and ripped a plate of chitin from its shoulder.

It shrieked.

A second rune hung in the air.

He couldn't see Tony although it was obvious that Tony was there. Not obvious to the demon, thank God. It continued to keep clear of the runes but made no attempt to find the wizard drawing them.

◆

Henry was hurt.

Leah wasn't. The world rearranged itself so that that demon kept missing her. The resulting contortions would have tied a human spine in knots. Demons were more flexible.

Lots more flexible, Tony realized as, chitin plates creaking, the demon curled around limbs wrapped in rope and charged toward Henry from a completely unexpected angle.

*Concentrate on the rune!*

He'd already screwed the third rune up once tonight. He couldn't afford to do it again. More specifically, Henry couldn't afford for him to do it again.

Three runes.

His head pounded as he began the fourth, keeping it next to the third as he finished it. If he drew the final rune in its proper place, the demon might realize his intent before he finished and go after him instead of Leah and Henry. The demon wouldn't be able to see him, not if the Notice Me Not was still working, but any kind of a charge in his direction would take it out from between the runes.

With any luck, his ability to move energy around was unique enough it would be unexpected. After all, how many wizards got trapped in haunted houses redolent with the waxy buildup of evil and ended up symbolically branding themselves in order to save the day? Well, the rune on his palm was symbolic; the branding part had been agonizingly real.

Tony'd just sketched in the final swooping crosspiece when the door between the offices and the soundstage bounced off the wall of Raymond Dark's sanctuary and crashed to the floor.

The wall swayed but stayed up.

It had been a soundproof door. Big, and thick, and heavy, it used to be attached to the wall with large metal hinges. The demon that had thrown it was mostly two enormous arms and the supporting torso. No head to speak of but just under where logic insisted the lower edges of its ribs should be—had logic not decided discretion was the better part of valor and buggered off for coffee—was a huge fang-filled mouth. There were no runes or glyphs or Post-it notes allowing it to take out Leah.

Jack and Lee's demon.

*It had fucking well b*etter *be Jack and Lee's demon!* Because if it wasn't, they'd missed a hole, and if they'd missed one, then they could have missed a dozen and a dozen extra demons were twelve more than Tony wanted to deal with.

He finished the final rune but didn't move it into place, waiting until the second demon joined the first under the gate.

It stood, weight forward on its knuckles, and watched the fight. Maybe it sensed the trap—hardly surprising with three blue patterns of glowing energy suspended in the air and nothing distracting it. Maybe it was waiting until the first demon took the edge off a common enemy. Maybe demons liked to see other demons get the chitin kicked off them. Whatever the reason, the gate wasn't enough to draw it between the runes.

What could he add as enticement?

What did demons want?

Foot on knee, on elbow, on shoulder—Leah leaped for the light grid, kicking the demon hard in the face. It fell back, she dangled, and Tony called her jacket and shirt into his hand.

Fabric tore, buttons bounced off demon, vampire, and concrete.

Most of the Demongate was exposed between track pants and white lace bra.

The oldest operating spell in the world. Leah'd said it was what had drawn the Demonic Convergence, so demons were obviously interested in it even when they hadn't been marked to destroy her. Since they hadn't been marked, Leah was half dressed but still completely safe, protected by the spell.

From the look on Leah's face, if this didn't save the day, demons would be a minor problem as far as Tony, personally, was concerned.

The second demon roared and charged forward.

Tossing the handful of white silk aside, Tony shouted out the words for the clean cantrip.

Scrubbing bubbles covered the floor of the soundstage, knee-deep.

The second demon started to slide, threw out a massive hand to stop itself, overbalanced and, other arm flailing, slammed into the first demon. Chiton cracked. They both went down.

Tony threw the fourth rune into place.

Leah dropped onto a spotlessly clean circle of floor empty of demons and bubbles both, landing in a deep crouch as her knees took up the shock of the landing. Henry straightened, left arm held tightly against his side, blood soaking through the shoulder of his cream-colored sweater. The empty loops of yellow nylon rope gleamed, cleaner than they'd ever been.

Slipping and sliding through the scrubbing bubbles, picking up speed once he hit the dry concrete, Tony raced to Henry's side. This was where he'd been dragged into the story, back in Toronto after another demon attack had left Henry nearly dead. He had his jacket off before he stopped moving.

Henry's gaze slid past him. "Tony?"

Crap. The Notice Me Not.

"Where are you, you little shit! How dare you use me as

bait!" Leah stomped across the soundstage toward the place the fourth rune had been, kicking bubbles out of the way.

How did he turn this thing off?

"Quit screwing around, Tony. Turn the spell off."

He waggled the tab on his fly. Nothing. "I don't know how."

Henry cocked his head.

Leah threw up her hands. "I bet you don't know how to turn it off, do you? I'm telling you, square pegs round holes and if I ever get my hands on this Arra person, I'm going to kick her ass."

"He's here," Henry murmured, his eyes darkening.

"No shit, Nightwalker. I think the overactive cleaning supplies are a dead giveaway."

This time when Henry called him, there was no question, no doubt that Tony would answer. He said, "Tony."

Tony heard, *"Mine."* and stepped forward to meet the darkness in Henry's eyes.

They stood for a moment, barely an arm's length apart, Tony breathing heavily, listening to the song of his blood responding to the call. When Henry made no move to close the distance between them, he swallowed and said, "You're hurt."

Henry glanced at the wound on his shoulder. "So it seems." And back at Tony. "I've been hurt worse."

"Not because of me."

"This wasn't your fault."

"You have to feed." Tony watched the Hunger rise, and offered his wrist. Ignored the way his hand was trembling.

To his surprise, Henry shook his head and his eyes lightened. Not completely, but it was clear he'd locked the Hunger down. His good arm reached for Tony, pulled him close. Cool fingers clasped the back of his neck, drew his head down onto a broad shoulder. That Tony was a good two inches taller didn't seem to matter. "We can't go back to the way we were."

"I don't want to go back." But he did. Right now, right at this moment, right after sending two very large demons back to their hell, right after stopping a third, right after sending friends out into danger, he wanted nothing more than to go back to when Henry made the decisions. When life went on around him without him having to be so damned involved. "You need blood."

"Yes."

He drew in a deep breath and let it out slowly. "But not from me."

Fingertips caressed the bite on his throat that was still only partially healed. "It's too soon. And the wrong time."

They meant the same thing. Except they didn't.

The wizard in charge didn't get to lie down and have it done to him, no matter what the current value of *it*.

"Will you Hunt?"

"No."

"Amy'll be back later tonight." Is this how Vicki had felt? Like she was pimping for Henry? "She'd be thrilled." She'd be impossible to live with, but since he only had to work with her, he thought he might survive.

"Kevin Gross is in Raymond Dark's office."

"Ah." Tony stepped back, Henry's hand falling away. "Is he . . . you know, okay with it?"

Henry smiled, his teeth very white. "He likes that I tell him the truth."

"Yeah? I kind of preferred it when you lied."

"No." Again fingertips touched the bite on his throat. "You didn't."

Tony turned before he had to watch Henry walk into the office set. He drew in a long breath, let it out slowly, and noticed Leah staring at him as she shrugged into her shirt.

"I'm fine." Tying the front tails into a knot, she yanked it tight. "Thanks for asking."

"You were protected."

"That didn't give you the right to use me as bait."

"I know. I'm sorry."

The apology seemed to take her by surprise. "Oh. Okay, then. And it worked—so good idea."

"Thank you."

"Just a thought, you might want to avoid that invisible wizard thing until you learn how to turn it off."

Had Henry not been here, how long would he have remained unnoticed? "I'm planning on it."

"Good. So, about these bubbles . . ."

The remaining bubbles, those that had been outside the runes, were continuing to clean, moving out and over the soundstage.

"Just ignore them. Eventually, they'll dry out and pop."

"Leaving a sticky magic residue?"

"How do you make that sound so smutty?"

"Practice." She grinned and shrugged back into her track jacket, ignoring the ruined zipper. "Now what?"

"Now I need a confab with Ryne Cyratane."

"A what?"

Tony squared his shoulders and looked as resolute as a man could with a clump of scrubbing bubbles halfway up his leg. "We need to talk."

# Twelve

"ALL RIGHT, LET'S ASSUME, just for interest's sake, that you haven't completely lost your mind." Finger combing hair disheveled by the fight, Leah crossed over to the chaise lounge, waited until a wave of scrubbing bubbles finished cleaning the last bit of grimy upholstery, and sat, staring up at Tony as though his lost mind was a forgone conclusion. "Why do you want to talk to Ryne Cyratane?"

"Dealing with two demons at once almost got our collective butts kicked. I'm still finding it a little hard to believe that the slapstick defense actually worked."

"You're suggesting that we're not in a Three Stooges movie?"

He snorted, and ran a hand back up through his hair. "Look, even if I deal with most of the weak spots before they open—and that's doubtful because they're not all going to be in easy-to-access places—we're still screwed. Three demons would have won that fight, and if they win the fight, they'll open your gate."

"What about the rest of the troops?"

"We don't have troops!"

"Okay, fine. Keep them out of it." Leah rolled her eyes. "You're still missing the obvious solution."

"Okay?"

"I get on a plane as soon as possible and get the hell away from here. Ryne Cyratane has committed his power to bringing the demons through at *those* points in *this* place. He's not going to be able to follow me."

Tony frowned. That seemed so reasonable he automatically suspected it. "So he'll break off the attack?"

"Are you listening to me? I just said he's committed his power."

"So he won't break off the attack?"

Her smile was scathing. "As you kids today say: duh."

"Then that's only a solution for you. And only a temporary one. He'll know where you are because of the gate, right? Then as long as the Demonic Convergence is still going on," Tony continued when she nodded, "he'll redirect things and just shove the next demons through there. Where you'll face them alone. Without the wizard. Because I'll probably die when the studio gets swarmed. And then you'll be dead," he elaborated when she didn't look convinced, "just like you would have been with that first demon if I hadn't been there."

She crossed her legs and scowled at the toe of her shoe. "You don't know that."

"Yeah, I do. So, your obvious solution is crap. The only way we're all going to survive this is by staying together and stopping that swarm."

"By talking to the Demonlord who's sending it?"

"I don't think it's him."

Brows drawn in, she peered up at him. "Did you get hit on the head?"

"No!" He bent to pick up the rope just to give his hands something to do. The scrubbing bubbles had left it not only clean but smelling faintly of lemons and free of static cling. "Jack asked me the same question yesterday," he muttered, feeling slightly picked on.

"It's a reasonable assumption when you're saying things like you don't think the demon who created the gate is trying to reopen the gate by taking out the person he created the gate on that only he'd know about," she snapped.

"Why?"

"What?"

Holding one end of the rope in his left hand, Tony began to coil it between hand and elbow. "Why would Ryne Cyratane be the only who knows about you? There's clearly more than one demon down there. Out there. Wherever the hell their hell is. Odds are good they talk to each other. Get together Friday nights, drink a little demonic beer, play a little demonic poker, talk about gates they've got set up to get back into a world where the inhabitants are easy to rend and will worship you in order to keep from being rended."

"Demonic beer?" Leah tossed her hair back over her shoulder. "Please."

"Stop fixating on the details. The theory is sound and those other Demonlords have also had thirty-five hundred years to make plans about how they'll use the gate yours left behind. And besides . . ."

*The Demonlord didn't look happy, that was for sure. He looked frustrated. Like he knew the thing he was looking for was right there, right in front of him, but he couldn't find it.*

". . . he wants to talk to me."

"He wants to feast on your steaming entrails."

"Maybe."

"You're not his type. Trust me."

"Look, he's been appearing when these attacks are going on, even when you're not aroused. The first time, he looked angry, and I figured it was his motivation showing and he was angry at not getting back here to the worship and the slaughter. Or maybe it was the too-close-to-water thing. Who knew? Then, after it became obvious to anyone with half a brain that there was a wizard involved, he showed up looking for me. But I don't react to you, so he couldn't find me and that was making him frustrated. Then I had a dream about him . . ."

"Oh, that's a good reason for me to stick around. You had a dream."

Tony ignored her, both hands working the rope. "He was wearing the same expression L . . . other people do when I'm obviously not getting their message."

Leah snorted. "Good luck with that since he hasn't decided what message he's sending."

"What? Wait, you're not talking about Ryne Cyratane there, are you?" No. She wasn't. "You think we could deal with one communication problem at a time?"

"He's conflicted."

"I got that," Tony sighed, tying off the coil. "Now could we . . ."

"You should kick his feet out from under him and beat him to the floor."

"Is that what you did?"

Dimples flashed. "I never have to work that hard."

That answered that question. Lee wasn't just using the women as a blind; he liked women, or he wouldn't have fallen for the primal "do me, baby" Leah was offering. Of course, liking women didn't necessarily preclude liking men. Take Henry, for example. He was about as enthusiastically nondiscriminating as they came.

Not that Lee had ever been enthusiastic.

Except that once.

With him, anyway.

He could have been enthusiastic with any number of other men for all Tony knew and was just being carefully closeted at work. Or all the metaphysical shit Lee'd been through in the last six months combined with Tony's not so secret attraction had seriously fucked with his head.

*Yeah. Let's not forget option B.*

*Or that a whole herd of demons on the way is more important than your pathetic lack of a love life.*

He leaned the coil of rope against the far wall of the set where it would be out of the way but still convenient for immobilizing creatures from hell and turned to face the immortal Demongate. "Ryne Cyratane has something to say to me, and I need to hear it."

The immortal Demongate snorted again. "Well, unless you have a really good calling plan, you're out of luck, aren't you?"

"You said you'd been in contact with him. That you meditate . . ."

"It's a postcoital meditation, Tony, and one thing I'm sure of is that since you and I have no coital in our future, there's going to be no post. Oh, wait, I have an idea. You, me, and Lee. Might be just the thing to break the ice." Grinning, she leaned back on her hands and crossed her legs. "You're thinking about it."

He was.

But then he was a guy and he wasn't dead, so that was pretty much a gimme. Actually, the evidence suggested a growing number of guys didn't let being dead stop them.

"I'm not kidding about this." Tony tried to look like he wasn't kidding. "So unless you know another way to contact him . . ."

"You could always try switching your long distance service and then having a fast wank."

"Leah."

She stared at him for a long moment. "You're serious," she said in amazement, sitting up straight.

"Completely. We'll have to use Henry as a conduit between us."

"Henry? Well," she admittedly slowly, one hand disappearing under the knot in her shirt, "that'll definitely get his attention."

"Yeah." Tony touched his throat, the skin still puckered under his fingertips.

Leah still didn't look entirely convinced when she raised her head and locked her gaze with his. "Do you even know *how* to meditate?"

"I don't think I'll have to. I think your Demonlord wants to talk to me badly enough that as soon as he has a way to grab onto me, he'll make the connection. And with any luck, he'll want to talk to me more than he'll want to destroy Henry for messing with you."

"Do you think Henry will go along with this?"

"Along with what?"

Tony turned as Leah answered. "A threesome to save the world."

Red-gold brows rose briefly and dipped again when he realized that no one was kidding. "Whose idea is that?"

"Not mine," Leah smirked. "Guy rips your clothes off, and suddenly he wants to get hinky."

The hazel eyes darkened just a little as he turned a disbelieving gaze on Tony. "I can't wait for the explanation."

♥

"Because your place is a dump, Henry doesn't trust me enough to let me into his sanctuary, and I have a king-size bed."

"No surprise," Tony grunted.

Leah leaned over CB's desk to poke him in the chest. Hard. "I can still get on that plane."

He waved her quiet as Amy finally answered her phone.

"Tony!" He could hear sirens and angry shouting in the background. "There was like this massive accident by the stadium!"

"Arc you all right?"

"Yeah, we're good, but there's no way we can get by. Boundary's just this total mass of twisted metal and emergency vehicles—fire, police, ambulance. We can't even go around 'cause we're in the middle of the block. CB's a little annoyed."

That explained the angry shouting. "Where is he?"

"Right in the thick of things. I think he's trying to get the road cleared."

"When he stops shouting, tell him that we took out the two demons and the soundstage has never looked cleaner."

"Cleaner?"

"Long story." The scrubbing bubbles had petered out just past Raymond Dark's coffin. "Downside, the big steel door got bent, the soundstage door is now lying on the floor of Raymond Dark's office, and the front door got shattered. If you guys can't make it back . . ."

"We can't friggin' move!"

"Okay, then can you call the security guy and have him come around? Henry and Leah and I have something we have to do."

"Something kinky?"

His jaw dropped. *Not a lucky guess,* he reminded himself picking it up. *Just a smart-ass Amyism.*

"Oh, my God! Is it something kinky?"

Shit. He'd paused too long. "No, it isn't! It's something demonic."

"Demonic doesn't preclude kinky."

"You're right," Tony told her, hoping that the whole best defense is a good offense thing wasn't just blowing air. "It *is* something kinky and will likely involve a pair of handcuffs and a couple of liters of maple syrup."

Her snort came through loud and clear. "What, is Jack playing, too? Fine, don't tell me, and the number for the security company is on the list by Rachel's phone. Call them yourself. I'll find a phone booth and look up twenty-four-hour glass companies. Zev's gonna be so pissed he missed this."

"In what universe?"

"You know he likes to be around when things are happening."

"So we'll try not to have things happen on the Sabbath from now on."

"It's good to have a plan. Oops, I gotta go; CB just assaulted a taxi."

"A taxi driver?" Leah asked when Tony repeated the high points of the conversation.

He shook his head as he thumbed in the number for Lee's phone. "Probably not."

Lee answered partway through the second ring. "Tony? Are you all right?"

"Henry took a couple of hits, but Leah and I are fine and the demons are gone. You?"

"We're still at the site. They're digging for a custodian buried in the rubble and so far they've only found part of him. Jack's dealing with the emergency crews, but I can get a cab back to the studio if you need me."

For sex to save the world.

"Tony?"

"Sorry. Got distracted for a minute. Um, Leah and Henry and I just have some loose ends to tie up . . ." He turned his back on Leah's obscene gesture. ". . . before I start dealing with all those other weak spots, so when you want to leave there, you guys can call it a night."

"You sure?"

Sex to save the world. The perfect excuse.

"Yeah. This is wizard work now, so unless Harry Potter and Gandalf drop by to help out, I'm on my own for this next part."

"Be careful, then."

"You, too."

"So I'll see you Monday unless the world ends or something."

"Yeah, or something."

"You'll call me if I can help?"

"Sure."

"Tony."

"I promise."

"You're lying."

"I'm not." If anything came up he thought an actor in the highest-rated vampire detective show on syndicated television could handle, he'd call Lee first.

"Well, thanks for letting me help tonight . . ."

*Even if it wasn't my choice.*

". . . even if it wasn't your choice."

Okay. That was a little scary. "No problem."

"I mean it."

"I know."

He listened to Lee breathing for a moment, enjoying the sound.

"I uh, think my battery's dying. I've got to go."

"Right." And thank God for dying batteries, Tony thought, hanging up. So much more believable than "there's someone at the door" or "my appendix just ruptured." He looked up to see Leah watching him, wearing a frankly speculative expression. "Life was a lot easier when I thought he was completely straight," he sighed, tossing plausible deniability into the toilet.

"If there's one thing I've learned in thirty-five hundred years," Leah told him as they crossed the office, "it's that almost no one is completely anything. We're in the minority."

"That doesn't change the fact that life was easier when I thought he was completely straight."

"Can't handle the thought of reality intruding on your fantasy life?"

"Something like that."

"Listen, if Harry Potter and Gandalf do drop by, we're going to need a bigger bed."

Tony ignored her. The moment the words had left his mouth, he figured that comment was going to come back and bite him on the ass and, all things considered, that was barely a nibble. "There's at least one dead out by Simon Fraser," he told Henry as they exited into the outer office. "And Amy says there's a shitload of injuries in a pileup on Boundary by the stadium."

"We got lucky." Henry dumped a dustpan of broken glass into the garbage and straightened. "The residual power of the gate is keeping the death toll down by drawing them directly here where they can be immediately dealt with, and your forcing both weak points to blow open tonight made sure the explosions occurred when there was almost no one at either site. Things could have been a lot worse."

"You had to feed off Kevin Groves."

"I've fed off worse."

"He's a tabloid reporter," Tony muttered as he picked up Rachel's phone to call the security company, absolutely not thinking of what else Henry did when he fed. "If there's worse, I don't want to know."

Tony put down his toothbrush and stared into the mirror in Leah's guest bathroom. Quick shower to get the higher bits the scrubbing bubbles missed. Debris from the recent half dozen soft tacos—gone. Was there anything else he should do to prepare?

"Tony! Sunrise is at 6:52—pick up the pace."

Apparently not.

Leah and Henry were in the bed when he got to the bedroom, carefully not touching, their respective powers dialed way back.

"Making sure there's no premature communication?" he asked, turning to stroke glyphs into the doorjamb with one toothpaste-covered finger.

"Practicing safe context," Leah corrected. "What are you doing?"

"Warding the room."

"With toothpaste?"

"You didn't have any cough syrup." With any luck, cavity protection plus whitening and mouthwash would work as well. "This may be dangerous."

"This? Using a vampire as a conduit to contact a Demonlord? Can't imagine why you'd think so, especially considering that the last time it almost happened you stopped it with your throat." She folded her arms under the swell of her breasts. "Tell me again why I'm going along with this?"

"Because you haven't said no to sex in thirty-five hundred years."

One dimple flickered. "Well, it's not a good reason, but it's a reason."

"And you don't want to die."

"That's a good reason."

Wiping the remains of the toothpaste on the towel wrapped around his waist, he set the tube down on the edge of the dresser and approached the bed. "Henry . . ."

A pale hand rose to cut him off. "If you hadn't convinced me, I wouldn't be here."

"Sure." He'd been hoping for some kind of reassurance that this was the right thing to do. That attempting to contact Ryne Cyratane was the right decision. It seemed like a naked vampire was as much reassurance as he was going to get.

Tony half expected commentary as he dropped the towel,

but either Henry's presence or what they were about to attempt—metaphysically—kept Leah silent. He slipped into the bed on Henry's side as Henry shuffled over and let out a breath he hadn't realized he was holding. "Okay. Henry has to be in contact with both Leah and me when this goes down, so I think we need to . . ."

"Relax."

"What?"

Leah rolled onto her side and up on one elbow. "You need to relax," she said, sliding her upper hand along Henry's chest. "You're not suddenly directing an X-rated episode of *Darkest Night,* so let's just forget about hitting our marks, shall we? We're taking part in an ancient sacrament. With a twist." She frowned. "And a small chance of death and dismemberment. You just lie back," she continued before he could respond, "and think about whatever you have to. Leave this up to me; I used to do it professionally."

Her superior tone brought him up to mirror her position. "You're not the only one with a past."

"In this bed? I wouldn't assume I was."

She still sounded patronizing. "Just remember, I know things you don't."

"About what?"

Tony slid his hand under the sheets. Henry gasped. "About him."

♥

Henry had not initially gone along with the idea of contacting the Demonlord. Or rather, he'd agreed with the idea but not the method suggested. Sex with Leah, given what they were, could never be anything but a power struggle, and even the possibility of sex had resulted in a loss of control he didn't want to remember. Couldn't help but remember given that his Hunger still marked Tony's throat.

*"That won't happen this time because you've just fought a demon and that has to have taken some kind of physical edge off and, besides, I'll be plugged in from the beginning. When the power starts*

*to rise—metaphysically speaking—I'll grab it and ride it to Ryne Cyratane."*

*"It's a dumb idea,"* Leah had put in, adding, *"but it might work."*

Tony ignored her, concentrating on Henry. *"There won't be a risk of you biting Leah and pissing her Demonlord off—wham bam feedback blows you into little pieces—because I'll be there for any tooth action, and because you've been topped up recently, there's no chance of you getting carried away."*

Henry had stared at the younger man for a long moment, unable to look away from the visible part of the damage he'd already done. *"You'd trust me that much?"*

*"Jesus, Henry, what kind of a question is that? I've trusted you with my life from the moment we met. I've always known what you are."*

That, in the end, was what had brought Henry to this place, to this bed.

He had intended to take a more active role, but perhaps between a wizard and an immortal Demongate it was safest to lie back and be used. To not be drawn into competition. He breathed in the warm, rich scent of their arousal mixed with his own and let the Hunger rise just enough to let them know they used him at his pleasure, that he had power of his own.

Tony knew how to keep himself separate from what his body was involved in—he couldn't have survived the streets if he hadn't—but separate wouldn't get Ryne Cyratane's attention. He had to be as much a part of what was going on as Leah and Henry. This was not, as it turned out, particularly difficult. Familiar skin, familiar hands, familiar need got him over the small hurdle of girly bits doing their thing off to one side and in a very short time, he was fighting to remember that he couldn't be drawn into the maelstrom—it had to be drawn into him.

Then Leah cried out.

Henry's teeth closed through a fold of his skin.

As he arced up off the bed, he could feel a fourth presence

and opening himself up to the surging currents of power, he raced to meet it.

It was a lot like absorbing the fire he'd set in Leah's curtains.

Except this fire burned.

His heart pounded, he couldn't catch his breath, and bits of his life were passing before his eyes. No. Wait. That wasn't his life. He wasn't double-jointed. And then he was back in the white and two very large, hot hands were wrapped around his biceps and lifting him into the air.

Someone was talking. Deep rumbling. Shades of Barry White.

Tony struggled to focus and finally managed to hear words.

"What place is this, Wizard?"

Good question. It took him a moment to figure out how his mouth worked, but he finally managed to form the words, "Neutral ground."

It was a guess, but it seemed to be enough of an answer since the hands released him and he found himself sprawling at the feet of Ryne Cyratane.

The view from down there was pretty damned amazing.

"You risked much to speak with me, Wizard."

"Did I?" That was news. Did he want to know what he'd risked? No, he decided, getting carefully to his feet. "You wanted to talk to me, big guy. I made it happen. Say what you have to so I can go put on some pants."

The Demonlord's lip curled, exposing long ivory-colored teeth. Recognizing one of Henry's expressions, Tony realized Ryne Cyratane had just hung out a sign saying *Want to be eaten? Ask me how.* "You speak bravado out of fear."

"Duh." Had he come into this cold, without all those years of Henry behind him, he'd be a gibbering wreck.

"You desire me."

That was too obvious to require a response. Tony had no idea where the energy was coming from, considering the rocket ride he'd taken to get here as well as the mentioned and admitted fear.

"You have been protecting my handmaiden from the attacks of an Arjh Lord."

"No, she's been attacked by . . . Hang on." He could feel his brain begin to sluggishly work. "What's an Arjh Lord?"

"I am an Arjh Lord. Sye Mckaseeh is another." The first statement was very nearly a roar. The second merely a comment.

"Right." They'd hardly call themselves demons. And, apparently, the new one was a Scot. Which brought up another point. "Why are you speaking English?"

Massive arms crossed over a hairless chest. "I am speaking what you are hearing."

"Sure. Okay." That made as much sense as most things in his life these days and was, at least, useful. Absently scratching at his left palm, Tony backed up a few steps, hoping a little distance would help clear his head. "Look, why don't I tell you what I think is going down, and you can yay or nay the synopsis?"

Dark brows drew in. "I am unaware of your meaning."

"Just listen." He laid it all out. An Arjh Lord directing the Demonic Convergence to create specific weak spots he could use to push through his own minions, marking them so they could kill Leah, thus opening the gate and allowing the Arjh Lord to enter their world and try to take it over.

Minions needed explaining, and Tony downplayed just how easy that takeover would be. No point in giving the big guy ideas.

When he finished talking, Ryne Cyratane nodded. "It is as you say; Sye Mckaseeh is warping what you call the Convergence to her own place."

"Sye Mckaseeh is a wo . . . is female?"

"Yes. And a mighty warrior among the Arjh Lords."

"Great. A mighty warrior." Tony cleared his throat. "Look, you wanted to talk to me, what did you want to say?"

"I wished to give you, as the wizard protecting my handmaiden, the information you already possess. Your people have grown wiser since last I walked your world." He didn't sound like he approved.

"Probably not wiser, we're just more used to processing information. But if that's all you wanted, let's move on to what

I want . . . need." The Arjh Lord's expression suggested Tony's needs were so low on his list of priorities they were essentially nonexistent. Time to evoke vested self-interest. "I need your help, or your handmaiden is going to buy it—die, she'll die—and you'll lose all that energy she keeps sending you, not to mention any chance you might have of using the gate yourself sometime in the future. You know, in case she finally gets depressed enough to . . ." He drew a finger across his throat.

The gesture didn't need explaining. "Go on."

"Sye Mckaseeh is creating twenty-seven weak spots between your world and mine." He'd finally taken a moment to actually count them. "Apparently three nines are a mystic number or something, but that's not the point. Very shortly we'll be ass-deep in arjh and the odds are good one of them will get through to your handmaiden and kill her to open the gate."

"You are a wizard; you hold the eternal cosmos in your hand. Strengthen the weakness before it tears. With power drawn to so many places, it will take time before the arjh are through."

"Not enough time. My world is a complicated place, and I don't think I'll be able to get to all the weak spots before they rip open. I need you—your handmaiden needs you—to slow things down on this end. The arjh end. We need you to interfere with Sye Mckaseeh's plan."

"No. I am not one who battles with the other lords for power."

Tony blinked as that sank in. "You're kidding me. You're a lover, not a fighter?"

"As I understand your use of the language, yes. And there is disunity between Sye Mckaseeh and I."

"Disunity?"

The Arjh Lord shrugged. "Once there was unity. Now there is not."

Standing on that featureless white plane, Tony had a sudden strong desire for a wall, so he could bang his head against it. "She was your girlfriend and you guys broke up and that's how she knows about the Demongate and that's why she's trying to get it open, to screw you." Same old story, add a truck and a dog and they could set it to country music.

Ryne Cyratane shrugged again. "Her arjh watch for me. I could not get close to her should I desire it."

"Hey, you fighting your way through a few of her arjh would be a distraction, at least. We could use that."

"No."

"Yeah, we could."

"No, I will not fight."

"Yeah, but this isn't a power struggle with another lord," Tony reminded him. "You'll just be smacking around a few arjh."

"I do not fight."

"Then what the hell are those horns for?"

"They are a symbol."

Oh, that was useful. Not. "Fucking great. You're nothing but Bambi's dad."

Ryne Cyratane may not have understood the reference, but he definitely understood the tone.

Actually, Tony figured as he was once again lifted off his feet, it was probably a good thing the reference sailed right on over. "I'm sorry, okay! I'm just worried about your handmaiden!" He could see himself reflected in the onyx eyes—which was more than a little disconcerting since the hands holding him did not appear in the reflection.

"I do not wish my handmaiden to die." This close, the Arjh Lord's teeth were as out of proportion as certain other parts of his anatomy—only not in a good way.

"Bonus, because she doesn't *want* to die."

"But neither will I put myself in danger."

"Not even for her?"

This new expression was not one of Henry's. Tony'd last seen it on Mason's face when CB had set up an interview with one of the science fiction media magazines. The expression of the innately selfish forced to acknowledge they had responsibilities they didn't much like.

"If Sye Mckaseeh is indeed attempting to control so many

entries to your world, she will not be able to watch all of her lesser arjh," Ryne Cyratane admitted reluctantly after a moment. "It seems her continuing defeat at your puny hands has caused her to rage against you and to overextend." He smiled but, whether at Sye Mckaseeh overextending or at her continuing defeat, Tony wasn't sure. "While she is distracted by the great effort she makes, I will mark one of her waiting arjh with my sigil so that when it breaks through to your world, it will fight at your side and rend the others of its kind." Rend was pronounced with enough relish to supply an infinite number of hot dog carts.

"If you could mark one of her arjh," Tony pointed out, "you could kill it. And if you could kill one . . ."

"Death of her arjh, she would most definitely notice."

"Okay, back to your original plan." Tony's lower arms were going numb, but the Arjh Lord didn't seem to be tiring. "Problem is, I'm closing as many of these things as I can before they open. What if I close the weak spot you've coopted?"

"Do not."

Yeah. That was helpful.

"If my handmaiden, my priestess, my love is with you, she will know which weakness I use as mine."

Okay, that actually *was* helpful.

"Tell the Nightwalker I will allow his interference with what is mine this one time and this one time only. If you desire to speak with me again, find another way. Now go."

Tony bounced a little as he hit the ground. Bounced a little higher. The white began to darken. Higher still. Fighting a rush of nausea, he closed his eyes.

"Tony?"

Opened them to find Henry bending over him. "Bucket," he gasped, rolling for the edge of the bed. It was a good thing the wicker garbage container had a plastic bag in it because there wasn't time to forage any farther out.

A familiar growl. "Your arms are bleeding."

"Not . . . now!" His blood was Henry's. He got that. Given that no one else had ever wanted it, that usually wasn't a problem. At the moment he was a little too busy to deal with vampire issues.

He started shaking just before he finished vomiting and barely made it to the bathroom in time to empty the rest of his digestive tract. Things got a little messy anyway, and he closed the door on the scrubbing bubbles bleaching the color out of Leah's towels.

The bedroom was empty when he got back, his clothes folded neatly on the end of the bed. Reaching for his jeans, he caught sight of his reflection in the full-length mirror and paused. Purple-and-green handprints covered most of both biceps, the soft inner skin of his arms scored by Ryne Cyratanc's claws. Tony scratched at a dribble of dried blood, decided against risking the bathroom while the bubbles were still working, and reached for his jeans.

They seemed loose. Barefoot and holding his T-shirt, he staggered out into the condo, following his nose.

Leah was in the kitchen stirring what looked like a large pan of scrambled eggs.

"Where's Henry?"

"Gone. Apparently, he didn't trust my closet space. I put some cheese and some cold ham into these," she continued without turning. "You're going to need the fats as well as the protein."

Considering the fun he'd been having since he got back, the last thing Tony wanted was food. "I'm not hungry," he groaned, dropping onto a stool by the breakfast counter.

"I know. You're starving." When he snorted, she turned and glared. "Do you have any idea how much energy you used tonight?" She gestured at his arms with the spatula. "You created a physical form, you idiot. Okay, maybe that was partly because of how we made contact, but I still can't believe you were so stupid!"

"I'm fine," Tony protested as she began to scrape the eggs out onto a platter. "I just got a little bruised."

"You could have been killed. How many times do I have to remind you that demons gain power by slaughter? You're just lucky that slaughtering you didn't occur to him."

"It didn't occur to him, because I was right; it's not him sending the demons. He needs me to protect you." Tony frowned, suddenly realizing that Leah's eyes were bright with unshed tears. "You're really upset."

"Of course I'm upset!" Holding the full sleeve of her dark green dressing gown back with one hand, she slammed the platter down on the counter in front of him with the other. "If you'd gotten yourself killed, what would have prevented all those demons from coming through and killing me!"

Of course she was upset.

Strangely comforted by this indication of normalcy—within his current fluctuating definition of the word—Tony flicked a bit of scrambled egg out of his chest hair and back onto the plate. "He's going to do what he can to help."

"You're sure."

"Positive." By the time he finished repeating everything that had been said in the white, the platter was empty. He didn't remember eating, but since he was holding a dirty fork, it seemed safe to assume he had.

"Sye Mckaseeh?"

"That's what he said."

"Scottish?"

"I didn't ask."

"I can't believe I'm in danger and I could die because Ryne Cyratane broke up with his girlfriend."

"She's definitely holding a grudge. And I think he's a bit afraid of her."

"He could have been lying to you."

"I know. I don't think he was, but . . ."

"But you don't have a lot of experience judging demonic veracity."

"Uh . . ."

"You had no way of knowing if he was telling the truth."

"Right." Tony tapped the fork against the edge of the platter. "Maybe I should have taken Kevin Groves with me. You and Henry have already had him, it wouldn't have been that much of a stretch."

He'd been kidding, but Leah rolled her eyes and snatched the fork out of his hand. "Fine time to think of that now."

"Eww."

"Oh, grow up. And get dressed so we can get started on saving the world. We've got twenty-seven weak spots to find and close before my god's ex-girlfriend stomps through and tries to take over the world."

"Yeah, well, you know what they say. Hell hath no fury like a demon scorned." A broad wave at her robe. "You'll be going out in that?"

"I dress very quickly."

The obvious comment was, well, too obvious to bother with. His T-shirt seemed to have more holes than he remembered, but eventually he got it over his head and both his arms. His arms hurt, but that was hardly surprising. His shoes and socks were still in the bedroom, but when he stood up to go and get them, the floor moved.

"Or maybe you should sleep for a few hours first," Leah sighed, walking around the edge of the counter and peering down at him.

# Thirteen

HE HADN'T HAD ENOUGH sleep, and in the last—he counted back on his fingers Saturday to Wednesday—four days he'd probably lost a good ten pounds. *That's right, folks, it's not only a Demonic Convergence, it's a workout plan. Sign up now and we'll throw in the Sye Mckaseeh Diet free! All the carbs you ever wanted, but you have to get them away from an Arjh Lord before you can eat them.*

"Tony!"

The level of pissyness suggested Leah had been calling his name for a while now. "What?"

"We're here."

Here was Richmond, in a company parking lot nearly empty except for a premillennia Buick and two Smart Cars.

"The weak spot is in the lot?" he asked hopefully. With any luck, number one of twenty-seven would be an easy fix.

"The weak spot is in the building."

So much for easy. "Of course it is."

"It's a Saturday," Leah reminded him, opening her door. "I'll distract the security guard, you close things up, slam bam, we move on."

"Isn't that supposed to rhyme," he muttered getting out of the car. His knees hurt and his back was stiff; he felt about seventy-five. "You know, Gandalf was probably no more than thirty and the whole gray hair and beard thing was payback for being a wizard. Explains the break dancing with Saruman," he added as they walked toward the front doors. " 'Cause that'd make them the right age in the backstory."

Leah turned to stare at him in confusion. "What are you babbling about?"

"The break dancing scene in the movie. Okay, it was supposed to be a fight, but, man, the fight choreographer really fell down on the job."

She rolled her eyes. "For pity's sake, read a book."

"There was a book?"

The building containing the weak spot belonged to a company called Seanix Technology Inc.

"Number one PC manufacturer in Canada," Tony announced as they moved out of the fine mist and into the shelter under the concrete overhang bordering the front of the single story building.

"You know that and you didn't know Peter Jackson made *Lord of the Rings* from a book?"

He shrugged. "I've never had time to watch the appendices. And we have a problem."

"Besides your appalling ignorance of anything besides television or movies?"

"The security guard is a woman."

"What? That was on the sign, too?"

Tony sighed and pointed.

The tall blonde sitting behind the desk in the main lobby was intent on one of her monitors and hadn't seen them.

"You're right. We have a problem."

"Fortunately, I have a solution."

"You know a spell to take care of her?"

"Nope. I don't need magic for this."

Leah patted him gently on the shoulder. "Tony, you're gay."

"That'll help," he said, quietly pulling open the heavy glass door, "but more importantly, I'm in television."

The door got the guard's attention. Wearing a professionally neutral expression, she watched them cross to her desk. "Can I help you?" she asked, the neutrality touched with suspicion.

Tony smiled and pulled a business card out of his wallet. "I hope so," he told her, passing it over. "My boss sent me out to find a location for our next episode and with any luck, this building will have the perfect space."

"You work on *Darkest Night*?"

"I do."

"Oh, wow. I love that show! Lee Nicholas is so hot! That episode where he got captured by the coven and they were going to sacrifice him unless Raymond Dark—who they'd been hunting for centuries—surrendered to them and he was tied out over that altar; that was just brilliant! And that scene where he was chasing that mad scientist down the street after he was exsanguinating people and blaming it on vampires, that went right past my mother's best friend's ex-husband's store!" Her enthusiasm dropped about five years off her age. "It says here you're a TAD?"

He cranked up the camp, just a little. "I'm also a location scout, the photocopier repair person, decorating consultant, and, occasionally, second dead body on the right." He leaned in. "That leg at the edge of the screen after the massacre on that container ship at VanTerm—mine." CB had been way too cheap to have a leg made when he had any number of them walking around collecting a paycheck.

"No."

"Yes."

She rose up on her toes and peered over the edge of the desk. "Oh, my God, it was your leg! I recognize the shoe!"

No she didn't, it was a different shoe entirely, but Tony wasn't going to mention that. "Look . . . Donna . . ." Her name tag, now close enough to read, said *Donna Hardle*. ". . . I know you can't leave your post, but would it be possible for us to wander very carefully around the building—not touching anything, I promise—to see if we can find the space my boss is looking for?"

"I don't know; it's Saturday, and . . ."

"And there won't be many people working, so we won't disturb them. We thought about that. And besides, we'll want to shoot on a Saturday."

"On a Saturday?"

"Uh-huh."

"I'm here on Saturdays!"

"Hey . . ." His cheeks were beginning to hurt from all the lunatic smiling. ". . . that's great. You know, Lee loves to meet his fans."

Her cheeks went pink. "He does?"

"Loves to."

Donna glanced down at the card, looked over the bank of six monitors, bit her lip, and said, "I guess it's okay if you don't touch anything, and I'll have to make sure you're not carrying cameras."

"That's fair." Because if they were intent on industrial espionage, they'd surely have their corporate spy supplies out where they could be easily found. On the other hand, as he turned out the front pockets on his jeans and patted down his jacket, he gave her points for even considering it. Leah had his car keys, so all he was carrying was his wallet.

"And you . . ." Donna frowned at Leah. "Are you with the show, too?"

"Stunts," Leah said shortly, holding out her bag. "The location needs a safe fall site. Why don't you just hold onto this."

"You do stunts? That is so cool!" Setting the bag down on her desk, she keyed in a fast run of numbers and the door at the end of the lobby buzzed. "Go on through. There's a couple of guys working today; don't disturb them, okay?"

"We'll be as quiet as the mold man in episode nine."

"That was a great episode!"

Leah snorted as the door closed behind them. "Somebody should tell Donna that womb to tomb she only gets so many exclamation points and she's wasting them."

"Be nice," Tony muttered, massaging the inside of his cheeks with his tongue.

"No."

Sye Mckaseeh's potential entrance was in a multidesk office with windows overlooking what was probably a manufacturing area. There were long tables and individual stations of tools, and if it wasn't manufacturing, Tony had no idea what it was. "I don't see the two guys the guard mentioned."

"They're probably in R&D if they're in on the weekend," Leah told him, down on her knees running a hand over the teal blue carpet. "It's under here. There's a bit of a bump. I think there was a wall taken down and the office made bigger."

When he cocked his head, he could see the shimmer. "Back up."

♠

"What was with all the hand waving?" Donna asked as they came back out into the lobby. "I could see you on the security monitors," she added before they could ask how she knew.

"I was setting up the shots," Tony told her, peering at her through the square of his fingers. You know."

"Of course! So cool! Did you find what you needed?"

"I think so, but now I have to tell the boss. He makes all the final decisions."

"So you don't know what Saturday you'll be here?"

"Not yet."

"That's okay, I wrote down all my days off until after Christmas, so can you try and be here when I am?"

As Tony took the piece of paper, he laid his other hand over his heart. "I will do my best."

"That's just so great!" She was handing Leah back her bag, but her attention never left him. "Tony, can I ask you a question?"

He noted the impressive amount of information conveyed by Leah's *we have another twenty-six of these things to close and not nearly enough time so we need to haul ass* expression and then ignored it. Donna had done them an enormous favor and right now was definitely not the time to be acquiring a karmic burden. "Sure."

"It's about Raymond Dark and James Taylor Grant." She lowered her voice and glanced to both sides, as if worried about eavesdroppers. "Is there, you know, a subtext there on purpose because they always stand so close together?"

"Sorry, that's standard blocking for television," Tony told

her. "Actors have to be well within each other's personal space in order to get them both in a small screen closeup. There's no subtext; they're just hitting their marks."

Donna clearly didn't entirely believe him. "But they're so perfect together."

He winked, and gave his best imitation of a lascivious screaming queen. "You don't think James Taylor Grant would prefer a younger man?"

Giggling, she waved them toward the exit. "Go on. I have work to do!"

"Subtext?" Leah demanded incredulously as they walked to the car. "What was she talking about?"

"You don't spend much time online, do you?"

"I have a life. And what was with the *Queer Eye* schtick?

He snorted as he dropped into the passenger seat and let his head fall back. "I know our fan base. Be sure to hit a drive-through on the way to number twenty-six."

♠

"This is looking very familiar." Tony finished his coffee and tossed the empty cup into the back seat. "Isn't this near . . . ?"

"The place the tentacled demon broke through and terrorized your friend's coffee shop? Yes. Same neighborhood. And this is where our next stop is." Leah pulled into the parking lot at the Four Points Sheraton, narrowly missing two middle-aged women dragging an impressive amount of luggage.

"It's not just a residual reading from the old place that blew?"

"No. But I'd have thought it was if you hadn't mapped it and I'd have gone right on by and we wouldn't have closed it and it might have spat out the demon ready to destroy the world as we know it. Not to mention me." The parking space she chose was some distance from the building. "Probably Sye Mckaseeh's intent. Good thing she doesn't know what you're capable of."

"Yeah. Good thing." Right at the moment, he didn't feel capable of much.

"There's a few too many men in there for me to distract them all, not to mention women."

"Not to mention."

"So how do we play this?"

He sighed and unfastened his seat belt. "We get lost in the crowd."

"And if the weak spot's in one of the rooms or one of the offices or in the middle of the lobby?"

"Why don't we just cross that bridge when we come to it? And speaking of Bridge . . ." Standing just outside the car, he stared at the hotel.

"Superficial resemblance at best," Leah snorted. "Come on. Let's do this."

Dark girders held the Four Points sign out over the main entrance. Tony stared up at them, noticed a spot where a bit of paint was missing, and closed his hand around Leah's arm. "Tell me it's not up there."

"It's not up there."

"Thank you. Just look like you're supposed to be here," he murmured as they entered the building. "There's hundreds of people in and out every day. We're just two more faces in the crowd."

"You've done this before?"

Why not. It would look better if they were talking. He kept his voice low. "Big hotels with conference rooms have bathrooms tucked away in odd unwatched corners. If you're not so filthy you get noticed right off, you can use them to clean up as long as you miss the suits having their post-conference piss. Sometimes, you can score a coffee and some food from outside the rooms."

Leah looked intrigued as she guided them past the front desk. "The hotel rooms?"

"Them, too. Half-eaten room service beats Dumpster diving any day, but I meant from outside the conference rooms. Pastries and stuff. Handful of creamers if nothing else."

"For all it's been short, you've had an interesting life."

"Yeah, and getting more interesting by the day."

The weak spot they were searching for wasn't in the lobby.

Or by the pool.

Or in the Business Center.

It was in the ballroom. Although there were round tables draped in peach tablecloths set up for later in the day, at the moment, the ballroom was empty.

"And we catch a break. Go us."

"Maybe." Frowning, Leah trailed her hand along one of the long walls until she came to a narrow wallpaper-covered door. Opening it exposed a dark, empty cubbyhole.

"It's where those folding walls go," Tony said, peering over her shoulder and squinting a little to see the familiar shimmer. "You know, the kind that divides the room into smaller rooms."

"I guess this one's missing." Motioning him forward, Leah stepped back out of his way.

"Excuse me? What are you doing?"

They turned to see a man in a navy blue suit staring at them suspiciously from just inside one set of double doors. He was wearing a Four Points Sheridan name tag and the slight bulge at the waist of his jacket was either a radio or the hotel business in Vancouver was excessively competitive.

"I've got it," Leah murmured and started across the room.

For the first couple of steps, she was just a good-looking woman walking, then even Tony could see the difference as she cranked up the metaphysical attraction. Checking on the hotel employee's reaction, Tony noticed the gleam of a gold band against a dark finger.

The guy was married.

*Just fucking great.*

He sketched out the first rune at full speed, shoved it through the shimmer, and glanced over his shoulder.

Leah was almost at the door, the translucent image of her Arjh Lord flickering around her. "You're the manager?" he heard her purr. "Just who I wanted."

Second rune.

She had her hand against the manager's chest and he was smiling.

Third rune. At little slower because this was the one that gave him trouble.

Tony turned in time to see the door close.

*Crap.*

Fourth rune and he was sprinting across the ballroom before the shimmer had entirely disappeared. Fighting off a wave of dizziness, he crashed through the door, stumbled, apologized as he bounced off a passing luggage rack, and caught sight of Leah and the manager going into a conference room.

If the door closed, he wouldn't be able to stop her.

As it swung shut, he called.

The door jerked out of Leah's grip. Brass hinges creaked but held.

The look she shot him through Ryne Cyratane's torso promised a thousand years of torment and an immediate butt kicking. Tony let his arm drop back to his side and croaked, "Come on. We're on a tight schedule."

"There's time . . ."

"No." He sounded definite. Go him. He had no idea of what he'd do if she refused to listen.

Fortunately, he didn't have to find out. Leaving the manager standing confused and unfulfilled in the conference room, Leah stomped down the corridor, right past him and out into the lobby, heading for the exit. Half expecting to see smoking footprints in the carpet, Tony followed.

Disoriented by the unexpected sunshine, he had to dance around a shuttle bus and a pair of taxis vying for the same spot. By the time he was in the clear, she was already at the car. "That manager," he said before she got a chance to speak, "he was married."

"So?"

"So he was married."

Leah settled back against the trunk and crossed her arms. "Are you telling me you never got into a car or went into an alley with a married man? Most hustlers can't afford those kinds of scruples."

He didn't remember telling her in so many words that he used to hustle. Still, took one to know one. "That was different."

"How?"

"This guy, the manager, he didn't make that choice. You didn't *give* him a choice."

Her eyes widened incredulously. "So you were saving his marriage?"

"Maybe."

"You know nothing about him. He could be putting it to half the cleaning staff."

"That has nothing to do with me. This did. If he decides to betray his wife, that's his business, but we don't get to make that choice for him." Suddenly, the pavement was a lot closer than it had been. "Ow." Why was he on his knees?

"Tony?"

He blinked up at her.

"You didn't take the time to focus properly, did you? You used your own internal power for those runes, didn't you?"

"Could have." He honestly didn't remember. "I was in a bit of a hurry," he reminded her as she helped him back onto his feet. "You don't generally demand a lot of foreplay."

He expected more argument, but she was quiet as she opened the car door and eased him down onto the seat. He couldn't read her expression and he didn't trust the silence, so just before she slid the key into the ignition, he grabbed her arm. "What?"

To his surprise, she leaned over and kissed him gently on the cheek. "You're a good man, Tony Foster. A good man with power. I'm not sure if I find that terrifyingly hopeful or just terrifying."

As she effortlessly shook free of his grip, Tony sagged back against the seat and frowned. "Yeah, well, that and five ninety-nine will get you a meal deal," he said after a moment, unable to decide if he should be flattered or insulted. "Which reminds me; you'll need to . . ."

"Hit a drive-through on the way to number twenty-five. Yeah, I figured."

♠

"Tony, wake up!"

There was a certain, *this is the last time I'm going to say this* tone to Leah's voice that dragged his eyes open. He could see trees silhouetted against a sapphire sky. "It's almost dark."

"I know. You ate and then you fell asleep, and I couldn't wake you."

"Why am I wet?"

"I said I couldn't wake you," she snapped, tossing the empty cup into the back seat and starting the car.

Now he thought about it, it was a pretty stupid question. Although she'd reclined his seat as far as it would go, sleeping in the car had left him stiff. And not in a good way. "Oh, man, I have really got to take a piss."

"There's a gas station on the corner."

"Where are we?"

"Just down the road from number twenty-five," she told him, pulling up to the pumps. "It's on a private house. Give me your credit card. For gas!" she added when he stared at her blankly.

"What's wrong with your cards?"

"The gas is going into your car."

"Right. Fine. Whatever." It wasn't until he was getting back into the car having visited both the bathroom and the convenience store, holding a bag of beef jerky and a giant sport drink and feeling much better that he realized what she'd said. "On a private house? Not in?"

"There's a piece of soffit missing. Do you know what that is?"

"Sure. I'm a wizard. We know things."

"It's the piece that fills in the angle between the roof to the house."

"Ah." He chewed a piece of jerky as she pulled out into traffic. "Bungalow?"

"Two stories."

Two stories with a porch and a flagstone walk and some bushes clipped into tight little spheres. Dark curtains were drawn over lace sheers in the front window, but a thin line of light seemed to indicate someone was home.

Standing on the sidewalk and craning his head, he could just barely make out the shimmer. "I can get it from here."

The first rune slammed up against the eaves trough and rained down in a shower of blue sparks. Tony threw the remains of his sport drink on a smoldering spherical bush. *Good thing neighbor in the city means minding your own business.* "Son of a bitch. I can't get the right angle on it, the porch is in the way. I'm going to have to lean out that second-story window."

"And how," Leah snorted, peering up at the house, "are you going to get to that second-story window?"

"I guess we're hunting for another location," he said as he headed back to the car.

She caught his wrist as he was opening the trunk. "Tony, people with that kind of repressed shrubbery are not likely to be fans of *Darkest Night.*"

"So we expand our demographic." Shaking free, he pulled out his show jacket and shrugged into it, dropping his jean jacket into the trunk. It was the ubiquitous black satin with a blood red logo across the back, and he didn't wear it often—there were only so many Donnas a guy could face in a day—but it made him look more official and at past seven on a Saturday evening, that could only help. "We'll get whoever's in there to take me to that room because we want to use the view out of it on the show."

"They won't care."

"And we'll offer them a great deal of money."

Leah glanced at the shrubs as they walked up the front path. "That might work. Except," she added, "I get the impression CB's not going to sanction that."

"We're not actually going to use the view," he reminded her, heading up the porch stairs.

"Fair enough. But once you're in the room, they're not just going to let you lean out the window."

"No, you're going to distract them. Or him. Or her. Or the Brady Bunch. Without forcing he, she, or them to break any vows."

"Okay, Mr. I've-got-an-answer-for-everything: if it's not a him, how?"

"We'll be on the second floor."

"So?"

Tony sighed and pressed the doorbell. "You're a stuntwoman, right? Fall down the stairs."

♠

"I don't understand." Mrs. Chin clutched at the front of her pale blue sweater with one hand and peered anxiously from Tony's card to Tony. "There'll be a television show on our front lawn?"

"No, ma'am. We just want to shoot . . . film," he corrected when she looked startled. "We want to film the scene out the window just like it is."

"But why?"

"For the television show."

"Yes, you said that, but why?"

"It'll be what one of the characters sees when they look out *their* window, Mrs. Chin."

"Except they won't ever be in your room," Leah added quickly. "We'll put the pieces of film together back at the studio."

"I see." Either she didn't, or she was confused about something else. "And you'll pay me money for this?"

That was almost a statement and definitely not what she might be confused about.

"Yes, ma'am."

"Because you always hear about how much money there is in television." She glanced at the card again. "How much money?"

"I can't say exactly, ma'am. I need to take a look and see if it's suitable and then . . ." He pulled his cell phone from his pocket. ". . . send a couple of pictures to the boss."

Her eyes narrowed. "You're not taking pictures of the inside of my house."

"No ma'am. Just the view out the window."

"And you want to do this now?"

"The sooner the boss makes a decision, the sooner we can cut you a check."

"But it's dark out," she protested, leaning just enough to see past them and get confirmation.

"That's okay. It's a television show about a vampire. But a good vampire," he qualified as her eyes began to narrow again. "It's about a vampire detective who solves crimes and protects people."

Mrs. Chin nodded, slowly. "That sounds familiar. What's it called again?"

*"Darkest Night."* He half turned so she could see the logo on his back. "We shoot right here in Burnaby."

"I've never heard of you," she declared, but she stepped back and let them into the house.

"Oh, good heavens! Miss? Are you all right?"

Tony hadn't seen the fall, but it had certainly sounded impressive; lots of bumping, lots of crashing, and finally some very believable moaning. As Mrs. Chin ran out of the room, he leaned out of the window—fortunately, one of the old-fashioned kind that lifted up and had no screen—twisted around and, using the frame, pulled himself up to sit on the ledge. He had to lean away from the building, left arm stretched right out to get the runes through the weak spot and although all four slid through, he wasn't entirely positive that it had closed. He leaned a little farther. Squinted . . .

The world tilted in an interesting way, but there was definitely no shimmer.

No window ledge either.

Porch roof, though.

And then a bush.

A bush that turned out to be just a little sturdier than he was.

*Oh, that's just fucking great,* he thought, rolling out onto the lawn, breathing fast and shallow through his teeth so as not to scream. *Four days of fighting demons, and I get taken out by shrubbery.*

Lying there and bleeding seemed like his best option, but

unless they wanted to deal with more questions than he was prepared to answer, he had to get away from Mrs. Chin before he fell over. More specifically, he had to stand up and then get away from Mrs. Chin before he could fall over again.

Bright side, nothing was broken.

Nothing important anyway.

Thankful he seemed to be in marginally better shape than the bush, he staggered up the porch steps and peered into the front hall. Leah was sitting on a wooden chair, head in her hands. Mrs. Chin was nowhere in sight. Opening the door, he waved Leah quiet and moved as quickly as he could to her side as Mrs. Chin came from the back of the house with a glass of water.

"Oh, there you are," she snapped, her gaze flicking to the stairs as she handed Leah the glass. She obviously thought he'd just come down them and just as obviously disapproved of his lack of concern for his companion. "This young woman should be taken to the hospital."

Hospital? Was the spell no longer protecting her? "Are you hurt?"

"She fell down the stairs," Mrs. Chin told him grimly. "There could be all sorts of internal damage and I am not responsible. Those stairs are safe. I wasn't near her when she fell. I gave her a glass of water."

"Of course not."

"If you try to sue me, that's what I'll tell the judge."

"Okay, sure."

"Maybe you're right about the hospital." Leah stood and handed back the glass. "We should go now."

Tony was all in favor of that. Left arm pressed tight against his side, he extended his right. "I'll help you out to the car."

Somehow Leah managed to support most of his weight and still make it look like he was helping her. A lot of stunties were better actors than the industry gave them credit for, he acknowledged silently as he thanked Mrs. Chin for her time and the two of them moved as quickly as possible toward the street.

Leah tipped her head toward his. "You fell out the window?"

"What was your first clue?"

"Could have been the way you were upstairs and then came in through the front door. Or it could have been the crash you made as you hit the porch roof."

"Mrs. Chin . . . ?"

"Kitchen's in the back of the house. She might not have heard it."

"Is she still watching?"

Clothing rustled as Leah half turned. "Yes."

"Then let's move a little faster before she comes outside and sees what I did to her bush."

"You damaged one of her bushes!"

"The damage was mutual."

"If I let you go, can you lean on the car until I get the door open?"

"Sure." Or not so sure. The adrenaline was wearing off, he hurt in more places than he cared to catalog, and the world was beginning to tilt again. Fuck that. Tilted world had got him into this mess. Mess. Messed. Missed. Didn't miss that damned bush. Wouldn't miss it. It could just lay there and well, rot.

"Come on, Tony. Into the car."

Leah's voice seemed to come from very far away and she seemed taller. Or he had gotten shorter. And that would suck.

"God fucking damn it!" Cracking his head on the edge of the car roof helped him focus. He collapsed into the seat and whimpered a little as Leah buckled him in. *You know what needs seat belts? Fucking window ledges, that's what.*

"This isn't good."

She was sitting beside him in the driver's seat and, since he couldn't remember her going around the car, it seemed he'd lost a few minutes somewhere. She was looking at a dark stain on the palm of her hand.

"Shit. You're bleeding!"

"No, Tony. *You're* bleeding. It's soaking into your jacket. That's why I didn't see it before. How badly are you hurt?"

"I can't feel the fingers of my left hand." When he lifted them up into the light of the streetlamp, they looked kind of like sausages. "But that's good I can't feel them," he added. "Because when I could feel them, they hurt like fuck."

"Let me see where you're bleeding."

"I'm bleeding? Oh that's just great. Henry's going to kill me. He hates it when I waste . . . Um . . ." The word just wasn't there. And then a good chunk of the world wasn't there. Then what was left started beeping.

♠

Henry pulled up behind Tony's car and was out of his own almost before the engine stopped.

"The supplies you asked for are in the backseat," he snarled, pushing past the Demongate and yanking open the passenger side door. The blood scent, no longer confined but spilling out to almost overwhelm the night, would have been dangerous had his anger at the circumstances not been so great.

Scooping Tony up into his arms, he led the way into the apartment building.

♠

"Hey, Henry. I was just thinking about you."

"Were you?" Henry sat on the edge of the bed, his cool fingers gently gripping Tony's jaw.

"Yeah. I was thinking you'd . . . uh . . ." Interesting that it hurt so much to frown. "I don't remember. But you were there." His gaze flicked up over Henry's shoulder to Leah and he snorted. "And you were there. And there was a wizard. Oh, wait. That was me."

Smiling, Henry released him. "Don't frighten me like that again."

"You're frightened of me misquoting *The Wizard of Oz?*"

"You've been in and out of delirium for the last two hours. We were just discussing whether or not we should take you to a hospital."

"What happened?"

"Apparently, you fell out a window."

It all came rushing painfully back. The window. The bush. The bleeding.

And now?

He was in his own bed, in his own apartment. His left arm was on top of the covers, forearm wrapped in a tensor bandage, the fingers an ugly shade of grayish purple and still sausagelike. With his right hand, he explored the gauze corset wrapped around his torso. If he hadn't been to a hospital . . .

"Leah does a decent field dressing," Henry said, reading the question off his face. "We don't think the wrist is broken, but you won't be able to use the hand for a few days. What happened?"

Duh. "I fell out a window."

"He got careless," Leah muttered, stomping to the kitchen.

"I didn't." Was her bad mood because she cared, or was that just lingering delirium talking? "The world tilted."

"I thought as much."

A little surprised, Tony turned his attention back to Henry. "You expected a tilted world? What? It was part of the whole Demonic Convergence thing? Next time, warn a guy."

"I expected something *like* this to happen. Not this specifically."

"Cryptic much. I thought you'd be more pissed."

"Oh, he was." Leah reappeared holding a mug. "The anger and the yelling and the accusing me of trying to kill you went on for a while. Henry, lift him into a sitting position."

Tony wasn't given a chance to protest, and it didn't hurt as much as he expected it to.

"Now, drink this."

Henry had to help him get his working arm out from under the covers, but once he had his fingers wrapped around the mug, they seemed to be holding. His mouth filled with saliva as he breathed in the meaty scent of the soup and he had to swallow spit before he could get to the good stuff. Since he didn't think he'd survive another alphabet noodle out the nose, he drank slowly without being told.

No one said anything until he finished.

"There's more."

"Good." He passed Leah the mug. "I'm starving."

"Literally."

And back to Henry again. "What?"

"You are literally starving. Your body is not up to the demands you've been making on it. That we've *all* been making on it."

"You haven't been . . ." Cool fingers brushed the scar on his throat. "Yeah, okay, maybe a couple."

"We've been forcing a couch potato to run a marathon," Leah told him handing him the refilled mug. "For the last four days, you've been using your power almost constantly. You're not in good enough shape for this."

"Thanks."

"I'm serious. The world didn't tilt, Tony. You fainted. Well, almost fainted," she qualified, stepping back from the bed and folding her arms. "That's why you fell."

"I almost fainted?"

"Yes."

"That was remarkably unbutch of me."

"This isn't something to joke about, Tony." Henry pressed his palm against the gauze. "You need to rest, regain your strength, heal."

Tony glanced down at Henry's hand. The gentle pressure remained just this side of pain. He was either saying, *I don't want you getting hurt.* Or *I'll hurt you if you try to get up.* Tony wasn't sure which. "How long do you want me to rest?"

"For as long as it takes."

"I can't . . ."

"You don't have a choice," Leah pointed out, sounding no happier about it than Tony felt. "Your body is setting the agenda now."

"Yeah, but there's still two dozen demons coming through."

"Tomorrow," Henry told him in a tone that suggested he not bother arguing, "Leah and Jack will go out and get detailed information on as many of the weak points as they can."

"Doesn't Jack have a job?"

"He has Sunday off. Amy will be here, sitting with you. Making sure you sleep and eat and don't do anything stupid."

"*Amy* will be making sure *I* don't do anything stupid? She attacked a demon with a candle."

Henry smiled. "Which is why we assume she can handle you. As soon as you can use your left hand again, you'll be driven to the easier points. You'll leave those in more difficult positions until you're in better shape and, hopefully, by then they'll be less difficult. CB thought using a location search to gain access to private property was a good idea. When we find out where the weak spots are, exactly, he'll call in some favors if he has to. Lee's willing to use his celebrity as a distraction when there's no stairs for Leah to fall down."

"You've got everything planned." Didn't mention Kevin Groves, but Tony wasn't going to remind him. He could think of a use for a man who knew a lie when he heard it and didn't want that use to occur to Henry.

He drank his soup. He slept for a bit. He ate a plate of eggs when he woke up. And he complained just enough to keep Henry from getting suspicious.

♠

On his way out of the bathroom some hours later, having stumbled out of bed and to the toilet without actually opening his eyes, he realized the apartment smelled like lasagna and patchouli. That gave him enough warning that he didn't embarrass himself when Amy rose up out of his single armchair like the shark from *Jaws* rising out of the sea. Except it was a great white and she was all in pink-and-black plaid and . . . Okay, it wasn't a very good metaphor, but he'd just woken up so tough.

"Hey."

One of the kitchen chairs was closest to hand, so he sat on that before he fell down. "Hey, back."

"You look like crap."

"Funny, that." His wrist ached, he had enough bruises he

looked like the one hundred and second Dalmatian, and his stomach felt as if it was lying flat against his spine.

Amy handed him a bunch of bananas and dropped into the other chair. "Henry said I'm supposed to keep feeding you whenever you wake up, but the lasagna isn't ready so you'll have to eat something healthy. Should you be sitting?"

"Instead of?"

"Lying down."

"Up is good for a while." That was the best banana . . . best *two* bananas he'd ever eaten.

"You're not chewing."

"It's a banana," he protested around a third. "You made lasagna?"

"Please," she snorted. "I bought lasagna; family-sized and frozen. You fell out a window?"

By the time he finished telling her the adventures of Wizardman and Stuntwoman, the food was ready. By the time he finished eating, he could barely keep his eyes open.

"Hey, have Lee send Donna a signed picture, care of Seanix Tech, okay?"

"For the third and final time," she sighed as she lowered him onto the sofa bed, "okay."

The next time he woke up, his apartment smelled like chicken, and Amy was watching *The Princess Diaries III.* He must have made some kind of noise because without turning she said, "Yes, I enjoy movies made for teenage girls. Before you make something of it, remember that in your weakened state I can kick your ass."

Figuring he had enough going on with two dozen demons, he staggered silently to the bathroom.

"How long was I out?" he asked, returning to his kitchen chair.

"Almost three hours. I was just going to take the chicken out of the oven. Leah said this time you'd need food more than sleep."

"You cooked a chicken?"

"Like it's hard. The oven does all the work. You didn't have a roasting pan, though, so I had to make one out of three aluminum pie plates, half a roll of aluminum foil and the lid off the jar of pickles."

He didn't really want to know.

"Jack called," she told him while he ate. "They—not him but you know, they the cops—found the leg of that guard from out on Eastlake Drive halfway to the studio."

"The whole leg?"

"Most of it." She plopped another spoonful of instant mashed potatoes onto his plate. "I guess the demon got tired of carrying it. What do you figure; snack or weapon?"

"Either. Both."

"Yeah. So you're not going to have time to close all those new weak spots, are you?"

"Not if I have to lie around here much longer." Since he couldn't walk to the can and back without holding the walls, lying around seemed like the best bet.

"If you don't take time to recover, Henry says you'll die and then where will we be? At least with you alive when they come through, we have a chance. What do you think they'll look like?"

"Who?"

She rolled her eyes. "The new demons, dipshit."

"What difference does it make?"

"I'm curious, okay?"

"Leah says the more human evil looks the more dangerous it is."

"More dangerous than that one we chased from the coffee shop? Damned thing had tentacles and claws and spikes and mouths in weird places and . . ."

He held up a hand to cut short the litany. "Maybe it works better as a metaphor in this case."

"Ooooo, metaphors." Burgundy lips pursed. "Someone doesn't want to be a TAD all his life."

"I want to direct."

"You and half the lower mainland. Come on, sleepyhead, back to bed."

Next time he woke up, he definitely felt stronger. Still punctured, bruised, and unable to use his left hand, but stronger. There was a bit of blood soaked through the dressing on his side, but he could walk without holding the walls and he remembered to chew his food—at least as much as he ever did. He was back in control of his body instead of the other way around. But what would it hurt to give Jack and Leah the day to detail the weak spots? It *would* probably speed things up when he got back out there wizarding.

While Amy spooned red Jell-O into bowls, Tony phoned Zev because he wanted to talk about something that wasn't demonic, something normal. Too soon, he found he had almost nothing to say.

Depressing?

No shit, Sherlock.

As the apartment grew dark, he realized he was running out of time.

"I know that look."

"What look?"

She cocked her head and snorted. "The 'I'm about to do something stupid' look. Henry said I'm not to give you your laptop."

It didn't matter; he could call it to his hand no matter where it was.

It didn't matter; he didn't want it.

"I'm just going to lie down again."

"And sleep."

"Sure."

He closed his eyes. Concentrated. Twenty-four soon-to-be-arriving demons had a way of focusing the mind.

He needed to find the square hole to his square peg.

Or was he a round peg in a round hole?

He couldn't remember and wasn't sure it mattered.

If pain was a compulsory part of defining his place in the universe, he had it to spare. His wrist ached. Add it to the definition. His side hurt. Add it to the definition. His nose itched. What the hell . . .

The universe began to take shape around him.

There.

No.

There!

*This is pain. This is me. The part that doesn't hurt, that isn't me.*

*And this is how those parts fit together.*

*Ladies and gentlemen, we are the world.*

He really didn't have much time, but a quick look around from this vantage point might pick up some useful insights. Allowing his consciousness to move out from his body, he brushed against Amy and smiled to see her spirit as a blazing tower of light. Kind of like six or seven of those big opening night searchlights all shining up at the same point.

His wards were a gleaming crimson cage around the apartment, promising safety and danger simultaneously. Tony hoped they were supposed to, but what the hell did he know? Way too many of the last few scenes were being shot on the fly.

Beyond the wards, another tower of light blazed so brilliantly he didn't need contact to see it.

Henry.

Weird that a Nightwalker's spirit would be so bright.

Not weird at all considering it was Henry's.

Henry.

Crap.

No more time to play tourist.

No more time to be an invalid.

Sinking back into his own body, he took a calming breath and forced himself to relax into his place in the universe, his square and/or round hole.

Hesitated.

Remembered.

Bad idea.

Trying not to brace against the anticipated pain, he healed his wrist and the wounds the shrubbery had gouged in his side.

And then he rode that distilled pain deeper. He could see

the contradiction in using magic to heal the damage the use of magic had caused. He could also see how to get around it.

His back bowed until only his head and his heels were touching the mattress. Just before he lost consciousness, he heard Henry's voice and was glad Amy wouldn't have to explain the screaming on her own.

# Fourteen

TONY WAS HEARING VOICES. All things considered, that hardly seemed worth getting worked up about, so he lay there, drifting just below consciousness and listened to the rhythmic rise and fall of sound. After a while, he realized there were words involved.

Loud words.

"I said he was no use to us injured; that doesn't mean I told him to heal himself, and it doesn't mean he'd listen to me if I *had* told him, so just back off."

A woman's voice. He knew that voice.

Leah.

"I don't see the downside, guys." He knew that voice, too. Knew it better. Trusted it more. Amy. "Okay, he's gonna have to pig out again and get his strength back, but then he'll be good to go, and that'll happen a lot faster than it would have taken for his arm to heal."

His point exactly.

"Thank you," Leah agreed.

"This doesn't mean I'm on your side," Amy snorted. "I'm just saying."

"And what if, in his weakened state, his heart had given out? Or a blood vessel had burst in his brain? You couldn't hear his body fighting to survive what he'd done to it. I could." A new voice. A man's voice. A really, really pissed-off voice. Tony had been thinking about maybe trying to open his eyes, but it suddenly seemed smarter to wait until Henry had calmed down a little.

Leah sighed. "The point is, Henry, he did survive. He gambled and he won."

"He had no idea of what the stakes were."

"He's trying to keep the world from being overrun by demons. He's trying to prevent a mass slaughter of innocents. He knows how high the stakes are."

"And how could he have done that if he killed himself?"

"But he didn't kill himself! Have you always been such a pessimist?"

Oh, yeah. That was going to calm him right down. Realizing that if he waited for Henry he'd be lying here all night, he forced his eyes open. Leah and Henry were facing off by the table. Amy stood a careful distance away, leaning on the counter.

"Hey." It came out less like a word and more like a cough, but it was enough to get the attention of everyone in the room. "I smell honey garlic . . ." He needed a second breath to finish. ". . . ribs."

Amy grinned. "Leah stopped for Chinese. You hungry?"

"Star . . ." Catching sight of Henry's expression, Tony decided that admitting he was starving might not be the best response. "I could eat . . . a horse."

"That's too bad; she stopped at the good place." Grabbing a towel off the counter, Amy opened the oven door. "I stuck it in here to keep it warm."

"How domestic."

"Oh, about this much. It's a mess in here by the way. You should clean your oven."

"I figured I'd just . . . move."

"Men are disgusting," Leah announced stepping over to the bed. She pulled a can of nutritional supplement out of her shoulder bag, popped the tab, and held it out. "Drink this first. It'll take the edge off and keep you from choking."

Although nothing hurt, he was embarrassingly weak and just starting to wonder about sitting up when Henry's arm slid under his back and lifted him up to lean against the pile of rearranged pillows. "You're good at that."

"Too much practice."

"It was my choice, Henry."

The vampire's eyes were shadowed. "I know. But she suspected you'd try a healing when you were strong enough. She could have warned me or stopped you."

"She is the cat's mother," Leah muttered.

"My grandma used to say that." Amy appeared beside her holding a plate of food. "So you shouldn't. And you . . ." She switched her attention to Tony. ". . . should drink that so you can eat so you can get your strength back, so you can get back out there and kick demon ass."

Henry watched him while he drank. The supplement was supposed to taste like chocolate. It didn't. It tasted the way people who'd never had chocolate thought chocolate might taste based on descriptions of the cheap waxy shit they sculpted into rabbits at Easter.

Henry watched him while Leah quickly unwound the bandage on his left wrist and he flexed the fingers, checking that everything worked the way it was supposed to.

Henry watched him while he forked Chinese food into his mouth. Actually, all three of them watched, but Henry's gaze was the heaviest. Leah kept her expression neutral—probably so as not to provoke Henry—and Amy made pig noises.

"Want more?" she asked when he finished. "Never mind." She took the empty plate before he could reply. "Stupid question."

Beginning to feel better, Tony sat up straight and Leah leaned in to remove the gauze wrapped around his torso. Henry's hands were there first. She backed up, her own raised in exaggerated surrender.

Tony shivered as cool fingers touched his skin, checking that the punctures had healed and the bruises were gone. They lingered last against his throat where the bite mark had been. This time it was gone. The skin was smooth.

"Your choice," Henry said softly and straightened.

"What just happened?" Amy demanded as she set another filled plate of food on Tony's lap.

"Our little boy just grew up."

Pausing just long enough to glare in Leah's direction, Tony dug in as Amy snorted.

"As if."

♣

Just after three, Tony dropped Amy off at her apartment.

"Are you going to be okay?" he asked as she leaned back into the car.

"Me? I'm fine. Why?"

"You've got to be up in three hours for work."

"I sit on my ass most of the day, I'll be fine. Besides, I've never needed a lot of sleep. What about you?"

"Me? *I'm* fine." He'd damned well better be 'cause that whole healing thing had fucking hurt.

"Uh-huh." She looked as though she was planning to argue but thought better of it. "Just be careful, okay? And thanks for letting me help. This stuff is, you know, real."

He frowned, not sure he understood. "Real?"

"We're saving the world from demons who want to slaughter and enslave us, Tony, and it doesn't get more real than that." Straightening, she hung her *Vampire Princess Miju* backpack over one shoulder. "Keep me in the loop or it's chow mein noodles under the fingernails," she growled and quietly closed the car door.

Real demons. Two words guaranteed not to show up in the same sentence in most lives. Tony watched Amy trot into her building, waiting until he saw the light go on in her apartment before he turned the engine back on and put the car in gear. It was chivalry she wouldn't thank him for, but tough. Demons weren't the only metaphysical creatures wandering around the lower mainland and she had a big "I believe" stamped on her forehead.

Henry pulled out right behind him.

Tony'd slept all day and hadn't wanted to waste any more time, so the moment the calories kicked in, he left Leah asleep in his apartment and headed for the one easy access weak spot of the six she'd mapped out with Jack.

Separate cars because Henry had his own inflexible timetable.

New Westminster had been replacing old water mains for some time now. According to Leah, Mckaseeh had plans to pop a demon through in the trench on Fader Street. Tony drove past and stopped at the Hume Park end of the road.

"In case an insomniac across from where I'm working glances out the window and reports something hinky going on," he explained to Henry's raised eyebrow as the vampire got out of his car.

Henry made a noncommittal noise.

"It could happen," Tony muttered as they walked back.

"Is there no security on the site?"

"Just the kind that drives by every couple of hours. If they show up while I'm wizarding, you can go talk to them." He sketched a set of air quotes around the word talk.

"Thank you for letting me help."

Sarcasm? Tony didn't think so. Henry sounded just as sincere as Amy had and, come to think of it, just as sincere as Lee had earlier. He frowned. Why would people be grateful for a chance to die by demon? Because no one likes to sit around with their thumb up their butt when the world is ending, feeling help*less.*

Whoa. Epiphany. In a time of crisis no one wanted to feel they were less than they were.

He wasn't just sending his friends and coworkers out into danger, he was empowering them. Okay, except for Henry who was about as empowered as it got all on his own. This didn't mean he could thoughtlessly thrust them into danger, but he could stop feeling so friggin' guilty about the danger they were in.

*I wonder if I will . . .*

The Arjh Lord's weak point was at the bottom of the trench, the shimmer nearly indistinguishable in the dark patterns of turned earth and old pipes.

Tony peered down into the construction site, his weight sending a small avalanche of dirt off the crumbling edge. "If

I burn the rune then tip it on its side then shove it out over the trench and you hold me in place, I could push it down into the pit without having to climb down there."

A red-gold brow rose.

"Not going to happen, is it?"

Henry pointed along the trench. "I think you'll be safest climbing down there at the end where the new pipe has been laid. It's a gentler slope."

For not particularly large values of gentle.

Surfing the last meter on a wave of rubble, Tony hit bottom buried knee-deep in dirt. He glanced back at the new angle and sighed. Getting out was going to be fun.

But first the fun of dragging his lower legs free and then the fun of getting to the weak spot without breaking his neck.

Cocking his head, he could see the shimmer, but he couldn't see his footing.

*Memo to self. Next time, bring a flashlight.*

First, buy a flashlight since he didn't own one.

Because he didn't need one . . .

The first couple of weeks after the haunted house, he'd practiced the Wizard's Lamp spell obsessively, but it had been months and he wasn't 100 percent positive he remembered the wording.

Or, as it happened, how much juice to give it.

Any possibility of developing night vision was obliterated in the sudden flare of brilliant white light which broke his concentration so completely that it shut off again almost immediately.

"That was unpleasant," Henry snarled.

Tony peered up through the afterimages at where he thought Henry might be standing. "Sorry."

"Just do what you came to do and do it quickly before someone arrives to investigate that flare."

"You think someone saw it?"

"I think they saw it in Alberta."

He didn't so much find the shimmer as trip and fall into it. He expected it to feel unpleasant, but it actually felt anticipatory. A moment spent considering who was doing the anticipating added in the unpleasant.

After burning the first rune, he realized that they shed enough light for him to find a path.

"I should've just dragged a rune along with me," he muttered, shoving it through the weak point.

"Yes, you should have." Henry had, of course, been able to hear him. He wasn't sure why he could hear Henry, whether it was a vampire thing or a wizard thing or Henry just didn't care who he woke up, figuring he could handle anything that lived in New Westminster. "There's a car coming," he continued, breaking into Tony's musing. "If it stops, I'll deal with it."

"Sure." The musing was new. He never used to muse.

The car stopped right about the time Tony was pushing through the second rune. He waited until he heard Henry's quiet, "Can I help you, Officer?" and then burned the third rune on the air.

The car pulled away as he finished and he drew a two foot W—*Because today's show is brought to you by the words* wizard *and* whatever—to light his way out of the pit.

Almost out of the pit.

The slope began to crumble. "Henry!"

Strong fingers closed around his wrist and yanked, defying gravity and slamming him into the reassuringly solid barrier of Henry's chest.

"Do you have to make even the easy ones difficult?" the vampire murmured, the words cool against the back of his neck.

"I didn't make it difficult," Tony panted. "It was in a pit! What did the cop want?" he asked, pulling far enough away to see Henry's face.

"He wanted to know about the light."

"What did you tell him?"

A flash of teeth. "That he didn't want to know about the light."

Four down, twenty-three to go.

♣

"Okay, Jack and Leah will keep mapping out the sites, so we don't have to figure out how to deal on the fly—they get the information back to CB, he works out the plan. I use the location search cover for the shopping mall and the restaurant and the garage while Amy runs interference." Tony picked the list up off CB's desk and shoved it in his back pocket. "That's a start anyway."

"If you want, I could stay here and plan with CB while Lee runs interference," Amy offered.

"Mr. Nicholas is working this morning," CB growled. "In spite of the damage to my building, we are still attempting to shoot a television show here."

She rolled her eyes. "No point in saving the world if we can't save *Darkest Night?*"

"No point at all." He wasn't kidding.

"No, no, they'll walk through the actual mall, but the chase scene will play out here in the gritty back corridors of commerce." Amy's voice drifted around the corner to where Tony was pushing runes between the brackets that had once held some kind of storage rack. "It'll be an exotic locale with lots of atmospheric shadows and very little chance of anything expensive getting broken."

The head of mall security snorted. "That's almost exactly what your boss said when he called."

"Yeah, well, he's big on nothing expensive getting broken."

It was harder to spot the shimmers without Leah beside him playing Marco Polo with her belly, and a scrawled note directing them, "Toward the back of the restaurant," wasn't a lot of help. Tony took an embarrassingly long time to find the weak spot on the wall of the walk-in freezer.

"Is there something missing here?" he asked the restaurant manager.

"Yeah, used to be a set of shelves that bolted to the wall. We took 'em out about a month ago, why?"

"Just wondering."

"Yeah? Well, I'm wondering what a vampire's going to be detecting in my freezer."

"Aliens," Amy drew the manager back out into the kitchen. "Kept on ice by the CIA. But don't worry, no one will ever connect this freezer to your restaurant, so you won't be overrun by hoards of alien conspiracy freaks. Unless you want to be."

♣

"No, it's like there's this car accident, see, and they bring the car back here. But Raymond Dark suspects that it wasn't an accident and that the car didn't really hit a tree. Okay, it did hit a tree, but the tree really did jump out into the road."

The way the garage owner and both mechanics were hanging on Amy's every word, not to mention her cleavage and the very, very short skirt she was wearing over the black tights and combat boots, Tony figured he could have turned the '63 Thunderbird on the rack into a pumpkin and none of them would have noticed. Not that he'd do anything so heinous to such a wicked ride, but still.

Later, he mentioned that she was disturbingly good at coming up with freaky story ideas.

"I know." She slouched lower in the seat and pulled out her phone to call the office. "It scares me a bit, too."

♣

Seven down.

Tony had an entire barbecued chicken for lunch, a 500-gram tub of potato salad, and three organic bananas Amy made him eat for the potassium. He was hungry, sure, but he still felt great. That last healing had totally been worth it.

"Leah's marked two more construction sites I can do after dark. If I can get another three tears sealed up this afternoon, well, I'm starting to think we might actually be able to win this."

"I am uplifted by your confidence. Another banana?"

"No, thanks. Three's fine."

♣

"For the last time, Mr. White has been called away, and I don't care what television show you're from; no one goes into his office without his permission."

"I keep trying to tell *you,*" Amy sighed, "that my boss phoned and spoke to your boss, and he said it wouldn't be a problem. We'll just be in and out."

Mr. White's secretary—executive assistant? Pit bull? Tony had no idea—folded her hands into what shouldn't have even remotely resembled a threatening position. Shouldn't have. Did. "Mr. White left no such instructions with me. You'll have to come back tomorrow when Mr. White is in the building."

"But . . ."

"Tomorrow."

"Will he be in later today?"

One perfectly plucked brow rose. "What did I just say?"

"Come back tomorrow?"

She smiled, not exactly in approval. "Did you want to make an appointment?"

"We had an appointment!"

"So you say. Not that it matters as Mr. White isn't here."

"Okay. Fine. We'll make an appointment."

"I'm sorry. Mr. White has no time tomorrow. Would Thursday fit your schedule?"

"What happened to Wednesday?"

"He's in court on Wednesday."

Amy took a deep breath and let it out slowly. "Mr. Bane will call Mr. White again and set something up. We'll be back."

Mr. White's secretary seemed unimpressed.

"That was a fucking waste of time we don't have." Tony sagged against the elevator wall and glared at their reflections in the stainless steel. "I should come back with a Notice Me Not on and just boogie by."

"I thought you didn't know how to get noticed again after you did a Notice Me Not."

"Yeah, well. Flaw in a brilliant plan." Without Henry around to call him back, he'd be stuck unnoticed.

"I say we just let the demon trash Mr. White's office." Amy snorted, rocking forward and back, heel to toe.

"Works for me. This could be one of the ones I don't get to."

"Unless you get to all of them, shut Mckaseeh down cold."

"Not going to happen."

Her lip curled. "Not with that attitude."

"Not with only twenty-four hours in a day."

"Time travel!"

"No." He locked eyes with her reflection so she'd know he was serious. "No messing around with time. It's a lot more dangerous than demons."

"And you don't know how to give us more time anyway, do you?"

So much for that whole locking eyes thing. "Well, no."

She bounced, once, happy with her victory. "I wonder what's missing in Mr. White's office?"

"He's a lawyer," Tony muttered, as the elevator door opened and he pushed past a neoprene-covered bicycle messenger and out into the lobby. "Where to start . . ."

♣

"Ms. Wong, please. If you could just wait for a couple more minutes. We're stuck in traffic. Yes, I realize you'd like to go, but . . . We're coming in on Hastings. No, that probably wasn't the best idea at this time of day. Just give us fifteen . . ." Amy glanced over at Tony who raised his right hand, fingers spread. ". . . twenty minutes. No, we won't be long once we get there. I promise. Thank you. We won't be long, will we?" she asked, closing her phone.

"Hard to say, the old Carnegie Library probably has . . . Hey!" He broke off his explanation to yell at the car ahead of them. "What are your fucking turn signals for, asshole!" And broke back on at: ". . . a shitload of nooks and crannies. It could take a while to find the exact position of the weak spot without Leah."

"I don't think we're going to have a while."

"You said the library was open until ten every day, Sunday to Monday. And this is Monday."

"The person CB spoke to is only there until five and, if you'll recall, our plans did not enjoy much success in the absence of Mr. White."

Tony sighed and geared down. "I'm clinging to the hope that librarians are more helpful than lawyers."

Wizards had the same trouble everyone else did finding a parking space in Chinatown at nearly five on a weeknight. Or any other time for that matter. He thought about parking illegally and putting a Notice Me Not on the car but was afraid he wouldn't be able to find it again later. They got to the library at 5:21. Ms. Wong was not impressed. Nor was she impressed by their desire to just wander around and "get the feel of the place."

"You are not the first people who have wanted to use our interior in their television show." She folded her arms and the toe of one sensible black pump tapped lightly on the tile. "You're not even the first people this month. Tell me the effect you're looking for, and I will take you where you need to go. This does not have to take the rest of the evening."

"Couldn't you just hand us over to the evening staff?" Amy asked.

"No. You're my responsibility, and the evening staff has work of their own to do. What do you need?"

"Well . . ."

"We need a place where something's missing." Tony stepped into Amy's pause.

The librarian frowned, stared at him for a long moment, and said, "There's a cushion missing off one of the seats in the reading room. Someone walked off with it last week."

"That's a good place to start. If you could . . ." He gestured and waited.

She stared at him for a moment longer and then shrugged, the barest lifting of one worsted shoulder. "This way."

♣

Eight down; nineteen to go.

"Talk about a hot seat," Amy snickered. "Some guy's sitting there, reading a newspaper and pow, demon up the ass."

Tony suppressed any thought of Ryne Cyratane in that context.

"I called the office when you were closing that last one because Ms. Wong didn't need to be distracted, and CB says the next one is another private house and Lee's going to meet us there at seven."

"Why?"

"Teenage daughters."

Okay. "Why at seven?"

"Because you've got to eat. And," she added before he could suggest they hit a drive-through and eat in the car, "because CB's estimating another half hour before Peter's through with Lee for the day."

"Oh, for . . ." Tony accelerated through a yellow light. "I think saving the world from demons is more important than getting Lee's last shot."

Amy snorted. "No, you don't."

No, he didn't.

"So why'd you just tell that librarian you needed a place where something was missing?"

Good question. "Honesty is the best policy?"

"As if."

"I thought she'd understand. She looked like she'd been . . ." He searched desperately for a less PAX TV way of saying it and couldn't find one. ". . . touched by magic."

Folding her knees up by her chest, Amy propped her boots on the dashboard. "Touched by who?"

"I don't know."

But she was a good-looking woman and he knew Henry Hunted in that part of the city.

♣

"That sounds absolutely fascinating, ladies."

Tony could hear the smile in Lee's voice and knew that

Mom and both girls were basking in full-on Lee Nicholas charm. There'd been shrieking when the door had first been opened and constant babbling as the whole group of them headed upstairs. When it looked like the babbling might ease up, Lee merely asked a question or made a comment and they were off again.

Dad had retreated behind a copy of the *Vancouver Sun* pretty much immediately.

Tony faced the five closed doors at the top of the stairs and pointed toward the northeast corner where Leah had placed the weak spot. "That room."

"Oh, my God!" The fourteen-year-old grabbed at Lee's sleeve. "That's my room."

"May I see it?"

Tony would have shown him anything if asked in that tone. If the renewed shrieking was any indication, he wasn't the only one. Fourteen raced in to tidy up while her sixteen-year-old sister tried to convince Lee that her room was infinitely better. Mom pointed out that he'd find the master suite not only bigger but more comfortable. The wink, wink, nudge, nudge was strongly implied.

Once in fourteen's bedroom, after his vision adjusted to the Day-Glo *That '70s Show* decorating, Tony discovered that the closet door was missing, replaced by a curtain of multicolored beads. The weak spot filled the space. With any luck, it was practice making the shimmer easier to see, not the imminent arrival of a host of demons.

"I might need to look at the other bedrooms," Lee said thoughtfully, when Tony gave him the sign.

More shrieking.

It suddenly became clear why Lee was willing to face demons. Demons were quieter.

♣

Nine down. Eighteen demons were still eighteen demons too many.

"Where to after this?" Lee asked sotto voce as they walked side by side down the porch stairs. This prime space had opened up when Mom had been forced to physically intervene before an argument over who'd walk beside Lee to the curb had come to blows.

"I'm meeting Henry at a construction site," Tony told him as, behind them, fourteen accused sixteen of having been in her face her entire life. "You're okay driving Amy home?"

"Sure. You'll get some sleep? I mean, later."

"I don't need much."

"I have to admit you look better than you did." Lee's gaze skittered across the side of Tony's face and ended up locked on the path. "Better in a medical sense. We're all worried about you."

Tony took a few seconds to examine and abandon several possible responses before sticking with tradition. "I'm fine."

"You've lost a lot of weight."

"When this is over . . ." He paused as sixteen threw in an *oh, grow up* too vehement to talk over. ". . . I'll gain it back."

"I'm not saying you're looking less studly; I'm saying you look a bit thin is all."

Studly? Tony tripped over a bit of concrete edging. Lee grabbed his arm and yanked him roughly back onto his feet.

"Guys!" Amy's voice cut through the October evening like a siren. "We've got incoming fen!"

Fourteen and sixteen buried the hatchet and began yelling at their friends to hurry.

Several voices shrieked, "Oh, my God, it's Lee Nicholas!"

Several more shrieked, "Lee, I love you!"

Tony's car was across the street and half a dozen houses down. Lee had found a spot barely twenty meters away. "Run!" Tony gave him a shove. "You can make it to your car!"

"What about you?" Lee demanded as the shrieking lost vocabulary and degenerated into a primal fannish keen.

"Don't worry about me, once you're gone, they'll calm down."

"What if they don't?"

"Damn it, Lee, run!" Just for a second, Tony was sure he heard an overwrought soundtrack, then Lee turned and sprinted for his car, digging out his keys as he ran.

A chime as the doors of the new Mercedes SUV unlocked.

"Amy!"

"Already here." She glared across the hood as Lee raced for the driver's door. "And do you have any idea how much gas one of these things uses?"

"It's bio-diesel!"

"No shit?" Half in, she leaned out for another look and nearly went flying as Lee pulled away from the curb. She dragged herself in and as the door closed, Tony heard Lee getting an earful of Spanish profanity.

At least Tony thought it was profanity. He didn't speak Spanish.

News to him that Amy did.

As the crowd realized they'd lost a chance to get up close and personal with the actor second billed in the opening credits of the highest rated vampire detective show on syndicated television, they turned their nearly hysterical, thwarted gaze on Tony. Just in case Lee hadn't been impressive on his own, Tony was wearing his show jacket to impress the homeowners.

The crowd didn't know who he was or what he did, but they knew he was with the show.

They were between him and his car.

He'd never make it.

This was not the time for discretion.

Bright side, no one would believe this lot anyway.

Tony grabbed for his focus, reached for his fly, and snapped out the Notice Me not.

There was a security guard on duty at the first construction site. A six-foot-four ex-cop from Ghana, he was studying to be an EMT. With an exam coming up, the odds were good he'd have never noticed a quiet visit tucked in between his appointed rounds, but Henry leaned just enough to raise the odds a little more and then went out to meet Tony.

Although the last of the evening's commuters kept the traffic fairly heavy over on Norland Avenue, Ledger Avenue—where the condominium complex was being built—was nearly empty. Henry heard Tony's car before he saw it. Even knowing it was there, it was nearly impossible to keep his attention on it. He found himself distracted by the hearts beating all around him; by the scent of blood, warm and contained; by the hundreds of thousand of lives that could be his for the Hunting.

Snarling, he forced himself to watch as the car stopped and the driver's side door opened and . . .

There was a woman singing in a third-floor apartment across the road. The song was melancholy, and it told him he'd be welcomed should his Hunt take him to her door.

A touch on his shoulder.

He whirled, grabbed a fistful of fabric, and slammed someone, something to the pavement—the familiar scent registering a moment too late.

"Fucking ow, Henry! That hurt!"

"Tony." Lying at his feet. Heart racing. Glaring up at him as if this was somehow his fault. "I see. You used the Notice Me Not again."

"I didn't have a choice," Tony grunted, accepting Henry's hand and allowing himself to be lifted to his feet. "There was this horde of *Darkest Night* fans ready to tear me limb from limb."

A red-gold brow rose. "The show has enough fans to make up a horde?"

"Small horde," he admitted, checking to make sure everything worked. "More like a mob, really. Very feisty, though. And pissed. So, are you planning to apologize for dumping me on my ass?" Which felt distinctly bruised.

Henry smiled. "Your spell distracted me with thoughts of the Hunt."

"So you're saying I'm lucky I only got dumped on my ass?"

"Essentially."

"Okay, works for me." He turned to study the steel skeletons of the three towers. "Leah's notes say this one's tucked up in that first structure."

♣

Tony knew Henry wouldn't drop him. Knew it without question. His hindbrain however, currently dangling four stories up supported only by a vampire's grip on his ankles, was having none of that. As far as his hindbrain was concerned, they were going to die.

Painfully.

Messily.

On impact.

The hysterical background babbling of *OH, MY GOD!* was annoying. And distracting.

"I don't want to rush you, Tony, but the moon has risen and we're not exactly invisible up here. If a resident living on the upper floors of any of those buildings across the way should happen to glance out their window . . ."

"Yeah. I get it. We'd be screwed. Sorry."

The orientation of the runes didn't seem to matter.

*Good fucking thing, too, because I don't think I could draw them upside down.*

*Right side up. I'm upside down.*

*OHMYGODOHMYGODOHMYGOD!*

♣

Ten down. Seventeen to go.

The second weak spot of the night wasn't so much in a construction site as an excavation.

"What's with the attraction to holes in the ground?" Tony muttered as they walked down the packed dirt ramp left for the excavation equipment.

"They are creatures of hell. They would feel at home in a pit."

"It's not that kind of a hell, Henry."

"Would a man spend his time there in eternal torment?"

"I guess." Based on what they'd seen of the inhabitants, it seemed a fair assumption. Although *eternal* might be thinking a bit too long term.

"Then it's close enough for me."

Eleven to sixteen.

"Oh, no," Tony protested, backing away even though Henry had made no move in his direction. "There'll be time enough to sleep when this is over."

"If you could finish it tonight, I'd agree with you, but you can't and you're becoming visibly exhausted. When you're tired, you make mistakes. When you make mistakes, you get hurt. When you get hurt, you heal yourself and, as your body becomes progressively more worn down, there is always the chance you won't survive the process."

"There's not much room for argument when you put it like that."

Henry smiled his most irritating Prince of Man smile. "Which is why I put it like that."

Television meant early mornings and habit got Tony to the studio by seven, a mere ten minutes after sunrise even though Henry had set his alarm for eight before he left. CB and Leah and Jack were already in the office. Amy arrived minutes after Tony and Lee minutes after that, carrying a tray of coffee.

"You may be wondering why I've called you all here," Jack muttered.

Only Amy laughed.

One hand up under the edge of her sweater, Leah stared down at the map spread out over CB's desk. "Well, that confirms it. The tears are deeper than they were."

Sixteen of the burns on the map were noticeably darker.

The good news was, Leah had recognized Ryne Cyratane's ownership of the arjh coming through in the middle of the Willingdon overpass. And the bad news involved the Telus overpass and another weak spot.

While Tony and Lee had been dodging teenagers, CB had spent a couple of hours on the phone and called in some favors.

♣

At exactly 9:45, an RCMP patrol car, lights flashing pulled out into the middle lane of the Kingsway and parked just out from under the Telus overpass. Morning rush hour traffic, finally having dropped from insanely busy to annoyingly crowded began to flow around it. When the uniformed constable stopped traffic entirely, Tony helped manhandle the rented telescoping platform out under the overpass. As the guy who'd come with the platform locked it down, he set out orange traffic cones.

When CB had laid out the plan, Tony had stared at him in disbelief. *"What am I supposed to do while they're setting up?"* he'd demanded.

*"I suggest, Mr. Foster, that you do your job. Unless there happens to be a spell to turn straw into gold on that laptop of yours, in which case you may do whatever you please."*

As traffic began to move again, now including the area the platform occupied in their detour, he followed the steadicam operator up the short ladder and clutched the steel railing as the platform rose.

They were directly under the weak spot. He could burn the runes in the air just below it and then shove them quickly up and through. The steadicam operator had his back to Tony as he shot the traffic moving under the overpass. The occupants of the cars, used to having to accommodate a dozen studios plus visiting productions, didn't even look up.

He was finished in just under ten minutes.

"Okay, let's go."

"I don't think so, kid. Chester Bane is paying me for twenty minutes of brand spanking new stock footage and that's what I'm going to shoot for him."

"But . . ."

"Do I look stupid enough to cross Chester Bane, kid?"

Fair question. And no, he didn't. "Then just let me down."

"We have this spot for half an hour, kid, no more. That's bloody close to not enough time so, again, no."

He couldn't climb down; dangling then dropping made him think of broken legs and Henry's reaction. "I'm trying to save the fucking world here!"

"Yeah, well, I only have your word for that whereas I know what'll happen if Chester Bane pays for twenty minutes and gets nineteen fifty-nine. The end of the world will seem tame in comparison."

Since Tony didn't have an argument for that, he folded his arms and fumed.

♣

With the easy places already taken care of, he only got two closed that day and one closed after dark.

Fourteen to thirteen. They'd pulled ahead by one. Two if he put Ryne Cyratane's marked arjh on their side of the count.

As Tony fell into a fitful sleep, he held tight to the hope that they might have a shot at winning this after all.

Three closed the next day.

Seventeen to ten.

Only two the day after that, though, and the second was nearly a disaster.

"What the hell is he doing? Does he paint graffiti on the pool? I see him paint something! I don't believe you come from vampire television. You stay! You stay right there! I call the 911!"

The Notice Me Not kept him from getting arrested, but it also kept him from interacting with anything until long after sunset when Henry finally found him. The longer the spell was on, the harder it was to get off.

Nineteen to eight.

Twenty to seven.

Twenty-one to six.

Those last two had gone relatively easily, but now he was stuck in traffic with Leah singing along to the latest from Radiogram. They were a local band who'd recently rocketed off local playlists and into the international music scene. Tony liked the band and their music, but Leah's smug *I followed them before they were famous* attitude was driving him up the wall. She even sang along smugly.

*Like I don't have enough to do without sitting here and listening to her . . .*

Hang on. Had Radiogram worked the *Darkest Night* theme into their latest release?

No. That was his phone.

"Leah."

"I'm on it." She stretched an arm behind his seat, snagged his backpack, freed his phone, and stuffed it into the dock.

"Tony, it's Kevin Groves. I just got a call from one of our regulars. She says she saw something big with horns blow apart the Willingdon overpass."

Tony eased into the curb lane while he waited for the other shoe to drop.

"She wasn't lying."

And there it was.

"Thanks, Kevin. Hang up." The phone clicked off. He needed to get to the studio. He needed to get turned around. Diagonally through a gas station, out the other side, over a median strip, and into the left turn lane to more-or-less catch the final seconds of the advance green.

Half a block. Picking up speed. Cutting between two SUVs.

Sliding sideways on damp pavement, Tony fought the car back onto four tires. "Keep that map down. I need to see out that window!"

"You need your fucking head—BUS!—head examined! And you need to look at this."

Another half block before he could take his eyes off the road long enough to glance her way. The way Leah was holding the map, he could see six pinholes where the light showed through. Six weak points burned through. Six demons in the city. One of them was theoretically on their side, but somehow that didn't make him feel any better.

"Call CB, tell him to empty the studio. Then call Jack and Henry."

"Sun's not down. BIKE!"

He missed the cyclist by millimeters. "Leave a message."

"I have a better idea." Her fingernails had left half moon cuts in his dashboard. "Why don't you pull into that strip mall, then you can make the calls and I can get us to the studio alive."

Tony hesitated just for a second then bounced up over the curb and into the strip mall parking lot. This was not the time to let machismo get in the way of a professional stunt driver. Their odds would improve with stunt drivers in the surrounding cars, but he'd take what he could get. As he dove back into the passenger side and buckled up, he glanced at the clock. 5:07. More than an hour and a half until sunset.

As Leah stomped on the gas, he reached for the phone.

They'd be starting before Henry woke for the night. Then he'd have to drive out to Burnaby. They'd be fighting multiple demons without his strength and speed, and it was entirely possible they'd be finished without him. Fucking weak spots might as well have torn open at noon. "TAXI!"

"Please. I saw it. You know, we still have time to get on a plane and haul ass out of here."

Suspicion tightened his chest. "Was that why you wanted to drive?"

"No, no, I'm doing the responsible thing."

"ONE-WAY STREET!"

Leah snorted and drove half a block on the sidewalk. "You know, Tony, if you're going to save the world tonight, you really need to pace yourself."

# Fifteen

FIGHTING TO KEEP THE nutritional supplement pouring into his mouth instead of spraying around the inside of the car, Tony watched in amazement as Leah forced every possible ounce of power from the elderly engine, took a few highly illegal shortcuts, and beat the demons back to the soundstage. The previous two trips they'd taken had clearly been nothing more than a rehearsal for this.

"Bonus that there's never a cop around when you need one," he ground out through clenched teeth, really hoping he wasn't going to hurl as they bounced over the back curb of the CB Productions lot.

"We weren't on a major highway this time, so I doubt anyone called us in."

"You doubt?" His voice went up embarrassingly high on the second word. "You went the wrong way down a Tim Horton's drive-through!"

"Please, in this area . . ." Leah yanked the wheel hard to the left and skidded to a stop, spraying gravel over the craft services truck. ". . . they probably thought we were filming."

She had a point. A month earlier, Vancouverites had applauded an armed bank robbery; bank security hadn't intervened, apparently waiting for someone to yell *"Cut!"*

"There're too many vehicles still in the lot," Tony grumbled, getting out of the car. Sure they'd been speedy, but he'd seen CB clear the building in less time. When the big guy said go, it took a stupidly reckless man to linger.

Leah grabbed his arm. "Hang on." Dragging him around to face her, she licked the edge of a tissue and scrubbed at his upper lip.

"What the . . ."

"Supplement mustache. Sets a bad example for the troops."

"We don't have any troops!"

"And the demons will laugh at you." One final swipe. "There."

"Thank you." It was as sarcastic an appreciation as he could manage. "Do I look like I should be taken seriously now?" he demanded as they raced for the rear door.

"Not so much, no."

Big surprise. Not. Maybe he should get a pointy hat. Or a big sword. Or his head examined.

Charging down the center aisle, he jumped cables, dodged around equipment, stopped dead as he emerged out into the open area by Adam's desk. "What the . . . ?" He whirled to glare at Leah. "Did you know this was going to happen?"

She spread her hands. "Hey, I'm as surprised as you are."

"You mentioned troops!"

"I was being facetious."

"They want to help," CB explained, stepping forward,

"Help?" Tony moved his attention from Leah to his boss. "What did you tell them?"

"That the battle would be joined tonight. Not as part of a general announcement, but to those who knew enough to ask."

Zev, Amy, Lee—no surprise, although Tony would rather they were all somewhere safe, like New Zealand—Mouse, Peter . . .

"Sorge and Adam and Tina have kids," Peter said, one thigh propped on Adam's desk next to a half-full box of flares last used in episode seven. "Kids who actually live with them," he amended. "We sent them home."

. . . Saleen, Pavin, and Kate.

They'd all been in the house last summer. They'd survived

Creighton Caulfield and they'd heard about what had happened in the spring with the Shadowlord. They knew what Tony was, and they thought they knew what he could do.

"Your fan club seems to be growing," Leah murmured, warm breath lifting the hair on the back of his neck.

Yeah, right. Kate had never liked him.

"Guys, there's half a dozen demons on their way. Demons. Just like in the most clichéd screenplay; all claws and horns and tentacles and bad attitude. Ask Zev, ask Amy, ask CB, they've all seen them. Well, one." He frowned. "Okay, I think CB saw a couple of them, but . . ."

"Shut up," Kate snarled. "We asked. We know." She snapped the loops of yellow nylon rope between her hands. "We need to knock them down and tie them up so you can send them back right? It's a physical fight—slam, bam, kick a little demonic ass?"

"It's not that easy . . ."

"Did I say it was going to be easy? We get that they're big and strong. What we don't get is how you thought you could take them out with only the boss and a Mountie at your side."

"Hey!" Amy protested. "Lee and I were always staying!"

"Yeah, an actor and a receptionist, that'll make a lot of difference," Saleen muttered. The grip slapped a length of steel pipe into his left hand. "These things have no special powers, right?"

"Well, they . . ."

"No," Leah interrupted. "They're just big and strong."

"And ugly," Zev snorted, fingering the sleeve of his sweater.

"Then it's time we get some of our own back."

"Some of your own back from what?" Tony demanded, wondering when he'd lost control of the situation. The words "stupidly reckless" were repeating on a background loop in his head.

"The Shadowlord. Creighton Caulfield." Mouse never said much, so the big cameraman's words carried a deliberate weight.

"They're not doing this for you, Tony." Lee crossed to stand barely an arm's length away. "They're fighting for themselves. Because this time, they can."

*They're not? They?* The next obvious question had to be *What about you?* or maybe *Who writes your dialogue?* But he knew the answer to the second and this wasn't the time to hear the answer to the first, and anyway, there were half a dozen demons making tracks to the studio. He took a deep breath and one step to the side so that the others could see him. Everyone accounted for but Mason, and Mason's absence was hardly sur . . .

"goddamned thing got buried in the closet!" Clutching the double-handed broadsword from episode twelve and wearing the slightly squibbed camouflage jacket from episode sixteen, Mason rocked to a stop by CB's side. "What did I miss?"

"Tony questioning our right to be here," Kate deadpanned.

Mason snorted. "*Tony* questioning? Who's the star of this show, him or me?"

"Heads up, people!" Jack charged into the group, glanced around, and obviously decided not to ask. "I just got off the phone with Geetha. There're six kinds of hell breaking lose and heading this way."

"You've been waiting your whole career to say that, haven't you?" Amy asked, snickering.

He flashed her a broad smile. "Pretty much, yeah."

"Okay." It wouldn't be in a few minutes, but right now it was. When they all turned to look at him, Tony said it again just because he liked the sound of it. "Okay. Jack, help Leah and CB position the troops. Pavin, bring one of the Fresnos to the back. I'm going to try and stop a demon at the door." He ran for the back without waiting for an answer. If they wanted to help, they could damned well be helpful.

He'd finished burning the first two runes by the time Pavin wrestled one of the small spotlights over from the office set. "Does light hurt them?"

"No. Set up here. Aim the beam through that pattern and right out the door."

"Blinding it?" Pavin asked, remarkably blasé about bright blue squiggles just hanging in the air. He used the knob on the back of the casing to adjust the beam. "So it can't see what you wrote?"

Let's hear it for tech support. "Yeah. That's the idea." He stepped out into the parking lot and drew the third rune with his eyes nearly squinted shut. "You'd better get back with the others."

The light blazed out the open door, significantly brighter than the late afternoon sun and definitely blinding. He couldn't see the rune from any angle that would get him through the door. Hopefully, the demon didn't know how this world worked, so it wouldn't realize the light was too bright. If they were lucky, it might wonder about the sudden change in illumination and pause in the doorway giving him time to get the final rune in place. With a little more luck, it wouldn't be Ryne Cyratane's arjh who showed up, wasting a perfectly good trap or trapping one of their best chances of surviving this.

*Good idea, Tony, use up all your luck before the fight even starts.*

As he burned the fourth rune, he realized there was something not quite right about the ambient noise. The familiar background sounds of the city were less familiar than they should be. He'd nearly finished when those sounds separated into squealing tires and breaking glass. Less screaming than he'd expected, but there'd likely be time for that later.

Half a Honda Civic rolled past the edge of the building. Tony slapped the last curl on the fourth rune and dove behind the garbage can at the craft services truck, rune clutched in his left hand. The demon charged around the corner still holding the other half of the car.

*What I'm holding beats what you're holding . . .*

*. . . unless you decide to throw the car at me. Crap!*

The twisted hunk of metal crashed into the gravel right in front of the garbage can, covering Tony in glittering bits of safety glass and slamming the can into his shoulder.

He didn't think he made much of a noise, but when the dust settled, the demon stood just outside the beam of light, eyestalks turned toward him, the bit on its face that corresponded to a nose twitching and testing the air.

Not good on a couple of levels.

The runes wouldn't hang forever and a little experimentation over the last few days had proved that the longer they were in place, the less kick ass they became.

Also, the plan was to avoid the ultimate wizard and demon one-on-one for as long as possible. A Powershot would knock him on his ass and out of the fight, so if it turned out to be inevitable it had to happen late in the game.

From inside the soundstage, a girlie shriek. It sounded like Mason.

The demon's head went up, exposing the get-Leah rune cut into its chest. Hard to tell, given the arrangement of its features, but it looked embarrassed. Maybe not Mason, then. Maybe some demons were less demonic than others. Grumbling under its breath, it stepped into the light, hissed and reared back, eyestalks withdrawing into the top of its head.

Tony had started moving as the demon moved. As it reared, he shoved the fourth rune into position.

It had time for only a truncated howl before the runes flared and it disappeared.

"Yes! One down!" He'd just started breathing normally for what seemed like the first time in half an hour when a clawed hand closed on his bruised shoulder.

There were only three entrances to the soundstage.

Three entrances. Six demons. Basic math.

*Crap.*

*And fucking OW!*

"Wizard."

Talking? That was new.

Ignoring the blood dribbling down from the points of the claws, Tony twisted as far as he could in the demon's grip. It looked sort of like a miniature Ryne Cyratane, although more Texas longhorn than Bambi's dad, and it wore the most obvious of the Arjh Lord's attributes sheathed up like a dog's. Unlike the single rune on the chest of the first demon, the black runes carved into mini-Ryne's chest were oozing blood over a pattern very nearly as complex as Leah's. It seemed that slipping an arjh into another lord's plan took more than a fake mustache, but since Sye Mckaseeh seemed to recruit from farther out on the horror show spectrum, that wasn't really surprising.

"Help wizard."

"Yeah. Fine. Release wizard!" The claws hurt as much on the way out as they had on the way in. "All right, if you're going to . . . never mind." The completely blank expression suggested he keep it simple. "Follow wizard!"

*It's a little like live action* Zork, he thought as he ran into the soundstage, the demon hard on his heels. *Eat snake. Thank you, that was delicious. I can't believe Henry still has that game on his system. And not a good time for silent babbling, Tony. Pull it togeth— Fuck.*

Three of the other four demons had arrived.

There wasn't room for all three of them directly under the gate, so they'd spread out within the confines of the set, turning the entire area into a seething mass of multicolored flesh and weaponry. Kate and Pavin were trying to loop a tentacled lime-green demon in rope while Saleen whaled on any bits he could get close to with his pipe. Amy, Lee, and Zev had another cornered. No, it had Zev cornered. No, they had it cornered. Jack was down on one knee, blood dribbling from the corner of his mouth. Mason was fighting sword to claw with the upper right arm of another of the chitin-covered demons yelling something that sounded like "Parry, thrust, riposte!" while Mouse silently fought the lower right, and CB dealt with the left side. Peter sagged against the wall, gasping for breath, arms wrapped around his torso. Leah was nowhere in sight. Since the point of this exercise from the invaders perspective was to open the Demongate, CB had stashed Leah somewhere safe.

And a good thing, too, since all three demons had a single, familiar rune etched into their chests. Or the equivalent area.

Tony pointed mini-Ryne toward the battle. "Fight demons!"

Mini-Ryne seemed less than enthused. "Help wizard."

"Fight demons!"

"Guard gate."

Left palm flat against the center of his back, Tony shoved

him forward. "Fight demons!" Whether the pressure of the rune convinced him or he'd run out of excuses, mini-Ryne finally charged into the fray, and Tony raced for the extension ladder. CB and Jack had been insistent that he not be in the middle of the fight; there were too many demons and if one of them realized he was the wizard, in the absence of the Demongate he'd be the center of all the demonic attention by default.

From the top of the ladder, he crawled out onto the lighting grid. Technically, this was not someplace he should be, but the grid was built to hold hundreds of pounds of lights and sooner or later, every electrician or light tech in the business ended up with his feet off the ladder or scaffold. Since he was neither, it was a good thing CB ran a flexible studio. Had demons been attacking a CBC studio, the world would be screwed.

He burned all four runes into the air beside him before he looked down.

Lime-green-and-tentacles had moved away from the corner. Amy had danced inside the tentacles and was pounding a second, foot-long ash stake into the main bulk of its body. Lee bashed the end of a tentacle against the floor with an antique mace, ducked a second, and slammed a third away from his head at the last minute. Zev stood to one side cocking a crossbow, a length of the yellow nylon rope tied to one end of the quarrel.

They weren't bringing it down, but they were definitely holding it in place.

"Welcome to the set of *Darkest Night,*" he muttered, stretching along the grid. Vampire shows inevitably acquired a lot of interesting weaponry. He dropped the first two runes into place and was ready with the third when Amy screamed, her leg caught in one of the demon's unexpected mouths. Distracted, Lee went down, lime-green coils around his torso. *You don't get to be distracted!* he reminded himself. He was already doing the best thing he could do to help. Third rune down. Placing the fourth rune got tricky until Zev got off his shot, dropped the crossbow and tried to tangle the demon's legs with attached rope. A glancing blow from the chitin-covered demon drove him forward into the grasp of another tentacle. Adjusting for Zev's weight, the demon jerked back against the first three runes. It shrieked as it brushed up against the power. As it charged forward, Tony threw the fourth rune into position.

"And action!"

Light flared.

Amy, Lee, Zev, and a meter of tentacle that had been reaching beyond the area the runes enclosed lay panting on the floor—although strictly speaking the tentacle wasn't panting as much as twitching. Amy had both hands clamped against her thigh, blood seeping between her fingers. Rows of tiny holes in Lee's jeans were beginning to darken. Holding the quarrel with the rope in one hand, Zev crawled toward the crossbow.

*Focus on the demons!*

Something grabbed his ankle.

He probably should have wrapped both arms around the grid and hung on, but that occurred to him a second late. Turning, Tony caught a glimpse of a familiar mouth with too many rows of black teeth between red scaled lips.

The sixth demon.

And then he was falling.

He curled in the air, landed on his right side, heard a bone snap. Since it wasn't his skull, he was actually okay with that. Arm maybe. No. Higher. Something in his shoulder. It hurt to breathe.

Then it really hurt as red-and-scaly flipped him over and raised a hand, trio of ten-centimeter claws extended. As the claws swung down for a disemboweling stroke, Jack caught the arm, shoved his gun in the demon's armpit, and pulled the trigger.

On a good day, which this wasn't, Tony had no idea how many bullets Jack's gun fired, but it seemed to go on for a while. Five, ten minutes. Or maybe his sense of time had gotten scrambled by the fall because there was no way the demon should have waited that long to bring its tail around and smack Jack off his feet.

On the other hand, its arm flopped uselessly, so who knew?

One arm flopped. The other was working fine. The first strike removed the front of Tony's jacket and most of the T-shirt under it. For some reason, losing a second jean jacket in the line of duty really pissed him off, and as the demon threw back its head and screamed in trumph, Tony cocked his right elbow just enough to raise his hand off the floor.

He'd spoken the first four words of the Powershot when Kate appeared holding two lit flares that she slam-dunked into the demon's gaping, tooth-lined throat.

The explosion was unexpected.

Welcome, but messy.

"Too fucking gross," Kate muttered as Jack returned, kicked aside a twitching slab of meat and grabbed Tony's raised hand. On the way up onto his feet, Tony discovered he'd broken his collarbone.

"You okay?" Lip curled, Jack flicked a wet, lavender glob off Tony's shoulder.

Lavender?

"Hey! Tony! Are you okay?"

"Sure." He was standing. He was breathing. Everything from his eyelashes to the ends of broken bone grating in his chest hurt, but he'd deal with that later. Out of the corner of one eye, he saw something long and green whipping toward him. He ducked before he realized the tentacle was no longer attached.

Jack hauled him upright again. "Tony?"

"I'm fine."

What he first thought was a disbelieving snort turned out to be the sound of another tentacle being ripped free. Mini-Ryne, his horns dripping dark fluids, sat on top of the remaining lime-green demon, removing tentacles and deftly avoiding the many mouths trying to take a piece out of him. His victory would have been more impressive had the demon not been wrapped in enough rope it looked like it had been swept up by some kind of deep-sea fishing net.

*This tuna is not demon safe. StarKist doesn't want demons with good taste, they want . . .*

"Tony! Focus!"

Right. Focusing.

"Not the face! Not the face!"

Mason's shrieked protest spun Tony around in time to see the actor flung backward by the chitin demon, the sword he still held bent into a tight vee. Roaring a challenge, the demon charged after him. Mason was seconds from losing his face entirely when CB roared a challenge of his own, pounded across the soundstage, and slammed a shoulder into the demon's middle in a perfect offensive tackle.

The demon went down.

Buildings would have gone down.

Unfortunately, CB went down, too. Worse, the demon bounced back up again dangling ropes like fat yellow streamers. Zev had clearly gotten off a couple more shots with the crossbow and just as clearly no one had been able to take advantage of them. It bent enough for its upper left hand to grab one of CB's ankles, and when it straightened, CB came off the floor.

Which pretty much proved that the demon was as strong as it looked.

The demon swatted Mouse away with its right hands. It seemed obvious that CB's head was about to be slammed into the concrete.

Tony jerked out of Jack's hold, grabbed his right wrist with his left, lifted the right arm to shoulder height then whipped it back and around while screaming out the words for the Powershot. Given the broken collarbone, the screaming was nonnegotiable. As his arm started back down, his right wrist slapped into his left palm, aiming the blast of energy that burned through chitin breastplates.

CB hit the floor with a solid thud, momentarily obscured by clouds of falling ash drifting back and forth.

*No, wait. That back and forth, that's me.* Swaying, Tony sank to one knee. "Check CB," he panted as Jack began to bend. He needed time to recover, and if turned out they were going to have to buy that time, they'd need CB's strength. Fortunately, Jack got the subtext.

Keeping his breathing shallow and his right arm supported by his knee, he turned just his head toward the only surviving demon. Mini-Ryne seemed to have eaten his way through to the life-sustaining bits and was now clearly sitting on nothing but meat.

For a long moment, the loudest noise on the soundstage was enthusiastic chewing and swallowing.

"Did we win?"

All eyes turned to Mason who was crawling out from behind the upturned chaise lounge. When he looked up and realized he was the center of attention, he tried to pull the sleeve of the camouflage jacket up over his bare arm. "Well?" he demanded petulantly as he realized the sleeve wasn't going to stay. "Did we win or not?"

The only demon in the room seemed to be on their side.

"Yeah." Tony sucked in as much air as he could, hoping for enough volume to carry over the rising tide of sound. "It looks like we did." The nail on his baby finger curled up, dropped off, and wafted slowly to the floor.

Mason was limping on a wrenched knee but unbloodied. Besides innumerable small cuts, CB had broken three fingers on one hand but ordered Jack away to deal with his own injuries. Mouse's nose had been broken again. Peter, Saleen, and Jack had cracked or broken ribs. Jack also had a split lip and a broken tooth. Amy and Pavin had been bitten. Amy had also got a bit of demon in the eye when Kate had blown it up. Lee, Zev, and Kate had long lines of tiny cuts from teeth in the edge of some of the tentacles. Zev had a line across his back and Kate's went around one arm. Lee's leather jacket had protected most of his torso but his pale jeans were marked with spiral blotches of blood.

"Should've worn your motorcycle chaps," Amy noted from the floor as Zev cut away the leg of her 100 percent organic hemp cargo pants.

"Good thing he didn't," Zev snorted. "We needed Tony's mind on the job."

Tony considered protesting, but it was a fair assessment, so he saved his strength. CB was the only one not coming up in varying shades of purple and black, but that was because CB was the only one too dark for the bruising to show. They were walking wounded, all twelve of them. Emphasis on walking.

"No one died," he said. And then because it was important, he said it again. Louder. "No one died."

It was almost funny watching the various gazes tracking around the space, checking to make sure.

Jack pulled his T-shirt down over the binding Kate had just wrapped around his ribs. "Not in here," he reminded them grimly, "but Geetha told me there were at least seven dead out on the street before this started, plus a shitload of critical injuries. We didn't avoid a body count, not by a fuck of a long shot."

"No one here died." CB's tone suggested no one argue this time. "Right now, I think we deserve to celebrate that."

Tony was thinking about that lawyer, the one with the weak spot in his office and when he caught Amy's eye, he knew she was thinking the same. Nothing they could have done about it then. Nothing they could do about it now. He'd just have to keep telling himself that. He didn't remember sitting down, but since he was on the floor, his back up against the underside of the yellow chaise, he must have. Little bits of broken glass surrounded him like glittering confetti. One of the lights had fallen at some point during the battle; crashed to the floor where every part of it that could shatter, had shattered into the smallest pieces possible. They'd been lucky. If it hadn't hit so hard, they could have added shards of flying glass to the *"things trying to kill us"* list. Tony had no memory of hearing the impact.

"Now then," CB stepped over the headless body of the red-scaled demon like it was of no consequence, and swept an imperious gaze around his domain, "we can't all hit an emergency room at the same time. Ms. Anderson, you're in the best shape. I want you to drive . . ." He stared at his crew standing clumped together and came to the obvious decision to save time. ". . . Peter, Mouse, Saleen, and Pavin to Burnaby General. They're used to the strange accidents of the entertainment industry, and with all the chaos in the area, there should be no problem."

"What about . . ." Kate jerked a thumb at mini-Ryne, currently pulling a line of linked opalescent bladders from deep inside the body of his meal.

"I doubt Tony will need all of us if he has to deal with . . . him."

Tony expected a protest, but Kate merely rolled her eyes. "Okay, but I can't fit five in my car."

"We'll take my van." Peter went to pull the scraps of his shirt back on, sighed, and tossed it on the floor. He waved those mentioned toward the exit. "It seats seven."

Limping heavily, using his piece of pipe as a cane, Saleen fell into step beside the director. "Dude, why do you have a van that seats seven?"

"Garage band."

"Seriously?"

"No."

"Hey!" Tony wasn't sure they heard him—given the distance and the whole about-to-pass-out thing—but all five paused. He needed to say something but wasn't sure what. Finally, he shrugged his one usable shoulder. "Thanks."

Weirdly, Mouse spoke for the group. He moved the dripping handful of flannel shirt away from his nose and grinned, the bloodstained teeth and eyes already swelling shut making him look particularly disreputable. "Wouldn't have missed it."

The other four, even Kate, nodded.

"Hang on," Amy called out, head cocked so she could glare through her nonwatering eye. "If they leave, who's going to clean this mess up?"

They were gone before she finished asking.

Tony braced himself for her protest, but CB began a second set of instructions before she got the chance. "Zev, take Amy and Lee out to Eagle Ridge. One of the demons came through near there. That gives us a ready-made explanation for the bite and the claw marks. If they ask, you were all out there because we're thinking of shooting at Heritage Mountain."

"And if they ask why we waited before coming in?"

Formal cadences returned with the raised brow. "I think Mr. Nicholas' talent extends to providing a little attitude."

"I could," Lee admitted, folding his arms. "But I'm not going anywhere until this is over."

Amy echoed his action from the floor. "Neither am I."

"Hardly seems worth going all the way to Eagle Ridge on my own," Zev pointed out with a careful shrug.

"You're all bleeding," Jack began, but Amy cut him off.

"You call this bleeding," she scoffed, folding her good leg under her and using Zev's uninjured arm to pull herself to her feet. "I lose more monthly. Besides, you're bleeding, CB's bleeding, Tony's bleeding . . ."

He was? He glanced down at his bare chest between the shredded wings of jacket and shirt and blearily focused on the lines of red rolling down from his right shoulder. Oh, yeah.

". . . and you guys aren't leaving."

"There is still a demon to deal with," CB told her. "Not to mention, as you so helpfully pointed out, the mess."

"Wizard!"

"Whoa!" Amy's head whipped around so fast her hair separated into bicolored layers. "This one talks?"

"Yeah." Tony shifted position slightly and regretted it a lot. "He talks. What do you want?"

It was hard to tell because of the gore encrusting his face—plus Tony's vision was a bit wonky—but mini-Ryne looked worried. "Demongate?"

"Safe." Frowning hurt, too. Quel surprise. Not. "At least I think . . ." He turned to CB who took three long strides and dropped to one knee beside him.

"If you cannot send this creature back, Mr. Foster . . ."

"I can do it." It might be the last thing he did for a while, but he figured he had enough left in him to draw four final runes. *Let's hear it for endorphins. Yay endorphins.* As long as he didn't have to hurry. Or, apparently, stand up. "Uh, Boss? Little help."

The big difference between being lifted onto his feet by Henry and CB was, well, about a foot vertically and at least that much horizontally. CB was a big guy and Henry was . . .

Henry wasn't.

That meant something. Tony frowned. Winced.

"Ms. Burnett is outside in my car." CB's voice was a low growl against his ear. "Parked up against that outside wall . . ." He nodded across the soundstage to the wall closest to the gate. ". . . she is close enough to the gate and to you that her own metaphysical signature should be masked but able to make a fast getaway should we have lost this fight. I doubt very much that any demon would have been able to catch her."

"Drove the Jag today?"

"I did."

It seemed like a plan. Actually, it seemed like a good plan, especially the masked signature part. "Have you been reading up on this shit?"

"Mr. Groves has suggested a number of very helpful publications."

"I'll bet. And she's going to stay out there . . . ?"

"Until one of us goes and gets her."

"Demongate."

"I told you, she's safe." Hang on. That wasn't a question. The first time the demon had asked. This time . . .

"Would whoever's been calling for me, please shut the fuck up. I'm not deaf, and I'm moving as fast as I can."

Most of his weight still on CB's arm, Tony turned in time to see Leah stop walking and raise a hand to her nose. The other hand was tucked under her clothes, pressed up against the skin of her stomach.

"Oh, wow. It stinks in here. Smells like offal and peppermint with the faintest hint of sulfur." She frowned over her hand at Tony. "You had to ash one?"

"Yeah. Leah . . ."

"Demongate!"

"What the hell?" She jumped back, then stopped and blushed. "Right. This is the one that's here to help and . . ."

When she stopped talking, Tony turned and stared at mini-Ryne. Standing on the partially eaten demon, he was, in turn, staring at Leah. His eyes were black, lid to lid, and even six meters away, he could see his reflection burning in them.

A heartbeat earlier, Tony would have denied any ability to move without help, but he pulled free of CB's hold before Leah's lips started to form the question and was standing in front of her before she asked it.

"Lord?"

"Boss!" Even as a physical barrier, he sucked right now, but when Leah tried to go through him instead of around, it gave CB enough time to grab her arms and hold her in place. Tony was pretty sure he was still standing, not exactly upright, not unless the studio had acquired a recent lean to the left, but standing. As he tried to straighten, he caught sight of Jack beginning to move.

Circle of yellow rope dropped around the demon's shoulders.

Jack in the air, then crumpled motionless against the base of the wall.

Lee on one knee, one of the demon's arms wrapped round his throat.

Amy's scream lingering.

And the tableau froze.

It happened just that fast.

Ryne Cyratane smiled, now clearly in control of mini-Ryne's body, his attributes no longer sheathed. "I think we should talk trade, Wizard."

"Trade?" It took a moment to sink in. Finally, he dragged his gaze away from the six inches of detached claw protruding from Jack's chest and shoved his reaction behind old familiar shields. "You want to trade Lee for Leah?"

The demon looked confused. "Who?"

"Her!" Tony jerked a thumb over his shoulder.

"Ah. That is not the name I knew her by when she was my handmaiden, my priestess, my love."

Leah leaned toward him, her arms angling back in CB's hold. "I am not your love!" she spat, tossing a curl of hair back off her face.

"Am I not?" He didn't seem too upset by her reaction. "Do you not remember . . ."

"I remember that you slaughtered my entire village!"

Hang on. "You said you were over that," Tony reminded her.

Her shrug was a bit truncated given her position. "Yeah, well, you were right. Maybe I still have some issues."

"So if CB lets you go?"

"I'd be in his arms in a heartbeat." No need to define whose arms. "Sorry. It's a built-in response, and guess who built it in."

The Arjh Lord cleared his throat. Tony turned to see Lee fighting for air, clawing at the arm around his throat. "You don't seem to be taking this seriously, Wizard."

"Stop it!"

He loosened his grip just enough for Lee to draw in a painful sounding breath. And then another. Tony breathed in with him. In. Out. Finally, clutching the demon's arm with white-knuckled fingers, Lee wheezed, "I'm so fucking tired of being the designated damsel in distress."

"Yes." Ryne Cyratane smiled down at him. "I can understand that." Even while wearing a body not his own, there was such understanding in his voice that Tony had a sudden epiphany about how he'd convinced Leah's people to worship him. Lee actually looked comforted.

"Okay." Tony cleared his throat and tried to sound a little more like he was in charge of the situation. "If we trade—Lee for your ex-handmaiden—then you'll kill Leah the moment you get her and the Demongate will open and you'll be here in the flesh, not just riding in the flesh of one of your arjh."

"Yes."

Tony fought the urge to preen under the Arjh Lord's approval. "This was your plan all along, wasn't it? You used Sye Mckaseeh as camouflage—while we were concentrating on her, you could slip in unnoticed."

"No. I took advantage of the situation when I had time enough to mark this body as a vessel rather than merely as mine."

"A spur of the moment kind of thing, then? With the added benefit of pissing off the ex?"

"As you say, an added benefit. And why should I not reclaim my handmaiden and then this world?"

"Because I'll stop you."

"You forget." The demon's grip tightened momentarily. Lee fought for air and then sagged, gasping.

"Okay, so we trade. What's in that for me? As I see it, Lee dies either way."

"The man dies now in front of you. Or later with you."

"Dude." Leaning on Zev's arm, Amy glared from between eyelashes clumped into damp spikes. "You'll kill him the instant the gate opens just like you killed Jack! He's the only thing here that's a danger to you."

"As I said, *later*. I did not specify how much later." He swept a dark gaze over her, head to toe. "You will enjoy my new world, little one. I promise you that."

"Bite me!"

"Perhaps." This was most definitely not the same smile he'd given Lee. Lee's had been compassionate enough to be believed in spite of the choke hold. This was pure seduction. Only the choke hold hadn't changed.

To Tony's surprise, Amy brushed a strand of hair behind her ear and limped forward, eyes locked on the demon. "Maybe we can . . . OW! Zev! What the hell was that for?"

"You were walking toward that!" Zev nodded toward Ryne Cyratane.

"I was not!" Measured the distance from Zev to the demon. Noticed how close she'd come. "Oh, crap, I was." She slipped the glare back on as the two of them began limping backward to the wall. "You're very convincing."

From seduction to amusement. "It's part of my charm."

"And it would be one hell of a lot more charming if you didn't have bits of that . . ." She jabbed a disdainful finger toward the remains of his meal. ". . . between your teeth."

"We will speak later, you and I."

"The hell we . . ."

"Slaughtered a whole village," Zev reminded her urgently.

"So what?" Behind the streaks of mascara, Amy wore the expression she usually reserved for those who wore fur. Or sweater sets in a nonironic manner.

"Your friends are intriguing, Wizard." The Arjh Lord gave Lee a little shake. "But not entirely correct."

"About?" Tony demanded. And then he had it. "I'm not the only danger to you, am I?" After that, it was one small step. There weren't a lot of names in Ryne Cyratane's current address book. "It's Henry, isn't it? He could take that body out, even now." Tony'd missed the implications when Kevin called to tell him the overpass had blown. The overpass had blown *first.* "You pushed this arjh through, creating a cascade like we did the other night because you had to be sure all this happened before sunset so Henry couldn't help." He knew he had it by the way the demon's lip curled. "Humans mean less than nothing to you, but he's another power."

"Um, Tony . . ." Amy rubbed her sleeve under her nose. "Henry's a romance writer."

CB rumbled an unnecessary caution behind him. Tony didn't need to be warned; he'd been keeping this secret a lot longer than the big guy had.

It had to be past sunset. Tony glanced at his watch. Crap. Not even close. How could they have destroyed five demons and been betrayed by a sixth in so little time? Okay, fine. So he couldn't keep things from happening until Henry got here. He'd just have to keep talking, to keep the demon talking until he'd regained enough strength to blast the Arjh Lord right out of his borrowed body.

Yeah. Like that was going to happen. He had no idea how he was still standing and the soundstage kept wavering in and out of focus like they were about to go to flashback.

Still, he had to try. Hopefully, Ryne Cyratane would see slouching as a sign of disrespect instead of an inability to straighten his spine. "The sun will set after you've taken over, you know. Henry'll still be around to kick your ass."

"Once the Gate is open, I will rule with many arjh. And I will gain power from slaughter."

He'd forgotten about that bit. "Killing Mckaseeh's arjh gave that demon you're wearing power enough to activate the runes on his chest, didn't it?"

"Yes."

"But you're using up that power maintaining the link."

This was the most unpleasant smile of all. "Yes."

"Ambitious change requires help; timing is everything." The fortune in Leah's cookie from way back when they'd first met. He'd forgotten it until now. "So I'm about out of my two hundred free minutes?"

The amount of bone necessary to hold up his borrowed horns, kept the Arjh Lord from frowning very deeply. "You make no sense, Wizard. But if you mean that you are out of time, then, yes." And he tightened his grip. "Choose."

Lee's face began to purple, green eyes bulging. He clawed at the demon's arm, head immobile, body twisting and thrashing.

Eyes locked on Lee, Tony almost missed Amy's charge.

"Zev!"

The music director's tackle took her to the floor, stopping her just short of the demon. Without the injured leg she might have made it.

"No! No! No! Bastard's not killing Lee like he killed Jack!"

"You're right, he's not; I'll trade!" Tony wasn't positive they'd heard him, but Amy stilled, Lee began to breathe again, and the demon beckoned with his free hand.

Tony turned just far enough to meet CB's eyes. He had to offer Leah to the demon, so this whole thing fell apart if the boss kept hanging on. Forcing his right hand high enough to close his fingers loosely around Leah's forearm, Tony saw CB's gaze flick, just for an instant, to his broken collarbone. Broken on the right side. *Come on, boss. If I'm using my right hand for this . . .*

Then, although he hoped it looked like he was jerking her away from safety, he hung on as Leah stumbled forward pushed by CB, the movement turning them both back to face the demon.

This demon was not Ryne Cyratane. The body was merely a meat puppet controlled by the Arjh Lord's energy. Back in Leah's condo he'd called energy into him. Called his own energy back. Called the fire.

These days, if he wanted something to come to him, it came. It took next to no power and it took almost no thought.

It came regardless of any solid object that might be in the way.

As Leah stepped out in front of him, Tony held his left palm against the small of her back and concentrated. Focused. Called.

The energy that was Ryne Cyratane tried to come to him through the only thing in the room designed to hold demons. He went through the Demongate.

Leah jerked once, made a noise somewhere between agony and ecstasy, and dropped to her knees, her arm pulling out of Tony's useless grip. On her knees, she curled forward, wrapped her arms around her stomach, and keened.

On the other side of the soundstage, the demon was merely a demon. Onyx eyes widened as the runes cut into his chest healed. He threw back his head and roared.

Still holding Lee.

Before Tony could figure out what to do next, Jack had the muzzle of his gun pressed into the soft tissue of the demon's throat and was emptying it up into the skull. There were no exit wounds. A skull with horns like that had to be hard. Tony half thought he could hear the ricochets as blood dribbled from the demon's eyes and ears and nose.

Ryne Cyratane's ex-puppet hit his knees much like Leah had. From his knees, he pitched forward to slam facefirst into the concrete.

Zev crawled to Lee's side while Amy threw herself at Jack.

"I thought you were dead, you son of a bitch!"

He groaned and stumbled back as she made contact, then moved her slightly to one side so he could pull out the claw. "I was wearing . . ."

"A flak jacket or Kevlar or whatever the hell you lot call those things now! I can't believe I fell for one of the oldest fucking clichés in the business."

"Actually, the claw got snagged on the bandages wrapped around my broken ribs and curved around instead of going in."

"Then why didn't you get up!"

"I thought I should reload."

"Bastard!"

"Ribs!"

As Tony hit the floor beside Leah, Jack and Amy moved into the traditional end-of-scene mind-the-broken-bones clinch. It'd never work, Amy was too out there and Jack hadn't gone out far enough but, what the hell, there was nothing like a traditional endi . . .

◆

"So it seems you managed nicely without me."

Tony blinked up at Henry's face and then past it at the ceiling of his apartment. Two things occurred to him. The first, that he had no memory of leaving the studio. The second, that Leah had a valid point about all the beige. He'd been looking at this ceiling a lot lately and boring didn't begin to cover it. Periwinkle, however, was out of the question. What the hell was up with her and periwinkle anyway?

"Tony?"

His gaze slid back to Henry's face. The eyes were a little dark, but it was mostly Prince of Man with just enough Prince of Darkness to command attention. He looked . . . worried? Crap.

Before he could ask, Henry had an arm around the back of his neck and a cup of water at his mouth. He drained it, and then another before he got the question out. "What did I miss?"

"A day and most of two nights."

"No." Attempting to get up on his elbows, he discovered he couldn't move his right arm. And that would be because it was strapped to his body. Holding the sheet up in one hand, he stared down at the bandages and then back up at Henry. "I broke my arm?"

"Collarbone."

The memory of pain. "Right."

"I know a very discreet doctor."

Impossible not to snort. "Well, you would, wouldn't you. But that wasn't what I meant. You look like there's shit hitting the fan and I've missed being there for it."

Henry took a moment to work that through and then he smiled, wrapping his left hand gently around Tony's jaw. "I was worried about you."

"Me?" His throat was sore. He wondered if he'd forgotten some screaming.

"You were unconscious for a day and most of two nights, Tony. Leah insisted you were fine, that your body needed a time out to recover from the metaphysical strain you've been putting on it, but I suspect she was saying that just to keep me calm."

"I've seen you not calm." The coolness of the vampire's touch felt good against heated skin. "Calm is better."

"Perhaps. Fortunately, although your heart had slowed, I could hear it beating strong and sure and was willing to wait a while. About an hour ago . . ." He moved his hand from Tony's jaw to rest it lightly on his chest. ". . . it began to speed up. It reached its normal rhythm just before you opened your eyes."

"My heart had slowed? I was hibernating?"

"Essentially."

"Cool."

"You need to . . ."

"Pee, Henry. It's been a day and two nights, I really need to pee." His stomach growled. "Is there food around here I can take with me into the can?"

Tony's memory returned as he ate. Not the part where they carried him from the studio but the rest: the battle, Ryne Cyratane's betrayal, and his defeat.

Betrayal . . .

"Lee!"

"Bruised but fine."

CB and Jack had gotten rid of the bodies. Henry didn't know where and hadn't asked. "Why would I? This wasn't my fight."

"You upset about that?" Tony wondered, his hand paused in the bucket of fried chicken. "That we didn't, you know, need you?"

"Honestly?" Red-gold brows dipped down. "A little." And

rose back up again. "It's a conceit of mine that I'm essential when it comes to saving the world. But mostly, I'm proud of the way you've grown into your power. Proud that you found a way to prevail against nearly unbeatable odds. Proud that you refused to quit and kept fighting long after many would have given up."

"Hey!" Tony jabbed a chicken bone indignantly in Henry's direction. "I couldn't give up; I was responsible for those people. They wouldn't have even been there if not for me."

"And, mostly, I am proud of that."

If his ears got any hotter, they were going to ignite and there was a suspiciously damp itch in his eyes. "Henry, I'm carrying some serious negative father shit, and you're creeping me out here."

"You'll have to get used to it if you're going to keep saving the world."

"Yeah, well I'm not . . ." He sighed as Henry smiled. "I am, aren't I? This kind of crap is just going to keep right on happening."

"You said it to me once; like is drawn to like."

"Yeah, yeah, and then I said it to Leah. I'm a font of freakin' wisdom." Looking into a future full of metaphysical bullshit, he sighed again and reached for the last piece of chicken. Paused, hand back in the bucket. "Leah. What happened with Leah?"

"Happened?"

"After I pulled Ryne Cyratane through the Demongate. Is she all right?"

"She's fine."

"She's really pissed, isn't she?"

"She's a little . . ." Henry visibly considered and discarded several words. ". . . annoyed."

♦

Tony didn't see Leah until early November—her agent had called while he was recovering and she'd gotten a job doubling on a CBC Movie of the Week being shot up in Hope.

*"Being immortal doesn't pay the bills; falling off a railway bridge in a corset and bloomers does. I'll see you when I get back."*

His entire response had consisted of: *"Yeah, but, Leah . . ."* and then he was talking to a dial tone.

The Demonic Convergence was still going on, but without Sye Mckaseeh's manipulations, things were coming through from a lot closer to home. Tony was out for no more than a couple of hours most nights tracking down weird little odds and ends and sending them back where they belonged. With the exception of a city employee working in the old sewer tunnel under Highbury Street who ran into a rat carrying a short sword, no one got hurt. Kevin Groves became an invaluable filter—most reports came first to him, and he could tell if the weirdness was real or homemade. In spite of a few very visible incidents, there was a remarkable lack of hysteria from the general population. The people of British Columbia had always been more willing than the rest of the country to adjust reality to suit them, and the contrary attitude of Vancouverites kept them from agreeing on just what exactly they'd seen.

During the day, they were so busy getting the last episode of *Darkest Night* in the can before going on hiatus there wasn't time to replay the whole climatic battle scene in any detail. Maybe a few people strutted—as soon as they stopped limping—and maybe Mason thought a little more of himself than usual, but his ego was so enormous already it was hard to tell. Mostly they worked at getting the stains off the floor under the gate and got on with the job. Where *they* included Tony. CB'd given him as much time off as he was getting if he wanted to remain employed.

TO: tfoster@darkestnight.ca
FROM: bestbane@darkestnight.ca
u r teh suckhead!

TO: bestbane@darkestnight.ca
FROM: tfoster@darkestnight.ca
when you get back, i'll teach you what i can

TO: tfoster@darkestnight.ca
FROM: bestbane@darkestnight.ca
OMG! I <3 U!

A small part of Tony held out a forlorn hope that something eldritch would attack and rip him limb from limb before he had to make good on his promise. Most of him had grown resigned to the inevitable where "the inevitable" had been defined by powers with a vicious sense of humor as his boss' youngest daughter.

♦

"Nothing." Amy hung up the phone and looked up at Tony and Zev. "That's four days since Kevin's had anyone call about something going bump in the night. Maybe Halloween was the last."

A pair of half-meter-wide, phosphorescent-green, eight-legged visitors had made the traditional Haunted Village at the Burnaby Village Museum out on Deer Lake a little more authentic than most years. By the time Tony found them hiding under the carousel, they'd been completely terrified by the giant bat on stilts and were more than willing to go home.

"Halloween does have a certain satisfying end-of-season feel about it," Zev admitted. "And that means this whole thing lasted about a month."

"Golly, Tony." Amy batted bright orange eyelashes suggestively in his general direction. "The Demonic Convergence is over and the show's going into hiatus, so *everyone* who works on it will have some free time. What are you going to do?"

Before Tony could answer her, the door to CB's office opened. A motorcycle helmet cradled under one arm, Leah paused on the threshold and grinned. "Ah, that's so sweet. Spanky and his gang. Oh, stop looking at me like that." Eyes rolling, she crossed toward them. "I got back last night. I would have called."

Tony ignored the excuse. "Henry says your tattoo changed."

"That was a little abrupt. What's up your skirt?"

"We were still in the Demonic Convergence. You should have checked in before you left, just to be on the safe side."

"Should have?" Arms folded. Lip curled. "You're not my keeper, Tony," she snarled.

She'd had millennia to work on that whole "don't fuck with me" thing, and it was definitely definitive. Zev took a step sideways, putting more of Amy's desk between them. Amy looked like she was taking notes. Tony didn't really give a crap. All things considered, attitude from an immortal stuntwoman was pretty fucking low on his list of things to be impressed by.

"I'm the only wizard we know of," he told her flatly, "and you're walking around with the oldest working magic in the world etched into your stomach. I need to know what's going on with it."

Leah's eyes narrowed, and she stared at him for a long moment. "You used me to defeat Ryne Cyratane. You had no idea what slamming him back through the gate would do to me, and yet you did it anyway."

"I knew what Ryne Cyratane would do to this world. Reshoot the scene and I'd play it the same way."

"Would you?"

"Yeah. I would."

Unexpectedly, she smiled, set down the helmet, and unzipped her jacket. "Okay, then."

"Can you say anticlimactic?" Amy muttered.

"Anticlimactic," Zev acknowledged.

Leah grinned and pulled her fuchsia turtleneck up off the tattoo. "You were expecting a fight? I made my point when I blew town, leaving him to his own devices, and besides, he's right. He should have a look at this, just in case."

"In case of what?" Amy demanded as Tony peered at the interlocking circles.

"These are new," Tony announced before Leah could answer. He traced the inner circle, his finger about a millimeter above the skin. "And there wasn't this much color before." Not only the new runes in the inner circle but a few of the unchanged runes were now a deep crimson. The color of fresh blood instead of dried. "What does it mean?"

"I don't know. You're the wizard."

"Yeah, but . . ."

No *but*, actually.

"I guess I'll have to find out," he said, straightening.

Letting the sweater drop, Leah leaned forward and kissed his cheek. She smelled like cinnamon. "I'm not going anywhere for a while, I'll help. There's not a lot about demonology I don't know."

"You didn't know Ryne Cyratane would betray us."

"Please!" She smirked and reached for her helmet. "He's a demon, what did you expect? Ciao, Antonio!" A second kiss on the other cheek and a wave with her free hand as she headed for the door. "Bye, kids. See you around."

"You going to stop her?" Zev asked quietly.

Tony shook his head. "No, if I need her, I just have to call." He rubbed the palm of his left hand against his thigh. "You guys want to go get a beer after work?"

"As if," Zev snorted. "CB wants the score for the last episode tweaked again. He's looking for a John Williams sound on a Chet Williams budget. I'll be here all night. Probably tomorrow night, too."

Amy leaned out and dropped a stack of old sides into the recycling box. "I'd love to, Tony, but Jack and I are going to a zombie retrospective."

That was unexpected. "Jack's into zombies?"

"He's not *into* so much. He thinks they're funny." She shrugged and pulled a strand of hair out from the inner workings of her skeleton earrings. "I figure as long as we're both enjoying ourselves, no harm no foul. Say, I know . . ."

Tony had always found ingenuous a worrying look on Amy.

". . . why don't you ask Lee if he wants to go for a beer?"

"Why don't you ask Lee if he wants to go for a . . ."

"Zev!"

Not at all repentant, Zev sighed. "You're willing to go mano a mano with invading wizards, haunted houses, and enough demons for a theatrical production of *The Inferno,* what are you so afraid of when it comes to Lee?"

"I'm not afraid. Lee's . . ."

"I swear, Tony, if you say straight, I'm going to feed you Amy's stapler."

"Hey!" Clutching her stapler protectively, Amy rolled her chair over to the other desk. "Use Rachel's. She's never in the office anyway."

Tony took one step back, just to be on the safe side. "It has to be Lee's choice."

"Why?" Zev folded his arms and glowered. It was a surprisingly impressive glower.

"His career . . ."

"Why would you affect his career?" Amy snorted. "You likely to do something kinky in public?"

"Actually . . ."

"Zev!"

"Earth to Tony; no one cares but you. So Lee likes guys as well as women. Big whoop. Most of the world has more important things to worry about than a bisexual actor in a third-rate, syndicated, vampire detective television show."

"Yeah, but . . ."

"Hey. No buts. End the freakin' suspense." She tossed Zev the stapler. He made threatening gestures with it, and Tony surrendered.

If the whole thing blew up in his face, he'd be able to blame his alleged friends. And office supplies. Which was a dubious comfort.

♦

Lee's dressing room door sat partly open and Tony had a moment's fear, relief, fear that he'd already left. There'd been talk about an offer to do an *Amazons in Space* movie in the Australian outback during hiatus, but he had no idea if Lee'd got the gig. Between the end of the Demonic Convergence and the end of the season, they'd been so busy they'd hardly said two words to each other.

Yeah. That was the reason.

*If he's not here, it's a sign and . . .*

He was just taking his cell phone out of the charger. He turned. Saw Tony. Froze.

*Okay. That's not exactly a welcoming expression. I should just back away slowly . . .*

On the other hand, he did have a very threatening stapler waiting for him.

*Oh, what the hell.*

Tony stepped into the dressing room, reached back, and closed the door. One of Lee's brows went up.

"I didn't know you could do that."

Both brows dipped down. "What?"

"The single brow thing."

"Oh. Yeah. Since I was kid."

"Cool."

A long moment of silence. It wasn't a very big room. They were no more than an arm's length apart.

Tony wasn't sure which one of them sighed first. He ran a hand back through his hair. "One of us needs to stop being such a guy about this."

"Yeah, except we're both guys."

"That's not a problem for me."

"Me either."

It happened just that fast.

Where "that fast" ignored the events of the preceding six months, all leading up to this moment with the possible exception of those events that had been leading up to world domination, mass slaughter, or actually shooting an episode of *Darkest Night.*

Now he finally knew where Lee was, Tony wanted nothing more than to make magic, to hold out his hand and call the other man to him—but the smoop levels had already risen to nauseating heights. He felt like he'd stumbled onto a Rainbow Network Movie of the Week and this was the part in the soundtrack where the female vocalist would come in with the power ballad. "So what do we do . . ."

Lee tossed his phone aside, grabbed Tony's jacket in both fists, and swallowed the last word along with the lower half of Tony's face.

Later, when they finally broke for air, Tony felt he needed to make one thing perfectly clear.

"I never once thought of you as the damsel."